T0247838

PRAISE FOR THE BRASS QUE

"Rollicking fun and sharp as a brass tack, this book is everything steampunk should be." — *Cat Rambo, Nebula Award winner*

"An intriguing alternate world, filled with sharply amusing dialog and lively characters. VERDICT: A delightful gaslamp fantasy that will please readers of Gail Carriger and Kate Locke." — *Library Journal*

"I loved *The Brass Queen*: hilarious, with a very tongue-in-cheek dry wit and delightful imagery. One of those books that you don't want to put down because they're just so much fun." — *Genevieve Cogman, author of the Invisible Library series*

"Razor-sharp wit and immaculate worldbuilding make this debut one to savor . . . a genre blockbuster." — *Leanna Renee Hieber, award-winning and bestselling author of* **The Spectral City**

"With a satisfying bite, this steampunk venture includes an insightful twist on the British Empire . . . Best of all, Constance stays center stage: a feisty, lovable heroine who is capable of rescuing herself, thank you very much." — *Foreword Reviews*

THE BRASS QUEEN II

GRAND TOUR

THE BRASS QUEEN II

GRAND TOUR

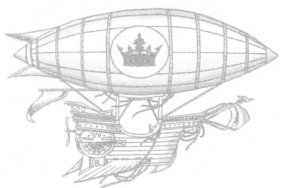

Elizabeth Chatsworth

CamCat
Books

CamCat Publishing, LLC
Fort Collins, Colorado 80524
camcatpublishing.com

Hardcover ISBN 9780744306293
Paperback ISBN 9780744306309
Large-Print Paperback ISBN 9780744306262
eBook ISBN 9780744306217
Audiobook ISBN 9780744306712

Library of Congress Control Number: 2023946744

Cover design by Lena Yang
Cover art and illustrations by James A. Owen
Book design by Olivia Croom Hammerman

5   3   1   2   4

Dedication

Amor da minha vida.

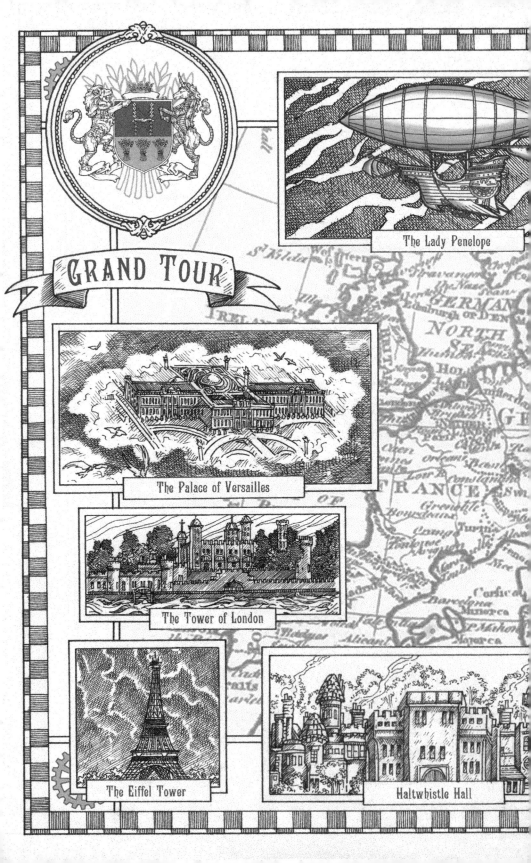

The Lady Penelope

GRAND TOUR

The Palace of Versailles

The Tower of London

The Eiffel Tower

Haltwhistle Hall

The Draugen

The Palace
of Stockholm

THE BRASS QUEEN

The Colosseum

PINDER'S
PRINT EMPORIUM
PINSTONE STREET
SHEFFIELD
ENGLAND

Tower of the Winds

Chapter 1:
A Night at the Opera

Saturday, June 5th, 1897:
Paris, France. 7:15 p.m.

The grass was always greener in another dimension. Miss Constance Haltwhistle imagined that in a parallel world, the tall, dark, and almost-handsome American cowboy, Liberty Trusdale, would be thrilled to attend a night at the Parisian opera by her side. He'd put aside his trademark attire of a black leather duster, battered Stetson hat, and clunky Western boots to wear a bespoke ensemble that precisely coordinated with her own.

His muscular six-two frame could only be enhanced by a top hat bedecked with shiny brass goggles, a white frilly shirt befitting a fashion-forward airship pirate, a green silk tailcoat embroidered with gamboling Yorkshire sheep, and the tightest calfskin jodhpurs his horseman's thighs could take without drawing indecency charges from the French authorities. She'd sent this outfit to his hotel room along with a note apologizing for accidentally electrocuting him atop the Eiffel Tower at lunchtime. The same note requested Trusdale to don his new outfit and join her in her carriage at precisely seven o'clock, that she might sweep him away to the opera for a night of forgiveness and festivity.

So where the hell was he?

As the glass doors of the Grand Hotel du Louvre had yet to reveal a blue-eyed cowboy ripe for reconciliation, Constance drew back from the carriage door's open window and settled her bustle upon its plush bench seat. She heaved as deep a sigh as her cruelly cinched corset allowed, absently tracing her fingertips over the faint tear stains on the seat's gold silk cushion where she'd wept herself to sleep on her fourteenth birthday.

Her eyes closed, transporting her back through the years to the iron balcony that surrounded the rooftop observatory at Haltwhistle Hall. The setting sun had painted the heavens a dusky pink above the Hall's crenellated towers, manicured rose gardens, well-stocked stables, and vast airship hanger. The hanger stood empty, as it had ever since Papa flew the *Lady Penelope* airship off to foreign climes on yet another hunt for alien relics. His obsession with scientific curiosities had grown exponentially since the death of her mother, his grief turning passion into mania.

But now, as the Hall's clock tower rang its farewell to the day, an unknown vehicle approached her ancestral home. Young Constance gripped the balcony's iron handrail, holding her breath as the mysterious carriage approached. The estate's prize-winning sheep stopped chewing their cud, staring in alarm at the carved red-and-gold Japanese dragon that wrapped three times around the vehicle's gilded frame.

Seated within the dragon's gaping jaws, the estate's bald, green-liveried Master of the Horse, Hearn, pushed the four chestnut Arabian ponies drawing the carriage into a trot. Only Papa would arrive in such monstrous style. For once, it seemed her explorer-father had not forgotten her special day.

She'd practically flown down the grand staircase to greet him, clambering up the carriage stairs without waiting for a helping hand from her aged retainer, Cawley. She'd flung open the door with a crash, breaking the latch that to this day would release itself at inopportune moments. A gloriously painted mural decorated the interior of the carriage. From floor to ceiling, an elaborate battle between two samurai armies raged across fields of gold-leaf splendor. The warriors' sacrifice stood as testament to the victories of the warlord empress who had originally commissioned the carriage to tour her newly conquered lands. Upon the golden bench seat, a note scrawled in Papa's own hand on a page torn from an etiquette book told her he might be home by next Christmas, maybe.

That was the last time she'd ever shed a tear for Papa.

Naturally, she'd claimed the carriage was her birthday present. None of her governesses, servants, or irregularly visiting family members were bold enough to challenge her on the point. When Papa returned two years later, he'd forgotten the carriage existed.

If a man could forget an imperial dragon carriage, what hope could a mere daughter have of being remembered?

Constance bit her lip to stop it from committing a very un-British wobble and snapped her eyes open. The doorway to the hotel still lacked a square-jawed cowboy dressed for a night at the opera. It even lacked the self-same cowboy dressed in his usual all-black Western garb, a gunfighter from every angle save for his lack of a six-gun. Was she repeating the pattern of waiting for a man to grace her with his presence?

It was time to seize control of the situation to save both face and sanity. Constance thumped the heel of her boot onto the floor of the carriage. She yelled to her driver, "Hearn, circle the hotel's immediate vicinity and return us to this very spot. We mustn't give the impression that we're waiting. In fact, let's all concur that we're running late to pick up Mr. Trusdale, who will be standing here upon our return, devastated that we left without him."

"Very good, miss," called back Hearn. The carriage lurched into motion as the four chestnut ponies out front surged into a spanking trot. The jolt caused the Yorkshire terrier puppy, Boo, curled into an impossibly small ball beside Constance's thigh, to awake with a startled bark. On the opposite bench, Lord Wellington Pendelroy fumbled his copy of the French court circular, *La Vue Royale.* The pink printed pages fell from his grip to scatter gossip and intrigue across the carriage floor atop the samurai warriors' heads.

"Wait, what are we concurring about?" asked Welli, tossing back his Byronic forelock with the panache that had earned him armies of admirers and scads of scandals, the latest of which were splashed across the court pages at his feet. After only two weeks in Paris, he was as sartorially resplendent as any continental count in his sky-blue silk tailcoat, pantaloons, and matching top hat so in vogue this season. He squinted down at his fallen newspaper as Constance rubbed Boo's ears and cooed at her, sending the puppy into a tail-chasing whirl of joy upon the golden bench seat.

Constance grinned at the puppy's antics. "We're concurring that we're not waiting any longer for Mr. Trusdale. Except that we are, in a roundabout manner. Don't tell him that we circled the hotel. I know the two of you have become drinking companions as of late." There was a wistfulness she hadn't intended to share in her tone.

Welli quirked a perfectly plucked eyebrow at her. "Everyone I meet becomes a drinking companion at some point or another. Don't worry, you haven't missed out on any tasty details on our enigmatic cowboy. The man is more tight-lipped about his past than a burlesque dancer turned Mother Superior. I always seem to end up talking about myself when we're sharing a beverage or two." He held up one finger as she opened her mouth. "And before you make any cracks about me constantly talking about myself, consider how much you want me to concur with your 'we weren't waiting for you, Mr. Trusdale,' story."

She chuckled, her heart lifting at her cousin's irrepressible *joie de vivre*. "You know me too well, cousin. Hold on, we're coming up to the hotel steps again." She perched on the edge of her seat and peered out the carriage window. The hotel's glass doors still stubbornly refused to expel a cowboy clad in a lamb-bedecked tailcoat. She heaved a dramatic sigh, then called out, "Once more around the hotel, Hearn, very, very slowly." The carriage reduced its speed to a sluggish creep along the cobble-stoned street.

Welli groaned. "Really? All right, third time lucky. If he's not standing here on the next drive by, we head straight for the opera, agreed?"

She furrowed her brow. "You don't think he's coming, do you?"

Welli shrugged. "That outfit you created for him could well be the straw that broke the cowboy's back. Impressed as I am that you managed to bribe a French seamstress into knocking up a gentleman's version of this monstrosity"—he waved a hand at her attire—"what makes you think he would wear it in public?"

"I'm sure he'll appreciate the sentiment and care that I put into designing such an elaborate gift. As our complementary outfits evoke a landscape that is of great importance to me, I'm obviously telling him that he is important too." She gazed down at her green gossamer ball gown, embroidered with innocent lambs and their ever-patient mothers on lush pastures enclosed by gray drystone walls. She could almost smell the moorland heather blooms that inspired the purple hue of her velvet hooded cloak, clasped by a bluebell brooch. Her bespoke ensemble showcased the bucolic hills and dales of Yorkshire to Paris, and well might the French be grateful for the view.

Welli sighed. "And as usual, you've overthought everything to a ludicrous degree. Is there any chance I can talk you into changing out of this crime against fashion before we head to the opera? Paris isn't ready for your sartorial gall, and Europe as a whole will no doubt be appalled by your unique brand of English eccentricity. I suppose I should be grateful that you didn't persuade the seamstress to include pigs on your attire."

No, those she'd saved to decorate her bloomers. Beneath her petticoats, a joyous tumble of pink piglets scampered through an apple orchard. Constance tilted up her chin. "It's British pastoral chic, a style that I just invented. I thought I should make a grand gesture to Mr. Trusdale, given the electrical unpleasantness at lunchtime. I assume, given that he was raised on a Kansas cattle ranch, that Mr. Trusdale adores farm animals as much as I do."

Welli chuckled. "Ah, Connie. It's your assumptions that get you into trouble. Like assuming that creating a fashion-forward farm ensemble is somehow better than making a face-to-face apology. Didn't you set the poor man alight with that ridiculous lightning gauntlet you're working on? He passed me heading out of the hotel at lunchtime in search of good whisky and I can only assume bad company. I swear his duster coat was still smoldering from your unprovoked attack."

She blinked at her cousin. "Trusdale told you about our altercation? First of all, you should know that it's *our* ridiculous lightning gauntlet. Mr. Trusdale and I are working on the Perambulating Kinetic Storm Battle Mitten #004 together, as equal partners. He wanted to take the device back to the drawing board due to its perilous instability. But due process takes forever, and I decided to do a few quick experiments of my own, to see if I could fix the problems."

"In other words, you kept working on it behind his back so that you could stun him with your brilliance."

"Was that so wrong?" She reached up to massage the tension from the back of her neck. "After doing him the favor of fixing the battle mitten's main issues, I decided the best way to demonstrate the new safety features was to take it to a potentially problematic location—"

"Such as the top of a thousand-foot-high iron landmark in a rainstorm—"

"Exactly. The Eiffel Tower in a sudden shower was the perfect place to prove to Trusdale that my clandestine tweaks to the battle mitten had solved all our technical problems. Cawley was carrying a large carpet bag that secreted a leg of ham which I intended to use for target practice. Once perfectly cooked by the electrical gauntlet, the ham would have taken pride of place in a lovely picnic luncheon atop the tower, with Cawley's extra-large polo umbrella providing us with shelter from the rain. We'd have perfect privacy, as no one goes up the tower in a storm. You know how skittish the continentals are about foul-weather picnics. Anyway, when I pulled back my lace sleeve to reveal the copper and brass glory of the battle mitten, the wretched thing went off and bang! Trusdale was blasted by a lightning bolt that shot him clear across the iron platform. Fortunately, he was only unconscious for a minute or so, and his leather coat saved him from any serious scorching. Once he regained the power to speak, he was perfectly fine, if a tad grumpy."

Welli's eyebrows grazed the brim of his top hat. "Only a tad?"

"Perhaps a little more than a tad." She rubbed her throbbing temples as the headache she'd suffered for much of the last week pounded anew. "I can't see why he was so upset. I've accidentally electrocuted myself with the gauntlet at least two dozen times this week, and does anyone hear me complain?"

Welli's eyes widened. "Good lord, were those your shrieks that echoed around our floor at the hotel every afternoon? I assumed Hearn had found himself a vocal new girlfriend—"

She tut-tutted and pointed toward the driver's box at front of the carriage, where Hearn and Cawley were no doubt eavesdropping on their conversation. This sensible precaution against being surprised by an aristocratic employer's latest whims allowed British servants to maintain the stone-faced demeanor they were famous for the world over. Such impassivity in the face of chaos and mayhem was a quality that Constance appreciated more than most.

"Hearn's affairs are no business of ours. The point is, some of us are stoic when we're electrocuted, while others seem to take such things personally. Which clearly they shouldn't. I'm sure Mr. Trusdale would acknowledge that, if he took the time to consider the situation more deeply."

Welli sniffed. "Not that I'm one to give relationship advice, but perhaps you shouldn't electrocute a man you clearly want to impress."

Heat flamed across her cheeks. "Who said I was trying to impress anyone?"

"You did, not one minute ago. You literally said that you wanted to impress him with all the wonderful improvements you'd made to your dangerously faulty lightning glove."

She folded her arms. "For the record, Miss Constance Aethelflaed Zenobia Haltwhistle, also known to a select few as the high-end weapons designer the *Brass Queen*"—she paused to give her cousin the opportunity to recall the pride he should feel at counting himself amongst that elite few—"has no one to impress but herself, and that's a difficult enough job without wondering what some itinerant cowboy thinks of me. Two weeks ago, Mr. Trusdale may have inadvertently saved my life, but I've also saved his. We're utterly even in terms of who is impressing whom, or not, as the case may be."

Welli snorted. "How *passionate* you are about not impressing Trusdale. What do you think, Boo? Doth the lady protest too much?"

Boo yapped enthusiastically and snuggled into her mistress's side, dissipating Constance's irritation instantly with her inherent cuteness. Constance tickled the puppy's belly, drawing happy grunts from the tiny terrier. "I simply believe that Mr. Trusdale could show a little more gratitude that the Brass Queen herself is collaborating with him on designing this nonlethal gauntlet. My arms-dealing ancestors are turning in their graves as I step away from the family business to build a future that doesn't involve hurting anyone."

"Except, it seems, our poor Mr. Trusdale." Welli raised an imaginary champagne glass in the air. "Well, here's a toast to your good intentions, Trusdale's tolerance to electrical shocks, and your desire to escape from a centuries-old arms business run by a long line of blue-blooded rogues, villains, and thieves. Cheers." He downed the nonexistent fluid in one gulp and smacked his lips appreciatively. "Mmm, delicious. And speaking of you turning your back on your nefarious ancestors, I'm delighted to inform you that according to page thirteen of the French court circular"—Welli tapped the toe of his boot on one of the printed pages littering the carriage floor —"after four years of being lost in the Congo, your father has been declared by the British court system to be legally dead."

It felt as if her heart might well burst through her corset, land on the lacquered floor, and flop there like a scarlet jellyfish. Constance pressed both hands against her chest as if to hold in the errant organ. "I beg your pardon?"

"Your father's been missing for so long that the high court has decreed that he's shuffled off this mortal coil. I'm sorry to inform you that in the eyes of the law, Connie, you're now an orphan. You have my deepest sympathies." He doffed his top hat and gave her a cheeky wink. "On the upside, this very week, Queen Victoria declared that women can now inherit both property and titles, just like men have for centuries. Who would have thought we'd see such egalitarianism in our lifetimes? That said, I do believe this magnanimous act was a direct response to your very public petition on this matter to her majesty before thousands of spectators at Endcliffe Park."

"I was only trying to—"

"Change the world as we know it, apparently. I can't believe that you, of all people, are now officially a baroness. That is, as long as your father doesn't show up from whatever foreign drinking den he's actually been holed up in for the last few years. I'm sure even death doesn't want to start a fight with Henry Haltwhistle unless it's absolutely necessary,"

She cradled her head in her hands as the carriage seemed to spin around her. "I'm taking Mama's title? Baroness Haltwhistle? It doesn't seem right. I'm no lady."

"Tell me about it. But the high court says otherwise, Lady Haltwhistle. Welcome to the upper echelons of the blue blood club. You can wear a baronial crown and an ermine cloak if that's a look you think you could pull off. At least it would be an improvement on your current get-up."

She did so love a fancy hat and cloak. She cleared her throat. "Actually, to start my ladyshipness off on the right foot, I have a small confession to make. Papa's intercontinental pub crawl with occasional excursions to raid hidden tombs and temples for treasure might, in fact, have been an *interdimensional* excursion powered by pilfered alien technology."

Welli refilled his imaginary glass and downed another drink. He wiped the back of his hand across his mouth indecorously. "Sorry, it seems I need a stiff one before sailing my yacht over the edge of this conversational whirlpool."

She grimaced. "Do forgive my reticence, but until recent events, I was concerned that if I had told you that Papa had used alien artifacts to rip apart reality so that he could go and live with an alternate version of my deceased mother in another dimension, you'd have had me committed."

"Please, I could never deal with that level of paperwork." Welli steepled his fingers together as he considered her curious confession. "I have to say, Constance, this really burns my breeches. A fortnight ago, I watched in shock as you maneuvered Haltwhistle Hall through a giant swirling aether portal to save it from being burned down by Prince Lucien's troops. It didn't occur to you then and there to mention that Uncle Henry had previously taken the same route to live with an alternate Auntie Annabella?"

"And her red-haired son, Constantine, who's apparently a male version of me. Papa finally got the son he always wanted instead of a mere girl. I hope they're all very happy together in their mirror world." Even she could hear the bitterness behind her words.

"A male you? Does that mean there's a female version of me out there? Ooh, I'm sure she's positively stunning. I'd love to meet her," smirked Welli.

She wrinkled her nose. "I won't ask why. Since father absconded, he's chatted to me occasionally through the use of a small-scale interdimensional portal, but our communications were, well . . . rather utilitarian. He had me ship him all his prized possessions through the tear in reality, but he never wanted to come back to visit me. And I had the estate staff to protect, so I couldn't go to him—not that I wanted to, as he's a selfish, pompous . . ." Her body trembled as the emotional dam inside her crumbled. If the British courts had declared Papa dead, surely she herself should relinquish any lingering hope that he might return? The tears she'd held back for so long flooded down her cheeks in a salty torrent of anguish. "Oh, Welli, why wasn't I good enough for him to want to stay home?"

Welli was beside her in an instant, his arm clasped tight around her shoulders, pressing a perfumed handkerchief into her hand.

She blinked down at the delicate lace square. "Dear lord, is this yours?"

"A token from a lady admirer. Or perhaps a male one with exquisite taste in accessories? It's not important. My dear, sweet girl, I'm so very, very, sorry. Your father's an absolute cad. Always has been, always will be."

"On that we agree. But I still miss him. What does that make me?"

"Human."

A smile haunted her lips. She trumpeted her nose into the handkerchief and tried to hand it back to him.

"Ah, no, that's yours to keep. Connie, I'm absolutely furious at Uncle Henry. How could he do this to you?" He gazed out the carriage window, lost in thought. She followed his stare, admiring the elegant marble-clad apartment buildings that Paris was famous for inching by the window. It seemed Hearn had taken her order to drive without haste to a pace that would make a snail impatient.

Welli stroked her hair softly as he murmured, "You know, when you were about ten years old, I questioned your father about the brutal training regime in martial arts he put you through, and his explanation was that you had to be strong enough to continue the Haltwhistle legacy. I asked him why he thought you were a blade that needed to be tempered. You were his daughter, not his weapon. He had no answer for me. But I can't tell you how much I regret not taking a stand against his lunacy."

She rested her hand upon his. "Had you stood up to him, he'd have cut you out of my life, and heaven knows how wretched I would've become if you hadn't kept visiting me after Mama died."

Welli wrapped his arms around her and pulled her closer. "It broke my heart to see you out there every

Sunday, rain or shine, laying fresh flowers on her grave. I always thought it was bizarre that your father made us bury a casket filled with rocks. He said he thought it was important that you had something concrete on which to focus your emotions. He claimed the Egyptian authorities wouldn't let him transport a person who died from malaria, but I know now that such bodies are transported all the time. I—"

She pushed him away, blinking up at the emerald eyes that mirrored her pain. "What do you mean, empty casket?"

Welli paled beneath his forelock. "Heavens, Constance, I'm sorry. I thought you knew. Not at the time, of course, you were a child, for heaven's sake. But since then, I assumed the servants had . . . I mean, surely Hearn or Cawley . . . or perhaps they didn't know?"

"They'd better not have known. I have more than enough liars in my family tree. I don't need my trusty retainers keeping things from me too."

The silence from the driver's cab was deafening. The carriage crawled on, drawing ever closer to the hotel steps and one more man who might let her down. What were the odds that Trusdale was any more noble than her carriage companions? *Trust no one*, as Papa used to say.

Welli reached once more for her hand, but she pulled it away. He said, "Come to think of it, the servants probably weren't in on the secret. Only the pallbearers knew for certain that something was amiss. That included myself, Father, and . . . well, who can remember back so far?"

She blinked up at him. "Are you telling me the truth, or are you covering for Hearn and Cawley so that I feel less betrayed?"

He cast his eyes down onto the floor, his cheeks as pink as the pages of the court circular. "Don't ask questions you don't want answered. I'm sure everyone on this carriage loves you in their own way, most of the time."

She pushed herself away from him on the seat and raised her voice so that the servants could hear her loud and clear. "Could we suppose, in honor of my new status as a baroness, that everyone in earshot will become a little more trustworthy? Is that too much to ask?" Mumbled affirmations from Hearn and Cawley seeped through the dragon's gilded walls.

Welli bowed his head. "Fair enough. If it helps, I'm sure if your mother were alive and well, she would have found a way to return to you."

Constance balled the handkerchief in her palm. "Or she abandoned me altogether, just like Papa did."

He shook his head. "That's not the Annabella I knew. She was caring and compassionate, with a kind word for anyone who crossed her path. Even your father. It takes a special soul to love an eccentric genius. She saw something in him none of us ever could."

Constance relaxed her grip on the handkerchief and said flatly, "I have so little of her left. Even my memories are fading with time. When I was young, she taught me to waltz, to sing, to shoot an arrow as straight and true as the goddess Artemis herself. All my happiest moments were spent with her."

She reached back into her hidden bustle pocket and pulled out her travel edition of *Babett's Modern Manners*. The bookplate inside the front cover declared in florid script that this edition belonged to Lady Annabella Pendelroy. She gently traced Mama's maiden name with her fingertips, the letters worn almost invisible through the years.

"This etiquette book is one of the few items I have left to physically link me to Mama. Papa decided to give it to me so that I might learn how to navigate social situations with a modicum of her civility and grace. She's the only Haltwhistle who possessed either virtue. Her other belongings were lost when I blasted the Hall through the aether portal."

Welli gave her the gentlest of smiles. "At least you know the Hall survived because of your actions. And if something can be lost, it can be found. Even a stately home in another dimension."

Constance dabbed her eyes with the handkerchief. "Or perhaps I need to let the Hall go, lock, stock, and treasure chambers. I don't know what my parents wanted for me in life, but I can do my best to seize the opportunity at hand. If the battle mitten is a commercial success, then I'll have the resources to live a somewhat normal life, a life beyond the Hall."

Welli shrugged. "Normalcy is overrated. Then again, I'm struck by the fact that you believe developing a nonlethal electrical weapon somehow makes you normal. Perhaps I should attempt an admittedly belated education in what it means to be a woman in the age of Queen Victoria? Have you ever considered taking up knitting? Or you could push the boat out and start collecting woodland ferns? Perhaps a nice seaweed scrapbook could set your heart alight?"

"Or maybe I could hold a séance or take up taxidermy? All lovely hobbies for ladies to pursue, I'm sure. But what if a single female, in search of a delectable fern, finds herself being followed by a ruffian through the woods? She could turn upon her pursuer, hold out her opera-glove clad arm, and demand the fellow state his business. Should his designs upon her be unsavory, a simple clench of her fist will ignite the battle mitten hidden beneath her glove and a net of pure electrical energy will fly forth to land upon the villain. Shocked into submission, the scoundrel will lie comatose at our lady's feet, allowing our heroine to set off once more in search of the perfect fern. No one is seriously harmed, and the miscreant will think twice before attempting to intimidate a lady in the woods."

Welli's eyes twinkled mischievously. "Am I to understand that you have identified poor Trusdale as an unsavory ruffian? Is that the real reason you zapped him into submission this lunchtime?"

Heat seared across her cheeks. "I told you that was an accident. And I certainly didn't expect him to be angry that I'd worked on the battle mitten alone. Heaven knows what he'd say if he found out about the extra special experiments I conducted in the midnight hours."

His eyes narrowed. "Oh lord. What kind of experiments? Nothing illegal, I hope?"

She shrugged. "Not in my book."

"You weren't shocking the servants, were you?"

Constance shook her head. "That would have been more convenient than my current strategy, but no. Hearn was game, of course. All those years of bare-knuckle boxing toughened Hearn up quite marvelously. It would take five electric battle mittens to bring down one so big, beefy, and brawny. I would have better luck attempting to take down a prize bull than flooring Hearn." She could practically hear the coachman beaming through the carriage walls. She lowered her voice, "But Cawley—"

"Must be a hundred years old. Tell me you didn't even think of shooting him with a lightning bolt."

"Only once. He hoped the jolt might help him with his arthritis. It did, but he also belched sparks for the rest of the day. We decided that I should formulate a new weapons testing protocol, which I duly named Plan 'V'."

"And what does the *V* stand for?"

Vigilante. But there was no reason for Welli to know all her secrets. Particularly the ones that could require plausible deniability to the constabulary of the reigning French monarch, King Louis XVIII. Rumor had it that British tourists were not currently the flavor of the month with Parisian law enforcers, given Queen Victoria's recent rumblings that she might well raise arms against France. Like mismatched lovers, the French and the British had an on-again, off-again relationship that had persisted through centuries of common sense and diplomacy. The two autocratic monarchies had much in common, a fact that neither the self-proclaimed Sun King nor his great-aunt Victoria could admit. Because of this royal tension, English aristocrats always started their grand tours of Europe in Paris. Not only was the city delightful, but the level of animosity shown toward tourists was an excellent barometer for the likelihood of a war, which could put a crimp in even the best-laid travel plans.

She wagged her finger at her cousin. "V stands for 'Very Top Secret, So Don't Ask Me Again.' And all my experiments were for a good cause, namely, scientific progress. Sadly, that progress didn't stop the battle mitten from misfiring today, or you, me, and Mr. Trusdale would already be enjoying a lovely night at the opera. Hopefully, he's decided to accept my heartfelt written apology and my carefully crafted gift and he's waiting for us as we speak."

The carriage trundled up to the steps that led up to the Grand Hotel du Louvre's glass doors. The lack of a cowboy caused Constance's heart to sink lower than the pages of the court circular.

Welli blew out his cheeks. "I hate to break it to you Connie, but I doubt Trusdale is coming. I thought perhaps he was pondering whether he was smitten with you enough to overcome his natural aversion to wearing farmyard beasts in public. But this goes much deeper than that. You owe him nothing less than a formal in-person apology for blasting him with electricity. And a second apology for working on this mitten behind his back. That's not exactly an equal business partnership, is it? Plus a third and final apology to apologize for leaving him an apology note rather than facing him yourself."

Constance gasped. "I'm sure I don't owe him an in-person anything. According to page fifty-seven of *Babett's Modern Manners* here, a well-crafted note is more than enough to smooth over any misunderstanding between friends, partners, or potentially, most countries. Mr. Liberty Trusdale should accept my thoughtful gift and . . ." She trailed off as Welli's words hit home. "What do you mean, was he smitten enough? You don't think Liberty is romantically interested in me, do you?" An odd flutter in her heartbeat caught her by surprise. "I mean, now and again, he looked at me a little too long, as if I had custard on my cheek that he desperately wanted to wipe off, but he never said or did anything to indicate romance was on his mind. Not so much as a single poem or a bunch of roses passed from him to me. And I must have told him at least ten times how much I loved poetry and roses. Not that I was dropping any hints, you understand."

"Heavens forefend." Welli clutched his imaginary pearls.

She mused, "Then again, perhaps he's intimidated by my British accent? Americans can be so peculiar about a properly inflected verb. Or the fact that I'm a member of the landed gentry, despite that land mostly being a large hole in the ground where the Hall used to stand. Or maybe—"

Welli held up his hand. "Or maybe he's looking for a companion who doesn't deceive him, shoot him, and then try and dress him as an accessory to an assault on fashion?"

Could it be that Welli has a point? Oh dear.

He continued, "And as pleased as I am that you're determined to chart a new course through life, switching one type of weapon for another, no matter how benign, doesn't sound like the sort of career that leads toward an upwardly mobile marriage to a member of the landed gentry. Flirting with foreigners aside, you don't want to be the last of the Haltwhistle line forever, do you? I hate to sound like our ill-tempered godmother, the Dowager Countess of Benchley, but—"

"Now I'm a baroness, even Auntie Madge might be persuaded that I don't need to marry the first chinless wonder who proposes matrimony. Not that I'd dare say this to her face, but I intend to surpass everyone's expectations for me. I'll become more than marriage material, more than a weapons expert, more than I can possibly begin to imagine. The world is my oyster, and I intend to swallow it whole in one salty gulp."

Welli winced. "And there's an image I don't want to dwell on. My dear, sweet Connie. I know that it's not easy for a bright, idiosyncratic woman to find a role in this world where she can thrive and not just survive, but perhaps you should just take a breath and pause for a moment? You've misplaced your childhood home, you're starting a new business with a man who's a virtual stranger, and your fashion sense seems to be going from bad to worse. How about setting aside your ambitions and enjoying all that Paris has to offer? Must everything be do or die the very moment you think of it?"

Constance scowled and thumped the heel of her boot against the carriage floor. She yelled, "Hearn, please take us directly to the opera. Mr. Trusdale has missed his chance to join our party."

"Very good, miss," called back her stalwart driver. The golden dragon carriage surged like a British dreadnought toward Queen Victoria's foe *du jour*.

As Welli hung on to his armrest for dear life, Constance said, "There you go, dear cousin. We're heading out to enjoy the night. Happy?"

"Not as happy as I'd be if you were dressed in the latest fashions. I'm certain the patrons of the Opéra Garnier aren't ready for this level of lamb at their chic event," grumbled the young lord.

Constance threw back her head and laughed. "Then the opera house had better gird its loins, because 'Miss Adventure,' as Trusdale likes to call me, is determined to have a bloody good time tonight. With or without him. Mark my words, Welli, this is the start of night to remember."

"And suddenly, that's what I'm most afraid of," said Welli as Boudicca yapped excitedly and bounced upon the silk cushions. Constance chuckled and stood to lean out the carriage door window to take in the Parisian air.

The most romantic city in Europe beguiled with its cherry-tree-lined walks, lush, manicured parks, elegant stone and iron buildings, bustling boutiques, and terraced cafés. Fine wine flowed, laughter drifted on the breeze, and the citrus perfume of pink peony flower beds mingled with the scent of fresh-baked goods from a thousand fine patisseries. The sweet fragrances almost overcame the tang of horse manure that carpeted the streets of the world's prettiest capital.

Along the paved sidewalk, besotted couples and their chaperones promenaded between stately matrons out for their evening constitutional and drunken aristocrats caught in the eternal circle between theater, restaurant, bar, and poker game.

Constance leaned out as far as she could over the carriage door, taking in the sights and sounds, reveling in a city that was almost as lovely as her hometown of Sheffield. Throw in a few extra fountains, and Paris might even rival her favorite soot-stained center of British industry.

Squinting, one might almost imagine the Seine to be as glorious as the River Don, glimmering in the soft evening sunshine that painted the city gold until the gas lamps were lit at ten.

Her breath caught beneath her corset. There, in between families strolling beside the river, a tall man in a black duster coat and a Stetson ran as if the hounds of hell were snapping at his heels. "What the—?"

Constance blinked, then roared, "Hearn, forget the opera." The carriage juddered to a halt in the middle of its lane, causing French hansom drivers to share their opinion of Hearn's driving with raised voices and whips.

Welli peered through the window. "Good heavens, is that—?"

"Let's find out." She bellowed to the driver's box, "Hearn, follow that cowboy!"

Welli gaped at her.

"Discreetly," she yelled. "Very, very, discreetly." She grinned at her cousin and leaned back out of the window, aware that this cautious approach was not one that would have occurred to her old impulsive self of an hour ago. The new, improved Baroness Haltwhistle was certainly full of surprises.

Constance couldn't wait to find out what she'd do next . . .

Chapter 2:
Springtime in Paris

The grass was always greener in another dimension. US secret agent and former cowboy Liberty Trusdale imagined that in a parallel world, he wasn't sprinting for his life in a Parisian park. Instead, he was enjoying the cool spring evening with a splendid stroll along the River Seine. By his side sashayed the indomitable British aristocrat Constance Haltwhistle. But this was not the wild-eyed woman who'd shot him at lunchtime, her long red hair a Medusan tangle swept into a tornado by rain and wind atop the Eiffel Tower. This Constance's smooth, combed tresses shone like a copper penny beneath her jauntily tilted yellow miniature bowler. Her snowy lace gown was cinched with an embroidered daffodil over-corset that sparked their conversation about botany in exotic locales she'd never seen but had read about in books. This joyous exchange during their first day in Paris was trapped in the amber of his mind. Such moments with Constance made life worth living. But would she also be the death of him?

Trusdale raced on through the park that traced a green line of tranquility alongside the river, his Western boots scattering gravel from the pristine path into the manicured flower beds. The scent of burnt leather filled his nostrils as his scorched duster coat flapped in the breeze. Since when had he become a laboratory rat in Constance's mad experiments? Had the gauntlet gone off accidentally, or was she truly that reckless? As he'd stomped away from her to find solace and whisky in the nearest underground cabaret, had she deigned to apologize, only to have her words blown away on the wind? He certainly hadn't heard an "I'm sorry" from her ruby lips, but should that surprise him from a woman whose understanding of modern manners was based on an out-of-date etiquette book?

More importantly, did his spy agency know that he'd been spending time with the ethereal high-end arms designer known only by the alias the Brass Queen?

The summons from his handler had come as they always did—when he least expected them. He'd tilted up his whisky glass to see a typed note stuck to the bottom. Lieutenant Godfrey Gillingham, code name God, wanted to catch up, right now, at an attic apartment in the seamier section of the city.

Refusal was not an option, and survival was uncertain. No handlers ever requested a face-to-face meeting unless something had gone very right or very wrong. And nothing had gone right for him since the moment he'd agreed to play the part of his deceased brother, the brilliant engineer J. F., to infiltrate Queen Victoria's Steamwerks.

The plan had been simple enough: Figure out if the imperial despot intended to send her redcoat army to reclaim the lost colony of America. It was complicated by a search for kidnapped scientists, a stolen invisibility serum, and the Swedish King Oscar II pulling strings to start a global war. And now here he was in Paris, chumming around with British aristocrats, ex-Steamwerks scientists, and a former arms dealer to the Queen herself, none of whom knew he was a spy.

He ran on, scattering pigeons as he tore by a dozen statues of Louis XVIII posturing with the confidence of an absolute monarch. Whereas other European royal families had fallen victim to revolution, France's kings had managed to quell all opposition to their reign with nooses and firing squads. The ancient kingdoms of France, Britain, and Spain all demanded their subjects to be loyal to their respective royals, and woe betide any who dared to be defiant in thought or deed. Such loyalty was identical to that demanded of field agents by his own shadowy employer. What if God thought he'd abandoned his secret mission in Sheffield because of his growing affection for a certain red-haired weapons designer with questionable morality? Was God about to terminate his contract and his life for failing his country? Being tardy would only make matters worse. Perhaps it was time for a shortcut?

He vaulted over the nearest flower bed and shot toward the busy six-carriage-wide boulevard that ran beside the public space. Like most pedestrians who risked death to cross the endless stream of horse-drawn vehicles, he mumbled a prayer as he dodged between hooves, wheels, and the whirling whips of irritated drivers. One stumble, and a stranger's carriage would send him to the afterlife, just as it had his brother. Constance had told him that in other dimensions, alternate versions of his beloved brother were alive and well. If true, he found comfort in that, but how far could he trust the word of a lady who lied so readily?

Admittedly, her father had indoctrinated her to put her family's survival above all else. Constance was a rough-cut diamond with facets that sparkled above deep fissures and flaws. Catch her in just the right light, and she was brighter than any star.

But only a fool would try to reach her.

He spotted what seemed to be a clear path through the traffic and leaped for safe passage. A flash of steel-shoed hooves flashed by his face, causing him to duck, as a pair of chestnut carriage ponies reared indignantly at his ill-timed dash. "Sorry," he shouted to their ginger underbellies, spinning and stumbling backward alongside their carriage. Its door swung open, and out tumbled its unfortunate occupant in whirl of purple velvet and green gossamer. He grabbed for and missed the falling victim as bicycle tires screeched behind him and an angry male voice roared, "*Écarte-toi, idiot.*" Confused, he jumped the exact wrong way and crashed to the cobblestones amidst a blur of metal spokes, a wicker basket, and a dozen chocolate croissants.

Trusdale groaned as pain raged through his ribs and a torrent of French insults from the hapless cyclist seared his ears. The Sorbonne linguistics program he'd attended years before on the agency's dime had trained him to understand conversational French. Sadly, the course had not covered being screamed at in the street by an irate baker casting dispersions upon one's ancestry. He lost the plot after his "grandmother had married a goat"—or was her groom an "artichoke"? The apron-wearing cyclist sprang to his feet, shook his fist, and continued the barrage of curses while stomping on his spilled croissants.

Apparently, Trusdale's grandmother had graduated to performing burlesque dances for airship pirates and other unsavory characters. Would that were true. It sure would have made the chat over his family's Thanksgiving dinners more entertaining than tales of birthing calves, dust storms, and dried-up water holes.

The fallen carriage victim was buried in a heaping mass of green gossamer tulle that had fortunately cushioned their fall as surely as an eiderdown. White bloomers emblazoned with joyful pink piglets led down to a pair of shapely knees atop green leather riding boots completely at odds with the feminine flounces, buttons, and bows decorating ten layers of petticoat.

Poor woman. Hope she's not hurt. What the heck is she wearing?

He pushed himself up to his feet, ignoring the uninjured cyclist for now and stepped toward the lady. "*Mademoiselle*, are you—Constance?"

With a splutter, the redhead emerged from her cocoon like an angry butterfly with a score to settle. "Mr. Trusdale. May I inquire why you're racing across the street like a fox chased by hounds?"

"Are you following me?" He glanced up at the carriage window. It was a perfect golden frame for a wide-eyed Welli holding a Yorkshire terrier puppy. "First you electrocute me, and now you're following me too?"

"Please, don't blame me for this latest display of insanity," said Welli. "We're innocent bystanders, aren't we, Boo?"

The puppy yapped its agreement.

"Traitors!" scowled Constance.

The cyclist unleashed another flight of creative invective and stomped over to Trusdale. He held out his palm expectantly, heedless of the continuing stream of carriages that thundered over the remains of his croissants.

Trusdale could only deal with one disaster at a time. He held out his hand to Constance to help her rise. "Are you hurt?"

"Not permanently."

"Good." He yanked her to her feet, none too gently. Their eyes met, and a tingle of natural electricity jolted through his hand as keenly as her gauntlet strike had. Did she feel it too?

"Static," she said. "Just to clarify, I'm not wearing the . . . you know what . . . under my opera glove."

"Oh, so now you're doing exactly what we agreed? You swore you wouldn't work on it without me, never mind wearing it in public and shooting me with the damned thing. You're unbelievable. Literally."

Her mouth flapped in goldfish style as he turned to the cyclist. He grudgingly dipped his hand into one of the many pockets hidden inside his black leather duster coat. His fingers closed upon two Louis d'or coins. The solid gold currency was emblazoned with a pompadour-wearing likeness of the reigning French monarch, King Louis XVIII. The self-proclaimed Sun King minted what was arguably the shiniest currency on the planet. Anti-monarchists quipped that the coins were polished to a sheen with the silky bloomers cast off by Louis's four hundred mistresses. But such comments were always spoken in hushed tones, even outside the boundaries of Louis's ever-expanding Empire.

The King's tolerance for criticism was as thin as the layer of gold leaf that covered the flying city of Versailles. Defended by a thousand airships, the mechanical marvel dwarfed Queen Victoria's paltry earthbound Buckingham Palace on every level. Victoria, the despotic royal battle-ax, had offered a bounty for any British airship that shot the city down.

It was a reward none would ever claim. Versailles's aerial cannons were as lethal as the sharpened hedge trimmers of the palace's famed gardeners.

He dropped the fancy coins into the cyclist's outstretched palm. The man wrinkled his nose in pretend disgust at the amount. Trusdale gave him a wry smile. "Oh, come on, now, be reasonable. You could buy ten new cycles and a hundred croissants with that amount. I'm a tourist, not an idiot."

The cyclist's eyes bulged in fury. He tilted back his head and shouted, "Gendarmes! Gendarmes!"

Trusdale held up his hands to placate the man. "Okay, I'll give you one more coin. There's no need to involve the—"

A blue-uniformed police officer appeared as if by magic behind Constance. Trusdale groaned as the cyclist told an exaggerated tale of aggravated assault by a cowboy. The police officer narrowed his eyes at all three non-French participants involved in the debacle.

Trusdale took a tentative step back away from the gendarme. No one should keep their God waiting. He was probably in enough trouble as it was. "This was merely an accident, officer. This good fellow's been paid for his pastries. I'm in a kind of a rush, so please forgive me for stepping away—"

"Is this your dragon vehicle, mademoiselle?" asked the police officer in perfect English to Constance. Boo took offense at the officer's tone and growled with all the ferocity that a two-pound puppy can muster.

The officer sneered at the dog's attempt to defend her mistress. "And is that your dog?"

"Yes, to both questions. Why?" asked Constance.

"Do you have a license for either?"

She placed her hands on her hips. "Oh, let me guess. Are these special 'licenses' you've created right now that we can only pay for in cash? What do they call that here, Welli?"

"The English tax," sighed Welli. "And I think you should pay the nice locals whatever they want and hop back into the carriage. The opera waits for no man, woman, or Yorkie."

Both the cyclist and the officer held their palms out toward Constance.

She scoffed. "Oh, no, you don't. The old me would have paid you off without a second thought, but the new me has principles. I'm making a brand-new start in life, and I refuse to be bullied in the street by scoundrels salivating to take advantage of innocent foreigners on their shores. If I give in, you'll pull the same stunt with another, and another. The rot stops here!"

Trusdale took two more steps back away from the fuming redhead. "Well, lady, gentlemen, and canine, much as I'd love to stay and discuss all this further, I have an urgent appointment to attend to."

Constance snapped her head around to stare at him. "An appointment with whom? Surely, you'll join us at the opera? Welli will be absolutely devastated if you don't come."

The young lord raised his eyebrows. "I will? I mean, yes, of course I will."

Trusdale shook his head.

"Not tonight, I'm afraid. I'll have to take a rain check."

"A what? It's not even raining," said Constance, gesturing at the heavens. "You're still sulking about being shot, aren't you? Well, that's the most childish thing I've ever heard. Here I am, standing in the middle of the street, offering you an olive branch—"

"If you do not pay the fine, mademoiselle, I shall drag you directly to jail," snarled the officer. "You now owe a third fine, for refusing to pay the first two fines. Plus, a boulevard fine."

"And my croissants," said the cyclist, gesturing at his fallen pastries. "Pay up, English lady."

"My dear girl, perhaps your principles could wait until after the opera?" said Welli.

"*Non!*" shouted Constance. "That's French for *no!* I shall not be harangued in the street by con artists and swindlers, no matter the state of their pastries."

Trusdale took another step back, casting a glance toward the far sidewalk and his route to God. Agency handlers were not known for their infinite patience.

Constance slammed the door closed on the carriage and stood her ground, eyes blazing, chin jutted to the firmament, fists clenched. All five feet of her curvaceous form sang with the power and authority of a queen, minus her crown.

Trusdale's breath caught in his throat. Even disheveled, furious, and in imminent danger of being hauled off to prison, Constance was a force to be reckoned with.

She spoke with a regal air. "Sirs, do you know who I am?"

The police officer and the deliveryman shook their heads.

"Good. Hearn, to the opera!" As the dragon carriage lurched forward, Welli and Boo were launched back into their seat.

Constance hitched up her petticoats and bolted for the park.

As the jaws of the police officer and cyclist hit the cobbles, Trusdale shot in the opposite direction, toward the far pavement, dodging horses and vehicles as he ran. He stumbled over the curb and onto the broad paving stones of the sidewalk.

Ignoring a startled shriek from a pompadour-wearing nobleman, Trusdale darted into an alleyway between two high-end jewelry stores. He risked a backward glance. Constance was sprinting like a madwoman through the park, startling pedestrians and pigeons alike as she ran. The police officer was giving chase as the cyclist pocketed his coins and strode away, leaving his cycle where it lay in the street.

Should I go help Constance?

Some things were more important than friends, family, and badly dressed wild women. His country called, and he would answer.

May God have mercy on his soul.

Chapter 3:
Mission Improbable

Trusdale had never known whether his agency handler was a single man or a committee.

His God had proved to be neither.

Sunlight streamed down through the garret skylight and cast a halo around God's snowy pompadour. She sat with the dignity of Athena behind a mahogany desk piled high with telegrams and newspapers from across the globe. Steel spectacles framed piercing gray eyes complemented by the silver and blue brocade of her sturdy travel gown. An agency-issue locket ring upon her finger no doubt carried the deadly poison that old-school spymasters loved to drop in a target's tea. The hidden sword walking cane propped against her desk would prove quick to hand if she chose to end their meeting with his death. He may have the weight advantage, but no woman would have reached the position of agency handler without leaving a sizable body count. It appeared that God was traveling incognito, dressed as a French aristocrat to better slide through the King's checkpoints with forged travel papers. Trusdale's own approach to spycraft relied less on stealth and more on exploiting his Americanness. It was rare that anyone assumed he was anything other than a good-natured tourist. To his mind, the goals of covert operations could best be achieved via generous bribes and supplying copious amounts of alcohol to loosen the tongues of local informants.

It was obvious this God was of a different persuasion. Even her letter opener carried a sinister air of being used to slice open more than letters. Peering over her glasses, she waved Trusdale to sit in what seemed to be a schoolboy's wooden chair someone had placed before the desk.

Trusdale gingerly perched his six-foot-two frame upon the chair and tilted up his chin to meet her gaze. The low chair was a classic Military Intelligence Corps tactic, designed to keep an informant off his game. *Just how much trouble am I in?*

God pursed her lips and held up a yellow telegram addressed to the fictional *Lieutenant Godfrey Gillingham.* "Dear God . . ." started every telegram across her desk, followed by banal musings on the weather that hid the correspondent's true message. God demanded regular reports from her undercover agents on the antics of America's allies and enemies alike.

Trusdale squinted at the telegram, stamped with the scarlet crown of the British Communications Service. He'd sent the sparsely worded missive from the tiny train station near Haltwhistle Hall, Constance's ancestral home. Moments later, he'd ridden for his life atop a headstrong black stallion named Beelzebub with a horde of redcoat cavalrymen on his heels, only to be scooped up to safety via an airship Constance had commandeered as Haltwhistle Hall was sucked through a giant aether portal into another dimension.

It was testament to spending several weeks in the company of Constance and her friends that his mind had already adapted to maintain an illusion of order in a chaotic universe. She may have led him on the path through the looking glass, but instinct told him he shouldn't provide a map there to just anyone, certainly not to an agency handler with a glacial stare and a frozen heart.

God inspected him as if he were a caterpillar she'd found munching on her salad at luncheon. "I received your telegram from Sheffield, agent. And your dossier on your Steamwerks assignment." She gestured at a thin manila folder tucked beneath yesterday's *Le Monde* newspaper. For once, King Louis didn't grace the front page. Over a sketch of a shadowy figure in a black hooded cloak and Venetian noblewoman's mask, the headline asked, *Qui est le justicier?*

God followed his gaze. "A vigilante is stalking the city's muggers. No one has a clue as to who she is, including the man who's about to walk through that door."

Behind Trusdale, the brass handle began to turn. Trusdale jumped to his feet, fists raised, ready to fight whoever or whatever . . .

"Sit down, you fool," God hissed. And down he sat.

Into the garret strode a tall, mustachioed French general in a tailored white uniform with royal-blue cuffs and a kepi flat-topped cap. Three gold medals pinned to the officer's chest celebrated command victories against British foes. The historic rivals were currently bickering over which of their empires got the best slice of Africa. As ever with imperial expansion, no one asked the indigenous people their opinions on the matter. *Maybe in another dimension, every human gets a fair slice of the pie?*

They sure didn't in this one.

The officer grinned, swept off his cap, and bowed. "Général Malaise, at your service, Madam."

God nodded. "Général, good of you to stop by. I was about to discuss your situation with my top agent here in Paris, Captain Cowpoke."

Trusdale blinked. Since when had he become the top agent anywhere? Also, exactly how many forms did he have to fill in to get that code name changed to something more dashing? Did the agency just file his name change request forms straight into the waste bin?

"Cowpoke here infiltrated the Royal Steamwerks mere days before coming to France," God continued. "He has intimate knowledge of our target. Cowpoke, you're honored to be in the presence of one of the senior brass in the French army. Général Malaise here is our mole in Louis XVIII's household guard. He's been feeding us tidbits about the royal court's antics for decades, and he represents a growing number of intellectuals, artists, proletarians, and military officers who want to build a more egalitarian future for France." She held up her right hand, eyes raised to the heavens above. "Imagine a glorious future where France stands as a republic, just like the US today. She could become our strongest ally in Europe against Victoria's redcoats. We shall stand as sister nations, free of all tyranny."

Malaise clapped his hands in delight. "Exactly, madam. All shall prosper. Together, our countries shall protect one another from the British storm."

Hmm. God sure knew how to sell hope in a jar when it served US interests. Trusdale leaned back in his chair as Malaise seated himself on the corner of God's desk. How difficult could it be to find two adult-sized guest chairs in all of Paris? Was she trying to keep the debonair Frenchman off his game, too? "Pardon my sayin', Général, but you don't exactly strike me as the revolutionary type."

Malaise chuckled. "Should I leave my boots unpolished and forgo my barber's shears? I look exactly as a military man should, no more, no less. As such, I rarely draw the King's eye, which is a good way to survive in his court. Louis is more paranoid by the day. Just this morning, he ordered twenty poets hung because of scurrilous sonnets about the size of his nose. What grown man is afraid of rhyming couplets? And did you know that he recently declared himself to be a deity? His ego is larger than the sun his flying palace blocks from shining down on the peasants' crops. They say ruined wheat fields follow Versailles's aerial meanderings across our great land."

"I guess that would rile folks up," said Trusdale.

"Indeed. Just as the brave US revolutionaries once got riled up at Britain's mad King George. America is our inspiration nation. But let me be clear, we strive to achieve a kind and peaceful revolution, not a war between the classes. Lord knows, we have all seen enough war in our time."

God nodded. "That we have, Malaise. You should know that Captain Cowpoke here won a few cavalry medals himself in his youth, fighting the Canadian Mounties.

I can only hope that Canada will one day escape the tyranny of Queen Victoria's yoke, just as the French people will throw off Louis's chains."

Malaise pressed his hand to his chest. "With your help, Madam."

"Absolutely. And together our countries shall stand firm against further imperial British encroachment." God pulled Trusdale's slim dossier toward her and tapped it, smiling at Malaise. "We have everything we need right here."

Trusdale knew damn well that the dossier held only his hand-drawn map of the Steamwerks armaments production facility, a count of the redcoat forces in Sheffield, and the barest details of how he'd been dragged into searching for kidnapped British scientists by Constance.

He'd left her name out of the report entirely, referring only to a local woman who had assisted him with transportation issues. There was no need to mention that his simple spy mission had turned into an interdimensional incident involving telepathic krakens, invisible assassins, and a plot to overthrow the Queen of England. Accidentally helping to save the life of Queen Victoria, imperial foe of both England and France, was not something he wanted to admit. Not even to himself.

Malaise said, "So, Captain Cowpoke, tell me all about Constance Haltwhistle and her eccentric entourage."

Ice ran through Trusdale's veins. He licked his lips and asked, in his most nonchalant tone, "Who, now? I can't recall that name."

God tut-tutted and slammed a wanted poster down on the desk in front of Trusdale. It offered a reward of a thousand British pounds and showed a line drawing of Constance in a flowing ball gown, seated upon a rearing mechanical unicorn. Her long red hair swirled artistically around her as she thrust a studded Prussian polo mallet to the clouds.

Even in miniature, her eyes blazed with fury and defiance. "*This* Constance Haltwhistle. The woman with whom you spent three days in England. The woman with whom you traveled to Paris. The woman who was Yorkshire's most wanted provocateur for a brief moment in time."

"Um . . ." Trusdale scratched his ear.

"Let's see if this jolts your memory." God slapped down another wanted poster.

Trusdale grimaced at the sight of himself atop a mechanical dodo, dressed in an Elizabethan-style sunflower costume with a large petal ruff around his neck, skin-tight silk stockings, and a puff of pansied hose around his hips.

"Oh, yeah, the costume ball. It's been a couple of weeks since then. I've kinda lost track of the details."

Malaise picked up Constance's poster and peered at the drawing. "This shapely siren doesn't look like a woman a man could easily forget."

"Ugh. Trust me, she's exactly the type of woman you'd want to forget. Her entire ancestry is made up of nothing but rogues, dilettantes, and thieves, and that's from her own lips! She's headstrong, opinionated—she's just impossible on every level."

"Ah, all the best women are." Malaise cocked a flirtatious eyebrow at God.

God groaned. "Please, gentlemen, spare me your thoughts on anything but the facts at hand. This woman flew her airship from England with two of Britain's top military scientists aboard—Doctors Maya Chauhan from India, and Zhi Huang from Hong Kong. Apparently, they are old friends of hers?"

Trusdale nodded. "Yup, with an emphasis on the *old* part. The pair of them are in their late sixties. Sweet, harmless old coots, on the whole. Now, I'm well aware they used to do military science stuff at Victoria's Royal Steamwerks, but that's all behind them. Their colleague, McKinley, runs the place now. Chauhan and Huang are retired from the British war machine. Truth be told, they're kinda sweet on each other. It's heartwarming to see folks that age finding someone to spend their golden years with."

"Ah, it is never too late for love. Not for any whose heart still beats with passion," said Malaise, with a waggle of his well-coiffed eyebrows at God.

Apparently, Malaise was important enough to God for her to overlook his flirtatious conduct. Or maybe she quite liked the uniform?

God snorted. She pushed her steel glasses up on her nose. "Let's cut to the chase, shall we? Cowpoke, have you ever heard of an underground arms dealer known only as the Brass Queen?"

Trusdale's throat dried. "Can't say that I have."

God reached for the fattest folder on her desk, boldly stamped in red with the words "Top Secret." She rapped her fingertips upon the folder. "I have here shipping reports that relate to certain goods linked to travelers on the *Lady Penelope* airship."

Tension seized Trusdale's shoulders with an iron grip. He forced himself to perform the most casual of casual shrugs. "A lot of people, goods, and animals get moved on that airship. It's manned by an itinerant crew who wouldn't look amiss on a pirate ship. The helmswoman carries a gold cutlass, for heaven's sake. Passengers include not only Chauhan and Huang, but numerous servants, aristocrats, and farmyard animals including horses, cows, pigs, and chickens. There's even a snappy little Yorkshire terrier—"

"I'm guessing the dog doesn't make arms shipments to India. Our conclusion is that the Brass Queen can only be one person. A woman skilled enough to manage an international armaments business for years without anyone suspecting that she was involved. A woman who designs the most advanced aether-guns and blunderbusses known to man. A woman who only sells her bespoke goods to royalty, aristocrats, and well-heeled despots. The Brass Queen is none other than"—

A bead of sweat ran down Trusdale's spine.

—"Dr. Maya Chauhan."

Trusdale marveled that his famously chiseled jaw didn't drop clean through the floorboards. "Maya? But, well, she seems so harmless. Are you absolutely sure?"

"We're sixty percent sure. And that's good enough for us."

Malaise added, "We have a grand plan, Cowpoke. We intend to compel Chauhan to design a very specific weapon—a kingslayer."

Trusdale gaped. "You want twinkle-eyed, almost-granny-like Maya to kill the King of France?"

Malaise smoothed his clipped mustache with a manicured finger. "Not exactly. After all, *we* are not the villains here. Understand, Cowpoke, that Louis's Versailles is the seat of his power. The palace has been held aloft by secret technology for the past one hundred years. Not once in all that time has it landed. *Mais jamais!* Records from the time of the launch state that at first, the palace floated a mere thirty feet off the ground, and supplies were simply catapulted up to it once a week. Now, it soars at two to three hundred feet and supplies are brought in by airship. If the palace crashes, Louis's self-proclaimed godhood crashes with it."

Trusdale nodded. "It would be an embarrassment for the King, I guess."

Malaise snorted. "It would be far more than that. The aristocracy would literally be brought down to the level of the common man, and a new democracy will rise in its place. We intend to blackmail the Brass Queen into developing a weapon that will force the palace to land in an uninhabited area. Then, my troops will escort Louis and his hangers-on off to the port of their choice to exit France. 'No blood, no mess—just a city brought down to rest.' This is a good rhyme for a good plan, *n'est-ce pas?*"

With the *thud-thud* of his heartbeat pounding in his ears, Trusdale took in a deep breath of the garret's dusty air and relaxed his tensed muscles. No need to alert anyone to his personal feelings. After all, they were all on the same side, weren't they? Then again, if his world could be just a little less fuzzy about what constituted good versus evil, he'd probably sleep better at night. "All right, it's an ambitious plan, Malaise, and I see where you're going with it. What I don't understand is: where do I fit into all this?"

God said, "Simple. You traveled with the crew of the *Lady Penelope*. You know her crew and passengers. You can use every single one of their lives as leverage to convince the Brass Queen, Dr. Chauhan, that cooperating with Malaise and me is in her best interest. Who knows? If she plays her cards right, there's a chance they might all live through this."

Trusdale rubbed his temples. If he refused to help, they'd send other agency operatives in his place. It was a sobering thought. Blackmail situations often blew up in unexpected ways, and the fallout could be lethal to all involved.

I need time to think . . .

God's unwavering stare told him his time was up. Trusdale gritted his teeth and stood. "May I?" He leaned over the desk and picked up the Brass Queen dossier, the wanted posters, and the newspaper for good luck. "Got to get my facts together, so I know exactly what to say to bring this 'queen' onto our side. Rest assured: You'll both get exactly what you want, on that I give my word. I just need a little time to sort out the details. Maybe a few months to—"

God snapped, "You have exactly one week, or I'll take care of the situation myself."

Trusdale beamed his widest tourist grin and tipped his Stetson at her. "Don't you worry yourself, ma'am. I'll have this situation handled lickety-split; I swear it on my life."

Malaise's eyes lit with genuine delight. "Ah, most excellent, Captain Cowpoke. You have my utmost confidence."

God's icy gaze suggested otherwise, but nevertheless, she dismissed him with a wave of her hand.

With his heart sinking into his Western boots, Trusdale clomped down the wooden stairs from the garret. He stuffed the fat dossier and other paperwork into the secret pockets that lined his coat.

He'd walked into the meeting afraid to die. Now, dying looked like a simpler option. Nausea claimed his stomach as his brain attempted to handle one more shift in perspective. In another dimension, was an alternate version of him content to be the bold American spy, putting his life on the line to manipulate people and events for America's gain? His poppa, the retired cavalry general, had pulled strings to induct him into the agency after Trusdale got himself shot one too many times on the battlefield while trying to save his men. He could never save them all, and seeing good men die to inch forward a meaningless battle line had worn on his soul. The agency had promised him service without having to see men make the ultimate sacrifice for their country. All he had to do was to pretend he was someone he wasn't.

The irony was that his late brother J. F. had also been employed by the agency. He'd served as an undercover operative at Nikola Tesla's company before winning a prized consultancy position at the Steamwerks. It wasn't until J. F.'s accident that he'd found out his own flesh and blood served the same God he did. Every family holds secrets, but two spies in the same family, with neither knowing the other's covert role, must be unusual. God had played both brothers perfectly, never revealing to either their shared role.

The stairs appeared to revolve around him as his spirits sank to a new low. What other secrets was God keeping from him? Or was it safer not to know?

He tripped on the bottom stair and stumbled out into cobbled alleyway between tenement buildings. Even the slums in Paris were tall and elegant and carried an air of looking down on him. He headed, shoulders slumped, not for the main boulevards but toward a flickering gaslit bar sign that promised drink, dance, and vaudeville delights.

There was a time he'd have put on his racing blinkers and run the race the way they wanted him to, never looking left or right, straight as an arrow with no swerving, head down to the finish line. But now . . . He couldn't deny that Welli and his faithful valet, Mr. Singh, had served in Her Majesty's redcoats. Doctors Chauhan and Huang had worked for decades in Victoria's war laboratory. And Constance had traded whimsical weapons across the globe without giving a single thought as to what they might be used for.

Yet somehow, the collection of misfits and miscreants that made up the crew of the *Lady Penelope* almost felt like family, right down to the bickering and affection lashed out in equal quantities to all who pulled up a chair.

His moral high ground sank into a swamp of doubt and self-loathing. Where in this was the noble purpose he thought he'd find working as a field agent? Where was the satisfaction of knowing he'd made the world a slightly better place? And who was he to judge who filled the role of hero or villain on the eternal stage?

He couldn't turn his back on his duty to his country and family back home, but there was a point at which a man still needed to be able to look himself in the eye in the mirror. Was there any way for him to navigate this sinking airship to a safe landing for all?

He set his jaw and strode into the bar, ready to formulate a plan over the best whisky in the house. He needed to satisfy both God and Malaise that he was committed to their purpose, lest they replace him with a deadlier agent whose first task would be to eliminate Cowpoke himself for failure in the field. Plus, he needed to persuade Constance into creating a kingslayer superweapon that could bring down a palace, all while keeping his role as a US spy hidden from the crew of the *Lady Penelope*. If Constance had shot him when she believed him to be a friend, how would she react if she thought he was an enemy agent spying on the Brass Queen? And how far should he go to protect a woman who clearly didn't want or need his protection?

One thing was clear.

What God wanted from him would take nothing short of a miracle.

Chapter 4:
La Femme Électrique

As the bells of Notre-Dame announced it was five a.m. to a city too sleepy to care, Baroness Constance Haltwhistle wished that she could meet a better class of criminal. The waning moon waltzed giddily with storm clouds overhead as she strode down the center of the dockland's alley with a black velvet cloak wrapped tight around her. The silver light of Artemis cast fleeting luminescence into dark tenement doorways that should have been teeming with villains. Yet, the three reprobates she sensed following her had sneakily taken to the tiled roofs above. The occasional clink of a hobnailed boot on slate was all that betrayed their presence. Constance held her breath as long as her corset allowed her to, straining to hear the movements of the thugs above the clack-clack of her pea-green wooden-heeled riding boots. The boots wouldn't have been a fashionista's choice of footwear to go with her now-filthy gamboling sheep ball gown, but comfort was king to the Brass Queen. Her sensible footwear had proven their worth as she'd spent the entire night running, hiding, and backtracking from the remarkably enthusiastic gendarme and the myriad of policemen he'd pulled in to scout the streets for Paris's most-wanted evader of fines. No tourist was allowed to escape the English tax once it had been imposed, and the police had left no stone unturned to find her. They'd even managed to trail her back to the Grand Hotel du Louvre. She'd shot in through the employees' entrance, avoiding the marble-columned lobby and the watchful eyes of the hotel manager. Bounding up the back stairs two at a time, she'd reached the third floor and the crew of the *Lady Penelope*'s block of suites.

Once inside her room, she'd barely had time to slip on her Venetian noblewoman's porcelain face mask, an emerald tiara, an electric battle mitten, pink opera gloves, and a black, hooded cloak. She'd bundled her old cloak and several pillows beneath her bed cover to present a reasonable approximation of her sleeping form. With the addition of a long red wig she kept in her bedside table for just such an occasion, the resulting body double would fool anyone who stayed at least ten feet away from her bed and didn't turn on the gas lamp.

Hot on her heels, the gendarme and his colleagues reached the third floor and began banging on every door, seeking their unnamed but entirely infuriating British quarry. They harangued the hotel manager into unlocking every door that wasn't answered, including her own. She'd hidden herself by squishing down inside the marble tub in her bathroom, occasionally popping her head up like a nervous bunny to peer out through the slightly ajar bathroom door.

Fortunately, her trusty servants had used the time bought by her evasive maneuverings to stash the dragon carriage and return to the hotel themselves. It took Hearn's massive bulk blocking the doorway to her bedchamber to halt the police search, as Cawley spluttered to all who would listen about the impropriety of disturbing a slumbering member of the landed gentry. Both servants attested that their mistress had not left her suite all day due to an acute case of languor brought on by too much poetry reading. Certainly, there had never been any attempts to venture out to the opera, which they claimed their mistress hated with a passion beyond reason.

Assured that Constance was an uncultured boor, the gendarmes who peered around Hearn's muscular frame into the bedroom were convinced that the pillows she'd hastily stuffed underneath the bed covers did indeed resemble the shape of a slumbering lady. Resigned to the fact that the tax-evading madwoman they sought was no longer within the grasp of the long arm of Parisian law, the police finally left.

Her servants knew better than to check the bed. They left her decoy pillows in place and retired, quietly closing the door behind them.

For a moment, she contemplated heading back into her room and taking a nap alongside her decoy. But there was science to do on the streets of Paris, and the bathroom window offered the perfect secret exit for a newly minted baroness to scramble down two drainpipes and drop into a back alley below.

Two hours later, dawn crept ever closer, as did the street ruffians who hunted her like cats following a solitary mouse. Constance reduced her pace to encourage the men to maintain their slow pursuit. It would be a shame to lose them now. After all, what was a science experiment without test subjects? And the conditions were absolutely perfect for this particular test. A spring evening in Paris allowed the city's crooks to take full advantage of unwary tourists who took a warm weather stroll beneath flickering gas lamps. By extinguishing certain lamps along the promenades, pools of darkness were created that allowed the innocent to be quickly relieved of their valuables. The hoodlums who followed her had managed to extinguish the lamps ahead so successfully that if it wasn't for the moonlight, she'd be effectively blind to their—hopefully imminent—attack.

The capricious moon abandoned her to lurk behind the deepening clouds. Fifty feet ahead, a man's rasping cough from the darkest of doorways caused Constance to halt. She cocked her head, mindful not to dislodge the emerald tiara she'd pinned onto her unkempt hair to catch the eye of bandits. *Is that the clink of a chain? What kind of would-be robber would carry a weapon that makes so much noise?* Then again, she had wandered a good half mile from the main thoroughfares. Perhaps the robbers didn't feel the need to hide their presence as carefully as they would in a more populated area.

What are they waiting for? It's not like I have all night to waste . . .

Hobnailed boots slammed onto the cobbles behind her.

Finally!

Constance spun on her heel to meet the cold eyes of a muscular thug squeezed into a three-piece suit. Two similarly clad compatriots were sliding down a rope from the roof. The well-dressed muggers couldn't possibly have had the time to tie a thick rope securely around a chimney stack just as she walked by. It must have been tied there prior to her arrival. Her throat tightened. She hadn't, by any chance, strolled into a trap, had she?

Ugh. That a blue-blooded heir to a hundred generations of rogues, scoundrels, and idiosyncratic inventors should find herself caught in a trap set by common crooks.

She might well die of embarrassment.

"Ahem," coughed a gruff voice behind her. Constance turned to see a bowler-hatted, silk-vested hoodlum with two mountains of muscle behind him. One bodyguard carried a ball-peen hammer and the other a four-foot length of heavy chain, which he had wrapped around his meaty fists. Both wore dark pin-striped waistcoats over burgundy shirts. Presumably, so as not to show the blood of any hapless victim they might leave behind in the night. It appeared that Parisian thieves dressed with more panache than all but the most avant-garde of British gentlemen, with the obvious exception of her Cousin Welli. His elegant ensembles would inspire lavish praise from even the notoriously stylish Italian muggers, right before they absconded with his latest diamond-pinned cravat and paisley tailcoat.

The two bodyguards hefted their weapons with an ease that suggested this was not their first night of midnight menacing. From behind her full-face porcelain mask, Constance graced them with a glare she considered far more threatening than their makeshift weapons. They gaped at her, then glanced at each other in confusion. She wrinkled her nose. *At least the hammer makes sense for a combat tool. It's quiet and somewhat concealable. The chain is just overkill.*

The bowler-hatted boss, apparently irritated by her glare, gestured a rude symbol at her and gushed forth an entire gutter of Gallic insults. A few words stood out in the torrent, including *justicier* and *va te tuer*. Constance's brow furrowed. Was he using a transitive verb? This was nothing like the formal French she'd learned at the knee of her governess. So far, she had been very careful not to speak during her evening excursions into the city's seedier streets so as not to betray her identity. But it appeared that a conversation was called for.

Using her finest French accent, she asked, "*Pardon, monsieur?*"

The boss narrowed his beady eyes to a slit. "You are English?"

"Certainly not," said Constance, genuinely offended. How did the Continentals always know exactly which country you were from even when you spoke to them in their native tongue?

Bowler-hat sneered, "You said that in English." His crew murmured in agreement.

It had been a *very* long night. She sighed. "Fine, so I'm English. What of it?"

"You've been making our lives very difficult, English. I ask my men, 'Where is the loot?' and they answer, 'The crazy masked woman took it all.' But they can never tell me *how*. You will answer both questions right now. Or else . . ." He made a slit across his throat with his hand.

How very dramatic. Constance squared her shoulders, hoping her full Venetian noblewoman's mask communicated the air of icy defiance this moment surely called for. "I have returned your stolen goods to their rightful owners." That is, she *would* return them. As soon as she'd figured out how to move the enormous stack of purloined watches, jewelry, and wallets she'd stashed beneath her bed at the hotel to the police without getting herself arrested.

Now that she stood facing six glowering hoodlums in an alley, it occurred to her that perhaps bringing Hearn along for backup might have been a prudent precaution. But then again, this new version of herself she was developing was an independent miss. After all, one can't rely on one's servants for everything, in spite of their stalwartness with Parisian gendarmes when the occasion called for it. The glory, and the danger, of this new life would be hers alone.

The boss thumped his barrel chest. "I am the loots' rightful owner. Me and the gang—"

"The gang and I," corrected Constance. "Both words are pronouns, but 'I' is a subject pronoun while 'me' is an object pronoun. Consider the English lesson my gift to you. I'd say that makes us even. Your loot, in return for my tutelage."

The hoodlums gasped and looked to their boss. His lips narrowed. "That's enough from you, crazy lady." He shook his fist and snarled, "We're going to end you, English. You will no longer be flying into our ointment. You will be as demised as a deceased dormouse." A smug smirk lit his flabby face as his followers grimly nodded their assent.

At least his English is becoming more colorful, if not more accurate.

Constance flung back her black velvet cloak to reveal her sheep-covered ball gown and pink leather opera gloves. Copper wiring traced a blooming rose pattern along the full length of the right glove to subtly mask the bumps and lumps of the device beneath. The baroness drew herself up to her full five-foot height and announced to the thugs, "This is your one and only chance, gentlemen, to go and surrender yourself to the local constabulary. Or I shall not be held responsible for the consequences." She raised the hefty weight of her pink right glove toward the boss as the men roared with laughter.

Constance blinked as the criminals ignored her glove to point and jeer at both her gown and pea-green boots. The boss snickered, "Had you never spoken a word,

English, one glance at your footwear and I would have known you were a subject of the dowdy Queen Victoria. But do not fret, for these monstrosities will still bring us a pretty penny. Perhaps we sell them to a museum of curiosities, yes?"

She stared down at her boots, "Well, I almost wore a lovely pair of pink dance slippers, but these are so much more comfortable . . ."

Without warning, they attacked *en masse.*

Constance swore and ducked as hammer, chain, and fists swung at her from all directions. Catching her footing on the cobbles, she used her lower center of gravity and an operatic sweep of her leather-lined velvet cloak to glide beneath the men's furious blows. *As water flows around the rocks,* as her kung fu instructor, Mistress Ying, used to say. The black cloak tossed like an angry sea as the men punched and kicked toward their luckless prey.

But Constance had swept like a leaf to the outer rim of their whirlpool of hate. Standing behind the boss with her right arm raised, she slapped her left palm onto her right forearm, hitting one of the five dials beneath the glove that controlled a range of shock levels from "Ouch" up to "Naptime." The brass gauntlet beneath the glove hummed as its copper wiring pulsed out a net of pure electricity toward the villains, right from her outstretched fingertips. For a split second, the net of lightning lit the alley as bright as winter stars above an iceberg. The monochrome scene crumbled into disarray as the electric current net dropped onto the gang members, shocking them down onto the cobbles in a series of satisfying thumps.

Constance relaxed her gauntlet arm and patted down a few tendrils of flame that ate through her ruined opera glove. An undergauntlet sleeve of reinforced rubber had protected her skin, but the danger of personal combustion was still a concern. On this test, no sparks had set her gown or hair temporarily ablaze, but additional tinkering on the gauntlet's safety features was clearly required. It seemed Trusdale hadn't been entirely wrong in suggesting that they work out the device's kinks on paper rather than on people.

She scowled into the night air. How dare he leave her to deal with the gendarmes while he took off to his mysterious meeting. Who could he know in Paris? Then again, she hadn't asked him too many questions about himself that might have revealed old friends, or worse, old flames. Whenever she'd gently try to pry information about his past, he delivered a stock tale of being raised on a cattle ranch, serving in the US cavalry, and then, he'd become a tourist, traveling the world with no clear plan in mind. By contrast, her Plan with a capital "P" was meticulously put together, with just enough wiggle room to allow for the changes required when facing an unpredictable enemy. She recoiled as one of the bodyguards groaned and started to push himself up from the cobbles. His fellow guard stirred as Constance took several steps back, eyes wide. No one had woken up from Naptime so quickly before. Had her latest tinkering decreased the voltage, or had Trusdale ruined the gauntlet with his massive bulk during the accidental shooting incident?

Her stomach knotted. The gauntlet could only carry one charge in the chamber. And they knew now that she was a tad more agile than the average bustled lady. Her element of surprise was gone.

The bodyguard swayed unsteadily and drew a folding knife out of his waistcoat. He flicked out the blade as his companion scrabbled to find his hammer beneath the snoring body of his boss. The two of them moved toward Constance with the menace of wolves approaching a lost lamb.

Constance took three steps back to feel the cold granite blocks of a tenement building press against her spine. She surreptitiously slipped her left hand into the hidden pocket she had sewn into her bustle. Grateful for her late mother's birth gift of ambidexterity, she fumbled inside the pocket and drew out the smallest aether ray gun in the Brass Queen's concealable protection line. By channeling the tiniest amount of interdimensional energy drawn from the fissures between realities, the gun could momentarily destabilize objects or areas, shimmering them directly into the void. She'd mostly used it to dispose of her chamber pots so that Cawley or another member of the Hall's domestic staff didn't have to empty them for her. Purchasing hundreds of chamber pots at a time had always raised eyebrows at the local porcelain works, but at least she'd negotiated a hefty discount for bulk delivery. As to where in the void the used chamber pots disappeared to, she'd never cared to investigate.

With a vicious roar, the hoodlums lunged for her. She pulled the trigger and a green flash of aether energy hit the cobbles beneath their boots. Her head snapped back to avoid a wild slash of the knife as the cobbles disintegrated beneath the men's feet. They tumbled down into the dark burial catacombs that ran beneath the city streets. Each shrieked like a schoolgirl as a mountain of skulls, bones, and dirt dislodged from the walls and collapsed around them.

Constance dusted centuries of deceased Parisians from her ball gown and strode off down the alleyway. Except for some minor damage to her cloak, the evening's experiment had been an absolute triumph. As the men behind her wailed for a helping hand out of the crypt, she glanced up at the moon, freed by the breeze to drift above the Paris skyline like the untamed goddess she was.

It was a freedom Constance could only dream of. She had Welli and the rest of the *Lady Penelope* crew to look after. Plus a cowboy to apologize to, apparently, for working on the gauntlet without him. Oh, and shooting him. Then again, who should apologize to whom for the altercation with the irate cyclist and the gendarme on the Boulevard? There wasn't an etiquette book in the world big enough to cover all the unfortunate incidents Trusdale witnessed or provoked. The man was an absolute menace. And yet . . .

Welli had said she owed Trusdale a face-to-face apology.

Ugh. She'd rather fight more street thugs, but beggars couldn't be choosers. The new, improved Baroness Haltwhistle would be gracious above all else. Trusdale was surely a man of principle, and as such, she owed him her best self. And her best self wouldn't keep track of who should apologize to whom. She would swallow her pride and beg his forgiveness. If not tonight, then tomorrow. Or at least very soon. Maybe Tuesday. Yes, Tuesday. In the meantime, she could create the very best Plan with a capital "P" to present a winning face-to-face apology that would dissolve Trusdale's ire on impact.

It was a big step, but the risk of Trusdale leaving on his own grand tour of Europe without her was too great. She adjusted her tiara upon her bird's nest mat of hair, wrapped her cloak tight around her shoulders, and straightened her posture. There was no reason she couldn't be somewhat elegant as she headed for the bright lights of the main promenades and the Grand Hotel du Louvre. Perhaps if any wandering cowboys spotted her in her ball gown scaling the drainpipes up to her bathroom window, they would be impressed by her grace under pressure.

Not that she cared about impressing anybody, of course.

Chapter 5:
Four Men, One Closet

As the sun rose over Paris, former Austrian officer Gunter Erhard, the disgraced right-hand man to the even more disgraced Prince Lucien, skulked in the broom closet of the city's most expensive hotel. The Grand Hotel du Louvre was a glittering confection of mirrored ballrooms, sumptuous buffets, and lavish suites. However, its broom closet had not been designed to accommodate three heavily armed Swedish henchmen and his own sturdy form without considerable discomfort.

Erhard's cocked general's hat, bedecked with a year's salary of gold braid and an enormous white ostrich plume, had tilted down over his right eye. The elbow of a blond giant, Lars, was wedged perilously close to his other eye, threatening to blind him at any moment. Ludwig's ax handle was shoved into Erhard's ribs while Johan's rumbling belly pressed up against his spine. His curved officer's sword, even in its brass scabbard, could potentially gut Johan should the poor man suffer the misfortune to sneeze. All four men were currently holding their breath and listening to the interminable conversation just beyond the closet's paneled door.

In the corridor, the burly coachman of one Lady Constance Haltwhistle, unaware of the mini-army stuffed like sardines mere inches from his broad backside, was flirting with a housemaid. She giggled as the Yorkshireman attempted to teach her the English language in four easy lessons. The first phrase she'd learned was "'Ow do," and now she was up to "Fancy a cocktail?" despite the early hour. It seemed the servants of the Haltwhistle family had chosen to schedule their personal lives around their employer's erratic hours.

Erhard's spies had confirmed that Hearn caroused with abandon from dawn until noon. From noon until six p.m., he spent his time polishing Constance's gold-leafed dragon-styled carriage, caring for her horses, and transporting his young mistress from store to store. It seemed the red-haired debutante had developed a penchant for Parisian seamstresses, perfumes, and confectionery.

In the evenings, Hearn drove Lord Wellington Pendelroy, Constance's rakish cousin, between the opera house, theaters, and the city's finest gambling dens. Frequent naps in the carriage kept Hearn bright-eyed and dangerous to any who sought to harm his employer or her family. His infamy as an underground fight champion was enough for Erhard and his crew to give the coachman a wide berth. Their plan was to kidnap Constance without anyone noticing her disappearance until she was well on her way to Sweden. An iron-barred cell awaited the blindfolded, bound, and gagged Baron's daughter on Erhard's airship. King Oscar had stressed that she must be taken alive, but no one had said she should enjoy the journey.

Erhard grimaced into the darkness of the closet. Give him a nice murder to do any day. Kidnappings were nothing but waiting, bashing, and bundling. It was the dullest form of miscellaneous villainy. He'd hoped to assist Oscar with his global domination strategy now that he was officially the King's Colonel of Skullduggery and Mayhem. But somehow, Oscar's sultry brunette adviser, Lady Nay, had stolen his advisory spot. *One day, Nay will pay for her chicanery. It was her vile whispering in Oscar's ear that led to me being here, stuck in a box surrounded by herring-breathed henchmen.*

Erhard's right hand drifted to the leather-wrapped handle of his officer's saber. He gripped the handle tight, comforted by its familiar heft. *Ah, sweet Sophie, my shining silver love. Your blade shall know the taste of blood once more . . .*

His reverie was broken as the maid's playful laugh drifted through the closet door. Erhard gritted his teeth and released his sword. Sophie would not be drawn today unless things went very, very wrong.

The maid's melodic voice poured praise upon Hearn as he gushed forth romantic poetry. The muscular British coachman was extremely smooth with the ladies, Erhard gave him that. Not many carriage drivers could quote Byron and Keats before breakfast.

Erhard exhaled as Hearn and his companion reached an international accord that cocktails at dawn were required. Cooing like lovestruck pigeons, they moved away from the closet door.

As their footsteps receded, Erhard squirmed to free himself from the press of his men. He writhed his way to the door and slowly turned the ornate brass handle. He pushed the door ajar and poked his head out into the corridor. The back of Hearn's bald head—shining in the gaslight above a green livery tailcoat, white breeches, and riding boots—was retreating toward the iron staircase that led down to the lobby. On Hearn's arm hung a shapely chambermaid in a long-skirted black-and-white uniform. Her feather duster was tucked into her belt above a voluminously bustled behind. She looked back over her shoulder and winked at Erhard, thrilled to have a walrus-mustached strongman on her arm plus two coins from Erhard's own wallet in her pocket.

The bribe was worth its weight in King Louis's gold. Since his last encounter with the Haltwhistle harpy, Erhard had done his homework on the woman's henchmen and hangers-on. Hearn was her muscle. The elderly servant Cawley was her errand-runner. Her cloistered friends, Doctors Chauhan and Huang, spent day and night in their suite ordering room meals and champagne at regular intervals. Constance's cousin Welli was an ex-British redcoat officer with a gambling addiction, and the mysterious American, Trusdale, had left Constance to the gendarmes in the middle of a busy French boulevard. Erhard and his men had sought to follow the police officers following Constance, but had lost both. It was a bad omen for the kidnapping, but this time, Erhard was prepared to face his red-haired foe. If he knew Constance at all, she'd have returned to her found family at the earliest possibility. Especially if she'd had her heart broken by the cowboy leaving her to her fate. That kind of thing could crack even a nut as hard-shelled as Constance.

He'd bet his last coin that the devil in bloomers was back in her room, plotting the cowboy's downfall for his lack of concern for her safety. Or cackling with glee that she'd managed to evade the gendarmes. Or perhaps, she was simply asleep, exhausted from the police chase. That would be his preferred option. He only had three men by his side. To take down Constance, he'd have preferred an entire platoon at his back, but Oscar demanded discretion in his dirty work.

Erhard looked forward to grilling the girl about her unusual martial skills on their flight up to Stockholm. Kidnapping victims always got chatty on long airship rides. Who knew what family secrets he might find out? There must surely be more to Oscar's obsession with Constance than a simple squabble over lost armaments. And knowledge was survival in Oscar's court these days, Lady Nay had seen to that. Gone was the wise King who had once pulled Erhard out of a deep depression over a lost love. Now, Oscar was little better than the tyrants he'd once scorned. Where was the man Erhard had grown to admire? How far had Nay's poison sunk into the old man's heart?

That was a question he'd try to answer another day. As Hearn and the maid disappeared down into the stairwell, Erhard stepped out into the corridor and straightened his cocked hat. A row of ten emergency cartridges was strapped securely against the side of his headgear. This surely wasn't enough to face the infamous Brass Queen. He prayed to all that was unholy that the girl would be sound asleep when they entered her room. The universe deserved him a good turn, for once.

A suite door opened ahead. The men instinctively flattened themselves against the wall as a bespectacled maid poked her head out from the doorway. She beckoned them to approach. Glancing over their shoulders, the four men scurried along the corridor. As they reached the maid, she pointed inside the suite behind her where a snoring, silver-haired septuagenarian in blue woolen long johns was sprawled out on the bed. A maid treated each of his hands to a manicure, and a third scrubbed his toenails with a brush and a sour look on her face.

"Monsieur Cawley believed our story that he'd won a free spa treatment by virtue of being the hundredth Yorkshireman to walk through the hotel door. He said that free was his favorite price," whispered the bespectacled maid. "He is very relaxed now."

"So I can tell," murmured Erhard, and slipped the maid an extra coin for her service. "Thank you for your help. Now, off you go." With his warmest smile, he shooed her into Cawley's room and closed the door.

At the end of the corridor stood Constance's suite. The men silently formed into an attack formation behind Erhard. Breathing softly, he crept to the door and slowly opened it. Inside the suite, all was cloaked in darkness thanks to the thick drapes pulled tight over the windows.

Followed by his men, Erhard squinted and padded silently into the orange-blossom-scented room. Lars locked the door behind them and pocketed the key.

As their eyes adjusted to the gloom, they tiptoed between two dozen hatboxes to approach the emperor-sized four-poster bed. They surrounded the mound of blankets that covered a sleeping form. Tendrils of long, red hair crept from beneath the blankets across a snowy white pillow.

The three Swedes raised their Nordic battle-axes, ready to fight the she-devil Erhard had warned them about for days. At first they'd laughed, but now they were grim and ready for battle. They were as prepared as they were going to be, and so was he. From an airtight rubber bag secured inside his tailcoat pocket, Erhard drew a chloroform-soaked handkerchief. Moist cloth in hand, he threw back the blankets and shoved the handkerchief toward Constance's . . .

Pile of cushions? A red wig? What the . . . where is she?

The sound of a window sliding closed came from the bathroom. A light flared beneath the bottom of the door as someone within lit a gas lamp.

Erhard shielded his eyes from the light as the bathroom door flew open. In clomped a short, curvaceous woman in a tattered ball gown, a muddy cloak, and riding boots.

She halted, gaping at the Viking raiding party in her bedroom.

As Erhard's hand flew to his saber, Constance let out a banshee roar that echoed around the chamber. Such a cry would surely wake the dead, never mind her neighbors.

The clock was ticking on this abduction. Time to take off the kid gloves and get brutal. He nodded at Johan. The blond behemoth charged at Constance like an enraged bull. The girl shrieked and bolted for the suite's main entry door. Lars raced to meet her there as Johan blocked her possible retreat into the bathroom. Making a bolt for the broken window within would have been her best move, but apparently the girl didn't know the meaning of the word *retreat*.

Constance rattled the locked brass handle and then thumped both fists on the paneled door. She squealed as Lars lunged for her corseted waist. With surprising grace and speed, she twirled out of Lars's reach and shot toward the bedchamber's curtained window.

Ludwig sprang to grab a handful of her long red hair. He caught hold of her pinned emerald tiara and yanked her toward him. Constance roared with fury and slammed the wooden heel of her right riding boot into his knee. Bones cracked, and the big man crumpled to the floor as Constance threw herself toward the bed. She leaped upon it and stood atop her mound of blankets, wild-eyed and panting with exertion in her off-kilter tiara.

Confused voices sounded in the corridor. Her piercing screams had raised her companions from their slumber.

But no one could help Lady Haltwhistle now. Even if they had to wrap her unconscious body in blankets and throw her out the window, she was leaving this hotel tonight.

Erhard scrambled up onto the mattress, knocking his general's hat over one eye on the four posters' curtain rail. He pushed his hat back into place, narrowly avoiding chloroforming himself as he did so.

Constance backed up against the upholstered headboard as Ludwig limped to the left side of the bed with murder blazing in his blue eyes. Lars flanked the right side of the bed, and Johan climbed up on the mattress to stand behind Erhard.

The fox was cornered.

Constance held up her right hand as if for protection as her left scrabbled underneath her cloak. Erhard leered at her helplessness and sprang to press the reeking handkerchief to her young face. A tiny gun appeared in Constance's left hand as he struggled to grab her throat. As if in slow motion, green light flared at his feet spreading out past the bed and lighting up the boots of his henchmen in a circle of lurid lime.

The world collapsed beneath him as the floor disintegrated. Down fell the bed, the Swedes, his prey, and himself in a stomach-turning tumble of blankets and pillows.

Down one floor, crashing through an empty bed.

Down another, smashing through splintered wood, plaster, and dust.

Next stop, the lobby.

Or death . . .

Chapter 6:
Banshee on Board

Trusdale stumbled up the stairs toward the Grand Hotel du Louvre's ornate glass doors. His head ached from the combination of his lunchtime lightning blast and too much fine whisky, not to mention way too much thought about how he could talk Constance into designing a kingslayer weapon without revealing he was working for God.

Mission improbable was almost certainly impossible without divine intervention. And he didn't mean his manipulative manager with her poison-filled ring and her venomous stare. What he needed was a sign from on high that somehow, someway, he could save Constance and her crew, start the French revolution, and maybe even survive without his handler's sword cane being inserted into his guts.

He shoved open the glass doors and strode across the polished marble tile of the hotel's extravagantly opulent lobby. If he prayed right now, would the heavens answer? Lord knew it was worth a shot. He placed his hands together as he walked, keeping his eyes and heart open to all eventualities. *Hello God, it's me, Liberty. I know it has been a while . . .*

Kaboom! A thunderous crash overhead rang in his ears like church bells.

What the . . .

He blinked up as the decorative plaster ceiling crumbled like icing on a wedding cake, exploding into a cloud of confectionery dust.

Kaboom!

Trusdale flung himself sideways as the ceiling collapsed next to him in a cloud of dust, splinters, and . . .

Constance?

He spied a flash of red hair atop the chaotic tangle of bed, blankets, and burly men who smashed into the polished floor. Cracks splintered across the marble tiles like ice shattered by a sun flare. From the hotel's mahogany-paneled check-in counter to the mirrored cocktail bar, wide-eyed guests and staff gawked at the spectacle before them. It appeared that the only bystander hurt was . . .

Me.

The cold tiles had smacked the side of his face like an irate lover. Pain throbbed from his left ribs. He'd landed sideways on his snub-nosed revolver, the Smallstack S50. The concealed weapon had done more damage to his ribs than it had ever done to an opponent. He raised himself gingerly onto one elbow, then pushed himself to an unsteady stand. Trusdale pressed his hand against his aching ribs. *Bruised, but not broken. That's a godsend.*

With the wind knocked out of them, Constance and her friends groaned and stirred upon the remains of a four-poster bed. Trusdale's brow furrowed. As ever, Constance had crashed into his world, and nothing made sense anymore. He stumbled toward her over the ceiling debris, concern overruling his agency training to bolt before the authorities arrived. Already, a portly hotel manager had shot out of an office behind the check-in counter. Like his guests and staff, he too stood gaping at the bizarre bed bombshell that had dropped into his lobby.

Trusdale had questions of his own he'd like to get answered before any official inquiry began. First: *Is Constance hurt?* Lord, he hoped not.

Who are her friends? He squashed a rising tide of jealousy that four men had somehow found their way into her bedchamber.

Even more curiously, *Why is a treasure trove of watches, wallets, and jewelry spilling out from under her bed? Does she have a secret life as a pickpocket?*

Trusdale glanced up through the hole in the ceiling as the crash of a door being kicked in echoed down from several floors above. Sure enough, Wellington's lanky frame, wrapped in a paisley dressing robe, appeared at the top of the series of holes that marked Constance's descent.

Next to him stood the silver-haired servant, Cawley, clad in blue long johns, and Doctors Chauhan and Huang. Welli raised a hand uncertainly and waved down at him.

Before he could wave back, Constance groaned and sat up. Her emerald tiara sat upon a disgrace of uncombed hair. Her green taffeta ball gown looked as if it was wearing half the soot off Paris's rooftops. Her right opera glove was scorched and charred. And her green eyes blazed with a fury, one that could set Hades alight, at the scar-faced man in a general's hat lying beside her.

The general stirred and glared at Constance before thrusting a handkerchief toward her face. She squealed and rolled backward off the pile of blankets that had cushioned her fall into the lobby. That roused the three Nordic giants sprawled upon the bed enough to extricate themselves from the wreckage as the scar-faced fellow scrambled after Constance.

Where have I seen scar-face before? Wait, is that . . .

"Erhard!" Trusdale yelled and launched himself at the Austrian. So, Prince Lucien's former right-hand man held a grudge against Constance, did he? Wasn't the prince still locked in the Tower of London awaiting Queen Victoria's sentence for attempted regicide? How was he pulling Erhard's strings from there?

Erhard whitened behind his dueling scars and scrambled out of Trusdale's reach. The Austrian's dark eyes scanned the lobby, surely noting the approach of the hotel manager with a troop of beefy porters and bellboys, not to mention Hearn, who ran out of the cocktail bar with a housemaid trailing behind him.

Constance regained her feet. As Erhard motioned to his men to head for the lobby's entrance, she stepped back, putting her weight onto her rear riding boot. With a banshee howl, she hefted up her ball gown skirt and kicked with the heel of her green riding boot toward Erhard's unmentionables. He flinched, taking a glancing blow to the thigh rather than the offspring-ending blow she'd sent to his privates. He howled with pain and limped for the lobby door with the three Vikings hot on his heels. Constance wasn't finished yet. She dropped to one knee and pulled a shining battle-ax out of the wreckage of her bed. She raised her arm and flung the ax after the departing men, slamming the ax blade into the lobby's mahogany doorframe mere inches from Erhard's head as he bolted out onto the street.

The manager blew out his chest, resplendent in his white wing-collared shirt and black tailcoat, and said with authority, "Baroness Haltwhistle will have to pay for this damage. " He swept his hand around airily, indicating the bed, the holes in the floors above, the acres of cracked marble flooring, and the battle-ax, which stuck out from the doorframe like a military banner.

Baroness? Since when?

Her ladyship spluttered, "How is this my fault? Go and arrest those men immediately. They were trying to kidnap me."

"I have no authority to arrest anyone. But I am happy to call the gendarmes," said the manager, peering down at the wallets and jewelry scattered amidst the ceiling rubble. He bent down and picked up a brown leather wallet. "This . . . this looks familiar." He opened the wallet and drew out a calling card stamped with the logo of the Grand Hotel du Louvre. "This is my wallet, stolen from me by a gang of street thugs last week. Would you care to explain, your ladyship?"

"I've never seen any of these things before in my life. But I did notice one of your maids running around the corridors in a cloak with a porcelain mask on. I don't know which one, of course."

A whisper around the lobby. "*La Femme Électrique, la vigilante.*"

Constance continued. "In her defense, I suppose someone had to step up and clean the mean boulevards of this city. Please feel free to take this entire treasure trove to the police station on her behalf so that it can be reunited with its proper owners. Frankly, I applaud the vigilante's courage in stepping in where the police failed to tread. I think a round of applause for this marvelous maid is in order, don't you?" Constance clapped her hands, staring wildly around the lobby for someone to join her. Hearn stopped at the edge of the debris pile and put his hands together in support of his mistress.

Her eyes settled on Trusdale next. He started to clap, slowly at first, and then more enthusiastically. Floors above, Welli and the rest of the crew of the *Lady Penelope* offered their standing ovation for the diva's performance. One by one, the hotel guests began to clap, and a half-hearted cheer arose from the hotel bellboys.

Constance met Trusdale's eyes and flashed him a genuine smile. She stood tall amidst the mayhem, and said in her ringing tone, "Even though it isn't Tuesday, I'm very sorry for my faux pas over the last few days, Mr. Trusdale."

"Faux pas?"

"It's French for—"

"I know what it's French for. And so does everyone here. Which particular transgression are you apologizing for? Shooting me? Deceiving me?"

"Both. I truly am most dreadfully sorry. And I should have been more conscious that a fancy outfit and a note are no substitute for an in-person apology."

Trusdale frowned. "Did you hit your head on the fall down here? What fancy outfit—?"

The hotel manager interrupted. "Sir, enough of your romantic squabbles. Baroness Haltwhistle, I'm awaiting your explanation as to why you and your ax-wielding associates have destroyed my beautiful lobby?"

She nodded. "Right. Oh, umm . . ." She placed the back of her hand against her forehead and staggered. "I feel a little . . ." She stepped toward Trusdale, her emerald eyes pleading for assistance.

Trusdale leaned toward her as she swooned into his arms with the theatrical flair of a veteran vaudeville player. How could he resist playing along? He shouted to the guests who milled around the lobby's edges, "My god, she's fainted. Fetch a doctor! Fetch two doctors!"

He lifted the comatose Constance, staring down at the grimy sheep that loped across her filthy green ball gown. Was she wearing this for a bet?

And yet, the design had a certain charm. Who didn't like farmyard animals?

He shouted at the manager's team, "All right gents, coming through. I'll drop the young mademoiselle here in her cousin's room. Looks like you folks have got yourselves some mighty big woodworm around here." He nodded up at the hole in the ceiling as the manager seethed.

"I assure you, sir, there are no woodworms." The manager raised his voice and turned to address the hum of gossip now emanating from the lobby's guests, "There are positively no woodworms at the Grand Hotel du Louvre."

Trusdale muttered at the manager, "Then you'd best let the Haltwhistle party check out nice and quiet if you don't want this incident splashed all over the city newspapers."

"The bill . . ."

"I'll wager there's a big reward for finding all this vigilante loot under the young lady's bed. If you hand this treasure trove over to the police as she suggested, I imagine that reward will pay for a good chunk of the repairs. If more is owed, Baroness Haltwhistle will make good on the debt. Right, Hearn?"

Hearn stepped forward and cracked his knuckles with a violence that caused the manager, porters, and bellhops to step back. "Oh, aye, she'll pay for all this. And then we'll leave, quiet like."

The manager eyed Hearn's wrestler's build and stepped aside. He hissed, "Not one of you will be welcome at a Paris hotel again. I will make sure of it."

Trusdale shrugged as well as he could with comatose Constance laid across his arms. He marched across the lobby toward the grand iron staircase that led up to the hotel's suites. The watching hotel guests applauded his "rescue" of the fallen maiden. It was nice to be seen as the hero for once. No matter how misplaced that appreciation might be.

It was just another crazy day with Constance. And he hadn't even had breakfast yet.

Lord help him.

Chapter 7:
The Captain's Cabin

I s there anything more annoying than having to pay an enormous bill for thwarting your own kidnapping? Constance stomped into the captain's cabin aboard the *Lady Penelope* airship and slammed the door behind her. She was now officially broke. Even worse, Welli was furious with her, having worked out that she was, in fact, the infamous vigilante *La Femme Électrique*. She'd forgotten that Welli could have a stern side as he lectured her about the dangers of seeking combat with random ruffians, despite her protestations that it was all in the name of science.

It didn't help that Trusdale had sat in the carriage with them as they drove to the airship port, listening to

Welli's tirade with his arms folded, his legs stretched out, and his Stetson pulled down over his eyes. The fact that he was wearing the exact same shirt in which she'd electrocuted him yesterday, plus a faint whiff of whisky, suggested that the cowboy had spent a night on the tiles. Hardly a good look for a member of the entourage of a newly minted baroness. In addition, she'd made a special effort to give the cowboy a very public apology in the devastated hotel lobby, which he'd yet to acknowledge. And now she owed him a debt of gratitude for carrying her away from the belligerent hotel manager. Did *Babett's Modern Manners* have a chapter that covered how best to thank an annoying cowboy for sweeping her off her feet?

She drew the book from her bustle pocket and flopped onto her alcove bed, taking care not to disturb the sleeping Boo. As ever, the puppy had found the comfiest place on the galleon to snooze as the humans aboard had fussed about stowing luggage in a hold already overloaded with all the Haltwhistle farm beasts Constance couldn't bear to leave behind in Yorkshire.

Technically, the airship belonged to Cousin Welli, but Constance had persuaded him to let her have the best cabin aboard. It was the one that Papa traveled in before he lost the airship to Welli in a poker game. Dozens of Papa's books still stood in dusty piles upon the floral rug, having spilled out from the bookshelves that lined the mahogany-paneled walls. Unlike his daughter, he'd never been able to create a portal large enough to allow him to take a huge object like an airship with him on his interdimensional travels. But he'd certainly managed to pick up a variety of alien artifacts that resembled sextants, hourglasses, and telescopes, many of which graced the cabin's shelves. These were the navigational aids for the strange new worlds he'd visited while Constance grew up alone and abandoned in their ancestral pile.

Constance leafed through her etiquette book, but failed to find anything regarding cowboys, feet, or the best way to escalate an unacknowledged apology. Perhaps such vital information had been on the ten or so pages that had been torn from the book by Papa when he couldn't find notepaper readily to hand? It was one of his few habits that had drawn a rebuke from his wife, usually so mild mannered and ready to forgive any rudeness on his part.

Did his alternate dimension wife scold him about such matters?

She would never know. Not that she cared.

A wave of self-pity swept over her. She set her jaw and suppressed the pity with the firm resolve of a Yorkshire-born woman. None of that nonsense. She would always find a way to survive—and maybe even to thrive—if she kept her spine straight and her upper lip sufficiently stiff. Who needs parents when you have a puppy by your side who loves you unconditionally?

She rubbed behind Boo's ears, and the tiny canine grunted with contentment.

She would always mother little Boo to the best of her maternal abilities. Which involved putting food in the puppy's crystal bowl three times a day. And sirloin steak didn't grow on trees. How was she to create an income now the Hall was gone and her electrical gauntlet was stubbornly refusing to become a marketable product to ladies keen to administer a zap of lightning to any ruffians at hand?

A Plan with a capital "P" began to form in her mind. If her income must now be gained from business opportunities other than selling farm goods or bespoke armaments, perhaps she should look to the assets around her. The *Lady Penelope* did boast an impressive array of hidden weaponry. This was mostly due to Papa's habit of shooting cannonballs at the stately homes of gentlemen scientists who disputed his theories regarding multiple universes. Scientific discourse could be remarkably violent when a Haltwhistle was involved.

Perhaps her Plan with a capital "P" could involve a touch of Piracy? She could imagine herself as a sky pirate queen, as brave and bold as those she'd read about in the penny dreadfuls. A brand-new wardrobe was undoubtedly called for, plus an eyepatch, and possibly a pet parrot for her shoulder . . .

A knock sounded upon her door.

"I'm not here," she called out.

"You sure about that?" asked a deep, American voice that conjured images of deserts, mountains, and rolling plains bestrewn with bison.

She wasn't feeling sure about anything at this particular moment. At least he was still talking to her. Then again, that wasn't necessarily a positive given the unpredictability of what he might say next. The servants she could predict with a ninety-nine percent accuracy; Welli, perhaps fifty percent. But Trusdale had a tendency to surprise her at every turn.

Has he gone?

The door handle started to turn. She gasped as it was pushed slightly ajar, and a man's hand holding a Stetson waved around the door at her. "I have some matters to discuss with you. Cawley's here with me as a chaperone."

Cawley's ancient voice crackled like dry leaves underfoot, "I have a pot of tea here for you, miss. Mrs. Singh is readying the airship for departure, but we'll be stuck in port for an hour while she checks over the engines."

An hour was a long time to go without tea.

"Very well, you may both enter." She stood and attempted unsuccessfully to adjust her off-kilter tiara in the mirror Papa had bolted to the wall between two brass portholes. The mirror's copper frame was remarkably utilitarian with its smooth design—not at all like the gilded baroque mirrors that decorated the hall. The image it showed her of herself was even more troubling than the frame. Her night in the alley and her tumble through the floors of the Grand Hotel du Louvre had done dreadful things to her attire. The sad sheep that trailed across her dirty ball gown would surely fail to win any prizes at the Norton Agricultural Show.

I'm a visual disgrace!

Trusdale stepped into her cabin, for once the better dressed of the two of them in his all-black ensemble of a scorched leather duster coat, Western frock coat, silk shirt, knotted neckerchief, svelte waistcoat, and pinstriped pants complemented by what appeared to be brand-new cowboy boots embroidered with silver airships. Where he'd purchased such garish footwear in Paris was a mystery as deep as to whom he'd run off to meet while leaving her to face the gendarmes of Paris alone. Trusdale's unkempt eyebrows crested ridiculously blue eyes, bright as sapphires against his shockingly tanned skin. Neatly trimmed sideburns and a square, clean-shaven jaw framed a nose that had been broken in brawls he claimed were all started by other men. Oddly, she believed him. He gave the impression of being a man who preferred to avoid unnecessary conflict. Perhaps he had come to tell her that life with the *Lady Penelope* crew was too dramatic for his taste.

Was this goodbye? A lump rose in her throat and stayed there.

The cowboy halted and surveyed the paneled cabin, looking everywhere but directly at her. He seemed particularly interested in the steam-powered radiator at the far end of the room. Once the *Lady Penelope* took flight, Constance would be able to warm the room courtesy of the airship's cutting-edge dual steam engines. The cast-iron radiator had been dignified with gold leaf and a marble mantel decorated with the Haltwhistle family crest. Exquisitely carved on a baronial shield, a tiny knight in armor kicked a dragon up the backside for all eternity.

Ah, no, it's Mama who's caught his eye. Above the mantel hung a stunning portrait of her probably deceased mother. Mama was a vision in elegance, gazing out a leaded glass window over Haltwhistle Hall's red and white rose gardens. Lady Annabella Pendelroy on the eve of her wedding, a brunette beauty in an off-shoulder scarlet ball gown lit to perfection by a setting sun.

Trusdale's eyes continued to roam. To the side of the mantelpiece stood an iron bistro table and two chairs strewn with a plethora of tiny bowler hats, cast-off corsets, and, embarrassingly, silk petticoats and bloomers. It hadn't occurred to her that she might end up with a gentleman in her cabin, particularly in its current state of disarray.

Then again, Trusdale was hardly a gentleman.

Cawley swept around Trusdale carrying a silver tray laden with tea for two. The gray-haired retainer wore an emerald tailcoat cut in an archaic style. Gold buttons, an ivory ruffled shirt, mint-green silk pantaloons, pristine white stockings, and black buckle shoes completed his antique ensemble. Cawley consistently refused to move with the times, preferring the Haltwhistle family's traditional livery style to Hearn's contemporary livery tailcoat, white breeches, and riding boots. Their fashion choices had stirred an inordinate amount of bickering between the two men, which Constance chose to ignore.

As long as she could spot their emerald livery in a crowd, the tailoring was theirs to decide. By allowing this creative fashion choice to remain with her staff, she considered herself to be an enlightened modern aristocrat. Papa would have forced every household member to wear their traditional garb until the end of time. But they were her staff now. Two stalwart servants left from an army of a hundred or more at the Hall.

With sixty years of experience as a household domestic, Cawley expertly balanced the tray on one of the bistro chairs and started to fold her unmentionables. Constance cringed. Hiring a new lady's maid was on her list of to-dos, right after she'd worked out the design kinks in her lady's lightning gauntlet. *Is that one of the matters Trusdale wishes to discuss? The suspense is killing me.*

Trusdale was staring at Cawley as the servant folded a pair of pink-and-white striped bloomers. The cowboy's cheeks flushed, as did her own. In the silence that followed, Cawley finished folding the clothes and tucked them into a chest on the wall beside the bistro table. With her underwear out of sight, Constance could finally begin a polite conversation with her gentleman caller.

"To what do I owe the honor of your presence, Mr. Trusdale?" she asked with what she hoped was a charming smile.

"And good morning to you too. I'll cut to the chase—are you injured? Do you need to see a doctor? You spent a good hour being comatose at the hotel while everyone packed."

Unpredictable as ever.

"Oh, well, I didn't want to answer any awkward questions from the hotel management. Thank you for handling that matter for me. And . . ." She swallowed hard. "I truly am sorry about shooting you, and before that, working on the gauntlet in secret. I hoped to jump a few steps in the development process, but patience may have been a virtue in this case. I could point out that, had my attempts at fixing the gauntlet been successful, an attack by four Vikings in one's bed is exactly the kind of situation where a working prototype of the Kinetic Storm Battle Mitten #004 would have come in useful. Perhaps we should start thinking of a catchier name? Together, as equal partners in this hopefully lucrative venture. What do you say?"

Trusdale blinked. "Four Vikings? Don't you mean three?"

She frowned. "I'm fairly certain I was fighting off four villains. One kept trying to thrust a cloth doused with chloroform over my face, so I assume they were not out to kill me. Given that both Prince Lucien and King Oscar have sent assassins after me before, a kidnapping is quite a step down in drama, don't you think?"

Trusdale's eyebrows almost blew through the top of his Stetson. "You mean to tell me that you didn't recognize Gunter Erhard, Prince Lucien's former right-hand man?"

"It's not as if I go around memorizing the faces of my enemy's retainers. Honestly, who has the time?"

"First of all, the fact that you have enemies with a taste for violence should concern you more than it does. Secondly, with Erhard here, I can only assume that Prince Lucien is out for revenge."

She blinked. "What, because I turned down his offer of marriage?"

"I'd say more like the fact that you ratted out his intention to murder his granny, Queen Victoria, and steal her throne for himself."

She sniffed. "Of the two, I'm sure it's the marriage refusal that irks him most."

"Yeah, you would think that."

Cawley cleared his throat, indicating that the tea service had been set out upon the bistro table. He pulled out one chair for his mistress.

It would be churlish not to sit. "Tea, Mr. Trusdale?"

He shrugged, and they sat as Cawley poured milk from a porcelain jug into two bluebell painted teacups from her favorite set. The cowboy said, "I need to talk to you about something . . . unpleasant."

"The fact that you abandoned me in the middle of the street to face two angry Frenchmen?"

"I wouldn't say abandoned, but yeah, sorry about that. I had an urgent—"

"Appointment, yes, so you said. May I ask with whom?"

He looked away from her. "Umm, my grandmother."

"In Paris? I thought you said your family lived in Kansas."

"Yeah, well, people do like to travel, even if they live in Kansas."

Cawley stirred the pot as Constance asked, "Paternal or maternal? Your grandmother, is she's mother's mother, or your father's—"

"My father's mother. She was just passing through, no need to make a fuss about it."

"Who's fussing? I was just making polite conversation. You hardly ever talk about your family."

"Kinda hard to get a word in edgewise when you're all, 'my great-grandfather moved a town that was obscuring the view from his hunting tower,' and 'my great-great-great-grandmother shot the first lord of the admiralty for making an improper suggestion to her at a ball.'"

She huffed. "It was only a village, and the first lord of the admiralty was merely slapped, with a poker, across his broadside. That said, I'd love to hear more about Kansas, and your family, and you, for that matter. You always seem so reticent to share. And after all, we are business partners, aren't we?"

She leaned forward on her chair, anxious to hear if that was still the case.

Trusdale picked up his teacup and slurped his way to the bottom of it before answering. "Yeah, I guess we are. But I need to ask you to do somethin'—"

A *tap, tap, tap* on the porthole window broke her attention. "Cawley, what is that? A seagull? Please shoo it away. You were saying, Mr. Trusdale?"

"Like I've said before, you can call me Liberty, if you want."

"*Babett's Modern Manners* suggests the use of a formal title is the proper way to address a business partner. Now, if I could possibly clarify whether we are also friends, then I could certainly start calling you by your first name."

He blinked at her. "You want a formal declaration of friendship?"

"Well, it's best to be clear in these matters, don't you think? A young lady might misconstrue a gentleman's attention. If we state here and now that we are business associates, friends, and possibly, maybe in the fullness of time, more than—"

Cawley shrieked louder than a first lord of the admiralty meeting the wrong end of a red-hot poker. Constance spun to see the porthole window open and a bronze mechanical scarab beetle clamped to Cawley's nose. Trusdale was at his side in an instant. He tore the clockwork dung beetle from Cawley's face and flung it across the room, where it smashed against the mahogany panels above Constance's bed before falling onto the covers on its back.

Boo dived upon the metal creature, barking and growling as its legs flayed helplessly.

"Hold on, stop, it's a message scarab," Constance yelled, launching herself toward the bed and snatching the bronze beetle away from Boo. The puppy yapped her displeasure at losing her prize.

"Sorry, darling," murmured Constance. She fiddled with the scarab's underbelly. It flicked open to reveal a devilishly complicated mosaic of colored tiles. She would need to slide the tiles into a pattern denoting the correct hieroglyphic to open the beetle. She groaned and set to work with her fingernail, starting with the names of ancient gods. "The British Museum sent a few similar clockwork beasts to Papa over the years. They usually only wanted confirmation that all the dangerous artifacts they'd paid him to store in the Hall's specially fortified treasure chambers were safe. Except for that one time when they sent a death threat because they'd got the impression that Papa was selling some of the less hazardous relics on the antiquities black market."

"And was he?" asked Trusdale.

"Of course he was. But he stopped as soon as the museum threatened to send RATT after him. The Royal Antiquities Tactical Team are the military arm of the British Museum. They're tasked with snatching treasures from Queen Victoria's conquered climes so they can safely be transported to England. Some they display, but the ones that caused them concern they would put into Papa's specialized care. He earned a pittance of a caretaker's fee, but he did relish the opportunity to use some of the relics in his more esoteric science experiments. He even came across an Enigma Key once, although we already had our own collection, of course, passed down from the eighth Baron Haltwhistle, Edwin the Stargazer. He's famed for building the Hall's Celestial Ballroom and its clock tower observatory . . ." She trailed off, not wanting to drone on about her family again without giving her poor guest a chance to share his own stories. "But I'm sure your ancestors built some lovely edifices, too, Mr. Trusdale. Please do tell me about them."

He gaped at her. "Uh, yeah, there's been a few barns and maybe a homestead or two. But could you just open the damned scarab? I'm dyin' of curiosity here."

Well! So much for being thoughtful, empathetic, and showing an interest in other people. She scrutinized the bug's belly of mosaic tiles.

Hmm. Dying of curiosity. The physical form of the messenger always gave a hint about the possible keyword, and to the ancients , the scarab represented birth, death, and rebirth. She slid the mosaics into the symbol of Anubis, the god of the dead.

She grinned as the final tile clicked into place and the puzzle bug opened like a metal daisy before her eyes. Hidden within was a piece of folded parchment covered in hieroglyphics.

Even Cawley looked momentarily impressed.

Trusdale whistled. "Well, ain't that a nice trick? What's the note say?"

She felt the blood drain from her face as the full weight of the message became clear. "Good lord, it's a missive from the Museum, but for me, not Papa. They've heard about the Hall vanishing from our plane of reality. They're demanding the return of all the artifacts held within its treasure chambers that Papa was supposed to protect." Fury blazed through her. "Dear lord, am I to be forever dealing with the mess he left behind? This is patently unfair."

The men nodded.

"They've given me exactly one week to return the relics, or RATT will terminate every member of the *Lady Penelope*'s crew. Even little Boo."

The puppy whimpered.

Constance cast aside the scarab and hugged the terrier. "Don't you worry, my sweet. I won't let them harm you or anyone aboard this ship, I promise." Her words held no power, and she knew it.

Trusdale pushed back his Stetson. "I don't suppose you know which dimension the Hall flew off to?"

She shook her head. "Not exactly. One that lacked sentient life, I believe. But there's literally an infinite number of such dimensions. Narrowing down the selection could take ten lifetimes, and I have seven days. Plus, to conduct a search, I'd have to open a portal, and that requires focusing the energy of multiple Enigma Keys. I broke mine asunder sending the Hall to is final resting place."

"And releasing the interdimensional aliens that were trapped inside each Key, as I recall. Giant telepathic krakens, weren't they?" said Trusdale.

"Yes. If only we'd kept in touch," she said. "I believe they took off to the dark side of the moon to live in peace, away from humanity's prying eyes. I could have asked them if they knew how many Keys there were in this reality."

"Figures," said Trusdale. "Okay. Well, I had come down here to discuss another matter with you. After the craziness in Paris, I was gonna suggest maybe we could take the airship on a nice, calm tourist trip. Nowhere special. Maybe the Palace of Versailles, if that's a place you think might be worth seeing. I know you're not the Brass Queen anymore, but hey, just for fun, if you still were, and someone wanted you to create a weapon that could shoot down a flying palace—"

She snapped her fingers. "Versailles! Trusdale, you're a genius. Louis XVIII possesses an Enigma Key. Papa desperately wanted it for his collection, but he decided it was too risky to attempt a burglary. It's so difficult to bypass the security of a paranoid king. If I can get one Key in hand, maybe I can find out if there are others we might access. Think of it as a grand tour itinerary in the making. If I had four or five Keys before me, I could potentially open a portal to try and locate the Hall. Then the Museum would get their relics back, and no one would have to suffer the wrath of RATT. There's nowhere on Earth that's safe from their tweed-jacketed terror."

Cawley and Trusdale stared at her. She said, "Oh come on, you two. This is as good a Plan as any. If you have any better ideas, now's the time to share them. I'm all ears."

The servant and the cowboy exchanged worried glances, but remained silent.

"That's exactly what I thought," she said with a sigh. "May heaven help me, the crew are going to be furious that RATT is gunning for them. I'll need to break the matter to our family of friends gently before I ask if any of them are willing to go with me to Versailles. This won't be a one-woman heist, of that, I'm sure. Cawley, I'll need you to crack open the best champagne and our finest nibbles for a luncheon that will lull everyone into an agreeable mood. Hopefully, the crew won't make me walk the plank for getting them into this mess. Although, to be fair, this is truly my father's fault. If he hadn't taken off—"

"I'm guessing you'd still have managed to find more than your share of trouble," said Trusdale.

Cawley nodded vigorously.

She shrugged. "We'll never know. In another dimension, I'm sure an alternate me is quietly gluing novelty seaweed into a scrapbook to while away the hours. But here in this dimension, I'm a woman on a mission to save all our lives. Are you both with me?"

"Yes, your ladyship," said Cawley.

Trusdale gave her the wryest of grins. "These relics that were kept at the family castle, were they cursed by any chance? Because lord knows, you have a habit of leaping from one hot frying pan to another, and it's a miracle you haven't yet fallen into the flames."

She snorted. "There are no such things as curses. Only luck and circumstance. I'm almost sure of it."

"It's the *almost* that bothers me. Until luncheon, Baroness Haltwhistle."

"I'm Constance to my friends," she said. "Not that we have to codify our relationship as more than business partners. Unless you want to, of course."

He grinned. "Not that we need to codify it, but yeah, we're partners and friends. Good friends, as long as you don't shoot me again."

"No promises," she said with a smile.

He tipped his hat to her and left the cabin, trailed by Cawley. Death may beckon, mayhem may call, but Constance knew one thing for certain. If you're forced to ride down the path to hell, your chances of making it back alive are better with a friend beside you. Everyone needed at least one person they could implicitly trust.

And Trusdale was her man.

Chapter 8:
The Lady Penelope

The Eiffel Tower was a smudge on the horizon as the *Lady Penelope* gained speed and distance away from Paris. Constance watched the edifice dwindle and disappear from the top deck of the airship's baroque pink-and-gold galleon. Above, the pink, cigar-shaped gasbag bobbed against snowy clouds and an azure sky. Constance licked her lips and dropped her eyes back to the assembled crew on the lower deck. Eight of the people she held nearest and dearest to her heart sat on an eclectic collection of chairs. Shock, anxiety, and bewilderment had been painted with a broad brush across their faces.

Only the airship's pilot, Mrs. Rani Singh, remained stoic at Constance's side. The retired pirate queen of the

West China Sea expertly spun the ship's large oak steering wheel. Rani was a vision of martial splendor in a scarlet sari with a curved gold cutlass strapped to her hip and silver streaks flowing through her long black hair.

Constance shifted her weight from one purple ankle boot to the other as she waited for her announcement about RATT and Versailles to sink in. Freshly washed and clad in her most demure violet lace gown with a cinched indigo over-corset and coordinating tiny bowler hat, she hoped she cut a sympathetic figure to her audience. It now appeared that Mrs. Singh, Trusdale, and Boo were the only members of the crew not actively scowling at Constance. Then again, Boo was fast asleep, curled into a tan-and-black ball of fluff on a floral silk cushion next to Constance's boots.

So, only Mrs. Singh and Trusdale aren't upset with me. Not the most promising start to my escapade.

Constance cleared her throat. "So, there you have it. For all of us to avoid certain death at the hands of the British Museum's Royal Antiquities Tactical Team, our grand tour must entail collecting enough Enigma Keys within the next week to open an interdimensional portal through which to bring back Haltwhistle Hall. Again, I sincerely apologize for the inconvenience. Any questions?"

Cousin Welli pushed back his Byronic forelock and raised his hand. Welli's legendary voice was rumored to soothe impatient horses and the cuckolded spouses of his many conquests with equal skill. In a tone dripping with sympathetic concern, he asked, "Not to be coarse, my dear, darling, cousin, but . . . has your sanity taken a leave of absence?"

She shrugged. "I'm not a physician. How would I know? The question is, will you, as a crew, pledge to assist me in this quest? Or would you rather toss me out at the next port of call and sail on your merry way, hoping that RATT doesn't follow up on their threat to terminate each and every one of you? May I point out that foreign armies turn and flee rather than face the Royal Antiquities Tactical Team? They reputedly have no mercy for anyone who stands in their way of snatching the best artifacts in the world for queen and country. Not that I intend to influence anyone's decision, of course. The choice is yours."

Mrs. Singh said, "I choose to sail on my merry way, Lady Haltwhistle. No offense."

"None taken." Constance bowed her head to the retired buccaneer. "I don't blame you one bit. It's an awfully large palace to search for one tiny trinket. Honestly, by attempting to outrun RATT, your chances of survival are probably greater than mine at Versailles. I could be wandering the sixteen acres of the palace itself, never mind its hundred acres of formal gardens, for days, or possibly weeks!"

She turned back to focus her attention on her cousin. It was technically his ship, after all. "Imagine me, Welli, tiptoeing around, desperately trying to avoid being captured by the palace guards as I poke into every closet, cabinet, and treasure room. Although, with my luck, Louis XVIII probably keeps the Enigma Key secured in his pantaloons. I might have to pickpocket it right off his person. Won't that be a fine story for the family dinner table this Christmas?"

Welli groaned. "Ugh, playing the jolly yuletide card. That's low, Constance. And for the record, I doubt you'll be able to get within pickpocketing distance of Louis. Before you go rummaging in a king's drawers, can't you locate an alternate Enigma Key?"

"Tell me how, and I will," she said. "Father took his secrets with him to another dimension, and it's not as if I own a tool that magically divines which pair of the King's pantaloons hold a one-inch triangle of alien metal. Do you possess such a device?"

Welli shook his head, hair flopping back over eyes as green as Constance's own. Sadly, his eyes were now tinged with despair.

Poor Welli. Should I survive this escapade, I must make this up to him.

Hearn, seated to Welli's left, leaned over and murmured comfort to the young lord. The burly carriage driver's muscular build strained to escape his modern-cut green tailcoat as he tested the physical limits of a folding deck chair. He hesitantly raised his hand. Cawley, seated beside him, kicked the champion wrestler hard with his buckled shoe. Hearn dropped his hand and folded his arms as his cheeks reddened.

Constance frowned. "Are you casting your vote, Hearn? Incidentally, I hope you've all noticed how incredibly democratic I'm being about this matter. Who knows, the *Lady Penelope* could become our very own republic!"

"I'm casting my vote to go to the flying palace," said Trusdale, lounging on a gilded throne chair brought up from Welli's cabin. The two men had agreed to share a double bunk room, with the proviso that Welli got the top bunk. "For what it's worth, these RATT agents sound dangerous. May as well take our chances with the palace guards. I just hope the whole thing doesn't come crashing to the ground, you know?"

Hearn cocked his head. "What, the mission or the palace?"

"Both," said Trusdale. "I'm kinda curious, though, if anyone has thoughts about what it would take to bring down a flying palace?"

Constance held up her hand. "That's not the mission." Honestly, why was he making this already dire situation sound even worse? Couldn't he try and help her a little less? "My Plan with a—"

"Capital 'P,'" chorused Cawley and Hearn.

Constance beamed at her loyal retainers. "Correct. My Plan is to snatch the Key and depart as quickly as possible. If luck is on our side, no one will even know the key is missing until we're well out of reach of the palace's cannons."

"One hundred cannons, to be exact," said Dr. Maya Chauhan.

Constance nodded. *Ugh. That's an overkill of firepower to avoid.* "But hopefully the cannons won't be our problem, because—"

"It's a sneak attack," said the doctor, with a wry grin. Maya's brown eyes twinkled with warmth for her one-time science student. As a child, Constance had adored attending Maya's public science classes at the Royal Steamwerks military laboratory in Sheffield. Maya was in many ways her role model for inventiveness, intelligence, and when the situation called for it, sass.

"Exactly," Constance replied, grateful for the support. "May I ask you and Dr. Huang for your votes?"

The two scientists were sitting with their thighs scandalously close on a rose-colored loveseat. Doctors Maya Chauhan and Zhi Gwan Huang were two of the brightest minds that had ever graced the hallowed halls of the

Steamwerks. For decades, the two had worked side by side, developing cutting-edge technology for Queen Victoria's vast redcoat army. Surprisingly, Queen Victoria had seen fit to allow the two to retire gracefully from the Steamwerks. Usually, scientists worked there until they dropped, but apparently the Queen admired Maya for her intellect and candor. The Delhi-born scientist had become a favorite confidante of Her Majesty in a court obsessed with scientific progress and world domination.

The sexagenarian couple had received Queen Victoria's royal decree releasing them from her service while they were staying at the Grand Hotel du Louvre. Now framed, the decree hung above their four-poster bed in what used to be Papa's shipboard laboratory. Old habits die hard, and the two were as happy in a room decorated with test tubes and Bunsen burners as they had been in the gilded finery of Paris's finest hotel.

Maya's gold and purple sari shimmered in the morning sun. She winked at Constance. "We vote for Versailles, don't we, Zhi?"

Hong Kong-born Zhi pushed his glasses up on his nose. He wore a shoulder-button tan lab coat with the ease of a man who didn't care a jot about fashion. "We do indeed. Versailles is a modern marvel of aerial engineering. We'd like to know what makes it tick. There's not one schematic of the engine room anywhere to be found. We know that for a fact because we searched high and low for one. The Queen wanted Windsor Castle to take flight. We had to tell her we didn't have the technology to levitate the palace. Let me assure you, she was not amused."

"I hear she rarely is," said Constance. "So, that's four votes for Versailles—me, Mr. Trusdale, Maya, and Zhi—and one against. Let's ask our second member of the Singh family for his vote."

Welli's longtime valet, Ajeet Singh, sat next to Welli's right hand. His uncut beard was frosted with silver. He was immaculately turned out in a black turban, a white collarless shirt, and loose gray pants. A curved dagger in his black sash belt and an iron bangle identified him as a Sikh warrior. Mr. Singh bowed his head. "As my wife votes, so do I. I vote against invading Versailles."

Now, that was a surprise. Constance had presumed that Mr. Singh wouldn't mind a bit of invading. After all, he'd served with Welli when the young lord was a Captain in Her Majesty's Fifth Foot and Mouth Brigade. Perhaps Ajeet's new comfortable quarters had made him soft? He and Rani shared the largest cabin on the ship, next to the engine room. After the airship's original three-man engine crew resigned back in Paris to crew one of the big European pleasure cruisers, Doctors Chauhan and Huang had whipped up a groundbreaking clockwork automaton in Papa's laboratory. Now, the engine room ran without human supervision, resulting in unprecedented space and privacy for the Singhs.

It was excruciatingly embarrassing that she'd managed to bring the wrath of the RATT down upon her quirky household. And overall, they were being so very nice about the whole matter. If the situation were reversed, would she be as reasonable about a crew member bringing doom down upon their heads? Probably not.

Despite Mr. Singh's no, Constance calculated that her odds of getting to Versailles were good. Including herself as a yes, she had Trusdale and the two scientists on her side. Four against two, with three votes yet to go. She almost had this in the bag.

"Welli, your vote, please?"

Welli slumped in his overstuffed blue armchair. "I'm sorry, Constance, but I can't condone taking this ship to Versailles. My father was furious that I supported you in keeping the Hall when he desired to burn the place to the ground. He's cut me off from my trust fund. This ship is the only home I have until I get my townhouse's bills paid off. Not to mention the fact that I believe there's a very good chance you'll be captured or killed. Probably both. I recommend we all try to outrun RATT, together."

Constance's stomach churned. "You don't understand how dangerous the militant-scholars can be." She reached back into her bustle and drew out the clockwork scarab to *oohs* and *aahs* from the crowd. "A mechanical messenger, a simple enough device to create. But consider the wealth and power of the organization that made this scarab. Where redcoats fear to tread, RATT agents—"

Welli held up his hands. "Spare me the amateur dramatics. I'm positively certain that palace guards take a dim view of uninvited guests. I vote for a graceful retreat. I hear Australia is nice, and I doubt the British Museum can find anything down there worth mounting an expeditionary force to retrieve."

Constance bowed her head to hide her disappointment and brushed at an imaginary wrinkle in her gown. She'd always assumed that Welli would take her side on any public matter. His independence here was troubling. She took in a deep breath, exhaled, and lifted her head.

"Thank you for your candor and clear-headedness, Welli. That's four votes for Versailles, three against. And finally, Cawley and Hearn, your votes, please."

She waited patiently for their inevitable yes. Thank heavens for loyal retainers. Her victory here was assured, if less one-sided than she'd hoped for.

The two servants glanced at each other.

"Well?" asked Constance.

"We're abstaining. Aren't we?" said Cawley to Hearn. The champion wrestler squirmed.

Constance gaped. "You can't abstain." If they did, she lost, and she'd find herself dropped off at the next European port with RATT on her tail. And that would make getting into Versailles even more problematic. Or even worse, Welli would drag her off to Australia. What on earth would she do in a land of koala bears and kangaroos?

Hearn cleared his throat. "The thing is, Miss Constance—"

"Don't you dare. We promised him," snapped Cawley.

Hearn continued, "We made a promise to your father not to discuss certain things. And this seems like a situation where some of those certain things seem uncertain. I'm certainly not saying that there might be a device to help track down Enigma Keys on this airship . . ."

Cawley groaned and put his head in his hands.

". . . but then again, I'm not *not* saying that. If it would help you to pinpoint the Key that may or may not be in the King's pantaloons, surely that would be a good thing?" Hearn gently placed his tattooed hand on Cawley's shoulder. "I mean, come on, Cawley. If we don't help, her ladyship will go charging off by herself. She'll either get herself killed by these museum thugs, or she'll sneak around a sixteen-acre palace until she gets caught. Baron Haltwhistle wouldn't want either of those things to happen, now would he?"

Cawley shrugged. "Who can say? He always was an odd bird, the Baron."

"What device? Where is it?" asked Constance.

Hearn held up his hands. "Now, don't get too excited, miss. Your father took a vital part out of it so that no one could start it accidentally. And he entrusted that part to the most sensible person he knew."

"The most . . . who's that?"

Hearn licked his lips and glanced between Constance and Welli. "Your godmother, the Countess of Benchley, Lady Margaret."

Oh lord, no.

Anyone but Auntie Madge.

Chapter 9:
The Fairy Godmother

It was ten minutes past teatime as Trusdale gazed out the leaded windows of the Dowager Countess of Benchley's magnificent château. High above the imposing round towers and turrets of the château, a smudge of tiny lights seemed to glitter against the azure sky. Trusdale closed his left eye, and the sky seemed empty. He blinked, and winked with his right eye. A blanket of clear blue sky stretched over the topiary gardens and pastures beyond. Cattle and sheep grazed together in perfect, natural harmony, unconcerned as to whether the sky above them could hold anything more dangerous than a hawk or eagle. Constance's purple ankle boot thudded into his shin. Trusdale winced and glared at the redhead. She motioned across her throat with an imaginary knife. Either she was telling him to stop winking at the sky, or . . .

"Are you quite well, Mr. Trusdale?" asked the dowager countess, Lady Margaret.

Trusdale straightened his posture upon his mahogany dining chair, which was chiseled with his host's snarling badger motif. "Yes, ma'am."

"Auntie Madge," as Constance called the countess, had fixed her gray eyes upon him from across the round tea table. Madge's expression was fierce enough to scare any badger into running for its burrow. Beneath a diamond tiara, her silver hair swelled into the massive pompadour hairstyle so loved by French aristocrats. Even fashion-shy Trusdale knew that her yellow lace gown and blue cinched over-corset embroidered with gold fleur-de-lis were all the latest rage in Paris. There was an air of his handler, God, about her, perhaps because of her utter confidence and supreme power, matched with bone-chilling eyes of gray. Even their jewelry echoed one another. The large locket ring on Madge's finger might not be agency issued, but he wouldn't be surprised if the dowager countess carried a pinch of poison in her ring. How had her numerous husbands died again?

He shivered. Could it be God who was the eye in the sky that even now he could sense was watching him from orbit? Was he experiencing good old-fashioned paranoia, or was he getting smarter the closer he got to thirty? Lord, what he wouldn't give to turn back time and never join the agency. Then again, if he hadn't, he would never have run into Constance.

If his handler was watching him from a hot air balloon or some other flying device, she must be wondering what the heck he was doing taking tea with aristocrats in front of the most stone-faced servants he'd ever seen. Behind the seated countess, apple logs flickered with flame in the baroque marble fireplace. The mantel was littered with gilt-edged letterpress invitations from France's ever-carousing gentry. Flanking the fireplace, almost melted into the blue-and-white chinoiserie wallpaper, stood Madge's butler and maid, stiller than statues. The effect was unnerving. Maybe that's why his spine kept crawling?

Constance and Welli sat on either side of him around the tea table set for four. Welli dazzled in a red paisley tailcoat, a frothy white shirt, breeches, and scarlet riding boots. The young lord reached for a minuscule cucumber sandwich on the tower of treats in the center of the table, and somehow resisted the urge to swallow it in one impolite bite.

Constance glared at Trusdale over the rim of her teacup. She was doing a fine impression of a prim and proper lady in her violet lace gown with its cinched indigo over-corset. She'd even straightened her tiny bowler hat from its usual rakish angle. The hat now perched upon a voluminous wave of pinned-up auburn hair as Constance attempted her own version of a pompadour. The pouf of hair made her ridiculous hat even sillier than usual. Yet, there was a method to her madness. The countess had yet to criticize Constance's looks, and Trusdale had even been invited to tea as her "plus one."

That Constance had classed him as such to her god-mother was surely his reward for backing her on the air-ship crew vote.

She'd seemed to be genuine in her request for them to be friends. It was an idea he could get behind. But lord knew what revenge she'd take on him if she found out he was spying on her and the crew.

And now RATT was doubling the danger for every-one on the *Lady Penelope*. Maybe Constance truly was cursed. Mayhem seemed to follow her no matter where she went.

Constance nudged him none too gently in the ribs with her elbow. Auntie Madge was glaring at him with an ice that took his breath away. Maybe she and God were related?

The countess cleared her throat. "Ahem. Your clown appears to be living in a world of his own making, Con-stance. Where do you meet these people?"

The redhead set down her teacup with a clatter. "Ah, no, Auntie. Not a clown. In fact, Mr. Trusdale is my security consultant—"

"I've never been a fan of the circus," sniffed Lady Margaret. "Who wants to sit in a tent to watch some fool eat a sword while another juggles live cats? The entire situation is preposterous."

"Live cats?" asked Welli, reaching for a miniature smoked salmon sandwich. "I'd pay to see that."

"Oh no you wouldn't," admonished Constance.

The countess put down her teacup and picked up her opera glasses. Trusdale squirmed as the seventy-three-year-old society maven studied his attire. "Perhaps you could clothe your clown in something more suitable for his occupation? The French are enamored with the traditional harlequin style. A diamond-patterned leotard, a tricorn hat, curled slippers, and so on. Such an outfit would surely be more amusing than this cowboy costume."

Constance groaned. "He's not a clown. But you make a fair point. This"—she waved a hand at Trusdale's outfit—"could use an overhaul. Mr. Trusdale, however, is uncommonly attached to his hat and coat."

Damn straight I am.

Stuffed inside the depths of his black leather duster were his secret dossier on the Brass Queen, his snubnosed revolver, and enough bribe money to get him out of most sticky situations. He wasn't going to take off the coat and risk Constance getting her sticky fingers on the dossier that contained concrete proof that he was a spy. And lord knew he wanted her to trust him.

More importantly, he wanted to become a man whom she could trust. He sagged into his chair, a shadow of the person he longed to be.

Welli shot him a supportive smile and said, "Ladies, with all due respect, you're embarrassing the poor chap. Not that I wouldn't mind seeing Trusdale's well-turned calf in harlequin hose, but we must respect that Americans approach fashion as we might an enraged bull. That is, with fear, boldness, or the casual tread of one who doesn't understand what all the fuss is about. As such, their style runs the gamut from overconfident to understated with a hint of laxness. I believe we should applaud Mr. Trusdale on what he surely believes is a practical choice of travel attire."

I'm sure there's a compliment in there somewhere.

"Would you define this hat as overconfident? Or leaning toward laxness?" Constance gestured at Trusdale's Stetson, resting inoffensively on his lap.

"I can assure you all, this is a classic design," said Trusdale. "Not to change the subject, but may I please borrow your opera glasses for a moment, Lady Margaret?" He held out his hand across the tower of treats.

The countess's snowy brows almost hit her tiara. "Is he short-sighted as well? The poor dear." Nevertheless, she handed him the long-handled opera glasses.

Trusdale put the silver glasses to his eyes and stared out the window. "I just . . ." The azure sky was entirely free of twinkling lights. "Did you ever get the feeling that someone was watching your every move?"

All three aristocrats chuckled. Trusdale placed the glasses onto the table and glanced around at his tea companions, confused at their display of good humor. The countess tilted her head toward her silent servants, still standing on either side of the fireplace like liveried bookends. They were stalwart representatives of the hundreds of staff who worked on the countess's sprawling estate.

"One would hope we are the center of our domestic's very existence," said the countess. "Without a watchful servant at hand, how on earth could one's every need be anticipated? Every action I take keeps the flow of activity through my household running like clockwork. For instance, should my teapot run close to empty, where would I be unless a servant noticed and hurried to the kitchen to request a new pot?"

As if on cue, the maid swept out of the parlor without so much as a rustle from her floor-length black gown and starched white apron. The countess nodded approvingly. "Do you see, Mr. Trusdale? This house is a well-oiled machine. You, I, and the staff all play our parts to perfection. Privacy would ruin everything."

Trusdale thought, *No wonder every aristocrat I meet is inept, insane, or at the very best, eccentric beyond belief. Still, must be nice to live on a planet where everything seems to revolve around you. Perhaps this explains why Constance always seems surprised when things don't go her own way?*

He'd surely score points with the redhead if he helped her to secure the mysterious component left behind by her dimension-hopping Papa. Trusdale picked up his teacup and said, "So, Constance, didn't you have something to ask your godmother about?"

A flush crossed Constance's cheeks. "Oh, for heaven's sake, man. We are still at the small talk part of teatime. We've yet to move on to social sniping and tittle-tattle. We don't begin serious conversations until the macaroons are served."

Welli nodded. "Yes, steady on, old boy. All things in good time."

Lady Margaret glanced between her two godchildren. "At my age, reaching the stage of macaroons at tea is not always assured. Let's get to the heart of the matter. What exactly are you after, Constance, other than the pleasure of my company?"

Constance brushed imaginary crumbs from the front of her corset. "It appears that my dear Papa entrusted you with an item that is vital for a scientific experiment I'm conducting."

Lady Margaret's expression soured. "And what have I told you about noble ladies studying the sciences?"

"But Dr. Chauhan says—"

"Is she either an aristocrat or married?"

Eyes downcast, Constance picked at the lace tablecloth. "Well, no, neither. I assume that Dr. Huang might propose one day, but not yet, as far as I know . . ."

Auntie Madge leaned forward and gently rested her hand upon Constance's arm. "My dear, the middle class may follow the wanton urges of their hearts, but we hold the future of our bloodlines dearer than any fleeting flirtation."

Welli nodded. "She's quite right, Constance. It's more than time for you to settle down with a handsome, malleable lord somewhere and start popping out baby Haltwhistles."

Constance exclaimed, "Welli! Of all the backstabbing—"

"Now, now, Constance. Your cousin is absolutely correct," said Madge, gazing at her goddaughter with genuine concern in her eyes. "You're twenty-one years old now, which is positively over the hill for most bachelors. Losing Haltwhistle Hall has certainly put a dent in your appeal. A pretty face alone won't catch you a viscount in today's Europe. You need either a fortune or enough dirt to blackmail a noble family until a younger son steps up to the matrimonial altar. As far as I know, you don't possess either."

"And that's exactly why I need to finish Papa's device. If I have it, I may be able to locate and bring back the Hall from . . . I mean . . . perhaps I can generate enough funds through scientific experimentation to build a new Hall that looks remarkably like the old one. It will be exactly the same in every detail. Isn't that a laudable goal?" Constance picked up her teacup and saucer with trembling hands and sipped her tea.

Lady Margaret sat back, steepled her fingers together, and considered the matter. "If you have a way to generate a fortune, whether it is to turn rocks into diamonds via alchemy, or whatever the current fad is amongst gentleman scientists these days, then I could turn a blind eye to a certain amount of scientific inquiry. But only if no one of import learns of your endeavors. You will never attain matrimonial harmony if your fiancé believes, even for one moment, that you could be more intelligent than he."

Trusdale said, "I would think any man would love to know that a highly intelligent woman chose them above all others."

Welli snorted. "Most men, or one man?"

"I . . . wait, what are you saying?"

The countess sighed. "My comments here are for Constance to reflect upon, not the two of you. Your journey through life will be a thousand times easier than that of any lady, by the mere fact that our society rewards maleness with opportunities that others are denied."

Trusdale couldn't deny this fact of life. He exchanged a glance with Welli and as one, both men busied themselves with the tower of treats.

Lady Margaret patted Constance's knee with her liver-spotted hand. "My audacious, naive, impetuous girl, you stand at the very precipice of womanhood. Don't fall to a stony path far below your station by gazing up at stars you will never reach. This world is unkind to bold women. Follow the road more traveled for both your own safety and my peace of mind."

Constance set down her teacup. "Then the world needs to change, not I. That said, am I to understand that you will entrust me with Papa's component? If so, Auntie, thank you, from the bottom of my heart. Please send the item over to my ship—"

"My ship," corrected Welli. He winced as Lady Margaret turned to survey him with eyes as sharp as cut diamonds.

The dowager countess pursed her lips. "I assume, Wellington, that you directed my attention to your cousin's matrimonial woes so that I would neglect to mention your own? Foolish boy. Twenty-six years old and unwed, with enough romantic conquests across the British Empire that one could speculate the blood of an Italian count runs in your veins."

Welli spluttered. "Now, hold on, Auntie. There haven't been that many conquests . . . I mean, well, there may have been a few dozen or so, but it's different for a boy . . ."

Madge glowered at him. "Not if that 'boy' has been cut off from his inheritance by his father and owes a considerable amount of money to an alarming number of European nobles."

Welli reddened. "Ah, well, I've had a run of bad luck at the poker table recently—"

"Good news for you, then," said the countess. "Your luck is about to change. I know several wealthy, if comely, maidens who might settle for a notorious dandy on their arm, if they can secure the title of Lady Pendelroy in due time."

Welli blanched and pushed back his forelock of Byronic hair. "I'm not yet ready to . . ."

The countess waved him silent. "Then it's settled. Constance, no, I shall not give you your thingamabob until such time as both you and Welli have proven yourselves to be the respectable, marriage-worthy nobles that you could be if you simply wouldn't give in to your passions, whether carnal, scientific, or otherwise. You're both more intelligent than you have a right to be, and I believe this does you no service in the greater world."

"But—" began Constance.

"Don't *but* me, young lady. I want to know that my godchildren are not the disreputable ends of their noble bloodlines. Wellington, you're merely a wandering viscount without income or land. Should you wish to one day inherit your father's earldom, you need to win him over."

"I couldn't care less about—"

"Then start caring. And Constance, Queen Victoria has just this week granted British women the right to inherit both property and titles. Given the apparent loss of your estate, is it in your best interests to reveal your eccentricities to the wider world? You should be striving to become the very model of a submissive Victorian lady, lest unkind gentlemen point at your foibles and say they exist because you have a legal right that shouldn't have been extended to you."

"So now I'm letting down the side of all women by not playing into a stereotype of passivity and feebleness?"

"Exactly. You're being monumentally selfish by not following *Babett's Modern Manners* to the letter. You need to be more ladylike than any lady ever born to prove that when given rights, true ladies still maintain their decorum, or the road to greater autonomy for all women will be difficult if not impossible to traverse. Queen Victoria won't live forever, and a male absolute monarch could nullify her reforms if they upset too many apple carts at the same time."

Constance blinked back tears. "I'm being selfish?"

Trusdale's heart ached for Constance as she dabbed her eyes with the drape of her lace sleeves.

"You are both acting selfishly," said the countess. "But then again, so am I. I want to see you married to respectable peers and producing legitimate offspring within the next year. Then I can rest in peace amongst the angels knowing that I have fulfilled my duty as godmother. This gives you two a limited time to shore up your fortunes and reputations enough to draw the right kind of attention. Fortunately, there are numerous events this season that may well provide you with the opportunity to meet your mates."

An acutely awkward silence settled upon the parlor as Lady Margaret's butler collected the gilt-edged invitations from the mantle and brought them to his mistress. She flicked through the invitations. "No, no . . . ah. Here we are!" She held up a large letter-pressed card dripping with florid calligraphy and a gold wax stamp. "My great-nephew is holding a masquerade ball tonight that would present the perfect opportunity for you both to mingle with more suitable companions. Whether or not Constance's alchemy resurrects your finances, you will be hard-pressed to marry well if you've never been seen at court."

She slapped the gilt-edged invitation down on the table with a bang as Constance and Welli stammered out their defenses against imminent matrimony. "Enough. No, don't thank me for my kindness in bringing you into my social circle. You can save your gratitude for after you walk down the aisle."

Constance and Welli gaped at each other, clearly stunned. Trusdale sat stock still, keen to avoid drawing the ire of the caustic countess.

To his surprise, Constance stood unsteadily and curtsied to her godmother. With tears welling, she said, "My sincere apologies, Auntie, that I am such a disappointment to you. However, I believe I have a greater purpose this day than seeking a noble marriage. You are absolutely correct that I should consider my part in continuing my bloodline. But my companions aboard the *Lady Penelope* are in danger because of my actions, which are themselves the direct consequence of selfish actions taken by my father. I am the last heir to a monumentally selfish bloodline. Perhaps the world will be better off if it dies with me. Goodbye, Auntie. I sincerely hope we will meet under better circumstances in the future." Lip trembling, Constance stumbled from the parlor.

Trusdale's jaw almost hit the floor. Just when he thought he knew Constance well enough to figure out what she would do next . . .

Welli groaned and sank his head into his hands. "Oh lord, I didn't mean to set her off with my teasing. I thought she would take any comments thrown her way in her usual indomitable stride. Her level of concern for the crew's well-being has increased since she encountered"— Welli blinked at Trusdale—"certain foreign influences. Still, I take full responsibility for her actions today. Please accept my heartfelt apologies, Auntie. Constance doesn't mean to be discourteous. She's just—"

"Her father's daughter. Henry was a bombastic blowhard, but one couldn't help but admire his backbone. She truly is a Haltwhistle, through and through." Lady Margaret sniffled as her butler produced a pressed handkerchief from his waistcoat pocket and presented it to her. She took it from him and dabbed at her nose. For the countess, this was surely the most emotional state she could present in front of witnesses. "I hadn't even got around to giving her a letter that arrived for her this very morning. The address was written in the most beautiful copperplate handwriting, just like the missives her dear mother Annabella used to send to me when she was off traveling with Henry on their ridiculous adventures. I'll send the letter over along with her thingamabob heirloom to your ship. Which I should tell you is nothing more than parts of an old picture frame wrapped in an inordinate amount of brown paper. Probably Henry's idea of a joke. Beyond this act of kindness, I shall have to cut her off completely."

"Naturally," Welli agreed. "She's clearly crossed the line in teatime decorum. However, in time, I'm sure she'll come around to your way of thinking. I hope at that point you will do her the courtesy of listening to her apology—"

"Hold on, now," said Trusdale, raising his hands to call for calm. "There's no need for anyone here to overreact. Family members fall out with each other all the time. But if you're smart, you forgive. If you're real smart, you'll also forget. Constance is being pulled in all directions here. Can't you both give her a break?"

Lady Margaret and Welli exchanged glances. Madge said, "*Babett's Modern Manners* states that—"

"Well, *Trusdale's Way of the World* states that life's too short to push away the ones we love. You can't control people, Lady Margaret." He gestured to her butler. "Maybe you can control your employees a little, but family is on a whole different level. Didn't you ever wish someone loved you so much that they told you the truth? You can't let etiquette rules stand between you and a girl who loves you for who you are. I know Constance thinks the world of you. Can't you give her a pass, just this once?"

Lady Margaret silently handed her used handkerchief back to the waiting butler, who walked over to the fireplace and threw it on the flames. The flames crackled as he returned to his post beside the fireplace. Somewhere in the depths of the house, a clock struck the half hour. The situation was dire.

Trusdale couldn't bear to think of Constance living with the pain of losing Auntie Madge's goodwill. She surely needed all the support she could get, given the sheer number of enemies she'd managed to make during her short time on earth.

Trusdale leaned in and picked up the letter-pressed invitation the countess had slammed onto the table. He scanned it and suppressed a smile. Constance's odd luck had kicked into life once more. It was time for a charm offensive. He gazed deep into the countess's gray eyes and said from the heart, "Lady Margaret, your wisdom and love for Constance is apparent to all. I beg you to consider the notion that there's a simple way to heal this family wound?"

"Not unless you are a magician as well as a clown," she said.

"I'd play the part of either if it helps you and Constance to move to a better place. What if I could talk

Constance into attending this ball by your side tonight? She will be attending a fancy party looking her best, just like you wanted. With your help, maybe she'll meet her future fiancé . . ." His heart ached at the very thought, but for Constance's sake, he pressed on. "Or maybe she won't. But she'll be there, in person. As the British often do, you can both pretend not to have had a falling out in the first place. Talk about the weather or something. And then you can move on from this ugly moment as if it never happened. What do you say?"

Lady Margaret slowly nodded. "There's more to you than meets the eye, Mr. Trusdale. Perhaps I have misjudged your usefulness to her, and to me. Do you honestly believe that you can persuade Constance to attend the ball . . .?"

"I'm sure I can," said Trusdale, ignoring Welli's look of alarm.

"Then, I agree to your proposal, Mr. Trusdale. Wellington, I will send my team of seamstresses to your ship with suitable masks and costumes for the three of you. I keep a selection on hand in case I or my guests spontaneously decide to attend an event. The French do so love their masquerades. The mandatory face masks give the attendees the chance to be anonymous for once in their lives. Naturally, that tends to lead to risqué behavior and occasional debauchery. Wellington, you must keep an eye on Constance. She knows so little of courtly intrigue and escapades, she may find herself saying or doing something she'll regret later."

The countess rose from her chair, and Trusdale and Welli stood up as gentlemen should. Madge bestowed a rare smile upon them.

"Sit, both of you, and finish your tea. Your airship may follow mine to the ball. For now, I shall take my leave of you so that I may sleep for a few hours. The ball begins two hours before midnight and will last until dawn. It's an exhausting enterprise for one of my years. Good afternoon, gentlemen."

Both men bowed as she swept from the parlor with the majesty of an antique dreadnought. Welli waited until the butler had followed his mistress out of the parlor before he punched Trusdale in the shoulder. "What are you thinking, man? The last thing Constance ever wants to do is go to a frivolous party, even more so now that she's trying to save the crew from RATT. Trust me, once she's got the bit in her teeth, there's no guiding the filly. And Margaret will never forgive her for standing her up at a society ball, whereas she might eventually have forgiven Constance for this teatime spat. You can't possibly understand the dynamics of—"

Trusdale waved the gilt-edged invitation in Welli's face.

The gilt matched the card's gold wax stamp imprinted with the sun symbol of King Louis XVIII. Welli squinted at the card and broke into a smile. "You're a sly dog, Trusdale. A sly, sly—"

"Dog. I know. Do you know what else I know? Constance loves a fine garden. And there's no garden on earth as fine as?"

"Versailles," chuckled Welli. "Our fairy godmother has given Constance a chance to go to a ball to find her true heart's desire—an Enigma Key. Here's to hoping it's not being kept in the King's pantaloons as Constance fears."

"Here's hoping," said Trusdale. "Say, you know where I might be able to send a telegram around here?"

"Auntie Madge hates telegrams. They're far too new-fangled for her. I might be able to set you up with one of her carrier pigeons, though. Color me curious about who you might be writing to. A lady friend, perchance?"

Trusdale shook his head. "Ah, no, my grandmother. Got to tell that fine lady that I'm heading to a royal ball. She'll be thrilled."

Or at least, God and Général Malaise will be less likely to reassign me if I'm seen as making progress on starting a revolution in France.

Welli chuckled. "You *are* moving up in the world, Trusdale. Next, you'll be prancing around Queen Victoria's court with a debutante on your arm."

Trusdale grimaced. "God forbid. Come on, let's go and find ourselves a pigeon before the next pot of tea arrives."

Welli sighed and stuffed several small sandwiches into his mouth. Cheeks bulging, he mumbled, "The sacrifices I make for Constance. She has no idea."

"But you love her anyway."

"Don't we all?" said Welli with an impish grin. "Not that we'd tell her that, of course. Or perhaps we might, if the circumstances are right?"

Trusdale ignored the twinkle in Welli's eye and placed his Stetson firmly on his head. He said in a mock-British accent, "One's so delighted to be invited to a royal masquerade ball. After you, Lord Pendelroy."

Welli laughed. "Ah, you're too kind, dear fellow. As the poets might say, 'And off we go to the city in the sky, the one, the only, Palace of Versailles!'"

Chapter 10:
A Dress to Impress

Alone in her cabin aboard the *Lady Penelope*, Constance studied the letter Auntie Madge had sent along with her mysterious heirloom. The letter had arrived in a plain envelope, addressed in a hand she knew only too well. Inside, she found a single page torn from the travel edition of *Babett's Modern Manners*. A page that fit exactly to the torn remnant left in her own copy. In copperplate letters, a warning had been written across the printed text.

My sweet nutmeg, beware the scar-faced man and the fallen king. They're coming for you! Love Mama xxx

Nutmeg had been Mama's pet name for her. Not everyone likes nutmeg, but those who do, love it. The name was supposed to help Constance as a toddler feel better when the world misunderstood her. Only family and servants knew of the pet name, and none would be so cruel as to use it. Was the letter a twisted joke on the part of some former household servant with an ax to grind over some imagined wrong? It had proved impossible to run a country estate without offending at least some of the staff with her helpful comments about their performance.

Not everyone took her purely constructive criticism well, as had been evidenced by staff quitting, sulking, or occasionally trying to shoot her with her own guns. But now that she was no longer mistress of an estate, surely no ex-servant would bother to pursue a personal vendetta. Plus, the envelope's freshly inked postmark revealed that the letter had been mailed three days prior from Stockholm, King Oscar's capital. Was he the fallen king? She didn't need a piece of paper to tell her that the King was her enemy. And the scar-faced man could only be Erhard.

Had Erhard mailed this letter days before his kidnapping attempt simply to torture her if she evaded his clutches? Unadulterated wickedness she could understand, but this was just petty. Surely even henchmen lived to some sort of code?

There was another possibility, one that she could barely begin to consider. The casket filled with rocks that Welli had mentioned was buried in Mama's grave. Was it possible that her mother wasn't dead, after all? Would Papa have lied about such a dreadful event to his only daughter?

Trust no one, he'd always said.

She ran her fingers back through her loose hair. No, that way lay madness. This was a joke, and a bad one at that. She balled up the envelope and torn page and tossed them onto the fire. There was no need to mention this to the rest of the crew. Her mail—weird, threatening or otherwise—was her concern alone. Mama was gone. It was time to focus on the present, literally. She walked to the center of the cabin to survey the four large sheets of brown wrapping paper that she'd pieced together on the oak-planked floor.

As ever with one of Papa's gifts, the wrapping was as important as the present itself. Each piece of paper was scrawled with Papa's coded handwriting, hieroglyphics, technical drawings, and surprisingly, a sonnet praising her late mother's giggle. Naturally, Papa had written everything in lemon juice to make it invisible to casual observers. It had taken Cawley two hours with a hot iron to oxidize the message into sepia tones that she could read. When viewed as a reflection in her cabin's large wall mirror, the sheets of paper had revealed their secrets on how to use the interdimensional aetherscope device.

The device had turned out to be eight sections of frame that clicked into place on top of the smooth copper frame of her wall mirror. Each section was adorned with delicate copper wiring that outlined constellations from various dimensions. A one-inch triangular socket at the bottom of the frame suggested that if she inserted a single Enigma Key, the energy released from the Key would surge through the mirror's circuitry to reveal . . .?

And this is where Papa's notes got hazy. Potentially, the mirror could reveal the location of other Enigma Keys throughout the multiverse. But he'd written some nonsense about "gazing into the void allows the void to gaze back," and unintelligible babble about devils. Or was it jellies? Papa wasn't a religious man, and she'd never seen him eat so much as a spoonful of jelly. Not even the wibbly-wobbly rhubarb-and-strawberry flavored jellies their family cook had created every Sunday throughout her childhood. They'd always been formed into fun shapes—crowns, castles, or severed heads. The jellies were a highlight of her childhood spent without friends her own age and under the tutelage of strict governesses.

Admittedly, Papa had picked governesses who could teach skills far beyond playing the pianoforte and embroidery. Fencing, jousting, kung fu, archery, dead languages, live electrical experiments—all the things he'd learned as a boy from his own gentleman-scientist father. By contrast, Mama had been keen on horse breeding and management of the estate staff. She'd always loved sharing a jelly with her beloved daughter.

Was there even the slightest chance she could still be alive?

Of course she isn't. Pull yourself together, girl. The universe doesn't bring back the dead, no matter how hard we might cry.

Constance heaved the heaviest of sighs within her new Tudor-style undergarments. Fortunately, her long, triangular corset was still loosely laced at her sides as she waited for the top layer of her costume to arrive. Auntie Madge's team of seamstresses had modified an Elizabethan-style court gown for Constance's short and curvy frame. Once the seamstresses had left the airship, Dr. Maya Chauhan had whisked the gown and petticoats away to her laboratory to add what she'd termed "a little sparkle."

Constance hoped the "sparkle" wouldn't be anything that would further offend her godmother. She'd been shocked to the core when Welli informed her that Madge was turning a blind eye to the teatime brouhaha. It had taken every ounce of strength she had to rebel against Madge, and by extension, every society maven's opinion that a woman's only value to the world was to become a wife and mother. In time, perhaps she would step into those roles if she so desired. But right now, the continuation of the Haltwhistle line could wait until she had dealt with her RATT problem.

Constance pointed her hands above her head and pirouetted like a ballerina to better study her historically inspired underwear in the freshly framed mirror. Her fashionable nineteenth-century hourglass figure had been transformed into the epitome of sixteenth-century feminine allure. Over a knee-length linen smock, her breasts were flattened beneath a triangular high-necked two-part corset.

Tied to this set of stays dangled a white farthingale hoop skirt, which bobbed jauntily over her blue silk stockings. A padded roll tied around her hips would add fullness to her underpetticoats and gown when they finally arrived from Maya's laboratory.

Tiny snores emanated from the alcove bed behind her as Boo snoozed contentedly. The black-and-tan Yorkshire terrier was curled into an impossibly small ball inside a heart-shaped Elizabethan neck ruff laid out on the green coverlet.

Hmmm. Should I take Boo with me to the ball? Many a fine lady at courts of old would have carried a pet to keep herself warm on a carriage ride. Perhaps Maya could fashion a coordinating sling in which she could carry the puppy?

Then again, I probably shouldn't take her with me. What if Boo makes an escape at Versailles? A sixteen-acre palace must hold a lot of places for a puppy to hide in. Not to mention a hundred acres of formal gardens she'd love to dig up. She could get herself into a world of trouble.

As could Constance herself. Keen to avoid wearing a historically accurate but unbearably itchy wig sent by her godmother, she spent the next half hour tormenting her waist-long red hair into an approximation of an Elizabethan hairstyle. She clipped drop pearl earrings fit for Tudor royalty onto her earlobes. Thirty pearl necklaces of varying lengths were laid out on the bed coverlet next to Boo, ready to be draped around her neck before the heart ruff was attached.

Madge had also sent over a bejeweled ostrich feather fan and eight diamond-and-sapphire rings that could be worn over long-fingered kidskin gloves. There was also a golden crown similar in design to the fanciful crown Constance used on her Brass Queen stationery. The crown was engraved upon her wax stamp that sealed secret documents about her weapons shipments.

She'd convinced herself that she'd created the Brass Queen's fanciful crown sigil from her imagination. But now, she realized that she'd based it on a joyful memory from her childhood. When Mama visited Auntie Madge at her stately mansion in Sheffield, Constance had been allowed to play with the treasures stored in Madge's curio chamber. This crown had been her favorite dress-up piece. Was this Madge's idea of a peace offering? If so, her godmother was more sentimental about her than she'd realized.

Her heart warmed by the thought, she picked up the crown and placed it atop her auburn hair. This precious, majestic hat was a gift directly from the heart of Lady Margaret. Had it been a mere pebble or a feather, she would have treasured it forever just the same.

She turned back to the wall mirror and admired her regal reflection. Tonight, she would transform to look like the greatest of Tudor queens, not a brass one. But the Brass Queen did possess some wonderful toys that even Elizabeth the First herself would surely have appreciated. Should she consider wearing her lady's lightning gauntlet under her right glove? The detachable lace cuffs of her gown would easily cover the mechanism.

Then again, the battle mitten seemed determined to misfire at every opportunity. She couldn't understand it. She'd asked Mrs. Singh to put her hand inside the mitten, and it had worked perfectly. Just so with Maya. But when she, the legendary Brass Queen, attempted to fire her own weapon, it would either fail to go off or, if it did ignite, it shot its lightning net too fast, too slow, or at the wrong intensity. It was almost as if she herself was the weak link in the mechanism.

But that made about as much sense as a letter from her deceased Mama. And the mitten must work for any woman who wore it, or it would never go on to become a commercial success.

A knock sounded upon her cabin door. From the other side, Dr. Chauhan announced, "It's me, Constance, and I come bearing gifts." After fifty years of working for the English crown, only a hint of Maya's delightful Delhi accent remained.

"Come on in," said Constance. "You're always welcome here, gifts or no gifts."

Dr. Chauhan entered beaming a grin brighter than a lighthouse on a stormy day. She'd changed from her purple sari to a yellow one decorated with red lotus blossoms. Cawley, ever constant, padded in behind her. He was carrying Constance's gown and petticoats draped across his arms as if he'd just caught a fainting debutante. He kept his rheumy eyes fixed on the night sky outside the cabin's porthole so as not to embarrass his mistress in her Tudor underpinnings.

"You look simply ridiculous, my dear," grinned Maya.

"Well, it's not as practical as a sari, I'll give you that. Look, my hoops wobble!" Constance gyrated around

Maya in her hoop skirt as Maya laughed. "And they say the bustle is impractical."

Maya nodded. "It is. But this is soooo much worse. Once we've stitched the top gown onto you, you'll be as cocooned as a caterpillar until we cut you out. Put this on first and close your eyes tight." Maya held out a lady's white porcelain face mask painted with red lips, a whisper of blush on high cheekbones, and thin arched brows over two cut eye holes. Two gold ribbons allowed the mask to be tied onto the wearer. "It's beautiful, isn't it? The seamstresses said it was cast in Venice over a century ago. It's delicate, so don't get in any fistfights."

"As if I would," said Constance. "It's far nicer than any mask I've owned. But why am I putting it on first?"

"So that when you open your eyes, you'll see the costume in its full glory. Don't worry, it should only take us about thirty minutes to get you stitched in there."

Constance groaned. "The things I do for fashion."

The next half hour dragged on for what felt like an eternity. Constance tried not to fidget as layers of aristocratic luxury were sewn upon her person. As each new piece added weight to her petite frame, she could almost feel the gravitas of becoming a Tudor queen. She felt somehow older and wiser as the final stitches were made and Maya pinned the golden crown to what felt like a permanent position on her head.

"That's it," breathed Maya. "Elizabeth the First, re-born on an airship in the sky. You may open your eyes."

Constance blinked at the image in the mirror of the queen she'd become. Her golden crown, curled red hair, perfect porcelain face mask, and heart-shaped ruff were stunning. But her narrow-waisted, puffy-sleeved, full-skirted white silk gown was sheer perfection. The white gown was richly embroidered with blue and silver waves, upon which bobbed a fleet of gold English galle-ons fighting an epic sea battle against the bronze Spanish Armada in 1588. And yet, Maya had added even more to the ensemble than Elizabeth herself could ever have imagined. A gossamer-thin web of silver wire draped over the gown. Metal replicas of the embroidered gal-leons sailed slowly along the net of wires like real ships on a stormy sea. Tiny cannons on each ship occasionally opened fire on their foes with a spark, a bang, and a wisp of gunpowder smoke.

"I'm a walking sea battle!"

Maya clapped her hands with glee. "That you are. If your godmother's goal is for you to attract male atten-tion at the royal court, I guarantee you this dress will do the trick! Boys do so love a battle. The control for your mechanical fleet lies here." She pointed at the British flagship sailing above Constance's belly button. "There's a clockwork mechanism sewn into your gown right there that will power the mechanical ships for a good twelve hours. Rotate the main mast clockwise to speed up your fleet, or tap the ship three times to fire all your cannons at once. Now, according to Mr. Trusdale's plan—"

"His what? If anyone's developing a plan for tonight, it should be me. Also, as wondrous as my sea battle is, do you think the addition of technology to this gorgeous gown could in any way offend Auntie Madge?"

Maya peered at a ship that was moving a little slower than its fleet mates. "Not when she sees how the explosions of cannon fire can draw potential suitors over to you. I'd stay away from presenting a detailed treatise on clockwork mechanics lest you bore them to death. Just tell them it runs on the honey of magic bees."

"That's ridiculous."

"But it's a fun conversation starter. Small talk has never been one of your greatest skills."

"Who has the time?"

"I would imagine it's the primary occupation of most of the guests at a royal ball. As for your godmother, I may only be a decade or so behind her in age, but I have found that many ladies of her age and breeding were brought up to believe that science was not to be trusted. A lady scientist was something of an oddity, even though throughout history, women have made important discoveries about the nature of this world and beyond. It is an irony that great minds like Ada Lovelace and her Difference Engine are not recognized for their brilliance. Instead, she is often only referred to in relation to her male partner, Babbage, or her rake of a father, Lord Byron. Or even worse, the fact that she gambled away her fortune backing the wrong horses at the races trying to raise funds to finish the engine."

"She did? Oh, that's simply dreadful. Did she manage to finish the device?"

Maya shook her head. "Alas, she did not. It was one of the many items on my to-do list as head of the Steamwerks, but all Queen Victoria wanted was ever more advanced imperial weaponry and troop transportation. It's only in the last few years that her mood has lightened. Now, she seems a tad more open to peacetime technology, and even a little fun, on occasion. She does love a masquerade ball. I'm sure she would adore your armada-defying gown." Maya drew a minute screwdriver out of her sari and kneeled to adjust a couple of the ships on Constance's dress. "Got a few stragglers. Here, hold on a moment."

Constance glanced at the cabin floor, now devoid of her wrapping paper puzzle. Cawley cleared his throat and nodded toward the campaign desk.

There, the wrapping paper flooring had been neatly folded just as he did with her clothing. Cawley tapped the side of his beak-like nose. That was his sign for secrets kept. So, Maya hadn't had time to study the diagrams before Cawley had swept them away.

Maya was the closest person Constance still had to a mother, but even so, she was a former Steamwerks director. And as much as Constance trusted her, she needed to remember that Maya might one day return there. If so, the less she knew about the Haltwhistles' knowledge of interdimensional portals, the safer the world would be. What if she gave Queen Victoria interdimensional technology? The Queen would be marching her redcoat troops into parallel versions of Earth before you could say, "please don't start a war of the worlds." Constance didn't need that on her conscience, thank you very much.

Maya stood back to admire her handiwork. "Now that's a fleet that could defend England. Between you and me, Elizabeth the First's great victory relied more upon bad weather and good fortune than her naval prowess. But there's nothing like a good story to cement a monarch's reputation. There's a small chance, given the stormy nature of past Anglo-Franco relations, that bringing up Britain's greatest naval victory might ruffle a few feathers at court. However, as France and England are currently at peace, I believe that your avant-garde fashion will draw attention most positively. Especially as Louis is rumored to be about to start a war against Spain. The Spanish boy-king has much to fear from the Sun King."

A volley of shots from her midriff toward the Spanish flagship made Constance jump clean out of her satin dance slippers. "Good heavens, am I going to be a fire risk?" She fumbled to find her slippers again since her feet were obscured beneath her vast skirts.

Maya laughed. "I should hope not. I've calculated the possibility of spontaneous combustion being less than one percent. I think your odds of surviving the night from cannon fire are good."

Constance shimmied back into her slippers. "Will I be the only attendee with mechanical fashion enhancements?"

"I doubt it, my dear. I've heard that the European aristocracy love enhanced fashions as much as Queen Victoria's courtiers, but with fewer of the brass goggles that she has so widely popularized. Technology is power, and almost every member of the nobility wants to show how rich and powerful they are. Fashion is a statement of status today, just as it was in the time of Elizabeth the First. But even without the drama of a sea battle gown, I'm sure you would have turned heads. You look stunning, Constance. I'm so glad I was able to enhance Mr. Trusdale's original idea that we sew firecrackers into your gown."

Constance's eyebrows almost hit her crown. "He wanted you to *what?*"

Footsteps approached the cabin, accompanied by a jingle of bells.

"You can ask him about it yourself. And yes, the codpiece came with his costume. Lord knows where your godmother picked that up."

Into the cabin strode Trusdale, dressed as a motley fool in a red-and-yellow jester costume with bells upon his three-horned hat. Pinpricks of white light pulsed across the costume as Trusdale moved. He glittered as if powdered with faerie dust from a magical realm. A large diamond-studded codpiece and curled diamond slippers dazzled almost as much as the dancing lights. In his hand, he held a porcelain nobleman's mask, half gold, half silver, with a comically large smile and cutout eyes.

Constance tried to avert her gaze from the twinkling codpiece.

Trusdale halted with a jingle of bells. He looked Constance up and down, then swept off his cap and bowed with a courtly flourish. "I am your most humble and obedient servant, your royal highness. Your majesty stuns with her queenly magnificence."

"And you're so very . . . sparkly, Mr. Trusdale."

He nodded, placing his belled hat upon his head. "Your godmother has a funny sense of humor. Apparently, she sees me as a lowly but wise fool who speaks the truth to power, therefore—"

"You're costumed as a Shakespearean court jester. Well, at least you complement my regal outfit. Pray tell, why did you suggest to Maya that I required live ammunition upon my dress?"

"For the same reason I asked her to add lights to my costume. We can't possibly search sixteen acres of a palace in one night. And staying there after the ball has finished is a real good way to get ourselves caught. We need to find out where the Enigma Key is kept, and the quickest way to get that information is with—"

"A bribe?"

Trusdale chuckled. "Boy, you should consider life as a secret agent. Yes, an irresistible bribe would be great, or well-placed flattery. To some types of folks, a compliment is worth more than gold. You can also try bonding with strangers by suggesting how similar the two of you are. Try to find shared experiences or philosophies. You don't have to believe a word you say, just as long as they think you're on their side. These are the oldest tricks in the book for persuading people to share information with you."

"I'm yet to hear why I need to wear a live armada and you need a constellation of moving lights."

"You and I are a distraction in case any one of our team gets into trouble. There's no way we'll be able to slip any weapons or burgling tools through royal security. King Louis is as paranoid as any absolute monarch with a flying palace can be. He prefers to keep his party guests corralled in the Hall of Mirrors for most of the night, where his guards can keep an eye on them. Traveling beyond the Hall so we can track down the Key will be difficult."

Trusdale gestured at his outfit. "But I can activate a single blinding flash of light from my costume, or you can fire all of your cannons at once to create an almighty bang. Either of these should be enough to draw the attention of every guard, king, servant, or aristocrat in the room. So, if you go bang, I may be able to sneak out and snatch the Enigma Key, or vice versa. With inside information to guide our path, astounding distractions, and a heap of good luck, we have a chance of pulling off the heist of the century."

"From whom, exactly, are you getting information about Louis's security?"

Trusdale wagged his finger. "Now, what kind of secret agents would we be if we shared our sources? The only other bit of information I have is that King Louis always dresses as a Greek god at masked events. Zeus, Ares, Hades, Apollo—you name it, he's played it."

"And that's why I'll be chumming it up with any Greek god who happens to be at the party," said Welli, sweeping into the cabin. "I got that tidbit about the King at my last poker game."

"Welli's your security source?"

"He's one of them. I have other sources in Paris."

Constance groaned. "Welli's information is usually as reliable as a broken wheel."

Welli spluttered. "Steady on, old girl. My pride has taken enough of a bruising this day." He waved his hand at his animal-themed costume.

She frowned at her cousin. "What are you dressed as, Welli? A goat?"

Welli grimaced. "Not exactly." In his hand, he held what appeared to be an ivory goat's mask embellished with gold ears, spiked horns, a sly smile, and a goatee beard. "I mean, I know Madge is annoyed with me, but honestly, a satyr? With a mink tailcoat, bearskin trousers, and golden hooves atop my boots? Should I wander into the woods, I could end the evening mounted as a prize over a hunter's fireplace."

"Then I'd stay out of the woods if I were you. On the plus side, it's stylishly cut, and shows off your slim figure to perfection," said Constance, hiding a smile. "I assume Madge's theory behind dressing you as a satyr is that you will attract women who relish a bad boy."

"And you'll attract men who like bossy women with a fetish for firearms."

Maya laughed. "Sounds to me like you'll both meet your perfect mate by the end of the night."

"And your godmother's work will be done," chuckled Trusdale.

"Not to disappoint her further, but I have plans of my own," said Constance. "Speaking of plans, what's your technological distraction, Welli?"

He reddened. "If absolutely necessary, I can break wind so loud it could shatter glass."

"Yes, but what's your distraction?"

Maya snorted. "He means I have sewn a faux bladder within his pants that will produce an extremely loud raspberry sound and release a vile but harmless gas. It's not my finest work, but I'd used most of my time on your own and Mr. Trusdale's costumes. Even with Huang's help, I can only do so much in six hours."

"I shall literally be the butt of all jokes in France if I have to use the blessed thing," said Welli. "I've sniffed the bladder, and the gas within will make your eyes water."

"Welli's distraction will be our last resort," said Trusdale. "But he's going to be playing to his strengths at the card table, so it shouldn't be needed."

The satyr nodded. "I have it on good authority that the King enjoys a good gamble as much as any well-heeled rake. The entire point of holding a masquerade ball is that the masks disguise everyone's identity. This gives the guests a chance to cut loose and be whoever they want to be. If the King likes to pretend to be a god, all I have to do is to befriend the godliest man in the room and sweet-talk him into letting me into the royal poker game."

"Given your recent run of bad luck at the card table, isn't that a terrible idea?" said Constance.

"Ouch. Well, yes, it's a gamble that might put me in a worse position than I'm in now. But with a good bluff and even better luck, I have a chance of finding out how valuable the Enigma Key is to the King. Does he even know it exists? Or could it be sitting atop a giant pile of precious jewels in the royal treasury? Or is it, in fact, tucked inside his pantaloons as you have suggested?"

"God forbid," said Constance.

Welli nodded. "Quite. You'd be surprised, Connie, at the secrets that men share over a hand of cards, especially if alcohol is involved. If this item is precious to the King, I guarantee he will have shown it to his closest friends after a boozy night of gambling. No man can resist showing off his greatest prize given the level of camaraderie which I intend to bestow upon this select group of lords."

"Ugh," said Constance, "to think our plan revolves around exploiting greed and pride. I would rather enter the palace like a cat burglar and prowl in the shadows until I locate my prey."

"Pah. Not in that dress, you can't," said Welli. "I must say, this getup truly suits you. You've never looked finer."

Trusdale nodded. "And you'll be a superb distraction if we need to go that far. Ain't nobody going to be paying attention to me or Welli if a stunning woman explodes a hundred cannons on her gown simultaneously."

He thinks I'm stunning? Constance fanned her suddenly warm cheeks with both hands. Precious little cool air reached her through the porcelain mask, but she didn't want to remove it and risk spoiling her regal facade. Impressing Trusdale was worth a little excess heat above her ruff.

"Here, my dear." Maya handed her the ostrich feather fan and Constance wafted herself slightly cooler. "Should you wish to draw the attention of everyone within hearing distance, tap your English flagship three times to fire every cannon on your gown. You will only be able to sound your salvo once, so don't set them off unless you have no other choice. Also, be careful with your feather fan. Don't waft too fast, or you may well inflame this battle beyond my calculations."

Constance slowed her wafts of the fan. Her gown might be a death trap, but it did wonders for her posture and confidence. Her experiments with the lady's protection gauntlet may be on hold for now, but perhaps there was a market for martial ball gowns? Imagine defeating surrounding foes with a tap of an ornament on one's dress. The idea reeked of genius; she was almost sure of it.

A bell rang out from the deck above. "We're here," said Constance and Trusdale simultaneously. He grinned, and Constance smiled behind her mask. As dangerous as this escapade was, she was glad to have the trustworthy Trusdale at her side. He might be playing a joker, but in a different circumstance, might she have played the fool for him tonight?

She shook her head. Like Queen Elizabeth before her, her first concern must not be romance, but power. Securing the energy of the Enigma Keys to bring back the Hall must be all that occupied her thoughts. Or doom would surely descend upon them all.

Awakened by the bell, Boo jumped down from the alcove bed and trotted beside Constance as she followed her party out of her cabin and up the stairs to the deck. Save for Mrs. Singh at the helm, the entire crew had packed onto the prow of the ship to catch a first glimpse of the Palace of Versailles atop its legendary vortex cloud.

At the very front of the ship, the *Lady Penelope*'s flying dragon figurehead perched upon the bowsprit pole. The scarlet dragon's snarling snout pointed directly at the tempered glass stern of her godmother's sightseeing airship. Moonlight gleamed along the ghostly lines of the galleon beneath its silver balloon. The transparent ship was dwarfed by the enormous white cloud that spiraled on the horizon above them like a lost galaxy. Over the next half hour, the two airships slowly rose up to enter the outer rim of the swirling cloud.

A freezing mist wrapped around the ship like a burial shroud. Icy crystals settled into Constance's lungs, and she coughed as the unnatural fog blinded her. She held up her fan in front of her face but could not make out its shape against the mist. Boo yapped and snarled at the fog somewhere near Constance's ankles. Before she could reach down to rescue the frightened puppy, the airship broke through the cloud and sailed beneath the midnight moon.

Gleaming in the moonlight, a vast golden platform shaped like a multiflamed sun spun slowly upon on a swirling bed of clouds. The twelve massive "flames" bursting out sideways from the sun's center circle served as docking bays for a hundred or more airships. From aristocratic galleons to sporty two-man speedsters, freight vessels, and floating vineyard ships, every dock bustled with activity even in the middle of the night. Lit by the stars, the moon, and a thousand glowing gas lamps, servants, merchants, and aristocrats alike hurried to impress the King as much as to escape his ire.

In the center of the sun platform, surrounded by acres of formal gardens boasting topiaries, fountains, canals, sculptures, and geometrically precise flower beds, stood the magnificent grand palace.

Constance's jaw hit the inside of her mask. Fortunately, the fragile porcelain didn't break.

She closed her mouth with a snap, marveling at the sheer audacity of using classical Greek architecture to build a temple dedicated to a mortal king's vanity.

As the original Sun King had viewed himself inexorably linked to the sun god Apollo, the flat-roofed palace and its many courtyards boasted dozens of flaming beacons that burned twenty-four hours a day.

The beacons added light and movement to the coldness of pristine marble walls, tall arched windows, fluted columns, and statuary produced by the world's master sculptors.

Beneath the threat of roof-mounted cannons, courtyards teemed with people scurrying between the palace's docks, kitchens, art galleries, boudoirs, theaters, and the golden glow of the famed Hall of Mirrors.

Maya murmured, "It's absolutely astonishing. The craftsmanship is simply exquisite. No wonder Victoria is jealous of this technological and artistic marvel. Did you know, the palace originally lifted off in 1773, a full eighty years before the world's first airship flight? It's so innovative, I confess I can't imagine how it holds its vast weight aloft. The cloud disguises whatever mechanics work beneath the palace. I wonder if I might wander the grounds to find out . . ."

Trusdale held up his hand. "Without a trade pass or a royal invitation, the guards won't allow you beyond the docks. Please, all of you, promise me you won't go any farther than that. With Constance, Welli, and me heading to the Hall of Mirrors, we're already more split up than I'd like. If something goes horribly wrong, you all need to be able to bolt back to the ship and take off without us."

Welli the satyr tut-tutted. "Such drama, Mr. Trusdale. We're only going to rob the King of France. What could possibly go wrong?"

Trusdale groaned. "Lord help me, you just had to say it, didn't ya? Now I know we're going to be cursed."

"With your light show, my cannons, and Welli's wind, I'm confident we can find the Key and escape long before dawn," said Constance. "As your noble leader . . ." she pointed to her crown, "I suggest we begin our escapade immediately. To the Hall of Mirrors, gentlemen."

She led Trusdale and Welli down the gangplank, ignoring their grumbles at her self-appointment to team leader. There was a lightness to her step despite her heavy gown.

Tonight, she would find an Enigma Key, or die trying. If this was to be her final evening on earth, she could imagine no finer outfit in which to meet the grim reaper.

With her fan gripped tightly in her gloved hand, Queen Constance of England and her mighty armada stepped off the gangplank and invaded France.

Chapter 11:
The Masquerade Ball

With the crown of the Brass Queen cresting her flaming red hair, a newfound power surged through Constance's veins. With every step she took through the Hall of Mirrors, she claimed her territory as surely as if she'd planted a flag straight through the parquet floor. High above, the vaulted ceiling's exquisite paintings celebrated the original Sun King's triumphs in war and peace. Yet the seventeen mirrored arches that dominated the back wall of the chamber appeared to exist only to reflect her awe-inspiring presence. Lit to perfection by a thousand flickering candles, her nautical fleet movements and exploding cannons drew the eye and ear of every aristocrat in the long chamber.

Safe from prying eyes behind her porcelain mask, she was free to play the role of the haughty monarch. With a wave of her fan, she dismissed inquiries about the gown's mechanics or herself. Her goal was to be "charming," a skill she had never needed to develop. The only way to approach this monumental task was to channel the intelligence, wit, and diplomacy that great queens such as Elizabeth the First must have possessed to survive their ruthless foes.

Within two hours, she was exhausted. But not one person in the chamber would have known it. Her feet ached from waltzing with countless admirers to the symphonic strains of the royal orchestra. Sweat ran down her spine, and her throat was parched from dancing and talking more than she would have thought possible. Never underestimate the power of a crown to keep a queen engaged when a mere woman might fade. The gold demanded more of her inner strength than she'd known existed. Floating on a cloud above a foreign land, she felt more grounded than she'd ever been.

With cool indifference, she waved away the next lord on her dance card. Even a long-beaked plague doctor's mask couldn't hide the disappointment in the anonymous lord's blue eyes.

Queen Constance didn't look back as she strode over to the tall French doors that opened onto the moonlit gardens. She took in several deep breaths of the chilly night air. The geometric swirls of the flower beds and the glistening fountains tempted her to wander. But the ghostly line of white-uniformed palace guards stationed a mere thirty yards from the doors gave her pause. Trusdale had insisted they should use charm, flattery, and bribes to find out the location of the Enigma Key. Trying to slip past the exterior guards, or even the two medal-wearing generals discreetly stationed at either end of the Hall of Mirrors, would probably get this Elizabethan queen thrown into the royal jail.

A jingle of bells sounded behind her over a soft footfall. Trusdale's resonant baritone was music to her ears, the voice of a friend in a room full of strangers. "May I ask Her Majesty for the honor of this dance?" She turned, and the bedazzled jester bowed as elegantly as any lord in the chamber. Her feet might ache, but how could she refuse such a charming invitation from a man with a sparkly codpiece?

She allowed Trusdale to take her gloved hand, and they whirled as one entity onto the dance area in the center of the candlelit chamber. The sound of the royal orchestra swelled into a slow waltz and Trusdale pulled her a little closer than her prior dance partners. Gone was his usual scent of leather and horses and fresh green meadows, replaced by a musky perfume with hints of cedar, jasmine, and vanilla. Constance leaned in and sniffed his neck, causing the jester to stumble on his long, curled slippers.

"Oops, sorry," she said, reddening beneath her mask. "You smell delicious."

"That's the first time anyone's ever said that to me," he chuckled. "Welli said perfume for both sexes was mandatory for a courtly ball."

"I have a gold pomander sewn inside my right sleeve," said Constance. "It's filled with . . ."

"Orange blossom and rose petals, your favorite flowers."

Constance tilted her head as they swept around the floor together to the *oohs* and *aahs* of two hundred watching aristocrats. The martial queen and the glittering fool. What a spectacle they must present. "I can't recall ever having told you that."

"You didn't have to. Cawley spritzes your clothes with floral scents every morning. More often than not, it's—"

"Roses and orange blossom. I had no idea you were paying such close attention to my person."

Trusdale chuckled. "Baroness Haltwhistle, you're always the main event in any room you enter. And not just tonight. That said, I believe you've captured the attention of almost everyone here. You should hire yourself out as a professional distraction. I could barely focus on our task.

How am I supposed to rob the King when the queen of hearts steals my breath away with her every move?"

Her heartbeat quickened beneath her Tudor corset. He'd told her that he could use flattery as a weapon against the unwary, yet somehow, she had no defense against his words. She wanted him to praise her, whether she deserved it or not. Where had this desire sprung from? She'd never cared what anyone outside the family said about her. Since when did a sweet-talking cowboy cause her pulse to race? She breathed in his warm scent and followed his lead across the floor. He danced with surprising grace for such a tall oak of a man. Was it her imagination, or were the masked ladies at the ball watching Trusdale just as closely as the lords watched her?

A wave of possessiveness washed over her. The thought of him holding any one of the blue-blooded ladies present in a cinch as tight as theirs caused her stomach to churn. She told herself that this made perfect sense, as Trusdale was a vital part of the plan to find the Key, and yet . . .

She moved a little closer to him and gazed up at his grinning mask. "I've been meaning to tell you how grateful I am for your vote to come with me to Versailles. You had no reason to risk your life here."

"No reason that you know of."

She chuckled. "Ever the man of mystery. Why don't you tell me something about your past?"

"Like what?"

"Like . . . your brothers. Poor J. F. was your older brother, correct? He must have been a brilliant man to come up with the design for the original Trusdale battle mitten."

Trusdale nodded. "He was the smartest man I've ever met, not that I ever told him that. You know, brothers. Can't build one another up too high, 'cos it's always a contest to see who's on top. J. F. was the one who could fix a steam locomotive's engine with baling twine and a prayer. He got a teaching job at West Point, even studied some with Tesla. Going to the Steamwerks to consult for Maya was a dream come true. If it hadn't have been for that damned carriage . . . but I've had to move on. Grief just gets you stuck on what you didn't do while they were here. I wish I'd told him how much I admired him. And so did Poppa, though he ain't the kind of man to say such things out loud. My younger brother, Freedom, he's the fastest gun I've ever seen. Real slick, a real tough guy, can handle any fight, any way, any how. But there's a soft spot to him. Any single gal who lived within fifty miles would come running whenever he visited home."

He gazed down at her. "It occurs to me, that between J. F.'s brains and Freedom's taste for firearms and charmin' ways, you might have liked either one of them more than me. I can't help thinking that you're dancing with the wrong Trusdale."

Perhaps it was the stirring swell of the violins, or the unexpected elegance of his dancing, but she found herself blurting out, "From where I stand, you're the right Trusdale. Time and again you've proven that I can trust you. And your integrity means the world to me. Left to my own devices, I'd stay here all night, dancing in your arms."

Trusdale kept perfect time with her sway. "And left to my own devices, I'd stay right here. But duty calls." He nodded at someone over her shoulder. Constance whipped her head around to see one of the white-uniformed generals guarding the end of the chamber slip out of the room. "Before I go, did you get to speak with your godmother?"

As he said this, they swept by Lady Margaret, resplendent as a silver-masked fairy with gossamer wings, an ice-blue high-collared gown, and a blue pompadour wig. With her trim figure, white opera gloves, and ankle boots, she could easily pass for a woman of Constance's age. Madge was surrounded by several lords whose own age was indeterminate. The freedom of taking on a disguise was exhilarating to those who spent their lives on display to the world. Madge nodded to her goddaughter as they passed by.

Constance nodded back at the society maven. She hoped she'd made Madge proud tonight, for once in their turbulent history. "We had a long discussion about the weather. I believe all is well between us, for now, at least. Interestingly, she and a few of the guests I chatted with shared some information that may help us. The King's treasure vault is only accessible to his personal servants and guards. But there's also a private maze that no one but the King and his mistresses may enter. And it's rumored that underground canals water the gardens on this platform, which suggests the entire structure somehow runs on hydroelectric power."

"You find all that out from dancing?"

"For once, people seemed to want to impress me. They were happy to share gossip and rumors about this place. I don't know how accurate any of this information might prove to be. I've been told that every cannon stationed on this platform is manned by a squad of elite troops handpicked by the monarch, and these squads are not allowed to interact with the palace guards. It seems the King has taken every precaution to prevent either military coups or the sabotage of his aerial defenses from within."

Trusdale groaned. "Ugh. Seems like King Louis keeps this place locked up tighter than a bullfrog's behind." Despair colored his tone, causing her to grasp his hand a little tighter through her kidskin gloves.

She said, "But we're here within the palace. In itself, this is something of a minor miracle, and it gives us a sliver of hope that we might find the Key. Welli's done a marvelous job working his way into the affections of the only Greek god in the room, Poseidon. Through skill or luck, he's managed to secure an invitation from Poseidon to a high-stakes poker game that will start shortly. He's putting the *Lady Penelope* up as his stake, so we may all be homeless by the end of the evening."

Trusdale shook his head. "That seems like a phenomenally bad idea. The ship's also our escape vessel if things go south. And I can't help feelin' . . . You ever get that sense that catastrophe is right around the corner? But somehow, you can't turn and walk away?"

She snorted. "I feel that every morning, the second I wake. The trick is to keep going and prove yourself wrong."

Even muffled by his mask, she could tell his laughter was genuine. "I don't know whether that's incredibly healthy or totally insane. Maybe it's a little of both." As the waltz drew to a close, he released her from his arms and bowed. "Thank you, Your Royal Highness. Even though disaster beckons us from every door, I'm glad I got to open them with you."

Her heart clenched. "You sound like you're saying goodbye."

He shrugged. "I've bribed my way out of this room. Welli's heading out shortly. I pray to all that's holy that one or both of us gets lucky. The information you've gathered here can only help." He placed his hand on his chest. "And may I say, Constance, it's been my honor to embark upon this escapade with you."

She put her hands on her hips. "What makes you think I'm letting you go alone?"

"It's too dangerous for you to leave this room. Welli and I both have military training, while you . . ."

"Ran a country estate and an arms empire. I'm more than capable—"

He held up his hands. "But tonight, you're a queen. Let the princes do the work. Stay here with your god-mother and enjoy the ball."

She stamped her slipper on the parquet. "You're only saying that because I'm female."

"I know you're a capable woman, Constance. But you've never been tested under fire on the front lines. This entire evening is about to take a sharp turn into trouble. You'll make my job a lot easier if I know you're safe and sound here."

Constance's rage swept through her like a firestorm. "How dare you—" But Trusdale turned his back and walked away. She spluttered into thin air as he strode over to Welli. The costumed satyr was one of a crowd clustered around a short man cloaked in an exceptional-ly opulent costume. The silver-masked Greek god of the sea, Poseidon, stunned in his blue velvet robes decorated with shoals of mechanical fish that shimmied across his person. Only Poseidon could match Queen Constance in finery and mechanical ingenuity. It wouldn't have surprised Constance to find out that he was an actual god who'd landed upon this flying cloud to party amongst the mortals.

Welli and Trusdale chatted as Constance clenched her fists. The two brothers in arms were clearly determined to leave her out of the perils of searching the place. Just like Papa had left her behind to travel the globe and the many worlds beyond this earth. Why was she never considered tough enough to brave any danger shoulder-to-shoulder with her male compatriots? What made her feminine form less deserving of respect than—

"Ahem," coughed a male voice behind her. She spun to see the plague doctor bowing before her. "It seems your jester was foolish enough to leave Your Majesty after only one dance. May I humbly request the honor of this waltz?" his soft, educated tone suggested he was English born. Either that, or he'd been well-schooled by a native tutor.

His black, floor-length coat was simply but elegantly tailored with a capelet over his slender shoulders. A double row of engraved silver buttons down the front of his coat displayed medicinal flowers in all their glory. The flowers gleamed in the golden candlelight cast by the chamber's numerous ceiling and standing chandeliers. Around the doctor's neck hung a silver pomander on a chain that emanated the sweetest scent of roses she had ever encountered. Through the cut-out eye holes of his black-beaked porcelain mask, ocean-blue eyes gazed at her. "Would Your Highness give this poor country doctor a chance to link hands with England's greatest queen?"

Constance felt her rage subside as the doctor held forth his gloved hand. She could vent her wrath on Trusdale and Welli later. Perhaps the two men would stand a better chance of slipping through the palace corridors without the cannons of a British armada firing beside them. Her dress was designed to attract attention, not for stealthy sneaking. For now, she could continue her charm offensive on the aristocracy.

She gave him her hand, and he whisked her into the rhythm of the waltz with ease.

He said, "Your Highness stuns with her mighty fleet. May I inquire as to the mechanisms behind your military might?"

"Would you believe they're powered by the honey of magical bees?"

He chuckled. "As a man of science, I would not." His step was light, as was his grip upon her hand.

"But I would not wish to bore the good doctor with a treatise on the latest developments in miniature firearm technology. Could we instead agree that clockwork cannons are a delight to behold?"

"As is the woman who commands the fleet with such grace and dignity. I've been watching you closely all night, Your Highness. Your step is stronger, and your gaze is bolder than many a court lady. I wonder whose eye it is you wish to draw?"

She blinked at him. "No one in particular. I'm here to placate familial pressure that I should enter polite society, even though I have no desire for an immediate husband. Given a choice, I would rather be outside, enjoying the roses that surely perfume the air with a scent as sweet as your own. But alas, we are confined to this one magnificent room by the King's paranoia. He would do well to have learned from the example of Elizabeth the First and held a more open court. Such obvious control can breed resentment. If I were him, I'd attempt to present an image of majesty that is fearless, not cautious."

The plague doctor's blue eyes widened behind his mask. "An interesting viewpoint, Your Majesty. Perhaps it is one you should keep submerged beneath your ocean gown, lest you bring a storm upon yourself."

"I believe the King has more immediate concerns than the opinions of mere women." She spat these words out with more than a little venom. Over the doctor's shoulder, Welli was now deep in conversation with Poseidon and his entourage. Trusdale was nowhere to be seen.

The plague doctor followed her gaze as they turned on the floor. "You seem perplexed, Your Highness. Are you troubled that you have not had the opportunity to speak with our host?"

She gasped behind her mask. "You know that Louis's costume is . . .?"

"Always a Greek god. It is a well-known secret amongst the higher echelons of the court. See how the sycophants crawl to catch his crumbs. I pity the man, always surrounded by a sea of untrustworthy souls."

She nodded. "Indeed. As Queen Elizabeth once said, 'To be a king and wear a crown is a thing more glorious to them that see it than it is pleasant to them that bear it.' I'm thrilled to view His Majesty from across the room. But at the end of this night, I can remove my golden crown and decide if I wish to wear it again. Ironically, I have more freedom than the King himself, trapped here in his gilded cage atop the clouds."

The plague doctor remained silent. Constance bit her tongue. How had she allowed her irritation at Welli and Trusdale to dissolve her newfound charm so quickly? She cast down her eyes. "Forgive me, good doctor. I speak too plainly for a passing visitor to this court. What do I know of freedom, or power, for that matter? I am as much a prisoner in this room as any other woman here. Our domain is the dance floor and the tea parlor, not guarding the ramparts or firing the cannons. What do I know of the troubles of the crown?"

The doctor chuckled. "Would you like to fire a cannon, Your Highness? Or, would you rather smell the roses?"

"In a perfect world, I would do both."

"You make an interesting choice; one that was not given but taken. I had thought to learn the secrets of your gown, but instead, I find the secrets of your heart even more fascinating. I cannot help you to fire a cannon, but I do possess a secret that few know. The rarest roses on this great platform are kept at the center of the King's private maze."

She sighed. "Then they may as well be on the surface of Mars, but I thank you for the information. Perhaps I can imagine them in my dreams, even though I will never see them with my eyes."

The orchestra brought the waltz to a close. The doctor released her hand and bowed low. Constance curtsied. He surprised her by leaning in and whispering, "Follow me, Your Highness. To a world beyond this world."

He turned and walked toward the far end of the Hall of Mirrors.

Constance started after him, then paused. She turned to see if Trusdale or Welli were in sight. Both men had gone, as had Poseidon and his sea of sycophants. Auntie Madge had extricated herself from her own circle of admirers.

She waved her fairy wand at Constance, indicating she was retiring for the night. Her godmother walked toward the exit, her hand resting for support upon the arm of a masked air pirate with a mechanical parrot on his shoulder.

Constance was left alone at court, and the lords scurried toward her like ants who'd spotted a fallen sandwich at a picnic. Eager to escape their hungry eyes, she spun on her heel and hurried after the plague doctor.

He was standing in the very corner of the mirrored hall, slightly less tall than the floor-standing candelabra beside him. The gold candle holder was one of twenty-six that lined the Hall of Mirrors. Their designs were varied, but this one displayed three angelic cherubim holding up a platter that bore an eight-candle crystal candelabra. Keeping one eye on the medal-wearing general guarding this end of the room, Constance approached the doctor.

He reached up with one black-gloved hand and extinguished four of the candles on the candelabra. Constance's breath caught in her throat as she turned to see if any other guests had noticed his audacity. The assembled aristocrats were dancing, gossiping, and laughing as they had throughout the night. No one was looking their way. Even the white-uniformed guard was staring at the center of the dance floor, apparently unaware of the doctor's foolhardy move.

The doctor stepped back into the sliver of shadow created by his bold actions.

She knew she should turn away and rejoin the party, but her feet kept walking toward him. As she drew close, he murmured, "Does Your Highness know that an ancestor of our great King fancied himself as a locksmith?"

"A what?"

"Allow me to demonstrate." With a furtive glance toward the guard, the doctor tweaked the ear of one of the cherubim on the candelabra. Silently, two mirror panels in the great arch of the wall slid back to reveal a passageway. He plucked a lit candle from the candelabra. "Locks, vaults, secret passageways. He used his skills to furnish himself with secret exits from occasions he found to be a bore."

"How do you know of such things?" asked Constance.

"Must I tell you of my family's great pride and hidden shame? My sister is a favorite courtesan of the current king. It is she who provided me access to the King's own roses. Follow me, and I'll share their scented splendor with you this night."

Constance looked back over her shoulder at the gilt-edged glamour of the masquerade ball. "I really shouldn't."

The doctor held out his gloved hand. "Isn't that what makes it fun? And what mortal man would dare tell Her Majesty, the Queen of England, where she can and cannot go?"

Constance set her jaw. "You're right. No mortal man can. Lead on, good doctor."

As she followed him into the dark passageway, the mirrored door silently slid closed behind them. Constance kept her eyes trained on the meager light cast by the doctor's candle. She held her full skirts high to keep them from catching on the rough-hewn floor, so different from the smooth parquetry of the hall she'd left behind.

Except for the occasional sparks from her fleet's cannon fire, darkness wrapped around her like a shroud.

Chapter 12:
The Maze of Wonders

The thrill of rebellion warmed Constance's heart as she followed the doctor through a labyrinth of dark passageways. Beneath her dance slippers, the floorboards hummed with hidden power.

She strained to hear the flow of water or the clank of gears above the doctor's history lesson about the building of the corridors, but could discern little beyond a distant howl of wind.

Over his shoulder the doctor said, ". . . and it is rumored that the King's great-grandfather added the final corridors that allowed him to access his private garden without passing by his guards. Even then, the family could never fully trust those who worked for them."

She nodded into the darkness. "It is ever difficult to know whom we can truly trust. Only this week, my supposedly loyal servants staged a rebellion by refusing to vote upon a matter I held close to my heart."

The doctor slowed his pace. "You allowed your servants to . . . vote? To share their thoughts and opinions? That is uncommonly progressive of you, Your Highness."

She snorted. "And how was I repaid for my trust? My servants abstained from the vote, leaving me in a predicament which I am still in the process of untangling. It seems the loyalty of our retainers becomes weaker with each passing generation. I've been told that my ancestors suffered no indignity from any man, lowborn or high, that was not met with wrath. I try to chart my own path through life, but my way is ever blocked by those who claim to have my best interests at heart."

The doctor glanced back over his shoulder. "Your Highness is wise. In the end, we have no one to rely on but ourselves. And perhaps, a few intimate acquaintances. It is difficult to maintain a facade when we are at our most vulnerable."

Constance frowned. She wasn't sure exactly what the good doctor meant. "Do you mean when we are outside our customary circumstances? If so, I know that I feel most vulnerable here tonight, despite the fiery fleet that sails upon my gown. Between you and me, I often wear a thin chainmail corset crafted from the Steamwerks' lightest steel alloy. Don't ask me how I got my hands on such a unique item, but I'll tell you this much. That corset has saved my life on more than one occasion from the knives of my enemies."

The doctor gasped. "You, too, face mortal foes? Does their mere existence not strike you with fear?"

"Not at all. It's not as if their attacks have caused me harm. Yet, I would feel more comfortable knowing that I had some defense against the unexpected."

"Sometimes the best defense is to be where your enemies cannot follow. And here we are, Your Majesty."

The doctor stopped before what appeared to be a solid stone wall. He fiddled with some hidden mechanism within it, and with a grating sound, a *trompe l'oeil* stone-painted panel slid aside to reveal an exit into the night.

The doctor walked on. Constance followed, her heart pounding in her ears. The doctor was an odd fellow, but likable. It was a rule at masquerade events that one didn't ask for a name, but she was curious about him. Perhaps, if she could find out the name of his courtesan sister, Auntie Madge would be able to identify him? It was rare to meet someone so easy to talk to.

Brilliant stars above rivaled the moon's pale glory. The celestial bodies seemed so close, and Constance fancied she could reach out and pluck them from the night sky to wear as jewels upon her Elizabethan gown. Ahead, the entrance to a yew maze beckoned. From somewhere behind the tall, clipped hedges drifted a scent of roses that was so intense she was almost overwhelmed by their heady perfume.

"Where are we?" she found herself whispering, although no one but the doctor was in sight.

"The King's astrological garden. As an enthusiast of the sciences, I suspect you will appreciate what he's accomplished here, building on the work of his forebears both botanically and mechanically. We follow this path through the yew maze, and then . . . well, you will just have to wait and see."

Constance hurried after the doctor as he headed for the garden. "A maze?"

"It's the second maze at Versailles. The first, which celebrated Aesop's fables, was destroyed to make way for new gardens. But this private maze has stood the test of time for over a hundred years. During its evolution, grottos were introduced at key points along the path so that visitors can rest and relax. Eighteen fountains reflect the maze's theme of universal exploration. The fountains each show a point of time in man's . . ." He coughed. "Ahem. As I should say, in both men and women's progress in the field of travel."

"Thank you for acknowledging that half of the human race is worth acknowledging."

The doctor chuckled. "You're a bold one, Your Highness. Let me point out our first fountain exhibit, showing a wingless dragon drawing the chariot of Zeus and Hera."

Constance blinked at the bubbling fountain. "That's a stegosaurus pulling a Celtic war chariot driven by a Neanderthal couple. They're wearing bear skins, not robes."

The doctor faltered in his step and turned to stare at the fountain. "But . . . that's not the legend that is carved on the fountain's base."

"Someone's got their historical details mixed up. I can't wait to see the next one! Unless . . . is it a canoe paddled by ancient Egyptians on the moon?"

"No, that's fountain number eight."

"Ah, brilliant. I believe I know the text this maze was based upon. Do continue with your tour."

"You know . . . how could you know?"

Because the original sixteenth-century text used to rest on a pedestal in Papa's study. Constance bit her lip to stop herself from blurting out that "Anonymous" was the favorite pen name of the eighth Baron Haltwhistle, Edwin the Stargazer. He'd also built Haltwhistle Hall's Celestial Ballroom and its clock tower observatory. From within its glass dome, she used to be able to gaze ten miles over her country estate. A wave of homesickness rocked her, one with the intensity that only comes when you've personally sent your home spinning off into another dimension with little hope of return.

Was she wrong to place her trust in Welli and Trusdale to find the Enigma Key tonight? Shouldn't she rely on her own investigative power? If the doctor knew so much about Versailles's gardens, perhaps he also knew where Louis might keep an interdimensional key?

The doctor stopped and turned to face her. "You didn't answer my question. How do you know of this text? It is extremely rare. There are only two copies known to be in—"

"Three," she lied. "The British Museum keeps one at hand in London. I went there with my governess as a child. It was delightful to see the engraved imaginings of the famous Anonymous. He, she, or they, was surely a genius of the first degree."

"The British Museum? Ugh. Is there any sacred item they haven't defiled?" The doctor walked on through the maze with Constance on his heels. The scent of roses grew ever stronger.

"I'm not sure it's a sacred text. My understanding was that the entire book is an allegory about humanity exploring different dimensions of themselves and their universe. Time isn't linear, solids aren't fixed in space, we are all merely pawns in a cosmic game far beyond our comprehension. You know, nonsense. Only half of it is true, but the museum could never figure out which half."

"Then let us skip ahead to the grand finale. Beyond the eighteenth fountain lies a part of this puzzle that isn't mentioned in the book."

Louis has got his hands on the addendum? That can't be right. Those copies only stayed within the family, or so I've been told.

Then again, her family was littered with liars, so anything was possible.

They walked on, traveling ever deeper into the heart of the maze.

Constance put aside her quest for the Key and followed the doctor. The maze now contained a mystery connected to her ancestral line of rogues, dilettantes, and thieves. That was more temptation than she was capable of resisting. She was lucky to have met a man as fascinating as the doctor.

His steps were sure and steady as they passed through identical passageways lined by evergreen hedges twelve feet in height. Multiple branches off his chosen path never once caused him to pause or take a wrong turn. Constance knew she would have spent hours if not days wandering through this hedge maze without his sure-footed navigation. The short, clipped grass of the path was now dusted with patches of white crystalline ash that glinted in the moonlight. Wisps of white smoke drifted up from long metal grates set every twenty feet or so along the edge of the path. Constance wafted her left hand through the tendrils of cloud as they walked by. The wisp froze her glove as surely as if she'd placed her hand within an icebox. She winced and patted at the flames she couldn't see but could feel through the kidskin.

Unnatural fumes, perhaps linked to the whirlpool cloud upon which the palace rests?

She raised her glove to her porcelain mask and cautiously sniffed. She detected ozone and a taste like burning walnuts set atop an iron plate. It was a curious combination, especially when overlaid with other smells: the sweet evergreen aroma of yew and the scent of roses that strengthened as they drew closer to the center of the maze.

Yew was known as the king of hedges, and it was possible its use here was more than ornamental. In folklore, the ancient tree species was often linked to both immortality and death, which had led to its planting in sacred places across Europe. Yew was almost indestructible to all but root rot and could live to be thousands of years old. The Magna Carta was sealed beneath a yew tree, and Henry VIII and poor Anne Boleyn were rumored to have met below a yew tree before they wed. Hadn't she read somewhere that the current Sun King's ancestor, Louis

XV, would sometimes dress as a yew tree at masquerade balls to mingle incognito with the crowds?

Papa had planted a yew grove at Haltwhistle Hall, adding to it every year he lived there. She'd loved clipping branches from it with him each Christmas to weave into festive wreaths to decorate the dining chamber. He'd told her that yew was a resonator species between dimensions; a yew tree in this world matched the exact shape, size, and age of other yews sharing the same space throughout the multiverse. A tree was more constant than a human or an animal, less solid than a mountain or a stone.

Constance's stomach churned beneath her gown. A yew maze coupled with fountains from Edwin the Stargazer's nascent scientific treatise on travel between worlds didn't bode well. His theories had been centuries ahead of their time. It wasn't until Papa perfected the first portal generator that Edwin's fantasies had become real.

Before them, a yew arch over the pathway promised an entrance into the center of the maze. The howling wind intensified, buffeting her with a scent of roses so intense she was close to fainting. Her companion seemed immune to the gusts of perfumed wind that blustered from the circular clearing ahead.

The doctor shouted back at her over the howling wind, "Do not be afraid, Your Highness. Today you will see what Galileo and Copernicus could not have dared to dream." He strode into the hundred-foot-wide clearing and cast his arms open. "I present to you a celestial wonder beyond the reach of all but the gods themselves. Behold! A working model of the universe!"

But it wasn't the universe she knew.

What have the Sun Kings built?

Around the perimeter of the clearing floated a ring of red and white rose bushes. The fragrant roses strained against silver chains that tethered their roots into cold white flames licking out of bronze grills set into the crystalline ash underfoot.

The ring of roses encircled an enormous cosmic armillary sphere. Hundreds of alternate planet earths on silver rings rotated around a blazing white sun. The huge, turning structure levitated above a hole that led straight down through Versailles's eight-story-deep platform to swirling purple clouds beneath. Presumably, falling through the clouds would lead to an unpleasant encounter with the ground below at a very high velocity. A howling wind gusted up the pipe from the clouds, blasting through the armillary sphere's rings before being caught and dissipated by a mirrored dome that kept the entire edifice hidden from passing airships.

Constance slowed her step, gaping at the cosmic armillary. These were the planet earths from other dimensions, other times, other universes. They all moved as if guided by clockwork on their insanely intricate planetary rotations, eternally driven by an energy source like no other. A sun that burned brighter and whiter than the north star, with a single, cool blue triangle at its core.

An Enigma Key.

Constance's heartbeat soared, drumming in her ears more loudly than a military tattoo. Versailles was flying because the Key was generating a weak interdimensional portal in the atmosphere below the platform. One blue Key alone was not powerful enough to punch a wormhole between dimensions, but apparently, it *was* strong enough to keep the palace elevated above the earth. The crystalline ash scattered across the clearing was most likely a byproduct from burning aether crystals blown up from the vortex clouds below. The white fire that illuminated the center of the maze was being used as ambient light.

Constance winced as the brightness of the sun-Key burned into her eyes. She focused instead on the back of the plague doctor's black cloak as he walked to a lectern-sized pedestal that arose from the ground in front of the armillary. He fiddled with controls upon the pedestal, and the wind from below dropped in intensity and sound.

"That's better," he said. "Is this not the most glorious contraption you have ever seen?" He continued to play with the controls as Constance approached. The cosmic wind eased to a breeze and the armillary globe slowed its rotational speed. The rose bushes bobbed gently on their chains, twirling slowly as if each were a figurine in a musical box. The white ash crunched beneath Constance's satin dance slippers as she walked up beside the doctor and peered at the controls. A plethora of dials, switches, and levers indicated that this device controlled Versailles's aerial platform in horizontal-only navigation, defense, and waste disposal. A speaker grille allowed communication with cannon crews, guard stations, servants, and gardeners located across the length and depth of the flying saucer platform.

This entire edifice was clearly the work of geniuses. But had those seventeenth-century scientists and engineers sought to power the palace with more than one Key, they could well have sent Versailles on an interdimensional trip to any one of the earths rotating in the armillary automation. Had the Sun Kings decided to stay put to consolidate their power over France, or had their subordinates fooled their masters by not informing them additional Keys would bring even greater power? Or was it possible that the kings simply never found additional Keys? If only she could ask the King himself about the armillary. What a fascinating conversation that would be.

The plague doctor hit a control, and a twenty-foot square section of the floor to the right of the control platform slid back, dropping white crystalline ash into a large bronze chamber below. A whirring of gears in the space beneath heralded the arrival of a new platform that rose to precisely fill the opening in the floor. An extra-large chaise longue, big enough for two people and piled high with red silk cushions, rested upon the newly arrived platform. A gold baroque table beside the chaise longue held a bottle of champagne in an ice bucket beside two glasses and a plate piled high with pink and yellow petit fours.

"May I entice you to taste a delightful confection?" asked the doctor, moving to sit upon the chaise longue. He picked up the iced champagne and expertly popped off the cork with his gloved thumbs.

Constance turned back to the control panel. "So, Versailles does not run upon hydroelectric power."

"Whoever thought it did? Come, sit beside me, Your Highness." He poured two glasses of champagne and patted the chaise longue beside him.

Constance frowned behind her mask. "Isn't that the King's champagne? Are you mad? You're going to get us into trouble. Now he'll know that someone has entered his private maze without his permission."

The doctor laughed. "The King would not begrudge us a single bottle of his finest bubbly. There are caverns filled with supplies below our feet. Upon our leaving, the bottle will be replaced by the royal gardeners who live down there, tending the canals and maintaining the horticultural excellence of this estate."

Constance looked down at the ground as if expecting the gardeners to burst forth from the ash before her. "They live down there permanently?"

"Indeed. They are the descendants of the original engineers and gardeners who crafted the platform of Versailles. The Sun King who first launched this palace into the heavens could not allow them to leave with their knowledge of our divine machinery. In his mercy, he ordered them and their families to live forever beneath the surface of the gardens. Over generations, they have become somewhat changed by the cosmic energy that powers the holy armillary. If one sees them, one might almost believe they are descended from fish or perhaps mermen." He shuddered. "Do not fear, Your Highness, they shall not bother us as we enjoy the light show from the dance of the planets beside you. The gardeners are the ultimate servants, never seen and never heard. This platform couldn't run without them."

Constance put one hand on her hip.

"Are they allowed to leave?"

The doctor snorted. "Of course not. As the great pharaohs of Egypt were sealed into their pyramids surrounded by their living retainers, so are these men and women bound forever to the Sun King. It is their honor to live to serve the majesty of the divine."

"Technology doesn't make a person divine."

The doctor tilted his head. "A curious statement. If we own the power to create or destroy at our whim, does that not make us divine? From that console, the Sun King can command Versailles's cannons to arc their fire down to the ground to destroy an ancient city. With a single proclamation, he can order a new city to be built in its place, peopled by those he deems worthy to live."

Constance pursed her lips beneath her mask. "You're describing a tyrannical ruler with an aerial armada, not a god."

The doctor clenched his fists for a moment. Then he laughed and lay back upon the chaise longue. "You are full of fire, Your Highness. Rest assured, we will have this celestial oasis all to ourselves for the next few hours. We shall watch the dawn rise together over the gardens of Versailles. But first, come over here and enjoy the planetary show before you from the best seat in the house."

Constance sauntered over and sat a little way apart from the doctor. She scanned the mirrored dome above the rotating armillary. "It seems the mirror deflects the wind and also protects the device from being seen by passing airships. The execution is brilliant. I wonder, where would the King keep the book that inspired his ancestors to construct this engine?"

The doctor moved closer to her on the chaise longue. "What does it matter? Now, My Queen, you must share with me the secrets of your armada's percussive power." He stroked one of the English galleons that sailed across her thigh. It fired its tiny cannon, causing him to pull his hand away with a laugh. "Delightful. I have seen movement in clockwork costumes, and I've even heard tiny bells ring from one or two ladies' gowns. But cannon fire is in a league by itself." He reached his hand toward her thigh once more.

Constance rapped his fingers with her closed fan. "The doctor has not been given permission to examine this patient."

He chuckled. "Perhaps the patient should take her medicine." He reached for the filled champagne glasses and held one out to her. "Remove your mask, Your Highness, that I might gaze upon you with no impediment."

She flicked open her fan between her body and the proffered champagne glass. "The good doctor is breaking the rules of the masquerade. We do not reveal our names or our faces."

"Yet you are a rule breaker, are you not? You followed me into this forbidden realm. You told me you did not wish to win yourself a husband this night. You speak your mind, uncaring upon whose ears your words fall. You evade the blades of assassins without fear. You, Your Majesty, are every inch as mighty as the Virgin Queen whose armada crests your gown. Now, surrender and allow France to conquer your English territory with love and pleasure."

Constance leaned in toward him and gazed into his blue eyes behind his black-beaked mask. "Where's the book?"

He blinked, casting a furtive glance toward the control console. "In the King's library, I assume. Where else would one keep a book? Now, Your Highness, tell me your name, that I may sing to the heavens of my new-found love."

Constance rose to her feet, and felt her gown tugged back by the doctor's hand. She halted as he said, "You are being ungrateful, Your Majesty. It does not become you. Be assured, you shall have the finest quarters in the palace with all the jewels and gowns you could ever desire. Servants will scatter rose petals at your feet as you dance through the courtesans' wing. You will befriend the most educated, the most skillful, and the loveliest women in France who have each committed to spending their lives here at Versailles. You shall want for nothing, I swear it."

"That's a pretty big promise for a poor country doctor."

He threw back his head and guffawed. "Have you not solved this riddle yet, Your Highness? I have the power to grant all things you desire, for I am divine, all-knowing, all-powerful. My love for you here tonight is as genuine as my royal bloodline. You have captured my heart, and a life of luxury and romance shall be yours forever."

Constance stared down at the black-gloved hand clutching at her skirts. "These women who stay at the palace, are they allowed to leave? Or, as the gardeners who live below our feet, are they held captive, with no hope of rescue?"

The doctor's grip on her gown tightened. "Why would any lady wish to leave the palace? They have everything they could desire. Who yearns for freedom when they can wear the finest gowns and jewels the world can offer?"

Constance leaned down and looked the doctor in the eye. "And what if a woman desires freedom above all else?"

"Then their beauty forever feeds my roses."

She gasped. "You . . . turn them into fertilizer?"

"The cosmic fire alone cannot keep these thorny beauties nourished. They are fed daily with the blood and bone of the enemies of my court. But you are no enemy. Come, girl, allow me to show you the heavens."

He dragged her gown sharply toward him. As he reached to grab her waist, Queen Constance fired every cannon upon her gown at once. With a blinding flash and a thunderous volley, France was blasted in the face by the English Armada. The doctor screamed as his porcelain face mask shattered in the blast. His face was one she had seen in profile on gold coins in Paris. A hook-nosed face with a slender jaw, it was the face of a man willing to kill or enslave her if she would not obey.

Constance closed her fan and stabbed it directly into the right eye of the Sun King.

Chapter 13:
Into the Darkness

It wasn't his jester costume that made Trusdale feel a fool.

It was the respect Général Malaise poured upon him as the Frenchman ordered a squad of his loyal palace guards to follow Trusdale to the death. Standing in the King's private wine cellar, the eight men saluted their Général and gazed at Trusdale with the admiration normally reserved for a war hero.

Trusdale licked his dry lips beneath his jester mask. As an undercover US agent, it made sense for him not to reveal his face, even to allies, unless absolutely necessary. It also hid the blush that had surely crept across his cheeks as Malaise painted him to be the champion who would save France from a monarch who'd squandered the country's wealth as peasants starved.

"At ease, gentlemen," said Captain Liberty Trusdale, using the same commanding tone he'd used to address his troops in the US armored cavalry. "As the Général stated, this will be a one-way mission, and the choice is yours as to whether you participate. Any man who does not wish to make the ultimate sacrifice this very night, step forward."

The white-uniformed troops stood their ground.

Great. That's eight souls I'm dragging with me to certain doom. Lord, help me. And them.

Trusdale bowed his head to their bravery. "Very well. I've been informed that this flying palace has no known engine room, that its cannon and airship defenses are manned by royalists, and that our mission is to bring this entire platform down to earth, hopefully without a bang. How we will achieve that goal is on a need-to-know basis. Our first step is to enter the canal system that runs below Versailles's gardens."

The soldiers gasped.

Général Malaise said, "I understand your surprise. Only the King knows if there is a secret entrance into this platform's innards. But the Captain," he gestured at Trusdale, "has a grand plan . . ."

Without a capital "g" or "p" . . .

". . . of outstanding audacity." Malaise pointed at a two-foot by one-foot grille set into the roughhewn boards of the wine cellar. "The dregs from the wine barrels are poured into this waste grille, where they land in the palace drains. Water floods the sewers at regular intervals, taking the waste to who-knows-where within the platform."

Trusdale nodded. "The drains don't immediately dump all waste into the sky. Like a giant bird, the palace drops its waste where it finds the most amusement. The King directs which of his enemies' homes or armies gain this unexpected gift."

He cleared his throat. "In other words, gentleman, there's a septic tank down there with our name on it. Our goal is to escape from the sewers into the platform's innards."

Before we drown or suffocate from the stench . . .

He continued, "We will then defeat Versailles from within with a secret weapon I carry upon my person. Once we land this platform, the Général will banish the King from this country, and an elected parliament will take his place. Long live democracy, and long live the new French Republic!"

The men cheered and set to work ripping up the grille and the surrounding floor with crowbars, shovels, and gusto.

Trusdale grimaced behind his mask. To think he was basing an entire mission on an imaginary superweapon and a throwaway comment from Constance in the Hall of Mirrors—he must be crazier than she was. And that was a very high bar to leap over, even at the best of times. She'd mentioned hydroelectricity as being a possible source of energy for Versailles. If he could escape from the drains and find a way to control the platform's water, maybe he had a shot of bringing Versailles down. The odds must be a billion to one, but still.

Whether God thought the Brass Queen was Dr. Maya Chauhan, Constance, or anyone else on the *Lady Penelope*, it was his sacrifice tonight that should buy the crew their freedom.

As the soldiers used their tools to widen the access shaft down into the sewers, Trusdale drew Malaise aside. "Général, do I have your word that, whether this mission succeeds or fails, you will release the Brass Queen and her companions from any further obligation to our agencies? This weapon I hold," he patted his ribs, causing a constellation of lights to sparkle on his jester costume, "is her final armament. She wishes to retire, and by helping you achieve your democratic state, I trust that you will allow her to do so?"

Malaise studied his twinkling costume. "I'm curious about this secret weapon you carry. What can possibly take down an aerial fortress yet be small enough to fit inside a jester's jacket?"

Trusdale clasped his hand to his ribs, shielding his imaginary superweapon. "I can't show you. It's . . . I swallowed it. It was the only way to get it past security."

Malaise gasped. "Is it a bomb?"

"No. It's far more sophisticated than that. My goal is to land Versailles gently on the ground, not send it hurtling to the earth with a gaping hole blown through it. There are thousands of people up here, and I wouldn't want to be responsible for harming any one of them. Even if some of them are loyal to your despotic king."

Malaise chuckled. "You are a good man, Captain, to care even for the lives of your enemies. I believe that beyond his elite guard, the King's loyalists are few. Most of the courtiers are only here because the King demands their presence at his endless parties. He often holds their friends and relations hostage, and death or imprisonment comes to all who dare to defy him. Rest assured, my republican allies do not want a bloody coup, Captain. This is 1897, after all. We stand on the cusp of a new century, one where the French people want only to live in a free republic as your own countrymen do."

"That's good to hear. Not to play the same wax cylinder, but I must have your personal pledge that the Brass Queen and her unwitting associates will leave here freely tonight. Even if my mission fails. Especially if my mission fails. If the worst comes to the worst, she has done her part, and I'm the only person who should be blamed for our failure."

Malaise put his hand on his heart. "I swear on all I hold dear that your shipmates will go free. I have discussed this matter with your lovely lady overlord, the woman you call God. Tempting as it is to continue to force a genius gunsmith to serve our needs, this superweapon you carry and your pledge of Dr. Chauhan's retirement is enough to buy her freedom. I wonder though"—he studied Trusdale, who shifted his weight uncomfortably in his jester slippers—"why is your concern for this wicked woman so strong? The Brass Queen is undoubtedly a villainess of the first degree. Why does she deserve to roam freely when her fantastical armaments have surely caused harm in this world?"

Trusdale threw his hands wide. "What choice did she have? Is an abandoned child to be faulted for surviving the only way she knew how? She used her brilliant mind to create fantastical weapons because that's what our dreadful world desired. But now, she's vowed never to craft a lethal weapon again. She's canceled her contracts with every one of her former customers, even though by doing so she risks their wrath."

Malaise stroked his mustache. "I see."

Trusdale sighed. "I don't know how much my word means to you, but I honestly believe she never meant anyone any harm. She doesn't always think through the end consequences of her actions, but who amongst us does? Her true passion is for science. Who knows, if left to her own devices, she may create something wonderful that will benefit all of mankind." This was true of both Constance and Maya—no wonder the two women had become close. Since the day eight-year-old Constance had first walked into Maya's Steamwerks science classes, the two had shared a bond almost as close as family. But everyone knew Constance's family tree had never borne a saint.

Malaise shrugged. "Or the Brass Queen might create something that will destroy us all. Science is a two-sided coin, Captain. No one can predict the uses new discoveries might lead to. Positive ethics must govern all who touch technology as either a creator or user, or what shall become of our shared humanity?"

Trusdale gestured at the troops, fearlessly digging to their doom. "You have to believe that at heart, most humans are decent. There will always be outliers, but the vast majority of us only want love, freedom, purpose, and respect, plus a warm hearth, a soft bed, and food on the table. Tonight, your troops and I will face our fates with purpose in our hearts, so that millions of people we'll never meet can pursue all of those things."

A grin lit across Malaise's face. "Ah, I see you are both an idealist and a romantic. I believe there may be a touch of French blood in your veins, Captain, for I surely see you as a brother this night. The Brass Queen is most fortunate to have a friend like you. I hope your faith in her good intentions is well placed. As far as myself and God are concerned, this woman will be allowed to retire as she desires, but not here in France. Anywhere but France."

"Thank you, Général."

Malaise bowed. "May the luck of the gods be with you."

Trusdale bowed in return. "Speaking of gods, King Louis's Neptune costume tonight was impressive. Out of curiosity, where would such a man keep his most precious items? For instance, a jewel or special trinket that he would not wish others to see?"

Malaise stroked his chin. "Such items would probably be kept in the courtesans' wing, where no men are allowed but the King and his body doubles. It is not known amongst the courtiers that the King sometimes sends a pretender to his parties when he wishes to meet new people. Of course, he has had his stand-ins tattooed with his cipher on their derriere so that none can usurp his throne."

Huh. Is Welli playing poker with the King or a pretender? Hopefully, he hasn't lost the Lady Penelope *to either. Why is nothing at Versailles ever what it seems?*

The white-uniformed troops finished their widening of the entrance to the drains. Two soldiers dutifully strapped on the backpack gas canisters with attached welding torches that would allow them to cut a way out of the pipes below if needed.

Less sophisticated dynamite sticks and flints were secured in a rubber case carried by one of their comrades. All of the men carried black waterproof pistol holders strapped to their thighs. From their pockets, each soldier drew out brass goggles and leather respirators and put them on.

Malaise said, "Sometimes violent storms sweep across Versailles. The waterproof holsters, goggles, and masks are issued to all the palace guards to protect us from foul weather. Here, take mine."

Trusdale strapped on the goggles over his jester mask. "Don't think I can accommodate the respirator, but I thank you for the pistol." He turned to the troops. "It's time for us to become the heroes of this revolution, gentlemen. I'll take point."

The troops saluted as he strode over to the access hole. With as much dignity as he could muster in his glittering codpiece and parti-colored costume, he clambered down into the dark drain. Stooping his jester hat low, he sloshed along the metal pipe, ankle-deep in foul-smelling brown water. The twinkling lights on his costume lent a festive air and much-needed luminescence to the sewer as his troops followed.

Not knowing when the cleansing surge of water might sweep through the drains and drown them all, he scurried as fast as his curved slippers allowed. In retrospect, he should have borrowed army boots as well as goggles from Malaise.

Why do I never think of these things in advance?

The pipe branched and split a dozen times. Trusdale trusted his gut, trying to picture the palace above and where the center of the platform might rest. If he were to build a flying fortress, he'd put the control center in the middle of the platform to better protect it from external attacks. But who knew how the Sun Kings designed this contraption? If even Doctors Chauhan and Huang couldn't figure out this platform's nerve center, what were his odds of finding it?

They were probably as good as his odds of seeing Constance again. Holding her close during their last waltz had been everything he could have dreamed of, except for the lack of a kiss at the end. If it hadn't been for their masquerade masks, would he have had the nerve to lean in to see if she leaned back? Would their lips have met for the first and last time, reflected in the mirrors of a golden palace? He sloshed on through the drain. When he left Constance on the dance floor to face his destiny, had she shed a tear for him? Had she been impressed by his bravery, and that he'd protected her by leaving the dangerous part of the escapade to Welli and himself?

He sighed into the sewer's foul air. When he released Constance from his arms, he could have shared that he cared for her like no other woman. But what good would it have done for her to hear that if she never got to see him again? Would he have forever lit a fire within her heart, or would a declaration open a wound that would never heal? Or worse, would she never think of him at all? The opposite of love wasn't hate; it was apathy. She said she trusted him, but she didn't know him as a spy and a liar. He'd danced with her in the very building he wanted to destroy. Did that make him a hero or a villain?

It all depended on which side of the looking glass you stood on. One of these days, he'd have to choose—one side, or the other. Or he'd have to walk away from both the agency and Constance, knowing he could never be enough for either.

A rumble of distant water far behind him down the drains drove him to increase his speed to a bell-jingling velocity. The metal beneath his slippers vibrated as he came to a fork in the pipe. From the right, gusts of strong wind buffeted him, threatening to send him tumbling down into the sludge. The horrid air gusting into his face mask bore a hint of roses.

To the left, the scent of sewage was borne away by the wind. Which way to choose?

Lord, send me a sign.

Cold water surged around his knees as he stared into the pitch-blackness of each tunnel. Behind him, a cleansing blast of water thundered toward his troops. He turned to face left, when a distant *crack* down the right-hand tunnel caused him to pause. Was that the sound of a hundred tiny cannons exploding at once? No, surely it must be a gunshot? And that meant dry land was somewhere to the right.

"Droite! Vite!" he yelled. "Turn right, go, go, go!"

The troops barreled down the right-hand drain as the sewer pipe hummed around them like a musical instrument. A cleansing torrent of icy water crashed into him with the force of a runaway steam train. Tossed head over heels like a tumbleweed, he held his breath and tried to keep his hands and feet from smashing into the side of the pipe. His glittering costume lights stayed on for ten seconds or so, showing him flashes of white-uniformed troops rolling in the dirty wave. None of them would last long under this punishment.

As his costume lights died, his lungs burned to draw in a breath of air that wasn't there. Deafened by the roaring water, he closed his eyes tight and tried to make peace with the inevitable.

Drowning in a sewer wasn't the way he'd wanted to enter the afterlife. But at least he'd seen a side of Versailles that no one else had. It was a distinctive end for a man who'd only wanted to serve his country with honor.

Damn my patriotism.

Fanciful fireflies flitted across his mind's eye as his lungs screamed for oxygen. His stomach lurched through his slippers as the pipe spewed him and his troops out over a ledge. Hard water slapped into his back, and he sank like a stone into an abyss of sewage. Icy, peaty water, thick with tastes he couldn't begin to identify, filled his mouth, nose, and throat. Consciousness ebbed away from him as something sharp and hard clawed at his back. He struggled to reach behind himself to bat the object away, but it evaded his hands and hooked into his jacket. It lurched him up out of the water as if he were a prize trout caught by a fisherman.

His limp body rotated on the fishing line as he blinked through the mud-streaked lenses of his goggles. It seemed it was the fish who were making a catch today. Otherworldly, silver scaled fish with human legs and long ghostly faces . . .

Then darkness took him.

Chapter 14:
The War of the Roses

Trusdale awoke on a cold bronze floor. The riveted plates of the metal dock provided a welcome resting place compared to the bottom of the vast sewage lake that stretched before him. Strangely, the toxic air that should have filled his lungs was thick with the scent of roses.

Constance's favorite.

But this dock was no place to bring even a pretend Queen of England.

He pushed himself up onto his elbows and gazed around the huge subterranean chamber. On the right, the sewage tank melted off into the darkness. To his left, the chamber was illuminated by an enormous ring of white fire that raged from the floor up to the ceiling and beyond through a circle of grilles. White ash drifted out like snow from the base, casting a curious presence over the dark bronze floor. In the center of the ring of fire, a circular opening in the ceiling and floor of the platform allowed an icy wind to gust in from who-knew-where.

Thirty feet in front of him, a wide path led through the fire ring toward a makeshift campsite populated by his troops and their unusual rescuers. His soldiers were recovering their strength on three tatty chaise longues that were long past their prime, the troops deep in conversation with a dozen men and women dressed in silver fish-scale armor. The fish folks' faces were pallid and unnaturally elongated, as if they had been painted in watercolor and smeared before drying.

One of his soldiers had noticed him stirring. The young man rushed over to Trusdale with a fish maiden on his heels carrying a steaming soup bowl.

The grimy soldier saluted and chattered excitedly in French.

Trusdale held up his filthy gloves. "Wait, hold on now. Private Martin, isn't it? What do you mean, they're gardeners? Are they friend or foe?" He eyed the fish maiden warily.

The soldier responded in English, "This lady, Chloe, has brought you a healing soup, if you will accept it. The people here represent several hundred who live in the levels below Versailles. They say they have been enslaved for generations by the Sun Kings. They want their freedom, but they've been too afraid of the King's wrath to attempt to escape. Tonight, our presence gives them hope that their long ordeal may soon be over."

"I sure hope so. Can they help us to safely bring this platform down? We don't want any casualties, just a nice soft landing somewhere." Trusdale bowed to Chloe but waved away the soup.

She nodded, flashing him a strangely alien grin that nevertheless set him at ease.

Private Martin gestured at the white fire ring. "The crystals the gardeners burn here absorb the noxious gasses from the sewage, but they have speculated that the ash produced may cause health side effects. All of the people down here have also been subjected to an unusual energy that emanates from the King's device overhead." Martin pointed up at the roof. "Apparently, up there in the center of the King's maze lies a control console that can move the entire platform laterally, but not up and down."

Martin tugged on his earlobe. "Sir, I must confess that I can't understand most of what the gardeners have said about the device, but apparently it has 'spoken' to one or two of them through their thoughts, but they can't comprehend its language."

Oh lord. Don't tell me there's a certain type of telepathic alien compressed inside a multidimensional triangle artifact right over my head? Where's Constance when you need her?

The soldier cocked his head. "Perhaps my English isn't too good? Did what I just said make any kind of sense to you?"

Trusdale sighed. "Sadly, it did." *Okay, so, the King has an Enigma Key, a weird control console, and a flying palace. It's gonna take a lot more than releasing water from the canals to bring this platform down. Plus . . .*

"I don't understand a few things here," he said. "Martin, can you ask them more about the King's device? The weird energy these poor folks have absorbed from the device, it changes them how—physically, mentally, both? What if, let's say, a girl had spent her entire life living maybe a few hundred feet away from nine of these devices. Let's say they were kept in an old dungeon at the bottom of a clock tower that doubled as an observatory. This girl loved to watch the sun, stars, and moon from the top of the tower at every opportunity. What would happen to her if she was exposed to the devices' energy every day of her life from birth until she was twenty-one years old?"

Martin translated to the gardeners and relayed their response. "There have been many gardeners through the years who have remained physically similar to any person who walks on the earth below. Some of them develop certain powers to hear and see things no others can. A few even develop minor telepathic abilities with the device above. But more often, they experience only physical changes. The gardeners' children are conceived and borne by their mothers as far away from this single device as is possible without drawing the King's attention. If the girl of whom you speak was conceived and then lived her entire life within close range of the nine devices, she would have absorbed their alien energy to an unfathomable degree. Who knows what changes the dark energy might have been wrought?"

Nausea rolled through his stomach. He had to tell Constance about this. Did her father know about the detrimental effects on a child brought up near Enigma Keys? If so, why hadn't he protected her from their energy? Unless . . . he hadn't wanted to. Was it possible that Constance was just one more experiment her mad scientist father had conducted? Is that why he'd never wanted her to leave the estate? The man was either the devil personified, or a careless fool. And no one had ever accused the Haltwhistle family of being fools.

He swallowed hard. If his theory was right, that the Baron had purposely exposed Constance to alien energy to further his studies, she'd be devastated. And here he was, risking his and everyone else's life here to bring her one more Enigma Key. If she got what she wanted, she'd be sipping once more from the poisoned chalice she seemed doomed to drink.

Private Martin waited patiently for his orders as Chloe drank the steaming soup from the bowl. "Is there any protection these folks use to shield them from the whisperings of the King's device?"

"The armor helps. It is made from an alloy the King's ancestors discovered in a book. But as you can see, they would require greater quantities of shielding to save them from these effects. They have been given enough to do their jobs, no more, no less."

The gardeners were merely cogs in the machine to the King. It was time to throw a spanner in the works. His agency language training had included a few weeks at the Sorbonne University.

From the few lessons he could remember, he issued a polite question directly to Chloe in her native tongue asking whether her people would help his troops access the King's console.

She grinned. "*Oui Monsieur, nous vous accompagnons,*" she said, beckoning for them to follow her over to the chaise longues.

As they walked behind her, Martin murmured, "Captain, if we bring down this platform, will there be a place in our brave new world for . . . unusual people like Chloe?"

Trusdale nodded. "I'll make damn sure of it with Général Malaise. They're helping us start a revolution, aren't they?"

Private Martin beamed. "Yes sir, they are."

"There you go then. We'll see everyone gets their due this day or die trying."

Martin nodded solemnly. "Our cause is just and God is with us."

In more ways than you know. Trusdale shivered, recalling God's icy stare as he left her garret in Paris. It was better to have God on your side than plotting against you, of that he was sure.

Trusdale's troops rose as he approached them. "At ease, men. I need my three demolition men and Martin here to follow me up to the surface. The rest of you please keep talking with our new friends and see if they can identify the platform's weak points. If things don't work out above, we'll need to figure out a plan B for landing Versailles."

The troops saluted and broke into their two groups.

Chloe pointed beyond the chaise longues to four twelve-foot square hydraulic platforms. One had been raised up to the ceiling, bearing who knew what to the surface. Two of the others held wheelbarrows and racks of gardening tools. Upon the final platform rested a gold baroque dining table, four chairs, and several crates of champagne.

Chloe spoke rapidly in archaic French. Martin translated, "The platforms can be raised up into the King's maze. It's his personal, private space where he takes his ladies to . . . well, let's just say the gardeners replenish champagne and victuals sent here from the royal kitchens. The King is likely to visit there tonight, should he meet a lady at his ball whom he wishes to keep for his collection."

"His . . . collection? Ugh." Trusdale balled his fists. "That better not mean what I think it means. No wonder Général Malaise wants to bring this man's palace down to earth."

Chloe said, "*Il est un monstre charmant.*" She motioned for the soldiers to clear the two wheelbarrow-bearing platforms as she stood before a lectern-sized control panel. Three male gardeners joined the troops as they assembled. The gardeners were armed with sharp, curved sickles. They nodded their allegiance to Trusdale.

Looks like I've got myself some new recruits.

Chloe flicked a toggle switch on the console and a panel in the roof slid back, creating a mini snow-shower of crystalline ash. She hit a button, and the platform bearing Trusdale and his makeshift army rose toward the opening in the bronze floor. The scent of roses grew stronger as they approached the surface. Trusdale braced himself against the movement of the platform, not knowing what he might encounter once he reached ground level. He reached down to his right thigh and flicked open the waterproof holster that carried his pistol.

As the platform rumbled up and his head poked above ground level, he gaped at the bizarre scene before him.

A Tudor queen of England was knocking the *foie gras* out of the King of France.

Chapter 15:
Into the Sun

To Constance's disappointment, smashing the King of France's head against the bronze, lectern-sized armillary control console did not cause the front panel to pop open. But this action was more satisfying than her prior attempts of hitting it with a champagne bottle or picking its lock with a hairpin.

The King gurgled from the ground, "I'll boil you in oil for this."

Constance stood back and folded her arms. "I told you what I'd do if you tried to sound an alarm through the panel. There's no need to act surprised when I do exactly what I said I would. Now, open the panel so I can retrieve the book, or I shall introduce you to each of my rings in a manner you won't appreciate." She unfolded her arms and cracked her knuckles through her white kidskin gloves. Hopefully, this action would be enough to persuade Louis to comply. Otherwise, she risked damaging the eight diamond-and-sapphire rings worn over the gloves that were serving as glamorous knuckle-dusters. It was a shame she wasn't wearing her electrical gauntlet, but the rings did add a certain regal glamour to her threats, which was particularly fitting given they were being addressed to a king. Louis rose to an unsteady stand and let loose a blistering flight of insults, few of which she understood and none of which she cared about.

"I've been insulted by better men than you, Louis XVIII," she said. "This is your last chance to open the console, or I'm afraid I will have to start getting a little"—she narrowed her eyes at him—"violent."

He gasped. "What do you call this?" He pointed at his swollen, bruised right eye. "I could have lost my sight."

She snorted. "I could have popped your eyeball right out of its socket with my fan if I wanted to do you lasting harm. But the longer you stall, the more unreasonable I'm going to get. Time's ticking away, Louis." She took a step toward him, fists raised.

He held up his hands to shield his face and whimpered. "Very well, I'll give you the book. But don't think for one minute you're going to leave this palace alive."

He reached inside the neck of his black shirt and pulled out a silver chain with a large oval locket. He opened the locket and drew out a bronze key. "Here, woman, take it."

Constance eyed him warily. "Put it on top of the console and back away."

"You don't trust me?" He scoffed. "After all our time together? I'm hurt."

"You will be if you don't put the key on top of the console."

The King stepped toward the console. As she had anticipated, he lunged for the communication button that linked to his elite guards.

He almost made it. But Constance's swift footwork was honed by years of dancing, fencing, and martial arts training. She closed the distance between them before he could hit the button. It was apparent that Louis had never been taught the finer points of street fighting by his coachman. Thanks to Hearn's patient lessons, her side-smash across the jaw with a knuckle-duster was one of her best moves.

Louis spun in a comically small circle and staggered back as Constance shot in to deliver a knockout blow. She needed at least ten seconds of peace and quiet to open the console, and an unconscious Louis was her best option.

Louis swung at her with a wild haymaker punch. She slipped inside the punch, holding up her left arm to deflect it as she smashed him across the nose with her right elbow. He yowled as bones crunched. The King fell to his knees, clutching his nose with his black-gloved hand. Inexplicably, he started laughing, tears streaming down his rouged cheeks. He sniped, "You are undone, Your Majesty. My guards are here. Prepare to die."

"As if I'd fall for that one," said Constance. "You think I'm going to turn around and let you . . ."

"Ahem," said an unknown voice from the back of the clearing.

Constance kept her fists raised and backed up at an angle so that she could see both Louis and the interloper.

She gaped at the new arrivals who stood silently on a platform sent up from below. A pack of unknown men stood before her, some clad in shining silver fishtail armor, others in uniforms of pure filth.

Louis cackled. "You are finished, Your Highness. Allow me to introduce my gardeners and . . . palace guards? Most excellent. Men, this palace party guest has outstayed her welcome. Kill this monstrous queen in as vile a manner as you please, and toss her body down through the clouds below to shatter upon the earth."

Constance licked her dry lips behind her porcelain mask. This wasn't going to be a fair fight. But she'd be damned if she wasn't going to take at least a few of them with her.

The men parted their ranks and out stepped a muddy savior. She'd know those bells anywhere.

"Tie up the King," ordered Trusdale the jester. "I need to interrogate this party guest."

Louis's slender jaw dropped to the ground. "What? Men, I order you to—Wait, no, what are you doing?" The troops surrounded the King as the gardeners pinned his arms behind his back and tied his wrists together with horticultural twine. Louis howled, swore, and pleaded to no avail as Trusdale walked over to Constance.

He stood before her, dirty, disheveled, and the closest thing to a knight in shining armor she could have hoped for on this absurd evening in the clouds.

He muttered, "Should I ask you why you're in the middle of a maze assaulting royalty?"

She shrugged. "Should I ask why you appear to be leading a palace coup?"

"I'd rather you didn't. I'm simply trying to keep everyone alive and happy. Seems the universe is fighting me every step of the way to make sure that doesn't happen."

"You can never please everyone. It's madness to even try."

He nodded. "You make an excellent point. I've spent what feels like a lifetime trying to find your damned—"

He gasped, looking over her shoulder at the cosmic armillary.

"If you're going to say, 'Enigma Key,' I've found it," she said. "Even though you told me to stay in the Hall of Mirrors, I nevertheless tracked it down before you did. Perhaps you'll take this as a sign that a woman is more than capable of handling the dangerous parts of any escapade as well as or better than a man."

He groaned. "Oh lord, is that what you're taking from this situation? What is wrong with you? No, on second thought, don't tell me, we'll be here all night."

Heat flared in her cheeks. "How dare you! I was handling everything perfectly well until you showed up."

"Yes, I saw. Maybe we can get you booked in as a ringer in a few underground cage-fighting matches? It could be a whole new sideline for you. You've gotta keep those Haltwhistle coffers full, right? Gotta push the boundaries of science, gotta ignore the dangers and charge ahead, right? You're more like your father than you'll admit."

She gaped. "To what do I owe this unwarranted attack?"

He pointed at the armillary's triangular power source. "That . . . thing . . . is dangerous. Look what it's done to the gardeners here. For generations, it's been warping their physical form and mental abilities. Yet your papa left you home sitting on top of a bunch of them. Do you think he cared what harm they might have done to you? Or was that all a part of his Plan with a capital 'P'?"

"Of course they're dangerous, but I know what I'm doing. Papa taught me . . . wait, are you suggesting he was experimenting on me?"

"Like a certain baroness who shot me with an electrical gauntlet."

"That was an accident."

"If you say so."

Constance spluttered. "I . . . that is . . . I'm putting this outburst down to fatigue on your part. My father's a cad, but he wouldn't . . ." She bit her lip.

He stepped closer to her, almost close enough to take her in his arms and dance again. He dropped his head, jingling the bells on his jester hat. "I'm sorry, this wasn't the right time or place. But maybe taking the Key isn't the best idea. Maybe we can buy RATT off, maybe we can hide, but right now, I need your help. Do you trust me?"

She blinked up at him. "I do."

"All right. Constance, I'm not gonna lie to you here. These men are following me because they think I've swallowed a superweapon that will bring down Versailles. I've got to figure out a way to safely land this palace. If this coup fails, we're all dead. I'm certain your boyfriend over there isn't the forgiving type."

She tilted up her chin.

"He's most definitely not my . . . ugh. You have no idea what I've been through. Last month, Prince Lucien of England proposed to me and then tried to kill me, and now the King of France propositioned me and then tried to kill me. I don't know if I'm moving up or down in the world."

"You definitely need to improve your taste in men."

She couldn't argue with that. "So, what do you want from me, exactly? To land the palace?"

"Can you do that?" he asked in wonder.

"I have a Plan in mind. A Plan with a capital 'P,' of course."

"I'll take it, 'capital P' and all. What do you need?"

She pointed at the bronze key that now rested on the crystalline ash. "That key Louis dropped should open the console panel. I'm hoping there's a book inside it that belongs to me."

"How could it possibly . . .?"

She glared at him.

He sighed. "Okay, it belongs to you. Then what?"

"There's a circle of navigation buttons on the console that allows the King to send it back and forth and sideways, but not up and down. The constraint of not being able to alter the altitude may have been built in by the original engineers for various reasons. Or, it could be that the interdimensional being, or beings, trapped inside the Enigma Key could resist responding to up and down commands if they didn't feel like being compliant."

She felt a tickle at the back of her brain. A warm, syrupy tickle that almost formed into words. "The poor thing has been trapped in this constant flying loop for over a hundred years, and I'm going to free it from the cycle."

As she said the words aloud to Trusdale, she also wrote them in chalk on a mental blackboard in order to communicate telepathically with the creature inside the Key.

"Gurble, narble, flurbel," it wrote back on the same chalkboard.

She'd made contact! Constance clapped her hands with glee.

Trusdale the jester cocked his head. "You're talking to the alien right now, aren't you? Dammit, Constance, isn't there any way we can do this without its help? Without you putting yourself at risk?"

"Not that I can think of. Don't worry, this one feels benign. It might be a single entity who is frankly worn thin from powering this palace for over a century. What it desires is a nice rest. Perhaps on board an airship?"

She drew a quick sketch of the *Lady Penelope*, with herself holding the Enigma Key aloft against a backdrop of a rainbow and fluffy clouds.

"Bedogle twerbe," said the Key, and drew itself as a triangle with a big cheesy grin and one eye.

"Oooh, cyclops creature, lovely."

Trusdale sighed. "Lord help me, and you. What exactly is your Plan?"

"First, to rescue my book. Then, you man the navigational buttons on the console while I slip into something more fiery." She nodded at the welding torch and gas canisters strapped to one of his demolition troops. "I'm going to ask the Key if it can lower the palace while you navigate us to a safe landing spot. I recommend mountains—fewer people around, and more chance to balance this platform rather than skid it across the ground and send sheep flying. Hit the purple button to blast air from the lower level that will temporarily clear the cloud cover below. I assume it's how Louis sees where he should drop things from the platform onto his enemies."

Trusdale shook his head. "Oh no, Constance. You can't possibly climb up a dozen rotating armillary rings wearing a Tudor gown, balancing over a hole that drops maybe a mile or so down to the ground. It's too dangerous."

"Watch me," she said, tilting up her chin. "If I can street fight a king into submission while wearing a hundred-pound dress, I can certainly hop up a few rings to grab an alien sun. My balance has been honed by years of dance, gymnastics, and martial arts training in a wide variety of costumes, from plate armor to leather catsuits. Papa insisted that I be able to defend myself in any given circumstance. He knew members of my family always stir the strongest passions in other people. The Brass Queen was born to face her enemies head on, and that is exactly what I will do. Don't even try to be the man who gets in my way."

Trusdale shook his head. "You give a woman a crown and it instantly goes to her head. Look, I'm not trying to dampen down your fire here, but what if I climbed up to the sun while you manned the console buttons?"

She scoffed. "And risk you mentally saying the wrong thing and insulting the Key? This job requires a Halt-whistle. And the longer you waste time arguing about this, the closer dawn approaches. At some point, the elite guards are going to notice the King hasn't returned to the palace."

"Ugh. All right. But let it go on record that your father is at least borderline evil. Who makes a child fight in armor?"

Constance shrugged. "I'm sure knights of old taught their children to fight that way. Papa wanted me to be as strong as my ancestors, regardless of my sex, height, or inclination to read novels all day. Welli was against it, apparently. But I don't believe it did me any harm."

Trusdale folded his arms. "And where was your mother in all this?"

"She often trained beside me. She said it was a wonderful way to keep her figure trim."

Trusdale sighed. "Of course she did. It's a wonder you're not even more—"

"If the next word out of your mouth isn't 'competent,' we're going to fall out permanently."

"Damn it. All right. Get your welding gear strapped on. By the way, don't talk to the guards if you can help it. It's important that they believe you are Dr. Maya Chauhan in disguise. Please don't ask—"

"Why?"

"You had to ask, didn't you? Let's just say I'm doing what I can to protect the crew of the *Lady Penelope*, and things have gotten slightly out of hand."

"In my experience, things always do." She strode toward the demolition guards with Trusdale trailing behind her.

Ten minutes later, Constance had strapped two twelve-inch-long gas canisters to her back. In her right hand, she held a welding wand attached to the canisters by a rubber pipe. She clipped the wand to the canisters on her back for safekeeping during the climb. Over the eye holes cut into her white porcelain mask, she'd lowered the demolition soldier's brass goggles. She admired her reflection in the mirrored goggles of another soldier, who carried a case of dynamite. Her new outfit read as "Tudor queen meets Steamwerks welder."

It was perfect in every way, even as she braced her spine to carry the weight of her ensemble. Her bragging was entirely based on truth. She had learned how to fight while wearing armor under her papa's expert tutelage, but this new heavy costume would test the limits of her strength and balance.

She walked slowly to the edge of the armillary globe and stood at the edge of the hole that led down through the platform, and studied the swirling vortex of clouds below. Her stomach gave an uncomfortable flip.

I'll be fine as long as I don't look down. She turned to see Trusdale standing ready at the console, the book written by her ancestors lying on the ash beside his curled slippers. The jester was standing by to hit the buttons to propel the platform to its new home.

Hopefully, that new home wouldn't be plastered all over the face of a mountain or upside-down in a lake.

"Clear the clouds," she yelled to him.

Trusdale moved his hands over the console, and a blast of air from the bottom of the platform blew a passageway through the clouds, revealing the dark French countryside a mile below. She took a deep breath and stepped onto the first six-inch-wide silver ring. Each slowly rotating ring held a silver earth about the size of a freestanding office globe, maybe three feet across. Now that she was closer, she could see that each Earth seemed to have different land masses. On some, England was still attached to Europe. On others, the island nation had disappeared beneath the waves.

She balanced carefully on the moving ring until it reached a point where she could safely hop to the next one. She swayed a little, catching a glimpse down into the open portal below. The ground looked a lot farther away when you were balancing over it on metal rings while wearing an enormously heavy dress.

As she swayed, she felt the Key ooze warm treacle into the back of her mind, steadying her. On her mental blackboard, the Key drew a human hand cupping a tiny stick figure wearing a big dress and a crown.

"Ah, you'll try to keep me steady so that I stay safe. Lovely. It's all mind over matter, isn't it?" She stepped onto the next ring, ducking another that twirled over her head. The dance of the rings carried on as she dodged and turned and hopped over ten of them until she was almost within arm's length of the sun.

The image of the Key's cold fire filled her brass goggles as she reached up and over her shoulder to pull down the welding torch wand. She hopped up onto the final ring, swaying in the breeze that gusted up from the portal.

She glanced down to see the yellow gas lamps of a town glowing far below her slippers. How fast must they be traveling? Slow enough to tug along the airships that were moored to the platform like children's balloons, but fast enough to pass over the town within a minute.

Heavens, are we going over thirty miles an hour? How terrifyingly fast.

On the blackboard in her mind, she drew a picture of herself cutting the key from its silver cage and the platform descending to balance on the peaks of three mountains.

The Key drew back a picture of the palace broken in two on either side of a single peak.

Ah, so it doesn't like my mountain landing idea. Constance frowned and drew the palace sitting atop a tasseled pillow like the ones on the King's chaise longue. She prayed the alien creature would understand this meant she needed a soft landing.

The Key's fire turned from white to blue and the entire platform of Versailles dropped fifty feet in a split second.

Constance faltered and fell forward, landing face-first across the rings with her nose six inches away from the Key. The sheer bulk of the massive dress had saved her from falling between the rings. With her right hand still holding the slender welding torch, she scrabbled for the one-inch alien triangle with her left. Her palm landed on the Key as the platform dropped another thirty feet, sending her stomach hurtling into the land of nausea.

How should I draw a picture of 'slow'? Would the Key understand what a snail is?

The Key drew a baby bird, with wings outstretched as a parent bird looked on.

I see. This is your first flight up or down for quite some time. You're a baby bird, doing your best. She drew a quick sketch of her own face smiling on her mental blackboard. Thank heavens she'd kept up her art lessons into adulthood. The likeness was rather good, given the circumstances.

The platform dropped again, this time forty feet. Constance groaned and tried to keep her stomach settled as she bounced her midriff along the still-moving ring. The wind from below was intensifying, and she could hear Trusdale shouting at her, although most of his words gusted away on the wind. Was he asking her if she was "all right"? She snorted at his compassionate cluelessness. She was balanced across thin metal bands thousands of feet above the Earth with a blowtorch in her hand and an alien in her mind. How "all right" could she possibly be? The rings around the armillary grated to a full stop as the Key's light turned yellow.

Thank you, my friend. She drew a heart shape onto her mental blackboard and set to work, cutting the Key from its silver cage as the palace platform dropped in fits and starts. The sparks from the welding torch blazed inches from her face as she cut through the final piece of metal holding the Key. The triangle dropped obediently into her left palm. She clutched it tightly as on her blackboard she drew the same baby bird the Key had drawn, this time standing in a meadow of flowers. *It's time to land, as gently as a bird, if you can.*

The platform tipped from side to side, then plunged like a stone toward the earth. The screams of the troops and the King behind her echoed in her ears as she hung on for grim life to the silver rings. The dark ground below raced toward her, with a glint of a dark river in the center. As the platform lurched, it seemed Trusdale was following the river's path.

The surface of the Earth rushed up as more water appeared below. *Was that a lake? Wouldn't the palace platform sink like a stone? Or would that depend on the depth? What if—*

Constance screamed as the platform slapped down with bone-jarring force onto the water and skipped like a pebble across the surface of a lake. A grating slide onto the rocks stopped the platform's velocity as the water rose in the center hole. Fortunately, it only rose a few feet. It seemed the palace was now a dock or island in a lake somewhere in the south of France. Who knew, perhaps it would become a grand destination for tourists?

Constance slipped the Key inside her left glove for safety. The cold metal tingled her palm with cosmic electricity as she drew a smiling version of herself on the blackboard. In return, the Key drew a jolly sun emblazoned with one eye and a grin. She attempted to push herself to a stand, but now that she was horizontal, the full weight of her gown pressed her to stay down.

Trusdale coughed behind her. She glanced back to see a dirty jester balanced behind her, ready to help her to her feet. She accepted his offer, ignoring the impropriety of his arms encircling her waist. As he pulled her up, they swayed together momentarily on the rings as if caught in the middle of another waltz.

Trusdale held on to her waist tightly. "Are you all right?"

"I am now," she gazed up at him. "It was all part of the—"

"Plan with a capital 'P.' Why did I ever doubt you?"

"Why indeed?" She grinned behind her mask. "Incidentally, is that a dynamite case your man is carrying? I'd like to borrow a stick or two."

"Borrow? For what?"

"You'll see," she smiled.

Chapter 16:
A Bird's Eye View

D awn cast pink-and-gold bunting across the sky to celebrate the birth of a new island. Gunter Erhard, Colonel of Skullduggery and Mayhem to the court of King Oscar, leaned on the handrail of the four-man stealth airship, *Draugen,* and studied the fallen Palace of Versailles. A team of white-uniformed palace guards labored to erect a makeshift bridge for carriages between the saucer-shaped platform and the rocky banks of the crystal-clear lake. They had so far managed to build a pedestrian walkway that thronged with ex-servants, freed prisoners, and former elite guards leaving the palace of their own volition. The air seemed festive, and the only signs of violence had been those left by Lady Constance

Haltwhistle upon the deposed King's maze. The fire still smoldered in the remains of the yew maze where the fiery redhead had tossed dynamite to destroy a mirrored cover that had once concealed a silver armillary. The sculpture lay smoldering, ruined.

Apart from this tragic blow to the garden statuary, the fall of King Louis XVIII was remarkably civilized.

To Erhard's right stood Ludwig, Lars, and Johan. Armed with telescopes and binoculars, the three blond giants were taking meticulous notes on the comings and goings at the fallen palace. Aristocrats were leaving, and peasants from a nearby town were wandering the King's gardens with awe and delight plastered across their faces, unaware of the spies in the sky above. The thirty-foot *Draugen* airship was rumored to be the world's finest aerial reconnaissance vessel. The top secret "ghost ship" was avant-garde from its virtually silent hydrogen engine to its soundproofed cell for transporting prisoners. Fast, light, and covered in a thousand external mirrors, both the ship and its cigar-shaped balloon reflected the clouds and sky around it. It was practically invisible to casual observers, even when using a telescope or binoculars. Sadly, the ship did kill a dozen birds daily as they collided head-first with the mirrored craft. On the plus side, this meant an endless source of fresh meat available for Erhard and his Swedish crew.

Two pigeons were currently roasting on the oven set atop the ship's engine, filling the air with the scent of roasting meat and the lingonberries stuffed inside. Ludwig had turned out to be a surprisingly good chef. The blond henchman wielded his Viking-style ax with true panache in the ship's kitchen corner, chopping vegetables and herbs with a speed most Parisian chefs would envy. Lars, Johan, and Erhard appreciated the giant's cooking skills as much as his ability to silently break a man's neck from behind.

Erhard sighed. He could stall no longer. It was time for him to give his report to King Oscar via the weird, wonderful, and slightly terrifying device the King had insisted he use. He drew the oval hand mirror from beneath his jacket. The copper-framed mirror was decorated with fine wiring and jewels that glittered an unusual shade of purple. A triangular indentation in the top of the mirror awaited the insertion of what the King referred to as an "Enigma Key." He popped the triangle into the slot, and the mirror hummed with alien life.

Once revered as a kind and benevolent ruler, the man whose face appeared in the glass had become preoccupied with starting a war on Europe in recent years. It was a senseless move, and one that Erhard would have opposed, had he been asked his opinion. He'd seen enough battles to know that no one wins once diplomacy has failed. Yet his particular skills were more in demand than ever as good men failed to use reason and logic.

For twenty minutes, the King barely said a word as Erhard tilted the mirror to display the totality of the palace's fall and its implications for France on the world stage. Oscar's voice sounded from the mirror, "And you believe this mighty edifice was brought down by the Haltwhistle girl? You've railed about her martial prowess, but surely this is beyond the work of one woman?"

Erhard turned the mirror to face him. King Oscar wore the face of a man two decades older than his sixty-eight years. What malady could draw so much strength from one who used to be able to carry four of his laughing grandchildren at one time? Oscar had always been strong in body and mind, a fine protector of his Swedish homeland, popular with his subjects and allies alike. How the mighty had fallen.

"Your Majesty, we saw the entire debacle unfold. Constance Haltwhistle, dressed as Elizabeth the First, entered the palace. Hours later, the palace fell, and we spied Constance striding through the palace's maze, tossing dynamite here and there, followed by a small army of palace guards and silver-armored men and women, with Louis XVIII tied up as her hostage."

Lady Nay's voice drifted from the mirror. "This is typical Haltwhistle behavior. If there is a heart of chaos at the center of the cosmos, you can guarantee a Haltwhistle is somewhere close by, bending it to their own ends. But this girl takes matters to heights that even her wretched father never imagined. The sooner you bring her to me, the better."

Oscar turned his mirror so that Lady Nay's emerald-green eyes could glower at Erhard across the miles. Her porcelain-perfect face was twisted by simmering rage, framed by tendrils of hair darker than a thunderstorm. She was beauty and the beast combined, both frightful and alluring. Yet Oscar trusted her above anyone else in his court.

Erhard kept his face composed and his tone unemotional. "Constance has now returned to her airship. We will follow her to her next destination, where we will capture her. She will be brought to Stockholm before this week ends."

The mirror turned back to Oscar, who carried it over to a window. "Take care as you enter our airspace, Colonel. We have been cursed with unusual weather." Oscar held the mirror aloft to show strange purple clouds, lit by the dawn, over the sleeping city of Stockholm. "These clouds bear no rain, but a purple fog descends from them each night, prowling the streets like a living being.

People are disappearing by the hundreds, with no trace of them left behind. We have attempted to keep word of the vanishings quiet so as not to stir panic. How many lives would be lost if all the citizens attempted to flee out of the city at the same time?"

Erhard frowned. "Perhaps you should retreat to the country, Your Majesty. You could reunite with the Queen." A plan which might loosen Lady Nay's hold upon the ailing king.

Her voice soothed the King from the shadows. "No king deserts their capital city because of a few stray clouds. Your leadership is required here. Rest assured, my scientists are creating a device that will end Stockholm's suffering for good. Now is the time to stand firm, Your Majesty."

Erhard gritted his teeth as the King's worn face filled the mirror once more. "Lady Nay is correct, of course. Her scientists will solve this puzzle for my people."

Erhard frowned. "Your Majesty, can you trust . . . these scientists . . . not to cause more harm than good? I strongly advise—"

Lady Nay snatched the mirror from the King's hand. "Your counsel is noted, Colonel. You have one job. Bring me . . . that is, bring to His Majesty, Constance Haltwhistle. She will play a vital role in our liberation of Stockholm from all that darkens its fine streets."

"Only her people walk those streets, Lady Nay."

Her thin-lipped smile sent ice daggers into his heart. "And they will be taken care of, I assure you. Do I need to stress what will happen to you and your crew if you fail to bring the Haltwhistle girl?"

The Vikings at Erhard's elbow dropped their telescopes and binoculars to stare at Erhard in alarm.

The witch was turning his own men against him. *Well played, Lady Nay.* It was a tactic he had used himself to good effect on many occasions.

He lifted his chin. "These men are the finest troops I've ever had the honor of commanding. We will not let down the King, I guarantee it." That was true, but he'd be more than happy to introduce his sword, Sophie, to Nay's black heart should the opportunity present itself.

"On your lives, then," said Lady Nay grimly, and the power from the mirror faded, freezing the image of her beautiful, cold face for a few seconds before fading.

Erhard tucked the mirror into his belt. With a confidence he didn't feel, he said, "You heard the King. Our mission remains the same. Capture the Brass Queen at all costs."

Chapter 17:
The Picnic

At long last, Trusdale could relax in the sunshine. He stretched out on a plaid blanket on the top deck of the *Lady Penelope*, which was still tethered to Versailles's main dock. A joyous picnic was exactly what the airship's crew needed to unwind after the tension they'd endured since leaving Paris. Trusdale munched happily through several plates of freshly baked crusty bread, stinky cheese, and sliced meats sent up from Versailles's kitchens by a grateful Général Malaise. The interim president of the new Republic of France had made good on his word of a peaceful coup.

Trusdale had watched in awe as the Général and his palace guards diffused tensions between incoming townsfolk and palace regulars with diplomacy, palace garden tours, and free bottles of wine for all. The Général had gifted Trusdale with several crates of vintage champagne liberated from the palace's wine cellar for his help with the coup. Other than securing a fine luncheon for his crew, Trusdale's part in the night's events had been kept secret from all but the brave troops who had dared to follow a jester into the depths of the palace sewers.

Doctors Huang and Chauhan had set off on a quest of their own to find the control room earlier that day; they were convinced it was located somewhere in the platform's lower levels. They had, of course, failed to find it, as Constance had been quite adamant about destroying all evidence of her family's scientific influence upon the Sun Kings, and Trusdale had been careful to keep her death-defying exploits at the armillary to himself. The two retired scientists were now sitting together on a blanket, toasting crystalline ash over a portable Bunsen burner and scribbling down multiple hypotheses in their notebooks. They were as happy as Boo, who was gnawing her way through the scientists' charcuterie leftovers as they speculated about the platform's mechanical systems.

Trusdale sat up and glanced around at the rest of the laughing, celebrating crew, scattered on blankets and chairs across the deck. Welli was boasting of his prowess at the royal poker table, claiming that he'd won the costume off Poseidon's back. It was a fine trophy to accompany the winnings he claimed would pay off all his debtors in one fell swoop.

Hearn and Cawley were sitting on deck chairs, eating pink petit fours and chatting with the Singhs. Neither of Constance's servants had left Yorkshire before this grand tour, and both loved to hear of Mrs. Singh's piratical exploits from her time flying over the waves of the West China Sea. They listened in wonder as she spoke of firing cannons across the bow of a British dreadnought, distracting the crew of the two-hundred-foot-long behemoth. It gave her pirate air fleet just long enough to scatter before the dreadnought's thirty cannons and two turret guns could blast them from the sky.

"And that was how I ended up being caught and sentenced to hang," said Mrs. Singh.

"And were you? Hung, that is?" asked Hearn, his eyes as big as saucers.

The ex-pirate queen guffawed. "Not that day, my friend. My crew and I escaped our bonds and managed to hop ship at the next port of call before anyone missed us. I even managed to pocket the dreadnought Captain's diary before we escaped, which contained the map he'd drawn that led me to find the lost treasure of Zheng He. But that's another story."

"Oooh, brilliant," said Hearn. "I hope you survived that adventure too."

"You'll just have to wait and see," grinned Mrs. Singh, winking at her husband across their picnic blanket. The stately Sikh warrior rolled his eyes and bit into a slice of cake proffered on a plate by Cawley. Constance's aged servant couldn't help but serve others, even when his tempestuous mistress was nowhere to be seen.

Just as Trusdale began to worry about her failure to appear, the door to the lower decks flew open, and out strode Constance dressed for adventure. A miniature white pith helmet perched at a jaunty angle upon her tumbling waist-length red tresses. Her crisp white high-necked, long-sleeved blouse was cinched by a brown leather corset dotted with brass rivets. Explorer's tools, including a compass, a pocket telescope, and a sheathed knife, were strapped to the corset with no attempt at disguising their function. She stomped across the deck in brass-toed ankle boots that flashed threateningly from beneath her long khaki skirt.

Welli gawked at his cousin's bold ensemble. "Good lord, Connie. Are we off to Africa?"

She shook her head. "Sadly, no. But as I had the outfit ready, I thought it best to give it a whirl. What do you think?" Constance twirled to enthusiastic applause from Mrs. Singh and Maya. "Thank you, ladies. It makes a lovely change from silk and lace. I now feel ready to face the next stop of our grand tour in style. With one Key safely in our possession, I have ascertained the location of several others. In short, once lunch is over, let's set course for the most magnificent of all cities."

Cawley gasped. "Are we flying back to Sheffield then, miss?"

Constance tilted her head. "Ah, good point Cawley. Now that I think about it, we are actually headed to the second most magnificent city in the whole world."

"Leeds?"

Constance shook her head, and Cawley's shoulders sank. She said, "Never fear, Cawley, soon we shall return to Yorkshire in triumph. But today we are headed to a city quite similar to Sheffield that, like our hometown, is encircled by seven great hills, has birthed an empire, and is famous for its great and noble citizens."

"Doncaster?" asked Cawley.

"Not quite. Friends, we are heading to Rome, Italy!" beamed Constance, throwing her arms to the heavens. "*La dolce vita* will be ours!"

The crew burst into champagne-enhanced applause and cheers. Constance continued, "And we'll find our next Enigma Key at the Vatican."

The applause stopped, and the crew exchanged worried glances.

Trusdale cleared his throat. "You're going to rob the Pope?"

She arched her perfect eyebrows. "Surely a religious man has no need of earthly treasure when he will find riches in the kingdom of heaven? I think a tiny trinket like an Enigma Key will be of no consequence to such a wise and powerful person."

"So, I'm right?" said Trusdale as he felt the blood drain from his cheeks. "You're going to rob the Pope? May I say that seems like a monumentally bad idea? There are the Pontifical Swiss Guards to contend with for a start."

Constance tilted up her chin. "Have no fear. My errant father was an honorary member of the Pyrrho Club, the best drinking and thinking enclave for international scientists anywhere in the world. As a family member, I should be able to arrange a tour of the papal observatories, the oldest of which is home to the Enigma Key. We'll go there after visiting the most popular tourist spots in the city, so that we appear to be enthusiastic tourists, not burglars. Once we've secured the second Key, we'll be well on our way to satisfying the British Museum's demand that we return their missing treasure via conjuring up an interdimensional portal. Rest assured, I have a Plan with a capital—"

"P," chorused the crew. To Trusdale's surprise, they didn't seem to be averse to following Constance quite literally through the gates of hell. What other fate awaited those who stole from the Vatican? "Are we having a vote?" he asked. "Because if so, I'm against robbing the Pope. There's no way that can end well."

Welli sighed. "I'd normally be with you, Trusdale. But against all odds, Constance did manage to secure the first Key with only short-term damage to a rotten king. I'll place my bet on her this time."

The remainder of the crew nodded in acquiescence.

"But, but . . ." spluttered Trusdale. "The Keys are inherently dangerous, especially to Constance. She's spent her life living with them, handling them, opening dimensional portals with them. Who knows what the long-term effects could be on her physical well-being, never mind her mental health. It's a wonder she hasn't gone stark raving mad with all that she's seen and done. And you, Cawley and Hearn, you helped her set up her experiments back at the Hall. How do you know the Keys didn't affect you too?"

The servants glanced at each other and shrugged. Hearn said, "Interdimensional energy absorption is all part of the job at Haltwhistle Hall. You get used to it."

"I think it's helped me live longer," said Cawley.

"Aye, well, there's a downside to everything," said Hearn with a grin.

Trusdale ground his teeth. "Can't anyone take this seriously? The more Enigma Keys we collect, the greater peril we face from interacting with the incomprehensively powerful beings imprisoned within. And ask yourselves this: What kind of creature is so ultrapowerful that it can jail such beings in the first place. Shouldn't we stop and consider—"

A whirring hum overhead drew his eyes to the heavens. Thirty feet above his head, a passenger pigeon was dropping a . . . *mechanical scorpion?*

"Look out," yelled Hearn, leaping to his feet and smashing Trusdale into the deck as the golden scorpion plunged toward the crew.

"It's a messenger beast. Don't anyone—no, Hearn, don't!" shouted Constance.

The burly coachman had already seized the metal scorpion by its curled tail and was bashing its delicate frame against the deck. The creature writhed and squirmed in his meaty hand, its coiled stinger desperately lashing out, trying to stab its attacker in the wrist to no avail. As cogs, springs, and colorful mosaic scales exploded across the deck, Constance rushed in to save what was left of the mechanical marvel. She picked it up by its one remaining leg as it shuddered to a stop.

Constance gingerly picked out a folded piece of parchment, then flung the scorpion's remains to the edge of the deck, where Boo pounced upon them with a growl. "Yes, you show it who's boss, Boo. Now, what do we have here?" She scanned the message. "Well, the British Museum is turning up the heat. Not content with killing us, this is a remarkably lurid description of how they intend to dispatch us. We'll be mummified alive, and our hideous screaming corpses will be put on display to amuse visiting school children. Even poor little Boo!"

Shock and horror rumbled around the deck. "Their threats are repulsive on every level," said Constance. "Again, I apologize heartily to you all for bringing the museum's wrath down upon you. I owe each of you more than I can possibly repay. Could I think of any other way to get them off our backs other than collecting the Enigma Keys"—she fixed her gaze on Trusdale—"I swear, any other way at all, I would take it. Should we accomplish our mission and return the Museum's lost treasures, I promise I will never go near another Enigma Key again. And I will certainly not drag any of you on any more death-defying adventures."

"Well, don't go mad, dear cousin," said Welli. "Perhaps we don't want a death-defying experience, but I think we all enjoy a little adventure here, don't we?"

"Not me," said Cawley.

"I can get in all the adventures I want down at my local pub," said Hearn. "The Hateful Baker is the favored drinking spot of a host of villains and ne'er-do-wells, most of whom are my lifelong friends. They're good lads to have at your back in a fight, bad lads if you want to leave the pub without getting your pocket picked on the way."

Welli chuckled. "It's fair to say that one man's adventure is another man's torture. But it's in our own best interests to make the best of the hand we've been dealt, even if the game we're playing seems to be rigged in favor of the dealer. Yes, we're facing a potentially grotesque death at the hands of crazed scholars, but let's enjoy the best of what this moment has to offer. This luncheon is delightful, and I for one am looking forward to visiting Rome. Who's with me?"

Constance clapped her hands together in delight. "That's the spirit, Welli! Mrs. Singh, please set the autopilot for Rome. Let's all eat, drink, and be merry, for tomorrow we shall sail over the Mediterranean Sea with nothing but blue skies and sunshine to escort us to our . . ."

"Doom," muttered Trusdale.

". . . next adventure. Please, raise your glasses to the *Lady Penelope*, the best airship there ever was or will be."

The crew raised their glasses and toasted the ship with cheers.

Beaming ear to ear, Constance accepted champagne and nibbles from Cawley. She sashayed across the deck and sat down beside Trusdale on the blanket. Without breaking her smile, she leaned toward him and whispered, "Trust me, Rome is the safest option. Don't ask."

"Oh, I'm askin'. You can bet your sweet bustle I'm askin'."

She flushed at the mention of her bustle. "Don't lower the tone. Now, I've investigated the matter with Daphnia—"

"Who?"

"The poor alien creature trapped inside our new Enigma Key. I named it Daphnia after the one-eyed water flea. It drew a picture of itself on my mental blackboard, and that's the closest creature shape that I could identify, although size-wise I think she might be as big as a train. Daphnia seemed to prefer she, but that could be because she was trying to make me feel comfortable with our sudden intimacy. She's trying to mimic me, if you will."

Trusdale's temples started to throb. Why was a headache the main result of any conversation he got into with Constance? "After all I've said about how hazardous these creatures are? No one should take the ability to link minds with an alien creature as casually as you do. It's not right. How do you know this train-sized telepathic water flea isn't sucking your soul from every pore as it chats about the weather?"

Constance blinked at him. "She's a prisoner held captive in another dimension. The Key is merely the physical protrusion of her jail into our world, where long ago a vile alien race used Daphnia and her kind's natural energy to power their engines. I feel dreadfully sorry for her."

"I feel sorry for you that you'd believe a word an alien says to you."

"I have to trust sometimes, don't I? I don't want to go through life alone and suspicious. I want to trust those around me, even if they are from foreign climes, like you." There was an earnest edge to her voice that was new. It felt like she'd stripped back a layer of armor to reveal herself as never before. She gazed at him with the sunshine lighting her eyes as bright as faceted emeralds in a queen's crown. He licked his lips, suddenly parched despite the two glasses of champagne he'd enjoyed before Constance joined the party.

He kept his voice soft, so that she would move a little closer toward him. "I'm concerned about you putting trust in this particular creature so readily. I know you've 'chatted' with interdimensional krakens before, but as far as I know, they never tried to mimic you to win you over. It reeks of trickery."

He leaned toward her, so close he could breathe in the soft scent of orange blossom from her perfumed clothes. "And for that matter, how do you know this new friend of yours isn't exploring parts of your mind you don't want to share? Telepathy seems to be an unnatural way to start a relationship to me. And unnatural always means trouble."

Constance held her champagne glass steady as the *Lady Penelope* swayed away from its moorings, setting a course for Rome. As the airship reached a comfortable cruising speed, she said, "The mental exchange of information may not be common on this earth, but it's perfectly natural and normal on other worlds. Human beings have apparently failed to fulfill their potential in this area. Daphnia believes our insistence on verbally chattering to each other or using body language to show our emotions has protected us against less friendly aliens. She refers to these antagonistic beings as Ma."

"Pronounced as in 'my ma baked me a birthday cake'?"

She shrugged. "To cut a long story short, it appears that Daphnia's species and many others were conquered by the Ma millennia ago. The survivors of this epic conflict were imprisoned in Keys and forced to provide their natural electrical energy to their captors." Constance tore a piece of bread on her plate into a triangle shape. She positioned it next to a square of cheese and a sliver of salami on her plate. "Imagine if you will that this triangle of bread is the Enigma Key used to power the vehicles that carried the Ma to our Earth."

She picked up the square of cheese. "Now imagine this cheese is one of those vehicles. It's made from a quicksilver-like element we humans call *Aurumvivax*. Like a soap bubble, Aurumvivax can be blown into a spherical shape that floats between dimensions, protecting travelers inside its malleable metal walls. Once the bubble arrives safely at its destination planet, the Ma would melt the bubbles into their liquid form and emerge to conquer all."

Trusdale nodded. "Okay, I understand all this science stuff so far—we've got a power source, a vehicle, and occupants. But what does the salami represent?"

"Nothing. I'm just hungry." She placed the sliver of meat upon the bread and wolfed it down in one bite. "Mmm, delicious."

Trusdale sighed. "So, if these Ma creatures invaded us long ago, where are they?"

Constance's eyes lit up. "Ah, that's where things get really interesting. So, the Keys energizing the bubble craft staged an act of rebellion. They coordinated a blast of energy that popped the Ma's bubbles as they entered our atmosphere. The Aurumvivax and the Keys were scattered over five continents, and the Ma were destroyed. The prisoners inside the Keys remain trapped, but at least this way they had hope that one day someone would come along and help them escape. Enter my ancestors, who tried to talk to the Keys when other people kept them as trinkets or occasionally forced them into servitude. As far as I know, only my family has been successful in chatting with the Keys as you and I might chat together." She kept her eyes steady on Trusdale as she took a sip of her champagne.

This is a test. She's admitting her family was mentally changed by these cosmic interlopers, just as the Sun Kings' gardeners were physically changed by burning cosmic crystals. She's telling me . . .

"You and your family have been transformed by your compassionate interactions with these creatures. And you're okay with that?"

"It's not as if I had a choice. But, yes, my circumstance was different to that of my forebears. None of them had nine Keys pulsing away below their feet each and every day. But the servants and I have clearly not suffered any physical changes. Their livery contains a rare alloy woven into the green fabric that protects them, and Papa always told me that I have a natural ability to resist alien change, which he enhanced with many lessons and experiments as I grew up. As you can see, I'm perfectly normal, except for an enhanced ability to chat with aliens."

He sat back. "So, you're still trusting your papa? Believing every word that he told you about your safety, when you know damned well he's a liar?"

Her face shadowed. "He may be a villain, he may have abandoned me, but I don't think he would use me so cruelly, just to further his scientific ambitions. I'm sure that I meant far more to him than being a laboratory test rat." This time, there was an edge of doubt in her voice. She broke her gaze with him, staring down at her plate. "If I thought for one minute that he'd used me, I . . . don't know what I'd do."

He placed his hand on hers, ignoring Cawley's raised eyebrows across the deck. "I'm not trying to hurt you. I only want you to be careful. Maybe you've changed in ways that you've yet to experience on a conscious level. Maybe you're as healthy as a horse, and I'm worrying unnecessarily. But I don't like maybes. Please, try to keep your interaction with this creature down to a minimum? I couldn't live with myself if you got hurt because I held my tongue." He downed his remaining champagne in one gulp and glanced around the deck to locate another bottle.

The silence between him and Constance seemed to last longer than a trip to the stars.

She twirled her champagne glass in her hand, eyes downcast on the bubbles dancing through the amber liquid. "Then . . . I take it you *don't* want to hear about my experiments with Daphnia."

"Your what, now?"

"With Daphnia's help, I've used the aetherscope mirror to chat with versions of me in other dimensions. Some alternate me's are absolute idiots, but with assistance from a couple of the more scientifically gifted Constances, we've figured out the locations of multiple Keys that scattered through our dimension when the Ma's bubble crafts exploded. To put it another way, the aetherscope showed me an ethereal treasure map, if you will, and the Key in Rome is the nearest option."

He put down his empty glass and rubbed both temples. "For God's sake, Constance. Despite everything I've said to you about being careful, you've gone looking yourself up in other dimensions? What the hell?"

Constance's smile slipped, and worry darkened her eyes. "It seemed like a good idea at the time. And the results have been most helpful. The only downside I can see is that the process is exhausting. I shall have to keep up my strength with fine victuals and excellent champagne. May I please continue my tale about how Daphnia came to France?"

He shrugged. "Do what you want. It's not like anything I say makes a difference."

She tut-tutted. "Don't be churlish. I'm trying to help everyone on this ship avoid becoming part of a mummy exhibit. Surely that's worth taking a risk or two? Anyway, our poor Daphnia crash-landed in the Alps millennia ago when the Ma's invasion went awry. In the seventeenth century, French explorers found her and brought her to the Sun King. With the aid of Edwin the Stargazer's book, the Sun King managed to construct a rudimentary void vehicle. That silver armillary cage essentially poked her nonstop with a stick, forcing her to generate cosmic energy that kept the platform aloft. I've apologized on behalf of the entire human race for the Sun Kings' insensitivity. Fortunately, she doesn't seem to be one to hold a grudge."

This was starting to feel like a time for a stronger drink than champagne. Maybe whisky? A lot of whisky.

Constance studied him. "Are you wondering if our planet is likely to be invaded again?"

I am now. "It did cross my mind. Tell me the truth. You're not using telepathy on me, are you?" He waggled his eyebrows at her to try and lighten the mood. There was no point in making her angry. All those years of playing the amiable tourist for the agency could help him mask the despair that was growing inside his heart. Constance was teetering on a precipice, and all he could do was watch to see if she'd fall.

She laughed, lifting his spirits, if only for a moment. "I wish I had that ability, but my meager skills don't work on humans. I tried for years to mentally ask Cawley to bring me snacks, but sadly, ringing a bell or yelling at the top of my lungs were my only options."

He snorted. "Yeah, life is hard. Still, part of the magic of getting to know someone is not knowing exactly what they'll say next. And lord knows, I can never predict the next words that will come out of your mouth."

She gasped. "I can't predict what you'll say, either. What a pair we make. Here's to living life beyond the predictable. I raise my glass to you, Liberty. May you continue to surprise me." She drained her champagne glass and held it up so that sunlight could refract a rainbow onto the teak deck. "You've certainly brought color into my life. And I thank you for it. I want you to know that I appreciated your assistance at the armillary. I couldn't have climbed up to the Key and manned the navigation buttons at the same time. Daphnia was doing her best, but skipping the platform across the lake was a terrific idea to reduce our velocity."

"Yeah. That wasn't entirely intentional," he muttered.

She chuckled. "And I truly appreciate your honesty in all things. Thank you for being there when I needed you most. You're a good man. I'm so glad that fate has brought us together."

Maybe it's the right time to tell her that I'm actually a lying, cheating spy?

Now that Versailles had fallen, he'd already sent three letters via Maya's mechanical pigeons to the agency resigning his commission. It was clear he'd done his job right, for once. The King was overthrown, Malaise was no doubt as happy as a French clam, and he'd achieved a miracle for God that he could barely believe himself.

Yet, she'd sent back two-word missives to his pleas to depart the agency.

Request denied.

There'd been no praise for his efforts, no explanation for her denial, no nothing on which he could plan his future life. Was he doomed to stay a spy forever, knowing his death would swiftly follow if he refused to return to the fold?

How does one get a god to change their mind?

"I . . . that is . . ." He sighed. Maybe it was all right to let at least one woman believe he was already the best version of himself. She deserved nothing less. "You're welcome, Constance."

I'm such a darn coward.

She moved a little closer to him. "If you stop by my cabin this evening around seven, I've got something to show you." Her eyes twinkled impishly.

He gaped, then shut his jaw with a snap. "Er . . . should I bring Cawley with me?"

She shook her head. "I don't need his judgmental silence today. This rendezvous will be our secret. Consider *Babett's Modern Manners* on hold for about an hour."

This feels like a trap. Or maybe a miracle? "Are you sure that's proper and all?"

She guffawed, throwing back her head and shaking so hard he thought her tiny pith helmet might go sailing off into the clouds. "I'm not sure at all. Maybe it's the champagne talking. Maybe I'm overtired from talking to too many versions of me. But, right now, I feel like you're the only person on this ship who truly understands me."

It's a miracle, definitely a miracle. "I'll be there."

"Of course you will," she grinned. "Now, this glass won't fill itself, will it?"

He was back by her side with a chilled bottle of champagne before she had time to change her mind.

Chapter 18: The Aetherscope

Constance stood alone in the center of her cabin, gazing at herself in the aetherscope mirror. The Constance staring back at her wore the same explorer's outfit she did. Her tiny white pith helmet was tilted at the same jaunty angle. An adorable gray kitten snoozed on the alcove bed behind the other Constance, in the exact same spot where, in this world, Boo was snoring off two plates of the scientists' charcuterie.

Across the dimensions, a knock sounded on two cabin doors. "Enter," called out both Constance and her alternate self, each turning their heads to see who would enter.

As Cawley walked into her other self's cabin carrying a tea tray, Constance grinned at her almost-handsome cowboy visitor. Trusdale was dressed in his least offensive all-black ensemble. A Western-cut frock coat, lariat tie, silk shirt, svelte waistcoat, and wool pants complemented his bespoke boots embroidered with silver airships. In his hands, he carried a champagne bottle and a pair of cut crystal glasses that oozed sophistication over alternate Cawley's mundane teacups.

Constance clapped her hands with glee. "I win," she said, glancing back at her alternate self's shocked face. Her other self pouted as her version of Cawley passed behind her, heading for the iron bistro table.

Trusdale frowned. "Are you well? Why are you . . ." he stepped forward and glanced between her and the mirror's image. "What the . . . is that a cat?"

"Is that a cowboy?" asked alternate Constance. "And no chaperone? You're a wild woman."

Alternate Cawley turned, saw Trusdale, and dropped his tea tray with a crash. Awoken by the sound, Boo barked at the cat with the ferocity of a Doberman pinscher.

"Boo, be quiet," said Constance to the yapping Yorkie as Welli shot into the cabin with a riding crop raised in his right hand.

"What's happening?" shouted Welli, staring wildly around the cabin. "Are we under attack? Is it sky pirates?" From his untucked pink silk shirt, bare feet, and crumpled linen pants, it appeared he'd been woken up by other Cawley's tea tray. He stared into the mirror. The other Constance waved at him. "Cousin Wellington. I haven't seen you in years. You've made it out of debtor's prison in your dimension then. Good for you. Third time lucky, eh?"

Welli blinked and lowered the riding crop and stared between the two Constances. "Like one wasn't enough to handle. Explain yourself, dear cousin. My Constance, that is, not you, Lady Phantasmagoria."

"Don't call her that. She's another me, in a world very similar to ours. Some of the other me's in other dimensions with whom I've chatted have been most strange. One poor girl was entirely preoccupied with seaweed scrapbooks. Another had willingly entered a convent. And in some dimensions, I don't exist at all. Imagine a world without me in it."

"Sounds like heaven," said Welli. "Is whatever it is you're doing safe?"

"No, it isn't," said Trusdale. "But your cousin here thinks it's the only way to stop RATT."

Constance in the mirror gasped. "Gosh, the same tweed-jacketed thugs who murdered poor Papa? I have his mummified corpse on display in the dining room back at the Hall. I feel this way he can still be part of the festivities on special occasions. You know, a paper crown at Christmas, a party hat at New Years. I make a special effort on his birthday. I— What are you doing?"

Constance twiddled with the remote control she'd fashioned to interface with the copper mirror. The Enigma Key, locked into the triangular socket at the bottom of the copper mirror, went from giving off a blue glow to a white one.

"There. The sound is off. My apologies for the other Constance's peculiar antics. It seems I'm not quite as down-to-earth in other dimensions as I am here." She frowned. "Why are you both staring at me like I'm out of order? I'm practicing science, not magic. As men of the world, surely you can see what I'm trying to accomplish here?"

Welli said, "Why don't you enlighten me." He stared at the two glasses and champagne bottle in Trusdale's hands. "And before you even try to suggest it, Constance, a Cawley in another dimension does not count as a legitimate chaperone for you and your friend here."

Trusdale stammered, "I . . . er . . . that is, I was just . . ."

Welli narrowed his eyes at Trusdale. "I can imagine what you were just. Follow *Babett's* rules, sir, or you and I shall come to fisticuffs. And that's not a threat I make lightly."

Constance groaned. "Oh, for heaven's sake, Welli. I merely invited Mr. Trusdale here to show him some science in action. There's nothing untoward going on."

Visibly disappointed to hear it, Trusdale walked over to the bistro table and put down the champagne. An unopened letter addressed in a fine copperplate hand lay on the table.

"Ignore that," said Constance. "A passenger pigeon dropped it off this morning. It's part of some horrendous joke someone's playing on me. But I'm not laughing, and I'm certainly not playing along."

Welli strode over to the table and picked up the letter. "This looks like . . . no, it couldn't be. Auntie Annabella used to write in the exact same style. She even had her own way of writing the letter C, with a tiny flower on the curl at the end. I've never seen anyone else do that. And look, there's her signature peacock sitting on the swirl of the *H*."

"Don't open it," said Constance. "Whoever sent it is mocking my loss. They're pretending to be Mama."

Trusdale and Welli both glanced up at the portrait of Constance's mother above the fireplace.

"It's the fifth such letter I've received. The first was delivered to Auntie Madge's château. But the others have been dropped here by carrier pigeon at irregular intervals. I'm supposed to believe that my long-lost mother is alive and well and living in Stockholm as a prisoner of King Oscar. She's allegedly locked in a tower, where she's persuaded a disgruntled courtier to slip out her notes to me, all written on pages that are missing from my own copy of *Babett's Modern Manners*. Let me ask you this: If she is being given envelopes to address, why doesn't she have notepaper? Her lack of stationery is suspect. I don't for one minute believe that—Welli, no, don't."

Welli tore open the envelope and read the handwriting sprawled across a torn printed page. "These torn pages directly correlate with tears in your own book? How long have your pages been missing?"

"For as long as I can remember. This book has always missed ten pages, which I always assumed Papa used as scrap paper. He was a devil for such things."

"He was a devil, period," said Welli. "This message says you're not to try and rescue her."

"No fear. I don't believe a word written in those letters. It's clearly an elaborate hoax."

Welli and Trusdale exchanged glances.

"What?" she asked, not wanting to hear their answer.

Trusdale cleared his voice. "But, what if . . . bear with me now, what if it this message truly is from her?"

"She calls you Nutmeg, Connie. Only a handful of people on this earth know that's her pet name for you," said Welli.

"And an infinitesimal number of people across all dimensions who also know my nickname. It's shockingly hard to keep a secret in the multiverse. Whatever I know, one of the other me's knows, and vice versa. This entire situation has given me the worst migraine." She rubbed her forehand with a hand that seemed even paler than was required for a fine lady. As white as a page torn from a book. "This endeavor is making me feel quite ill."

"How many of these worlds have you communicated with? Are the physical effects worse the more you do it?" asked Trusdale.

Constance sighed. "I suppose they are. But spare me your lectures; this is a short-term problem, after all. I'm inching closer to finding the correct Haltwhistle Hall, complete with the British Museum's treasures still intact. At first, I thought just any alternate Hall would do, but it seems that our collection of artifacts was unique. Curse my father for getting his hands on the best loot in the cosmos. Do you want to see the map of Enigma Keys that Daphnia and I have managed to create?"

Constance touched her fingertips to her temples and drew a triangle on her mental blackboard.

Daphnia instantly shimmered the mirror's image into a view of the planet Earth from the surface of the moon.

Welli and Trusdale gasped, leaning in to see the blue planet slowly turning in the darkness of space.

Across the globe, a dozen or so twinkles of purple light winked up at the stars. Constance pointed at the map.

"Those purple specks are Enigma Keys across our world. In time, I hope to rescue them all. But for now, I'm focusing on the ones in Europe. I'll show you how everything works. First, I'll ask Daphnia to show us her own location."

The image in the mirror swirled. Through clouds, a blue outline of the *Lady Penelope* as viewed from above appeared. Inside the line drawing, Daphnia twinkled as a purple speck.

Trusdale whistled. "That's amazing. How does it know where it is? Can it see?"

"*She* is able to see a three-dimensional model of our world, updated in real time. When the bubble fleet exploded millennia ago, one of the Enigma Keys was blasted up onto the surface of the moon. That Key appears to be able to relay limited information to the other Keys. Imagine the tragedy of it. It's like your family members are scattered all over the globe, and you can send each other postcards, but you can't afford the postage for a long letter. So, they communicate in these limited bites of information, but can't truly converse at length as we can here in this cabin."

Constance drew a circle in the air with her finger. "To illuminate the technical aspects of this process, Daphnia drew something on my mental blackboard that looked like a big ball of string or wool. One can only assume that the creatures trapped inside the Keys enjoy crochet or perhaps knitting. Maybe knit one, purl one, allows them to chat just as we use morse code to send telegrams?"

Welli grimaced. "Ugh. Science is positively ludicrous. The more I hear about it, the less I like it. Can you please backtrack for a moment? What do you mean by bubble craft?"

"I'll fill you in later," said Trusdale.

Welli cradled his head in his hands and groaned. "I should have stayed in bed."

"And miss all this fun? Now, if we back up a little . . ." Constance prompted Daphnia. A small outline of the *Lady Penelope* appeared on the left side of the mirror and on the right, a purple twinkle of the Key at the Vatican sparked in an outline of Italy's boot-like shape.

"What's that?" asked Trusdale, pointing at a red dot that flashed on and off just to the left of the *Lady Penelope*'s outline.

Constance frowned. "Oh, it's back, is it? Daphnia and I can't quite work out if it's an echo of her own form, or some kind of anomaly. Daphnia tried to send it a mental postcard, but her message was returned to sender."

Trusdale stood and walked to one of the two brass portholes that flanked the mirror. "You know, I've had the feeling that we were being followed for quite some time.

I think I sometimes see a glitter of . . . something . . . in the sky behind us."

Welli groaned. "So, we're being followed by a red dot? What does that even mean?"

Constance shrugged. "It could be dirt on the cosmic lens, for all I know."

"Maybe it's a really big seagull," said Welli. "Or a boat, somewhere below us in the ocean?"

"We're getting sidetracked. This is the important matter," she pointed at the blue outline of Italy. "See that purple twinkle in Rome? If Daphnia could focus right there . . ." She chatted with the giant alien water flea via her mental blackboard. "And *voilà.* There's a bird's-eye outline of the city, with the Key sitting in the old Papal Observatory at the Gregorian Tower, also known locally as the Tower of the Winds, a name they pilfered from an ancient meteorological station in Athens. Sadly, Daphnia only seems to be able to show us the outline of the building's roof, not the layout within. But I'm sure once we get there, I'll figure things out."

Further impressive displays of her collaboration with Daphnia ended prematurely when a wave of nausea swept over Constance. Beads of cold sweat trickled down her spine. It appeared her body didn't share her confidence in her mental abilities.

Blood pounded in her ears and her head felt oddly light as she studied the large red heart that Daphnia had drawn on her mental blackboard. Constance heaved several deep breaths, braced herself against the nausea, and drew a heart on the board. *Thank you for the love, Daphnia. This entire escapade is beyond exhausting. There's a thousand million other me's out there, but I've never felt so alone. Only I can save my family and friends. Only I can . . .*

She stopped midsentence, suddenly noticing that Trusdale and Welli were staring at her as if she were a madwoman. Had she been mouthing words to herself while she communicated with Daphnia? The gray line between telepathy, speaking, and control of her face was becoming more blurred by the moment. Something of her pain must have shown on her face, because Welli's stare softened.

He said, "Constance, I think you should get some rest. Your skin is as gray as ash. I think that all this science is sapping your strength. Maybe stop your experiments for tonight, at least. I'm going up on deck for a breath of fresh air. The carousing at Versailles took its toll on my body, and I certainly don't want to arrive in Rome looking like a wraith." He said pointedly to Trusdale, "Well, roomie, you look like you might need to leave and take a breather on deck too, don't you think? Otherwise I'll have to hunt down Cawley to sit in with you two."

Trusdale stood and stretched theatrically. "Good call, Lord Pendelroy. Fresh air and a stroll round the deck is exactly what I need right now. Good night, Constance. Maybe put a blanket over that mirror while you sleep. Who knows who might be watching you from other worlds."

Her breath caught. "Heavens, I hadn't thought about that. And I've been naked in here more times than I can remember."

Trusdale's cheeks flushed.

Welli groaned. "I wonder if the pages missing from your *Babett's* covered not talking about being naked in mixed company."

She blushed. "Sorry. Truly, I'm so very, very sorry for everything."

As the men left, she wriggled a coverlet out from beneath Boo and walked over to the mirror to cover it. She hung the blanket over one corner, then paused.

Could someone be spying on me? If so, could I catch them in the act?

It was time to see who else was out there in the multiverse, other than herself.

Infinity was waiting for her call.

Chapter 19:
When in Rome

Of all the world's great cities, Gunter Erhard hated Rome the most. He and his three Swedish henchmen had shadowed Constance and her party of misfits through countless picturesque piazzas. With every step he took, Erhard cursed the fiery redhead as he was forced to travel down paths he'd long sought to forget.

The Eternal City mocked him with its towering architecture, magnificent monuments, graceful fountains, and romantic ruins.

Was there anything more depressing than the Sistine Chapel's gloriously colorful frescoes? How nauseating was the Baroque splendor of the Trevi Fountain? And how utterly awful was it to walk through the masonry corridors that had in ancient times supported the wooden arena floor of the Colosseum?

Here, decades ago, under the light of the midnight moon, he'd fought a fateful duel up and down these haunted passageways. A fight for the hand of his dear Sophie, his sword's namesake, the only woman he'd ever loved. He heaved a sigh as he trailed behind Constance through the Colosseum's underworld. In a lifetime spent fighting other men for reasons both good and bad, why was it always women who caused him the most pain? How had Lady Nay become his nemesis in what was supposedly a patriarchal world? How had she learned to shine in Oscar's court, while his sun had slowly set?

His mind drifted back to the early days of her arrival. Once upon a time, Lady Nay, a noblewoman from a colony with a name no one could remember, had sought to win favor by entertaining the court with fantastical tales about exploring other worlds and dimensions. Always painting herself as the bold heroine, she spoke of traveling in a giant bubble to strange locales, some of which were populated by alternate versions of the courtiers. How she'd made Oscar and his courtiers laugh as she told lurid tales about these doppelgängers. She would colorfully describe how a bon vivant courtier in this world lived the life of a humble priest in one dimension and a notorious cat burglar in another. She spared no one with her characterizations, drawing guffaws and tears from her captivated audience. Such was her storytelling power, it was almost as if she'd seen these alternate beings through a magic window, spying on them to learn their darkest secrets and most hidden fantasies.

He could see her now, standing on a banquet table in a gold gossamer ball gown, her dark hair tumbling in loose waves down to her waist, enthralling Oscar and his court with a tale of passion. Her commanding voice compelled all within earshot to listen to every word that dropped from her ruby lips. With a vixen's smile she said, "My lords, ladies, and servants, the grass is always greener in another dimension. Imagine if you will our own Colonel of Skullduggery and Mayhem, Gunter Erhard, existing in a world in which he fights a secret duel in the Colosseum's shadowy catacombs for the hand of his lady love, Sophie. At a fateful moment, sweet Sophie throws herself between the two warriors, begging them to cease their quarrel, but alas, Erhard cannot stop the thrust of his blade."

The crowd gasped, turning their heads to see his reaction to her words. Seeking to spare Erhard further pain, King Oscar injected gruffly, "That's enough, Lady Nay."

"But let me finish, Your Majesty," she said, already willing to disregard the King she'd sworn to admire. "The wound he gives his lady love is but a flesh wound. He nurses her back to health, and they marry in Rome. The birth of five children—four sons and one girl—makes their loving circle complete in a gorgeous villa overlooking Erhard's very own vineyard. And they all lived happily ever after."

"Hurrah!" cheered the crowd, as Erhard gripped the hilt of his sword and stared daggers at Lady Nay. The corner of her perfect lips curled into a sneer.

How could she know?

Oscar stood, quieting the crowd. "That's enough fantasy for one day, Lady Nay. Erhard, with me."

They'd left the feast hall together, walking for hours through the portrait-laden halls of Stockholm Palace, the King and his liege. It was Oscar who had given him purpose as he'd wandered Europe, a broken man, after his dueling blade had pierced Sophie's heart. She'd bled out in his arms, murmuring forgiveness for his sins. Years of despair followed, until an old friend brought him to Sweden to give fencing lessons to the King's grandson. Oscar had been impressed by his skill with a sword, and moved by his tragic tale. He'd invited Erhard to join his court, back then a kinder and wiser place than before Nay's poison seeped into every soul.

But Erhard had lost his soul the night Sophie died. Nay's lies didn't twist his mind the way they did the King's. Was it through her machinations that Constance

Haltwhistle had come to Rome, perhaps to torture him with sights and sounds he longed to forget? Sometimes, he almost felt sorry for Constance. What sin had she committed to be such an object of fascination to Lady Nay? Then again, both women were nightmares in their own way. They were two peas in the same pod, two thorns in his side, two problems he had to solve before he could move to save his king. Good King Oscar still lived within the frail husk of a man he'd become under Nay's influence.

And only Erhard could save him. Even if it meant committing darker deeds than he'd ever thought he was capable of.

Erhard kept as many crowd members as he dared between himself and his future kidnap victim, the oblivious Constance Haltwhistle. Fortunately, her red hair flashed in the sun like a beacon, drawing him ever on through the Hypogeum's stone passageways.

His heart raw from remembering Sophie's death, he ground his teeth at Constance's obvious delight in touring the Colosseum's gladiator pits. She hung, wide-eyed, on every word offered by her local tour guide about bloody battles fought and won in this place to amuse the ancient Romans. What problems could trouble this girl, sashaying along in her explorer's outfit beside her rakish cousin with two servants trailing in her wake?

Her life, next to his, seemed to have been blessed. Behind her servants trailed the strange cowboy, Trusdale. He always walked in the center of the straggled-out crew of the *Lady Penelope* without ever looking as if he was part of the group. His leather duster was an inappropriate wardrobe choice given the intense sun that blazed overhead. What was the American hiding in the pockets of that heavy overcoat that he didn't want to leave back on the airship?

Doctors Chauhan and Huang lagged behind Trusdale, pointing at the stone walls, apparently discussing the structural genius of the amphitheater's design. They were the last of the *Lady Penelope*'s crew to remain on the walking tour. The Singhs had long since retreated to the airship docks. This suggested that the Haltwhistle rabble was not intending to stay in Rome for too long.

Good riddance to them. Once he'd grabbed Constance, where the remaining crew went was of no consequence. Although, he wouldn't mind garroting Trusdale if he had the chance. After all, the tall American had been instrumental in sending his former employer, Prince Lucien, off to rot in the Tower of London for treason.

He'd served as Lucien's right-hand man for years, egging him on to try and take his grandmother Queen Victoria's crown. Yet the prince never realized that Erhard's true master had always been King Oscar. *Who's the fool now, Lucien? How does it feel to be brought to your knees by a red-haired debutante and a wandering cowboy? And their scientist friends over there certainly played a part. Perhaps I should take revenge on the whole bally lot of them for thwarting our plot to assassinate Queen Victoria?* All he'd have to do is plant a bomb on the *Lady Penelope*. But the crew's suffering then would be merely physical. What could he take from them that would tug on their heartstrings, other than Constance herself? Perhaps the Yorkie puppy they all appeared to dote on? A dognapping would surely stick a knife into their collective hearts. What could hurt more than losing a pet who loves unconditionally?

He took a deep breath of the Colosseum's acrid air. A life of villainy was truly laborious. Ordinary folk never appreciated how much work went into orchestrating evil. The fact that he still knew wrong from right made his choices all the more exhausting. If only he could live inside the morally gray headspace that Lars, Johan, and Ludwig inhabited. How much easier life must be when the blame for your darkest deeds could be laid squarely at the feet of those who ordered you to commit them.

A flash of copper hair ahead as Constance glanced back over her shoulder prompted him to bolt to the passageway's wall, hoping to blend into the sunbaked stone. In retrospect, perhaps he should have left his ostrich-plumed hat back on his airship? He whipped off his hat and stuffed it under his armpit.

To his surprise, four of the half dozen or so unknown tourists who were strung out between him and Constance's crew also darted to the side of the passage. The quartet of stout women in bustled khaki traveling gowns, each holding a carpet bag, huddled together over a crumpled map. They kept glancing toward Constance as they conspired together.

That's odd.

Erhard turned to view the passageway behind him. Past the bowed heads and clasped hands of Johan, Lars, and Ludwig, each shrouded in one of the red velvet hooded cloaks favored by cardinals at that time of year, a trio of young women skulked suspiciously by the wall. Dressed in sumptuous jewel-toned silk gowns cinched with gold-embroidered over-corsets, the fashionistas were pretending to exchange calling cards, despite seeming to know one another.

They, too, kept glancing toward Constance as she resumed her stroll along the corridor, cocking her head to listen to her tour guide's ringing voice describe gladiatorial combat in gruesome detail.

Even odder. Seven women in two separate groups, following Constance Haltwhistle through the Colosseum. How long have they been on her tail?

That wasn't all, though. A silver-haired woman with eyes colder than a glacier framed by steel-rimmed glasses strode along the passageway at a brisk pace surprising for one of her years. She carried a silver-tipped sword cane with a casual ease that unnerved him.

An eighth woman. And of all the ladies, this grandmother appears to be the deadliest.

It was time to professionally dawdle. Erhard leaned back against the rough stone wall of the passageway and made a dramatic show of mopping his brow. As Constance's party moved on, the curious collection of women and his own cloaked cardinals padded along behind her. Erhard brought up the rear behind the well-armed grandmother, studying the backs of the women before him. *Are these operatives sent by Lady Nay to thwart my operation? Or has Lady Haltwhistle been making brand-new enemies as she travels through Europe? Or both?*

He gritted his teeth. Nothing was ever easy where women were concerned. He'd rather face an army of men any day. Men knew how to keep things simple.

Ahead, a four-way junction in the passageway loomed.

Constance's guide pointed to the right corridor, far narrower than the other three.

Good. Now I'll see how accomplished all those following the Haltwhistle girl are at their craft. As the crew of the *Lady Penelope* turned right, the four women in their khaki travel gowns conferred, and closely followed Constance and her crew. If any crew members looked back, they were sure to spot the women. Erhard snorted. *Amateurs.*

His own men wordlessly split up and took the other three corridors, no doubt intending to circle back when their shadowing of the crew would be less noticeable. As leader, he would be expected to stay on Constance's tail. *Professionals. Good.*

The trio of silk-dressed fashionistas also split up, two following his cardinals, and one following Constance at a distance. *Skilled professionals. Interesting.*

Somehow, he'd lost the grandmother. He spun on his heel, and there she was, pretending to read a map she'd whipped out of some hidden pocket. *Dear God, who is she?*

He turned and strolled on as nonchalantly as he could. For almost a minute, the grandmother kept an even pace behind him, and then . . . silence.

He glanced back over his shoulder to check her progress.

The passageway was empty.

Despite the heat, Erhard shivered.

Chapter 20:
The Tower of the Winds

T rusdale gazed up at the grand dome of Saint Peter's Basilica, looming like a curious giant over the honeyed stone buildings surrounding the Belvedere Courtyard. The sun beat down from an azure sky and sweat flowed down his spine like the Tiber River. Not for the first time this day, he cursed his prized coat for its cocoon-like warmth. He felt the weight of God's dossier on the Brass Queen tucked inside one of the coat's secret pockets. Sharing a cabin with Welli meant that he hadn't had any time alone to destroy the pages. He'd tried keeping them under his mattress, but Mr. Singh had a habit of making military-corner beds whenever Welli left the cabin.

During this exhausting day of guerrilla sightseeing, he'd made four attempts to fling the secret dossier into the Tiber; twice he'd tried to burn it, and once he'd attempted to feed it to a particularly hungry cart horse. Every time, his skullduggery had been interrupted by a member of the *Lady Penelope*'s crew. Constance had even gone so far as to purchase a large bunch of carrots from a passing vendor to help him feed the starving horse. Following a shouting match with the wretched animal's owner, she'd purchased both the horse and cart and sent them off with the servants to join the happy ranks of Haltwhistle Hall's remaining farm animals.

A menagerie of prize ponies, cows, pigs, and sheep called the spacious hold of the *Lady Penelope* home. Perhaps one day, Constance would be able to reunite them with the verdant fields of Yorkshire. Until then, the animals lived a supremely comfortable life. When the airship docked in port they enjoyed excursions to lush local pastures and fresh air when traveling, courtesy of the airship's open gunport hatches. The camouflaged hatches, historically opened only when air pirates foolish enough to consider attacking the flying galleon needed a few cannonballs launched their way, now whimsically served as sightseeing perches for two dozen Cochin chickens.

The majority of the crew had been delighted to return to the cool confines of the airship, worn out by their thrilling grand tour of Rome's magnificent attractions. Only Trusdale himself, Welli, and Constance had made it to the final leg of the tour. He and Welli were grimy with dust from the city streets. Somehow, Constance seemed to repel the dirt, almost as if she emanated a negative form of static electricity that refused to be filthy.

Above her pristine explorer's outfit, the late afternoon sunlight kissed her hair, burnishing the soft waves like a new copper penny. She cocked her head like an adorable Irish Setter puppy as their superb Vatican tour guide waxed lyrical about the history and architecture of the Papal Palace.

Constance caught him staring and shot him a sly wink. With a mischievous grin, she pointed up at the square stone tower rising before them. This was her not-so-discreet signal that they'd finally reached the resting place of the second Enigma Key. According to Daphnia, the Key was somewhere in the Gregorian Tower, a scientific landmark at the Vatican since the sixteenth century. Also known by the more romantic name, the *Torre dei Venti*, the Tower of the Winds housed an early anemoscope used to determine the direction of the wind. The tower also boasted frescoes of the celestial heavens, a science museum, and an astrological library.

A weathered bronze observatory dome dominated the roof of the square tower. According to their guide, the

Tower of the Winds had originally been commissioned by Pope Gregory XIII to determine whether the Julian calendar was accurate. A sunbeam cast through a pinhole in the tower wall lit upon a meridian line set into the floor, indicating that the ancient calendar was ten days off. The new Gregorian calendar was subsequently adopted by most of the world and was still in use.

"So, this tower is science incarnate," said Constance to their latest, and by far their greatest, tour guide, Sister Teresa of the Adoration of the Holy Heavens.

The elderly Sister beamed. "*Sì, signorina Haltwhistle.*" She was a gentle scholar-nun with tortoiseshell spectacles, a traditional black-and-white habit, and a specialist understanding of astronomy. Constance had discussed various arts and sciences with the whip-smart Sister throughout their tour, and the two women had clearly connected on a deep level.

Trusdale smiled to himself. This was a side of Constance he rarely saw except when she was with Maya. Given the opportunity, he'd like to learn more about the subject of Constance from A to Z, with extra credit. She was a topic he would surely never find boring, even if she was at times bewildering, if not downright baffling.

Sister Teresa concluded her oratory about the Tower of the Wind's history. "It is the most fascinating site, and it pains me to share that I will not be able to take you inside this wonderful building." Teresa's voice carried a warm, musical intonation that made even a negative statement sound pleasing. "Sadly, you will never be able to see the wonderful frescoes or peruse the books and artifacts in the astrological library and museum. The curator is not fond of nonecclesiastical visitors, and he guards the knowledge held within these walls most jealously. I've heard even Pope Luke himself had to be quite stern with the curator in order to gain the key to the observatory dome. It is rumored that the Pope has now adopted the dome as his private sanctuary for stargazing and solitary prayer."

Uh-oh. That's going to be a problem.

Constance nodded. "Of course, I absolutely understand."

She does? Since when has Constance been understanding about being thwarted?

Constance continued, "And thank you for a most enlightening tour. I believe I speak for myself, Lord Pendelroy, and Mr. Trusdale here when I say how appreciative we are for your time."

That's true.

Constance heaved a heavy sigh. "I only wish my gentleman-scientist father could have been here to hear your fascinating tour. I know he always loved visiting Vatican City, and he had nothing but praise for the research

conducted by your fine order. I hope that his many dona-
tions to your convent have helped you to continue your
studies. He always said that the Sisters of the Adoration
of the Holy Heavens were the finest, if most underappre-
ciated, scholars in the city."

Sister Teresa chuckled and pushed her spectacles up
her nose. "I had the pleasure of meeting Baron Haltwhistle a decade or so ago. Of all our celestial library's
visitors, he's the one most difficult to forget. Quite . . .
how do you say . . . larger than life? He made a huge
stir in the special archives, the *Archivum Secretum Apos-
tolicum Vaticanum*. Many rare and important historical
documents are kept there. The Baron claimed he could
tell that one of our most prized documents was a fake!
It was the letter that Henry VIII sent to Pope Clement
VII petitioning for the annulment of his marriage to
Catherine of Aragon. By coincidence, the Baron had
just invented a method of testing the authenticity of
wax seals."

Trusdale's internal alarm bells sounded as Constance
adopted a pose of wide-eyed innocence. She said to the
nun, "Heavens, what a stroke of luck. And did the ar-
chive staff let Papa test the document?"

Sister Teresa's gray eyebrows rose. "Why, yes, he was
allowed to test a dozen or so of the wax seals attached to
the document in an anteroom off the main library. To

the relief of all, his experiment proved that the letter was genuine."

"How fascinating," simpered Constance. "I recall Papa had his own copy of that same document. For reasons known only to himself, he was obsessed with Tudor documents. His interest might have been stirred by the fact that Elizabeth the First bestowed many fine gifts upon our ancestors. The most precious was a fabulous stained-glass window that Mr. Trusdale happened to break."

Trusdale gaped as the nun peered over her glasses at him disapprovingly. Burned forever into his memory, the decorative window at Haltwhistle Hall had been a true work of art. In glorious stained glass, a rearing unicorn mare, free of chains and rider, had balanced upon a Tudor rose. He held up his hands in protest. "Hey, I swear that window breaking wasn't my fault. One of Constance's crazy maids used an incendiary pistol to blast a heat ray straight through it. I just happened to be standing nearby when the glass exploded."

Sister Teresa tut-tutted at Trusdale. He hung his head. Even Episcopalians could be mortified by Catholic nuns at the drop of a hat. Shame was their superpower.

Constance said, "Of course, Haltwhistle Hall was full of many important historical artifacts, most of which Mr. Trusdale didn't see fit to destroy. For instance, in Papa's library, he displays a facsimile of that same letter from Henry VIII to the Pope. If you put that document side by side with the real thing in your library, I'm sure you'd be hard-pressed to tell them apart."

Where is she going with this?

She continued, "I'm currently on an important mission regarding the Hall. Should it be successful, I would be able to send that facsimile to you, so that you may compare the two letters, just to make sure that Papa didn't make any silly mistakes when he was testing your version. I have the feeling that he may have used his copy as part of the test."

Sister Teresa blinked. "Well, I am intrigued. I'm sure the Sisters would love to examine this document. You don't think that he managed to mix them up . . .?"

"Gosh, probably not. But he could be a little scatterbrained at times." Constance seemed to be waiting to see how badly Teresa wanted her copy of the letter.

Is she trying to tempt a nun? Heaven help us all.

Teresa shook her head. "As curious as I am about your letter, signorina, and I truly am, without the facsimile in hand, I do not believe I will be able to persuade the curator to leave the tower. I would need . . . more."

The nun smiled angelically. *And the score is Italy one, England zero.*

"Of course," said Constance diplomatically. "Not to worry. If it is physically possible for me to do so, I vow

I will send you the letter anyway, as a thank you for this tour."

"You are most gracious, signorina."

"It's the least I can do. Although . . ." Constance held her index finger in the air as if something new and startling had occurred to her. "Didn't you mention earlier that the Sisters of the Adoration of the Holy Heavens convent roof was in dire need of repair? I am sadly unable to access the mounds of treasure that fill Haltwhistle Hall's medieval cellars, but it just so happens that my cousin Welli here recently came into some monies."

Welli blanched and stared at Constance in alarm. *His gambling winnings from Versailles.* The young lord had paid off his debtors and was sitting on enough money to buy a small palace of his own.

Constance avoided making eye contact with her cousin as she said, "It occurs to me that we could use Welli's good fortune to make a generous donation to your fund."

The Sister joined her hands in prayer to show her gratitude. "Your gift will be most appreciated by my humble order."

Constance's grin widened. "Wonderful. I could write you a promissory note right here, in the square. Although . . . gosh, I would feel so much more comfortable doing so indoors, out of the sun. If I could be comfortably seated in say, this tower's astrological library, with a chair, a pen, and a piece of paper, I'm positive that my contribution to the fund could only be increased by my comfort."

And it's official. We're trying to bribe a nun. He could almost feel the flames of hell licking at his heels.

The Sister nodded thoughtfully but did not appear shocked. It seemed Sister Teresa had a practical streak when it came to helping her fellow nuns.

"Hmm. Would it be fair to assume, signorina, that, out here, in the blazing sun, you could write a promissory note for . . . ten percent of the roof?"

Welli licked his lips and stared at his cousin.

"Absolutely. But at a desk, well, maybe twenty percent?" said Constance.

The Sister pursed her lips. "A fair number, but I think, maybe, a desk is worth forty percent?"

Constance nodded. "An interesting thought, Sister. Perhaps if I was allowed to sit quietly at that desk alone, for say, thirty minutes, then I'm sure I will be able to gather my strength to write a promissory note for that exact amount."

Welli blurted out, "That's . . . *incredibly* generous of you, Constance. I'm sure the Sister isn't interested in—"

Sister Teresa held up her hand to silence him. "On the contrary, Lord Pendelroy, I believe Baroness Haltwhistle and I have reached an understanding." She studied

Constance. "Provided that you swear not to remove any books or documents from the library, I will do my very best to secure you thirty minutes at a desk, alone, to write an eloquent promissory note for a full one hundred percent of the roof repair fund. I will even try to arrange for a cushion for your chair."

Constance clapped her hands with glee. "Splendid. I wholeheartedly agree to your terms. I'm delighted that we can contribute to your worthy cause."

The Sister wagged her finger at Constance. "You swear you will remove no books, no documents."

"You have my word," Constance placed her hand on her heart and bowed her head.

Because it's an Enigma Key she's after. Well played, Constance. Your Papa would be proud. Sounds like he had sticky fingers, too.

The nun fixed Constance with a stern look that made the redhead squirm. "Your oath is sacred, signorina. Do not give it lightly. Now, if you will all please excuse me, I must prepare the custodian of this tower for your entry. He is a difficult man. This may take some time." Sister Teresa walked to the tower's studded oak door and rang an ancient brass bell hanging beside it. Moments later, the door was opened by a scowling monk, and she swept inside.

Welli folded his arms. "Would you like the shirt off my back too, cousin?"

Constance pursed her lips. "Didn't you say I should be more altruistic?"

"Not with my money, I didn't."

"You would have only wasted it on what I shall euphemistically refer to as good living."

Welli scoffed. "Like you're one to judge. And what's this about the Baron 'testing' church documents? It's clear that your Papa stole Henry VIII's letter and put a fake in its place. The apple doesn't fall far from the tree, does it, Constance?"

She flushed. "I'm returning that letter."

"Only so you can pinch something else."

"Well!" Constance's cheeks flamed into a vibrant magenta. "Now look here—"

Trusdale chopped his hand in the air between the two cousins as if separating boxers in a ring. "That's enough. You two have been sniping at each other all day, and I fear that it's my fault. Ever since I went alone to Constance's cabin—"

The cousins gaped at him, then hit him with a double-barreled blast of indignation.

Constance said, "We're arguing about money, and you had to add our last altercation to the mix? Why would you even—"

"—bring that up? Can't we have one fight at a time? We're talking about Constance's irresponsibility with my money, not her lack of decorum in inviting you to her cabin," said Welli.

"Which Welli had almost forgotten about—"

"Which I hadn't forgotten about at all. I just don't have the energy to be angry at her about everything at the same time. My god, who has the energy to deal with all this?" He waved his hand up and down Constance. "Except, maybe, you?"

Trusdale's cheeks burned. "Now, hold on, I'm only trying to help."

"Yes, it's a bad habit of yours. Please desist if you can," said Welli. He rubbed his temples. "Life's too short to spend it quarreling. Let's all just agree that no one donates my money to anything without asking me first."

"Agreed," said Constance and Trusdale in unison. Their eyes connected, and a shared smile thrilled Trusdale down to his toes.

Welli rolled his eyes. "I can't take much more of this day. Let's hope the good Sister does our dirty work fast."

Over Welli's shoulder, a movement on the far side of Belvedere Courtyard caught Trusdale's eye. Across the vast expanse of the courtyard's clipped lawn crisscrossed with gravel paths, four stout ladies in identical khaki travel gowns and straw boater hats observed their group with interest. A distinguished matron with salt-and-pepper hair pinned up beneath her hat was writing notes in a journalist's notepad. By her side, a pretty brunette squinted through opera glasses toward their party. A middle-aged motherly sort was pretending to read an upside-down Italian newspaper. The fourth woman, her black hair slicked back into a tight bun, stood with her arms folded across her broad chest. She appeared to be guarding four large carpet bags set upon the ground. Her physique reminded Trusdale of Hearn, if the coachman hid a secret penchant for wearing petticoats, puffy-sleeved twill gowns, and boater hats.

Trusdale chewed his lip. There was something familiar about the women. Had he seen them before at the Colosseum? And maybe three or four places before that? It was possible that the four ladies had chosen the same route as the crew of the *Lady Penelope* through the main tourist spots. But for them to be here, at the Tower of the Winds, suggested their presence was more than a coincidence. There were no other tourists in sight, only three hooded cardinals in red velvet robes. The exceptionally tall trio of holy men slowly made their way down the square's center path with their heads bowed and their hands clasped in prayer.

Trusdale murmured from the corner of his mouth to Welli and Constance, "Those ladies over there. I think they might be following us. No, don't look . . ."

Both cousins turned to stare at the women.

Trusdale groaned. "What did I just say? All right, you two wait here for the Sister to return. I'll mosey on over and see what's up, if anything."

"It would be better if a lady handled this," said Constance.

"Oh, do you know one we can send?" Welli's tone dripped honey.

Constance screwed her nose up at him. "Stay here." She marched with the confidence of a redcoat brigadier toward their observers.

"Oh yes, I'm sure this will go swimmingly," grumbled Welli.

The four women gaped at the approaching Constance. She'd almost reached the center of the square when she bellowed to them, "Well met, ladies. Are you, by any chance, following us?"

Lord help me. Is there a subtle bone in Constance's body?

The three tall cardinals halted as Constance marched across their path toward the nonplussed women.

Great, now she's interrupting men at prayer.

In a blur of red velvet, the cardinals pounced onto Constance like cats onto a well-dressed mouse. She squeaked in surprise as one man locked an arm around her throat and yanked her backward hard, his forearm clamped tight against her jugular to cut off the blood supply to her brain. Another cardinal shoved a white handkerchief into face as her eyes bulged and she clawed at the muscular forearm of the brute holding her, twisting her head to avoid the handkerchief.

What the—Poison? Knockout drops? Acid? Trusdale sprinted toward the cardinals, but his movements felt treacle-slow as Constance writhed in her attacker's grip, lashing out with fists and boots that failed to find a mark. The handkerchief-wielding cardinal dodged her heels and stepped back, nodding at her captor to finish the job as he turned with his companion to face the oncoming Welli and Trusdale.

Constance's captor clenched his arm tight and yanked the petite redhead clear off her feet. Her boots kicked twice as if she were drowning as her eyes rolled back in her head and her body succumbed to the stranglehold. She flopped like a rag doll as the brutish cardinal tossed her with ease onto his broad shoulder and turned to make his escape.

His fellow cardinals moved to cover his retreat, their full attention fixed on the approaching Welli and Trusdale. From the wide sleeves of their robes, the drew out silver throwing axes and flung them with venom toward the two men.

Without slowing his run, Trusdale leaned to his left as an ax flashed by his cheek. He could feel the breeze from its deadly blade as it whistled by his ear. The second villain's hurled ax narrowly missed Welli, who cursed like a sky pirate. The four men collided in a flurry of strikes and kicks. Trusdale punched, connecting his fist with a nose that shattered beneath his blow. Blood as red as the cardinal's vestments splattered warm and wet across Trusdale's face as the false holy man stumbled backward, clutching his ruined nose. His hood fell back to reveal a wild-eyed blond warrior with a Viking's plaited beard.

Oh hell no. They're the thugs from the lobby at the Grand Hotel du Louvre. He warily circled the Viking, seeking an opening in the giant's long-armed boxer-style defense to take him down. Trusdale snarled, "Where's your scar-faced boss, Erhard? I wanna know whose backside I'm kickin' after I'm done with yours."

The Viking leered and said with a Swedish lilt, "He's not here, cowboy. Johan will not be the man to spill the beans, but know this. You're too late to stop Erhard's diabolical revenge."

"He has sunk too low," added his colleague in villainy. "There are lines even the damned shouldn't cross. That bitch doesn't deserve . . . ouch!" Welli landed a punch across the man's jaw. He staggered back, blocking Welli's blows as the enraged former redcoat officer threw punch after punch at his foe. "How dare you refer to Constance that way!" he yelled, landing a blow that smashed into the fake cardinal's nose with a sickening crunch.

The man staggered backward clutching at his shattered nose, blood draining down between his fingers to disappear forever into his crimson robes. He gasped and protested, as if even hired thugs held scared standards that Welli had called into question, "It was not the *lady* I meant—"

Johan darted his eyes toward his wounded colleague, "Lars!"

The split-second distraction was all the time Trusdale needed. He snapped out a kick to the Viking's right kneecap with the heel of his Western boot.

The solid blow crunched into bone. The blond giant cried out in pain and grabbed for his injured knee with both hands, leaving his chin undefended against Trusdale's knee strike. The force lifted the cardinal clean off his feet to land on his back, sprawled out like a lumpy red velvet tablecloth across the gravel path. He groaned pitifully, his hand reaching for his fractured jaw.

Lars, still clutching his own shattered nose with his left hand, took a half-hearted swing at Welli. The lanky lord dodged the blow and shoved the man with all his might. He flew backward and landed with a crunch on his back on the gravel path. The fight knocked out of him, he moaned on the floor as Welli and Trusdale turned to face the final Viking as brothers in arms.

Trusdale's jaw almost hit his boots. To his surprise, Constance's robe-clad kidnapper was still in sight at the far edge of the square. The cardinal had dropped his limp victim onto the gravel. He stood astride her crumpled body, his left arm thrown up to protect his face as he threw punches with his right fist at the four khaki-clad female observers who surrounded him.

Armed with batons they'd pulled out of who-knew-where on their persons, they methodically rained blows down upon the wildly punching cardinal with the percussive fury of women protecting their own. With the two fallen cardinals temporarily out of the fight, Trusdale and Welli ran to aid the baton-wielding women against the final foe. His hood had fallen back to reveal the third blond henchman from Constance's hotel lobby disaster. The muscular Viking launched a forceful punch at his shortest enemy, the salt-and-pepper-haired matron. She delivered precise blows bartitsu-style with her baton to the Viking's wrist and elbow as his punch failed to find its mark. He cried out in pain and nursed his damaged wrist. The fallen Constance didn't stir as he charged directly at the short matron, knocking her to the ground as he broke through the circle of twill-clad Amazons. The coward hiked up his red robe and bolted out of the square with a trio of furious warrior ladies in hot pursuit.

The brim of the fallen matron's straw boater was broken, but her spirit was strong. She pushed herself up onto her knees and scrambled over to the deathly still body of Constance. She rolled the inert aristocrat onto her back and leaned in from the left to put her ear close to the girl's unmoving chest. Lips pressed tight, the woman sat back and brushed tendrils of copper-colored hair away from Constance's corpse-white face. She placed the back of her hand onto the aristocrat's smooth forehead and grimaced. Trusdale felt his concern mounting by the second as she reached for the aristocrat's left hand and pulled off the white kidskin travel glove. She held two fingers against her patient's wrist before gently laying the limp arm across Constance's unmoving chest. The matron glanced up as Trusdale and Welli loomed over her, tears glistening in her eyes.

"She's . . . not with us," said the matron, her voice catching in her throat. "I don't know if . . . can you please bring me my carpet bag? The blue one."

Trusdale was staring at Constance's lips, as blue as any carpet bag he'd ever seen. Purple bruises were starting to bloom on her slender neck where the Cardinal's choke-hold had suffocated the life out of her. Had he intended to kill her? Was that Erhard's ultimate revenge—not an abduction, but a murder? Or had the Viking simply misjudged the strength of his hold? Constance would have been furious to learn that it was blundering incompetence that had taken her from this world.

Invisible ice seemed to hold him in place, numbing his body and soul as he gazed down at her pale face, as cold and perfect as the alabaster statues they'd admired together earlier in the day. Even those sculptures had held more life than Constance right now, her eyes closed, her lips blackening from death's final kiss. He'd seen the same pallor freeze the faces of his fallen comrades on the battlefield. He hadn't been able to save them, and he'd failed to save Constance too. While she lived, he'd felt an energy between them, a spark that warmed his heart, knowing this wonderful wild woman shared the same world as him.

Now, he could only feel her absence. A hole in space and time that she should have occupied, her laughter, wit, and power filling the space as no one else could. She was a unique jewel, flawed in her perfection, magical to the bone. Wherever she was now, he wanted to be there, by her side, helping her to face the unknown.

The matron dug through her blue carpet bag as Welli crouched beside his cousin, his face almost as pale as hers. As a former soldier, he no doubt knew as well as Trusdale that Constance had drawn her last breath. Was he crushed by the same guilt he felt at failing the girl?

The matron drew a tiny white apothecary bottle out of her carpet bag. Keeping her eyes trained on Constance, she said to Welli, "I'm Esmeralda Effingham, a former chemist's assistant, and I mean Lady Haltwhistle no harm. May I?"

Welli nodded dumbly, apparently too sunk into grief to ask how the woman knew his cousin's name.

Perhaps it didn't matter anymore?

Perhaps nothing would ever matter again. Bands of iron seemed to contract around his chest as he fought to hold in a sob that would have torn his heart asunder.

Esmeralda pulled the cork stopper out of the bottle and slid her hand beneath Constance's head. With a mother's care, she tilted up the young aristocrat's head and wafted the bottle beneath her nose. "Smelling salts," said Esmeralda flatly. "It won't fix a crushed windpipe, but maybe . . . if there's a god in heaven . . ."

Welli bowed his head and clasped his hands together in prayer.

Trusdale stumbled forward and sank to his knees by Constance's side. She failed to stir, even with the searing scent of ammonia beneath her nose. Welli mumbled to himself as Trusdale reached out for Constance's right hand.

He hesitated to touch her, knowing the chill that death left upon its victims. But he had to say goodbye.

He laid his palm over her pristine kidskin glove. A jolt of static electricity shocked him, causing him to pull back his hand. *Is she wearing that blasted battle mitten?* Before he could investigate, a curl of white aether fire danced along the back of her glove. Almost imperceptibly, her little finger twitched.

Holding his breath, he reached out again and grabbed her gloved hand in his. There was no telltale bulk of a battle mitten under her glove beneath his grip, but once again a jolt of static electricity ran between them. Dust mysteriously levitated from the forearm of his leather coat and scattered into the air.

Her fingers closed around his.

He squeezed her hand with all his might, gazing at her ivory face, now warmed with a hint of pink in her cheeks. She stirred and coughed as Esmeralda wafted the smelling salts bottle beneath her nose. "Ugh," said Constance, raising her left arm to bat ineffectively at the bottle. "Stop that."

Wide-eyed, Esmeralda pulled away the bottle, keeping her hand behind Constance's head to support her.

The matron said, "I can't believe the salts worked in such a circumstance. Praise be the lord."

"Amen," said Welli, his hands still clamped together in prayer. "For heaven's sake, Connie. Don't ever scare me like that again."

Heart thudding with joy, Trusdale clasped her gloved hand to his chest. "You scared the hell outta me too. Welcome back to the land of the living."

Constance stared in bewilderment at her rescuers. "I died?"

"Only for a minute or so," said Esmeralda. "How do you feel?"

"I . . . think I saw the other side. There was no bright light, no flaming pits of punishment, only . . . me. A thousand different me's from other worlds, all screaming at me to wake up."

"So," said Welli. "Hell is other Constances. That makes sense."

A smile lifted the corners of Constance's lips, now losing their blueish tinge. "I don't think I was in hell. It was a sliver of time and space caught between the voids. I was there for an instant and then . . ." She switched her gaze to Trusdale, his hand still grasping hers as if her life depended on it. "You pulled me back, Mr. Trusdale. I can't thank you enough."

He shook his head. "I'm not sure it was me. I saw a lick of white fire curl out of your hand when I grabbed it. Maybe it was a remnant of energy left from your time at Versailles, or maybe using that aether mirror has caused some kind of interdimensional short circuit in your body."

The blue bruises on her neck were starting to fade beneath the sun's rays. She squeezed his hand and flashed a grateful smile. "Or maybe you can accept my thanks like a gentleman. And to think, you said that I should stop using that mirror, that it was beyond dangerous. But perhaps it has benefits we're not aware of?"

He grinned at her. "Whatever you say, Miss Adventure. But I still think you should reconsider interacting with artifacts you don't fully understand."

Reluctantly, he released her hand as Esmeralda helped Constance to sit up. "Please, Lady Haltwhistle, lean forward a little and breathe deeply, it will help you to recover. Are you in pain?"

"I have a pounding headache," said Constance, gingerly reaching up with her ungloved hand to touch her left temple. "I feel like I just drank an orchard's worth of Haltwhistle Hall's hard cider. Without the fun part where you think you can sing and dance better than anyone else in the whole world."

Trusdale chuckled. "That, I'd like to see."

Welli grunted. "I've seen it, and no, you wouldn't."

"But other than that, I merely feel bruised," said Constance, rubbing her neck. "What exactly happened to me?"

"You were assaulted by rogue cardinals. It was those three thugs who brought the house down in Paris," said Welli. "And this kind lady is called Esmeralda."

"But I'm Emmi to my friends," said the salt-and-pepper-haired matron. "I sincerely hope that we can become friends, Lady Haltwhistle. I'm a huge fan of your fight for women's rights."

"My what? I—Where are those damned monks? I've got a score to settle." She tried to push herself up to a stand but was prevented by all three of her attendants.

Welli said, "Oh no you don't. Why don't you rest for a minute or two before seeking vengeance."

As Constance huffed at her cousin, Trusdale scanned the courtyard for dastardly cardinals. It appeared that the two Vikings he and Welli had fought had limped away from the scene to lick their wounds. On the path where they had met their downfall, a trio of elegant young women promenaded. Their silk jewel-toned bustled gowns were cut so fashionably they would undoubtedly have been welcomed at any royal court. By contrast, Emmi's travel companions were now reentering the far side of the square with their straw boaters in various states of disrepair. It looked as if they had continued to scuffle with the fleeing cardinal until they lost him somewhere in Rome's bustling streets.

As the stout ladies puffed up to Emmi's side, she said, "I believe a formal introduction is in order, Lady Haltwhistle, Lord Pendelroy, and Mr. Trusdale. I hope you will accept my sincere apologies for any impropriety on our part, but I must admit that we have been following you since you left the smoky skies of Sheffield to conduct your grand tour of the continent. We"—she gestured at her three boater-hatted companions—"represent the Sheffield Sisterhood of Suffragettes."

The standing suffragettes gazed wide-eyed at Constance, as if she were a fallen angel and not the daughter of a dimension-tripping devil with more enemies than the Borgias.

"Here, let me show you," said Emmi, reaching both hands into her carpet bag. She drew out a stack of French and English newspapers. The main headlines indicated that back in England, Queen Victoria had passed the female inheritance law. In Paris, the famous vigilante, *La Femme Électrique* was stalking criminal gang members. And at Versailles, the King of France had fallen in a bloodless coup. Emmi continued, "Thanks to you, Lady Haltwhistle, single, married, and widowed women can now legally inherit property in the United Kingdom. What's more, the Queen has seen fit to revise the succession to the crown law in favor of absolute primogeniture. That means that her daughters have as much right to inherit her throne as her sons. Our next monarch will be her firstborn child, regardless of their sex. One day, Britain will crown Queen Victoria II, not Edward VII. Isn't that astonishing?"

Constance frowned. "I asked the Queen to consider changing the inheritance law to be fairer to all, but I had nothing to do with her reviewing the succession to the crown."

"But don't you see? You opened the floodgates to female emancipation. Even the Queen could not deny your righteous passion. We suffragettes have long fought to gain voting rights and other legal protections, but in one stroke you inspired a new generation of women to take on the fight for equality. It is notable that you used words rather than violence to compel the Queen to act, Lady Haltwhistle. The tension between those two elements has caused much discussion within our group."

The woman who resembled Hearn in a dress cleared her throat and curtsied to Constance.

She said in a broad Sheffield accent, "Beggin' your pardon, miss, Anne Tucker 'ere. Words are fine and good, but let's not forget a bit of violence here and there can turn a tide. The way you took on those gangsters in the Paris alleyways . . ." She one-two punched the air. "That was amazing to watch. Poetry in motion. And that electricity glove of yours is just astounding."

Constance glanced sideways at Trusdale, guilt etched across her pale face.

Anne continued, "And it was wonderful watching you toss that dynamite around the gardens of Versailles.

Boom, boom, boom, hedges on fire everywhere, and there you are, lit up like a goddess by the firelight. Nobody mentions you in the papers, but we know it was you at the head of the procession leading the shackled King Louis out of that maze. We were watching the explosions from our chartered airship with telescopes. They wouldn't let us land, you see. You need a fancy invitation or a trade license to dock at the palace. Probably not now though. I hear you only have to buy a ticket to go and wander around Versailles like a royal person. I mean, you're just like that lass, Joan of Arc, battling all foes with fire and gumption. But you're less French than her, of course."

Constance gasped. "I'm nothing like Joan of Arc."

Anne tugged at the low-cut neckline of her gown. Beneath the twill, the glint of a chainmail corset shimmered in the sunlight. "A few of us have even started wearing various levels of armored corsets, just like you've been known to do. Leather, a bit of chainmail, sometimes just a few studs here and there sewn into the silk. They provide much better protection against the policeman's batons than the cardboard we'd stuffed inside our corsets before you inspired us."

Constance blinked at the women's batons. "Am I to understand that you took those truncheons from the hands of the Sheffield constabulary?"

They nodded enthusiastically.

"Oh. I see. You know, you might want to investigate the unarmed martial arts too, as a last resort. You should check out kung fu, or judo—" said Constance.

Welli held up his hands. "Hold on, cousin, that's more than enough revolutionary talk for one day, thank you very much. I don't know who's leading whom here, but as a retired member of Her Majesty's armed forces, I'm against whatever is going on."

Ignoring Welli, Emmi leaned toward Constance. "We've been serializing your adventures in the daily Sheffield Suffrage Gazette. You've got a huge following."

Constance's eyes lit up. "Heavens, have I? How many followers, would you say?"

"That's it," snapped Welli. "Connie, we're leaving. It's bad enough that you're a baroness now; you get us in quite enough trouble without an army at your back. Are you well enough to stand?"

"I believe so."

Trusdale put his arm around her and helped pull her to her feet.

She swayed atop her ankle boots, still overly pallid but growing stronger by the minute. He leaned down and gazed deep into her eyes, drinking in their verdant depths. "Can you walk? How are you feeling?"

She gave a wry smile. "Honestly, my head feels like a bomb exploded inside it."

Anne said, "Oooh, bombs. That's another good idea to fight the good fight."

"No, it isn't. Not at all. Only criminals use bombs," said Welli. "Ladies, I must insist that you stop writing these lies about my cousin, lest I get litigious. You're spouting slander about my family, and I will not stand for it. I can assure you that my sweet Connie has nothing to do with any of the events in these newspapers, and I will take you all to court if you say otherwise. Do I make myself clear?"

The suffragettes kept their eyes trained on Constance. She glanced between her furious cousin and her impassioned new friends. With a sigh, she turned to the suffragettes and said, "It has been lovely to meet you all, ladies, and I thank you for your assistance in my hour of need. But I'm afraid Lord Pendelroy is correct, I am not the person you seek. There seems to have been a case of mistaken identity here regarding my involvement with certain—"

"World-changing events," said Emmi.

"Well, yes, world-changing events. Under any other circumstances, I would love to stay and chat. Unfortunately, I have obligations that draw me away. I believe I spy a nun beckoning to me over there by the Gregorian Tower. I know she wants me to make a substantial contribution to her charitable cause, and one simply doesn't make a Catholic Sister wait, if one knows what's good for one. Please excuse me, ladies."

Constance curtsied unsteadily to the suffragettes and ambled away toward the Tower of the Winds, where Sister Teresa waited by the open oak door.

"A substantial charitable donation. Is there no end to Lady Haltwhistle's magnanimity?" sighed Emmi.

Welli snorted. "There's no end to anything with Constance. She just goes on and on and on." With that, he strode off after his cousin.

"She's truly a shining example to us all," declared Anne, drawing vigorous nods from her companions. "Let's get to work writing our next dispatch about how she's now helping nuns."

Trusdale tipped his Stetson to the suffragettes. "Ladies, it was a pleasure. And thank you for fighting off that final cardinal with your batons. You saved Lady Haltwhistle, and for that I'm eternally grateful." He gave them a half bow before hurrying to catch up with the epitome of the "new woman": the incorrigible, impossible, Constance.

The woman he loved.

Chapter 21:
The Audience

The ink was drying on the promissory note as Constance searched every nook and cranny of the astrological library for the second Enigma Key. True to her word, Sister Teresa had provided a chair, a desk, a cushion, and solitude for Constance to write the note in private. But time was ticking away, and her half hour of hunting for the elusive Key was almost up.

Through the ancient floorboards beneath her chocolate-brown ankle boots, a conversation rumbled between the Sister, Welli, and Trusdale. Under Teresa's watchful eye, the two men were investigating the tower's museum on the lower floor, on the off chance the Key had been tucked inside an exhibit for safekeeping. Hopefully, the men were being as subtle in their search as Constance truly believed herself to be. Not upsetting Sister Teresa was a vital part of this plan.

Constance placed her hands on her hips and slowly turned on the spot, scanning every inch of the square room for the one-inch metal triangle. Oak bookcases lined the stone walls from floor to ceiling. Each shelf was stuffed with rolled documents in storage tubes, leather-bound books both large and small, and stacks of parchments decorated with glorious calligraphy. Apart from layers of tissue paper between the parchment sheets, the only protection from the ravages of time for the delicate works of art were heavy curtains that covered the windows. Teresa had opened one curtain to allow enough light in for Constance to write her note, but the gloom had made the search challenging.

She breathed in the warm, musty scent of paper, ink, and leather, and heaved a sigh. Her head was pounding like the beating the suffragettes had apparently given her would-be kidnapper. Overall, she would not recommend being choked half to death—or was it entirely to death, as Trusdale and Welli seemed to think?—as an ideal way to meet new friends. At least the four ladies had been enthusiastic about her escapades on the continent. How funny that they saw her everyday actions as world-changing progress. That was the sort of veneration she could get used to. It made up for Welli's eye rolling and Trusdale's worrying.

Waking to find Trusdale holding her hand, his ridiculously blue eyes darkened with concern, had been the highlight of her kidnapping experience. As with the chokehold, she wouldn't endorse being knocked unconscious as a means to hold hands with an almost-handsome man, but it had been a nice bonus. His neatly trimmed sideburns, that slightly crooked nose that had survived one too many bar fights, and his oh-so-square jaw with that charming dimple made a most pleasing sight to wake up to.

Even his ridiculous cowboy hat had given her a little shade as he leaned in close enough to make her knees weak. Thank heavens she'd already been on the ground, lest she embarrass herself in front of her new friends.

Or perhaps that's just a side-effect of passing out?

Constance shook her head, wincing as her migraine flashed stars through her aching brain. She must focus on the task at hand. If the Key wasn't in this room, that left her with only one option.

The riveted bronze door that led up to the off-limits observatory sang its siren song, tempting her to walk over and pick its lock.

I really shouldn't. She pulled two hairpins from beneath her pith helmet. *It would be an overstep of my agreement with Teresa.* She walked to the door and squatted to investigate its simple lock. *I should give up on ever finding this Key, right now.* She placed both hairpins into the lock and moved them independently of each other to provide pressure here and jiggles there. Papa's insistence that her early schooling covered the fundamentals of burglary had once again proved invaluable. At night as a seven-year-old, she'd often used her skills to break into the cook's securely locked pantry to steal forbidden sweet treats. Her ultimate loot had been a block of marzipan that she'd stashed in a hat box beneath her bed. The almond-flavored treat was still her favorite indulgence to this day, partly for the taste, but mostly for the flora and fauna she loved to sculpt before eating her creations.

The lock clicked open. *Well, if it's already unlocked, I may as well go through.*

From a slot window up high, a single sunbeam shone down through the darkness of the tower. It was the light from heaven above, illuminating her way up a narrow spiral staircase. She held her breath and stepped up onto the stairs, sliding her hand along the smooth metal banister as she rose toward the light. At the top of the stairs, a bronze door blocked her entry into the observatory dome itself.

She held her breath and reached for the round brass handle. It turned smoothly, with no clunk of a lock impeding her. *Finally, something goes my way.*

Constance pushed open the door and stepped into the hot metal dome. At night, the observatory was no doubt cool beneath the heavens; but in the daytime heat, the air baked her as surely as if she were a scone. Sunlight blazed into the circular room through an open vent panel in the ceiling. She winced as her migraine burst into a full cacophonic symphony, flashing fireworks and pain so sharp her teeth ached. She fell to her knees as if in prayer, holding her hands in front of her eyes. Through the gaps between her fingers, she blinked at the shapes and shadows before her.

An archaic brass telescope with its lens capped stood in the center of the round room. Next to the telescope, red and white ecclesiastical robes and a white silk skullcap were neatly stacked on a simple chair. On the dusty floor, a well-worn burgundy velvet cushion provided a comfortable place for elderly knees to pray.

And she wasn't alone.

Constance gulped. She'd seen the olive skinned, gray-haired person before her on the souvenir plates sold at every Roman tourist trap. Even without papal vestments, clad only in a long white undergown and a golden crucifix necklace, she knew that she was face-to-face with a startled Pope Luke.

And it would take more than a thin cotton gown to disguise the fact that . . .

The pope was a woman.

Bloody hell.

The wide-eyed pope sprang up from her prayer position with her black-and-silver bead rosary dangling from her right hand. She grabbed for her vestments, firing a torrent of Italian toward Constance as she fumbled to put on the heavy robes. The heat within the dome must have driven Her Holiness to remove them before she knelt to pray.

Still on her knees, Constance stuttered, "I'm-I'm so very sorry. I didn't know anyone was in here. I don't mean you any harm, I swear. I'm just looking for—"

The Pope, half dressed in the robes, scowled at her. "You're English? Why is it always the English who cause me problems? I suppose you saw . . . this." She gestured at her own body.

"Yes, but I promise I won't tell anyone, I swear." Her head hammered so hard it felt like it could explode at any moment. "I'm truly the soul of discretion. A secret is safer with me than a precious thing locked up in the Tower of London. That's pretty safe, in case you don't know."

Pope Luke wagged her finger. "Keep this secret between us alone, or . . ." She thought for a moment. "Or something unfortunate may happen to you."

"Something unfortunate is always happening to me." Constance rubbed her forehead. "Oh wait, you mean, like a threat? Am I correct in assuming that the pope is threatening me? Because if so, let me tell you, you are one in a long line of people who have done so. And things never go the way they . . . ugh." The room swirled around her like a whirlpool. "Am I still on my knees? I am, aren't I? I don't feel . . ."

The pope's brown eyes filled with concern, and she took a few cautious steps toward her unannounced guest. "You don't look well, child," she frowned. Compassion overcame her fear, and she knelt on the floor before Constance. "You've gone green."

"Good. My cousin Welli said I needed to get a little color in my cheeks." Constance laughed, then cringed as her migraine exploded once more. "I have the most dreadful headache. Believe it or not, I was roughed up by three cardinals less than an hour ago."

The pope groaned. "It's always something with the cardinals. It's enough to drive you to despair. That's why I . . ." She bit her lip, glancing around the observatory dome.

"That's why you come here, to get away from it all?"

The pope nodded. "It is the only place in the palace where I can find uninterrupted solitude, with no eyes upon me but Our Lord's. Peace and quiet is worth far more than gold in this city."

Constance sagged. "Then I can't begin to tell you how sorry I am that I barged in on your sanctuary. But where are my manners? May I please introduce myself? I'm Lady Constance Haltwhistle, daughter of Henry Halt-whistle of the British barony of Brampton-on-the-Wall. Like him, I'm a keen amateur scholar of astrology." She waved her hand at the telescope.

The pope eyed her warily.

Constance continued, "It's my real name, I swear. I wouldn't lie to you, of all people. And I didn't mean to insult you. Now I think about it, your threat that 'something unfortunate' might happen to me was pretty good. I think most people would be worried by it."

The pope sighed. "It was my first, and hopefully last, attempt at such a thing. Please forgive my harshness. I was startled, but there's no excuse for uttering such words."

"If it's any consolation, I've noticed that truly dangerous people never make veiled threats. They act, or they don't. No words are wasted. Why give a warning of actions that are best delivered as a surprise?"

Her Holiness the Pope chuckled. "A savvy observation, signorina. I will pray that your encounters with such people are limited."

"That's very kind of you. Please, call me Constance. Somehow, I'm guessing that Luke isn't the name you were given at birth?"

The Pope sat back on her heels and laughed. "I am the Contessa Lucretia Isabella Medici. I'm the fifth pope from my family. Through the ages, my ancestors were known as patrons of the arts and architecture. They were bankers, accountants, diplomats, and—"

"Astronomers? I believe I read something to that effect in the library downstairs. Do you find it difficult to reconcile religious faith and science?"

Lucretia grinned. "An excellent question, child. I find that one supports the other. The more I learn about the mechanics of the universe, the stronger my faith that there is a power and a purpose behind all things. We all have a divine spark within us that compels us to be kind, to be curious, to be our best selves. And that is why I will trust you, signorina, to keep my physicality secret. In return for your compassion, I will not hand you over to the Swiss Guards for trespassing."

Constance bowed her aching head. "Thank you, Holy Mother. Speaking of curiosity though, may I ask, why be the pope?"

Lucretia took a long breath. "I'm an accidental pope. I wanted to be a part of this great church, to make changes that could benefit our clergy, our parishioners, and the wider world. As women are often suppressed, not celebrated, both in this church and beyond, adopting male dress was the only way to have my voice heard. Even so, I have not managed to make the changes needed for all to feel welcome and valued. I do what I can within the confines I am given, and we inch toward progress. But I fear that I have failed Our Lord as my mission falters, and my time on this earth grows shorter by the year."

"You don't look that old. Maybe seventy? You've got years left to make changes." Constance rubbed the heels of her palms over her eyes, willing her headache to subside. Right now, the roots of her hair felt like they were somehow bruised and on fire at the same time. *What did the suffragettes say about me being at the center of world-changing events? It was my words that compelled Queen Victoria to allow women to inherit property. What if . . .*

She took a deep breath and gazed deeply into the pope's warm brown eyes. "Perhaps all things are pre-ordained, perhaps not. But I have just met the most extraordinary women who are fighting for equal rights for all to engage fully in society. However we identify ourselves here on earth, whether as male, female, other, none, or all, I'm positive that such physical details are insignificant across this universe and all the others. I may be female in this dimension, male in the next, and neither in the one after that. But it's my actions toward others, both positive and negative, that truly weigh my worth to the cosmos."

She placed her hand on her heart. "I am not my body alone. I am my thoughts, my feelings, my actions, and most of all, my love. Love for those around me, and love for myself, despite my flaws and failures. Perhaps even because of them."

She licked her dry lips and continued, "I beg of you, Lucretia, please don't punish yourself for your slow progress. Any step toward a great goal is a cause for joy, and a small action today could positively affect the future in ways we cannot foresee. Let's break down the man-made barriers that keep us trapped in intolerance and prejudice. We are one species under the heavens. I believe our only true mission is to bond over our shared humanity in the face of a vast cosmos we can never truly understand. Humanity is our family, and the purpose of our existence is love."

She leaned forward and lightly clasped the Pope's frail hands. A slight tingle of electricity seemed to flow between them. The two women gazed into each other's souls and both trembled. *Eternity is found in the eyes of every human. But how often do we take the time to share our infinite connection?*

Constance murmured, "You can do this, Lucretia. I believe in you."

"But do you believe in yourself, Constance? I see doubt and fear in your eyes. Of what are you so afraid, that it casts a shadow on your soul?"

Constance withdrew her hands, filled with sudden shame. "Bless me Mother, for I have sinned. On this earth, I've lied, I've cheated, I've manipulated people and events to go my own way, and for the most part, I never gave any of my misdeeds so much as a second thought. But I've been given an opportunity to see the consequences of some of my decisions played out in other realities through a cosmic mirror. For every innocuous Constance, there's a woman who cares for nothing but herself. It's not the reflection anyone wants to see in the mirror."

She slumped, exhausted to her bones. "I've seen myself from every angle, and it's not pretty. And I've spied on other versions of people I care about. My cousin, my servants, alternate versions of my parents, siblings I never had, even lovers I've never met. And perhaps it was wrong, but I tried to spy on a man I truly care about. His name is Liberty Trusdale. I saw his genius engineer older brother, his gunslinger younger brother, his sisters, his parents, all living lives of joy or misery depending on their choices and, sometimes, fate."

The Pope sighed. "Some things men aren't meant to know, Constance. You've searched too far for answers that don't exist."

She gazed into the Pope's warm eyes. "I've never found another Liberty Trusdale. He's not there, wherever I look. There is no middle son in the Trusdale family. He's unique, special. And there are thousands of me, most of whom I wouldn't want to be friends with. What does it mean that there's only one of him, and am I good enough to . . . I mean, am I the right one who could . . . Does fate want him to be with someone special, unique, like him?"

The Pope reached for her hands once more. "Dear girl, we are all unique. What is it that makes you feel that you're not good enough to win this man's heart, if that's what you desire?"

Constance swallowed hard. "Well, my father left me, my mother . . . she's either dead or she's sending me notes asking me not to visit her. I feel my servants stay with me because of the wages I pay them. My cousin stays close because of a sense of family obligation. People are by my side because of money and duty, but no one has chosen to be there just to spend time with me. Except—"

"The one and only Liberty Trusdale."

"Exactly. If I mess this up, if I'm the selfish, scattered, ridiculous person I am in so many other dimensions, there's no other Liberty Trusdale. He's one of a kind. And I can't learn from my other selves the best way to keep him by my side. And, beyond that, I'm wondering if—"

"There's a better person out there whom he could be with? My dear, I believe you're suffering from a crisis of insecurity. You don't have to be good enough to please anyone else. You can only strive to be the best person you can be. If you and Liberty are destined to be together, then it will happen. You must have faith. And I thank you for restoring mine. The heavens work in mysterious ways, and you have shown me the way forward."

Constance blinked. "I'm not sure anyone should be taking my advice. Least of all me, and definitely not you. You speak to a higher power."

The Pope nodded. "I have, and I will again. But you did not come here seeking enlightenment. What is it you need?"

Her cheeks flushed. "It seems churlish to ask, but have you ever spotted a one-inch metal triangle in here? It might glow now and then, if that's any help."

The Pope held out her right hand. Curled on her palm was a rosary chain crafted from jet-black beads punctuated with silver stars. A singular strand led off from the main circle to an Enigma Key secured by a silver pendant setting. Constance's jaw dropped.

Lucretia gave a wry smile. "This is the Celestial Rosary, kept here in the tower since the sixteenth century. For the last century, the rosary has hung upon this telescope, awaiting any who use the device to count their devotions after viewing the heavens. It sometimes glows at night, so this has led to speculation that it is divine in nature and may explain why this piece was crafted in the first place. When I first visited this observatory, I sensed there was a benign presence here. That feeling intensifies when I hold this rosary."

"Ah, you're sensitive to . . . May I share a secret of my own? That triangle contains a gateway, if you will, to a being from another dimension. I'm on a mission to release this unfortunate entity from its prison. It's a long story, but . . ."

The Pope beckoned her closer. "Give me your hand."

Constance obediently held out her right hand. The pope dropped the rosary onto her palm and pressed Constance's fingers closed around it.

Constance spluttered. "But, for all you know, I could be doing something nefarious with this, or at least selling it for my own gain. I mean, thank you so much, but . . ."

The Pope stood, and Constance followed suit. Her headache was finally easing, and the Key was safe in her hand. Even so, she felt compelled to say, "You're trusting me with something precious here. How do you know that my intentions are good?"

The Pope smiled. "I have faith that you're trying to walk the righteous path. We all stumble now and again. But keep going. Alas, our time here must end, and I must take on my male persona. Will you wait for me outside the tower?"

"Absolutely, Your Holiness." She stood and curtsied. "Thank you."

She bounded down the stairs two at a time and hurried her party outside into the square, deserted now of all but a handful of elderly tourists with their guide.

Trusdale seemed bemused by the surge in her energy. "No one could tell you were at death's door not an hour ago."

"I feel reborn, refreshed. The Key is in hand, and I've never felt more alive." She grabbed his hands and whirled as if in a country dance. "Isn't Rome wonderful? It's no Sheffield of course, but even so, I love it."

He laughed, whirling her around as Welli chuckled. Sister Teresa rolled her eyes and set off for her nunnery.

The door in the tower opened, and out walked His Holiness, the Bishop of Rome.

Welli and Trusdale paled as if they'd seen the Holy Ghost. Constance curtsied, and the group of elderly tourists suddenly found new energy as they rushed to bask in the presence of the Pope.

He smiled at all benevolently, with kindness in his heart and a twinkle in his eye. "Blessings to you all, and welcome to our humble city." He waved the tourists up from bows and curtsies as he walked amongst them. "No bows are needed today, my friends. We are all equal under the eyes of . . ."

He came face-to-face with a stately woman with silver hair, steel-rimmed glasses and a silver tipped walking cane. ". . . God." She bowed her neck, crossed her chest, and stepped out of his way.

Trusdale froze, his eyes wide with shock.

Constance grinned. "I know, it's the actual Pope. Isn't this amazing? He's given me the Key. We can head back to the airship, come on." She tugged at his sleeve. "Trusdale, what is it?" She glanced over her shoulder at the Pope's figure. The tourists were following him at a discreet distance, a spring in their geriatric step that had surely not been there before.

"I thought I saw . . ." Trusdale reached into his pocket and pulled out a typed note. "How does she do that?"

"How does who do what?" she asked.

"Umm, nothing. God sure works in mysterious ways. We're heading back to the ship then?"

"Yes. Mission accomplished."

"Yeah, that's what I thought," said Trusdale, gazing back at the receding group of tourists. He shook his head. "All right. Let's get out of here, Miss Adventure."

She linked arms with him and Welli. "To the ship, and the heavens above."

"Amen to that," said Welli.

Chapter 22:
A Snowy Day In Stockholm

Two days later, it was clear to Erhard that the crew of the *Draugen* was shattered in body and spirit. Ludwig, Johan, and Lars slouched sullenly upon their lookout stools atop the sun-drenched deck of their speeding airship. They spied upon the *Lady Penelope*, which flew far ahead and below the *Draugen*'s current trajectory. The Vikings gingerly held binoculars and telescopes against faces decorated with black eyes and smashed noses. Taking blows from the cowboy and the dandy—or in Ludwig's case, being chased through the streets of Rome by a pack of furious females—had been deeply humiliating for his Swedish henchmen. If he had been there to help them, would the outcome have been any different?

But Erhard had chosen to leave them alone to pursue his own mission for revenge.

His troops had not yet forgiven him for ordering them to attempt kidnapping Constance without his help. And he was finding it difficult to forgive them for almost killing the prize that Oscar desired above all else. How would he have explained to the King and Lady Nay that all their machinations to seize Constance Haltwhistle alive had ended with her being choked to death at the Papal Palace? As if his men's clumsiness was not enough to concern him, they clearly disapproved of the wicked revenge he had taken upon the entire crew of the *Lady Penelope.*

Erhard knew many ways to torture an enemy. Beatings and sleep deprivation were easy punishments for any hired henchman to administer. But emotional torture was far more effective and long-lasting. And what greater pain could he inflict upon Constance's crew than tearing the smallest, cutest member of their found family away from their collective bosom? He'd snatched her right from the deck of their ship while docked in Rome.

She'd been fast asleep, guarded only by the similarly snoozing servant Cawley. She'd succumbed to a deftly placed handkerchief over her snout without raising a single yap. Her youth and trust in the people around her had led directly to her undoing as she trusted them to keep her safe as she slumbered.

He leaned down to slip a sliver of roasted seagull to the Yorkie puppy securely locked in an iron-barred crate. Boo snarled and snapped, turning her nose up at the offered meat. "You're going nowhere, little dog. You'd best get used to eating the pigeon of the sea. It tastes just like chicken, more or less."

The tan-and-black canine, denied her favorite luncheon of steak tenderloin, turned up her button nose at his meager offering. The little bitch was clearly as stubborn as her red-haired mistress. Erhard dropped a second piece of meat into the cage. Boo turned her back and dug imaginary dirt back over the meat.

His men chuckled at the puppy's defiance. Here was his chance to reestablish a connection with his Swedish troops. They were all on the same side, after all. He enthusiastically joined in their laughter. "She's a fireball, this one. You can see why I stole her, can you not? How better to punish the crew of the *Lady Penelope* for thwarting the machinations of Prince Lucien and myself in England. Constance's crew dotes upon this feisty ball of fluff. What better way to hurt them than to snatch her from their warm embrace? They don't know if she was stolen, got lost, or was snatched from the deck by a ravenous seagull. It's the uncertainty over a lost loved one's fate that hurts people the most. Their minds can imagine dreadful dooms far more horrific than any I would ever inflict upon this adorable pooch."

Johan laid his telescope upon his lap and crossed his broad arms. "Then you do not intend to harm Boo? If our duty requires that we hurt people, so be it. But harming a puppy is out of the question."

Erhard spread his hands wide. "I absolutely agree. No harm shall come to the pup. In fact, she may become the *Draugen*'s mascot, should she choose to switch sides. You can rename her whatever you like. Boudicca is a fearsome name for such a sweet-natured beast."

Boo growled at him with all the ferocity her two-pound body could muster. Erhard ignored her and continued, "Snatching this pooch caused severe emotional pain to Oscar's enemies. Now that the crew mourns the loss of their pet, they're off their game. Our next attempt to kidnap Constance will come easier as she is no doubt exhausted from sobbing herself to sleep over the dog's imagined fate."

Johan nodded thoughtfully. "She has looked increasingly wan and bleary-eyed as she wanders the deck of the airship. Perhaps she is weaker now than she once was."

"Then we are united in our commitment to our mission, each other, and our great King Oscar?" said Erhard. When the Vikings nodded their affirmation, he said with a genuine smile, "Then let us continue our pursuit of Lady Haltwhistle with renewed vigor. I shall take the next watch. Perhaps you can teach our new crew member some tricks?" He leaned down to unlock the iron cage. Boo bolted out and raced around the deck yapping with joy.

The Viking warriors melted before her charm offensive. They abandoned their telescopes and binoculars to crouch upon the deck to play with the bouncing puppy.

Erhard held in a sigh at their soft-heartedness and raised his binoculars to view the three airships they had been shadowing since leaving Rome. The trio of ships ahead was strung out over five miles of airspace like porcelain ducks on a living room wall. Since he last checked her path, the *Lady Penelope* had pulled far ahead of the pack on her westbound trajectory. The shapely stern of Haltwhistle's ornate pink-and-gold baroque galleon contrasted sharply with the weathered teak rear end of the chartered airship, the *Shoulder of Mutton*.

On the deck of the *Mutton*, beneath awnings set up to protect them from the late afternoon sun, four stout women in twill travel gowns and battered straw boater hats tapped furiously away on Remington typewriters set atop sturdy teak desks. Perhaps the women were novelists? From the sound beating they had delivered to Ludwig, they certainly possessed the pent-up frustration of artists racked with the agony of creating universes from thin air. With no drinks before them except for several pots of steaming tea, they lacked the necessary measures of alcohol that helped many writers to appear like normal people in public. Was it possible that they were chasing Lady Haltwhistle in the hope she would become a patron of their art?

He swung his binoculars to the east, back toward Rome. On the edge of his vision, he could see the third airship, which was carefully keeping itself as far back as possible from both the *Mutton* and the *Lady Penelope*. On a reconnoiter swing around this final ship, Erhard had spotted the three ladies in jewel-toned bustled gowns and feather-bestrewn hats he'd seen following either Lady Haltwhistle's party, the fierce novelists, or potentially both groups, at the Colosseum.

The fancy ladies were definitely not following the authors for fashion tips, and Lady Haltwhistle's predilection for tiny hats didn't suggest they'd have any interest in her advice either. It was more likely they were following the retired redcoat captain, gambler, and dandy, Lord Pendelroy. Perhaps they were spurned lovers, or perchance he owed them money?

No, their ship was small and sleek, with an automaton crew crafted from brass and bronze. They did not seem to be lacking in funds, so chasing down a debt seemed unlikely. Could they be following the cowboy? Then again, such fashionable ladies surely wouldn't be seen dead with a Stetson-wearing buckaroo, which left only the scientists or the pirate captain. They could be interested in the *Lady Penelope*'s automaton, he supposed, but it had disappeared down to the furnace room for shoveling duty, a role fulfilled by Lars on his own ship.

One thing was sure, these many coincidences meant the sophisticated ladies could not be innocent bystanders in this game of fox and hounds. He must watch his step, lest another interested party interfere with his next kidnapping attempt of the irksome Lady Haltwhistle. Thank heavens he'd had no more sightings of the mysterious grandmother with the silver-tipped sword cane who'd spooked him at the Colosseum. He couldn't shake the feeling that she was out there, somewhere, watching him as closely as he watched Constance Haltwhistle.

Despite the heat of the sun's rays beating upon the deck, a shiver ran down his spine. But perhaps the chill was caused by his anticipation of his next odious task. It was time to activate the creepy communication device Lady Nay insisted he use to report his progress, or lack thereof, to the King.

Erhard drew the mysterious hand mirror from the pocket of his jacket. He kept the Enigma Key that caused the mirror to spring into life in a separate pocket, lest Lady Nay use the activated mirror to spy upon his movements. As he drew the cool metal triangle of the Key out into the sunlight, an electrical charge nipped at his palm. He scowled at the Key before placing it into its triangular socket. The Key glowed red from within, and the copper wiring around the mirror frame hummed to life. His reflected image in the handheld mirror dissolved into static, and then . . . snow? The device's identical receiving mirror appeared to have been left on a windowsill in the Palace of Stockholm. He could see the edge of an open window frame and flakes of snow falling against a backdrop of swirling purple clouds. Or was it ash that fell?

He waited, watching the snow, or ash, drift down. If the King did not have the mirror to hand, surely there was a footman assigned to watch the mirror for incoming messages? He cleared his throat. "Your Majesty?" he asked the snow. "Are you there?"

A chair rasped against floorboards somewhere close to the mirror, and shortly afterward the King appeared. His unshaven face was scored with deep wrinkles and despair clouded his rheumy eyes. "Erhard, is that you? Have you seen the storm?"

The King held his mirror up to the window. The beautiful city of Stockholm, the pride of the Swedish Empire, was blanketed by a layer of snow that glistened like violet crystals. Since winning the Battle of Poltava almost two hundred years before, the Swedes had enjoyed a lavish income from annexed Baltic states. With Russia weakened by corrupt leaders who cared nothing for their people, the Swedes had managed to gain the support of their subjects far and wide by the generous distribution of food and technology. Winning the goodwill of nobles and peasants alike had always taken precedence over imperial expansion for King Oscar, until Lady Nay appeared in his court. Where she'd come from was a mystery. Erhard's inquiries had found out only that she was nobility from a distant realm. People who asked too many questions about Nay tended to disappear in the night, so he'd not dared to take his investigations into her origins any further.

Stockholm's elegant streets and broad river alike were choked with purple snow. Not a boat or a soul was visible in the eerie wasteland.

The King whispered, "Where have they gone, Erhard? The people? My servants, my courtiers? I wake from sleep, and they have left me alone in the palace. Only Nay's people are here, working around the clock on that confounded device. What is it for, Erhard? She tells me, but then I can't remember what she said." The King turned the mirror back to his own face and whispered, "Am I going insane, Erhard?"

"No, Your Majesty. It's that woman. You must . . ."

The King jumped as a loud crash behind him indicated a door had been flung open. Lady Nay's voice purred, "There you are, my liege. I've been looking for you."

The King smiled at her faintly. "My lovely Lady Nay. Erhard is giving his report on—"

"Is he?" Nay crossed the floor between the door and the King with a surprising speed given the long train on her red, corseted ball gown. She had caused quite a stir in the royal court's fashion-conscious ladies with her extra-long gowns. It was as if she sought to take up the most space she could in any room.

"And what is your report, Colonel?" Her tone made a polite form of address carry the same weight as a death threat.

"My men . . . rendered Lady Haltwhistle unconscious in Rome."

Lady Nay leaned into the mirror, her green eyes glittering. "And?"

"Unbeknownst to us, she has hired an army of well-armed Amazons to defend her." Beyond the view of the mirror, his Vikings silently nodded their confirmation of his words. What self-respecting henchmen would want to admit that lady novelists had got the better of them in a fight?

"Amazons?" Lady Nay growled. "And where is Constance now?"

"She's back on her airship, heading full steam ahead for England."

Lady Nay grimaced into the mirror. "I'll wager she's heading back to Haltwhistle Hall, in Yorkshire. Her entire family is obsessed by that crumbling pile and its sheep-ridden pastures."

Erhard blinked. Could it be that he knew something Lady Nay didn't? "Ah, I doubt it, your ladyship. The Hall was swept away through a mysterious vortex on the very day my former employer, Prince Lucien, marched on it with an army of redcoats. I didn't see it myself, but apparently there is nothing left on the site but a massive hole in the ground."

Lady Nay gaped at him. He suppressed the smirk that so desperately wanted to dance across his face.

"Why didn't anyone tell me about this? Then that means . . . I thought only the Baron could generate a portal. How did his daughter persuade the Keys do her bidding?" She shook her head, her hair a dark, shining waterfall that could drown a man. Nay tapped a long, sharp fingernail against her chin. "I've watched a thousand versions of that girl across time and space, and none of them are this unpredictable. She's chaos incarnate."

"You never mentioned before that you knew Lady Haltwhistle personally," said Erhard, trying to find sense in Nay's words. Had she planted mirrors like this one in other dimensions? He'd discovered that alternate worlds existed while helping to track down an invisibility serum that dislodged humans into a void between dimensions. Their bodies disappeared from view to all onlookers, but they could still interact with physical objects in their original reality. The subjects of the experiments would have become the ultimate assassins, if only the experience of becoming invisible hadn't driven them all insane.

Lady Nay tilted her head and frowned. "I don't know this particular Constance, but I've viewed a thousand different versions of her. This Constance seems to be the worst by far. Perhaps it's because her father succeeded in crossing the void, or they may have developed some unique physiological or psychic ability. In any world, this girl is too smart for her own good, but our current target goes beyond the pale. This Constance is a threat and an opportunity, all wrapped into one irritating bundle."

She bit her lip, nonplussed, as the men who listened in from both sides of the mirror tried to grasp the meaning of her words. Ludwig petted Boo absently as the puppy snuffled in his pocket for possible treats. He scratched behind her ears, and the puppy grunted and yapped in appreciation.

Lady Nay leaned in toward her mirror. "What was that noise? Show me."

Erhard reluctantly turned around his mirror to show his Viking warriors lounging upon the deck to play with the stolen terrier puppy.

Nay gasped. "Is that . . . the hellhound of the devil's daughter?"

"The dog is Lady Haltwhistle's pet, if that's what you mean," said Erhard.

Nay clapped her hands together in delight. "Ah, you've outdone yourself, Erhard. What excellent bait with which to set our trap. I should have thought of this myself. I'd toyed with snatching a servant or the cowboy, but what version of Constance would ignore the plight of a beast? Her attachment to animals has always been one of her most baffling traits, but I had never seen it as a weakness until now. Well done, Colonel."

Erhard frowned. "I don't see how—"

"I will handle matters from now on. First, I'll prepare a gilded cage for the little beast. If Constance won't be tempted to rescue her incarcerated mother, then perhaps she will fling caution aside to rescue a pampered pet. That creature is the closest thing she has to having a child of her own. Her maternal instinct will no doubt be as fierce as that of her mother, Annabella, a sickeningly kind individual who I've had the equal misfortune of viewing across many worlds and variations. I'll bet that this Constance will risk everything to rescue her furry baby. But I will have to make some dangerous long-distance modifications to the Enigma Key you carry in your mirror to lay down a trail of electrical breadcrumbs that she can follow to Stockholm."

"Dangerous for whom?" He felt a pang of worry not just for himself, but also for his men.

She gave a sharp-toothed smile. "Dangerous for Lady Haltwhistle, of course. Give me exactly forty-eight hours, then pull your airship in as close as you can to the *Lady Penelope* without being spotted. When I give you the signal, you'll set off for Stockholm with Constance hot on your trail."

"But . . . this is a stealth airship. She won't be able to see . . ."

"There are other ways of seeing than by using human eyes, Colonel. Forty-eight hours. You have your orders."

Lady Nay's face dissolved into static. Erhard stared at his own face in the mirror once more. He pulled the Enigma Key from its socket and tucked it away.

Ludwig, Lars, and Johan's Nordic brows were uncharacteristically furrowed as Boo bounced between them, clearly convinced that her salvation lay with them and not Erhard.

The terrier wasn't wrong, but perhaps he could use the puppy's charismatic appeal to load the dice of fate to roll in his favor?

"Your guess is as good as mine as to what Lady Nay is planning for Boo, gentlemen," said Erhard. "But know this—she may be preparing a gilded cage for our canine guest, but I will not let her harm a hair on our puppy's head. You all no doubt remember that our good King Oscar of days long past was an avid animal lover. But Lady Nay . . . who knows what she's capable of? Why, some might almost say that the only pet she leads around on an invisible leash is . . ."

King Oscar. He didn't need to say it out loud. Understanding glimmered in his men's eyes, the secret thought that none had dared share even with his fellow warriors. The great King Oscar had become little more than Nay's pet monarch.

But would his men stand shoulder-to-shoulder with him if he attempted to save the King?

And was there enough of the old King left to save?

Chapter 23:
The Plan With a Capital "P"

The somber mood aboard the *Lady Penelope* had lasted a day too long for Welli's taste. After alerting every social contact he had in Europe to be on the lookout for an escaped Yorkie puppy, he'd set to work cheering the crew with assurances that she eventually would turn up. He'd put forward convincing arguments to combat whatever dreadful fate they'd imagined could have befallen the lost dog. In a final bid to lift the crew's spirits, he'd reinforced his psychological and emotional support of his companions by having a barrel of extra strong absinthe punch brought up to the top deck. Once tapped, he'd ordered all crew members to attend a party to celebrate young Boo's zest for life with mandatory fun, live music, and as much consumption of alcohol as their livers could stand.

Constance, as drunk as she definitely was, was supremely grateful for Welli's attempts to set the crew back on course despite their shared loss. RATT wouldn't care if their puppy was missing, of that she was certain. And she'd committed every coin she owned to paying a huge reward to anyone who found the missing pup. Combined with reward posters posted on every street corner in Rome, there was nothing more she could logically do to help find the dog. But logic didn't help a broken heart.

She sat alone on a picnic blanket on the deck, watching her shipmates console one another as best they could.

Welli plonked himself down next to her on the blanket. She blinked up at the lanky lord. "Perhaps we should have organized another search of the dock before we left?"

"Fifty searches were enough to prove she wasn't there. Don't worry, cousin," Welli assured her. "She can't have gone too far on those tiny legs. She probably chased a rat right off the ship through the docks out into the streets. Someone will spot her soon, I'm sure of it. Maya's mechanical messenger pigeons are flying on constant alert back and forth between us and Rome. If there's news, we'll hear it, no matter where we are."

She tilted her aching head. "Wait, we have rats on board the *Lady Penelope*?"

"Forget I said anything. Have another pint of punch." He tried to thrust a lurid green goblet of absinthe and friends into her hand.

She pushed it away. "Ugh, not another one. I can barely see straight now. Is that Hearn dancing a jig between two crossed cutlasses on the lower deck?"

Welli peered down at the dancing giant. "It is indeed. Come on, you have to join the party. Though our hearts ache, our spirits must stay strong."

"Speaking of strong spirits, this absinthe punch you've foisted upon us. Have you served it before? If so, did anyone die from it?"

He snorted. "You may wish you were dead when the hangover strikes, but no, no deaths have yet occurred from this particular punch recipe. All our crew members should be alive and somewhat well in the morning. I must say, Hearn is a nimble devil when he wants to be. Those cutlasses are two of Mrs. Singh's favorites. I'm surprised she trusts him not to stomp all over them."

"Rani's seen Hearn dance before at one of the Halt-whistle Hall Holiday parties. She knows he's practically a professional sword dancer."

Welli took a sip from the green goblet and winced. "Have you seen her collection of weapons? Even for a retired pirate, it's impressive."

"Seen it? How could I miss it?" Mrs. Singh's deadly collection had spilled out of her married quarters onto all four walls of the furnace room. A few of Rani's javelins had become permanent displays on the walls of the cargo hold that provided a cozy home to a select group of farmyard animals. Chickens loved to roost upon the safely capped spears, and eggs were often laid amidst piles of helmets and other armor the former pirate queen had been unable to fit into her small cabin wardrobe. Should the *Lady Penelope* ever go to war, Rani's weapons, in combination with the ship's camouflaged cannons and Constance's trunks of fantastical firearms, should make the ship a pink-and-gold force to be reckoned with.

As Hearn finished his sword dance by daringly kicking the cutlasses up into his hands, Constance rose unsteadily to her feet to applaud. "Bravo, Hearn!"

He bowed. "Thank you, m'lady."

Constance attempted to walk a straight line toward the tea urn that was set up beside a snoring Cawley sat in a wingback armchair. Despite the short distance, she tripped over the charging cables connected to the three armored exo-suits that knelt upon the deck and tumbled to the boards before them. Comfortably numb from the absinthe, she gazed up at the towering twelve-foot-high bronze-and-brass suits of mechanical armor. They were impressive to behold, even resting on their knees.

In shape, they strongly resembled the bulbous under-sea diving suits depicted in her *Girl's Guide To Imperial War Machines*. The book's author, one Dr. Maya Chauhan, had signed it and presented it to her for her eighth birthday. Constance carried it with her on her travels, tucked in a trunk beneath her self-designed ray guns of disintegration.

An updated version of the *Girl's Guide* would surely wax lyrical about the cutting-edge technology of the Steamwerks' exo-suits. The bulletproof glass door arched over the chest cockpit of every suit protected its pilot from enemy fire while providing an excellent view of the battlefield. When swung open, the glass door allowed easy entrance into a cockpit designed to be as plush and comfortable as any gentleman's library. The comfort of the cockpit's inhabitant was assured by a cushy, wingback pilot's chair upholstered in burgundy velvet and gold trim. The same velvet quilted the cockpit's bronze walls to muffle the sound of battle.

A gold-framed oil painting of Queen Victoria, resplendent in bejeweled goggles, a petite diamond crown, and a black leather battle corset cinched over a vast black gown, graced every cockpit. Perhaps she was there to stir the pilots on to greater acts of valor in her name. Or, more likely, to remind them that she was always watching. No British infantryman ever retreated in the face of the enemy and lived to talk about it. The grizzled Warrior Queen made sure of that.

Constance rolled herself up to a stand and staggered past the exo-suits to a gilded baroque throne that had once graced her mama's dressing room at Haltwhistle Hall. "May I please ask for everyone's attention for a moment?"

Hearn shouted, "Oi, you lot, all quiet for the Baroness."

She winced at his migraine-inducing volume. She'd certainly been more prone to headaches since her near-death experience at the Tower of the Winds. Or were her frequent calls to see alternate dimensions catching up with her? It was oddly addictive to see the shadow versions of the people she knew, similar but always different. Her visits made her appreciate how lucky she was to know the men and women gathered around her, right here in this moment. Of all the paths they could have taken in life, they'd chosen the ones that led them here, tonight. Didn't that make her the luckiest Constance in any dimension? "Thank you, Hearn. Let me ask, is everyone sitting comfortably?"

Some were lying comfortably. Mr. and Mrs. Singh dozed in each other's arms, curled in a hammock slung between the large brass telescopes bolted to either side of the raised foredeck of the ship. The conscious members of the crew, strewn about the main deck on chairs, blankets, exo-suit pilot seats, and cushions, raised their glasses in salute.

"Then I'll begin." She cleared her throat. "I appreciate everyone's help in looking for little Boo. Were we not being hounded by RATT over these wretched relics . . ." She glared at a smashed mechanical tarantula that Hearn had opened for her earlier in the day. The inclusion of a mummy's finger along with the usual threatening note was an especially tasteless move on their part. ". . . then I'm sure we would still be in Rome now. Welli's contacts are scouring the city for our lost crew member, and should we receive any news, rest assured, we will act upon it. Regrettably, the British Museum is forcing us ever onward, and our time is running out. The good news is that we now possess two Enigma Keys, and I've located a third. Mrs. Singh has had us running on autopilot toward one of the greatest cities in the world—no, not Sheffield, before anyone asks."

She eyed Cawley, now wide awake and pouring himself a cup of tea. "Shame, shame," he muttered to no one in particular.

"With the aid of my aether mirror . . ." She glanced at the lounging Trusdale, stretched out on what appeared to be a horse blanket. Even absinthe wasn't quite enough to banish the concern from his face. ". . . which I've used very sparingly and only when absolutely necessary . . ." That wasn't true, but there was no reason to upset Trusdale any further. ". . . I've discovered that another Enigma Key is located in London."

"Just don't say it's been stashed in the Queen Victoria's privy at Buckingham Palace," smiled Welli. The crew chuckled.

Constance grinned. "Of course not. It's located in the Jewel House in the Tower of London."

Everyone laughed uproariously. Constance's grin faltered. "No, really, it is."

The laughter died on the spot. Sea air gusted across the deck, bringing a chill that caused Constance to shiver.

"Are you out of your tiny mind?" said Welli. "You can't possibly waltz into the fortress that houses the crown jewels and whisk away anything larger than a speck of dust. There are Beefeater guards, clockwork surveillance ravens, redcoat patrols, armored mechanical warhorses—"

"But we have a secret weapon. Two of them, in fact." She gestured at the retired military scientists, Doctors Chauhan and Huang, snuggled together beneath a blanket in a cozy corner of the deck. The two scientists gaped at her from their unobtrusive love nest. "Maya and Zhi designed many of the mechanical security devices that patrol the Tower of London. As such, I'm sure they can provide us with an excellent strategy for getting in and out of the tower undetected."

The two former colleagues exchanged alarmed looks. Maya cleared her throat. "Constance, we may be retired from Her Majesty's service, but that doesn't mean we want to commit treason."

Constance frowned. "How could this possibly be treason? Trespassing, I'll grant you. If we actually find the Key, of which there is no guarantee, maybe we could be charged with a little light burglary. But surely not treason?"

"The crown jewels, Constance," said Maya. "The jewels of state. The shiny rock-covered hats that symbolize Victoria's majesty and authority. I've seen her charge gardeners with treason merely for failing to cut her lawn to the exact length she desired."

"I'll only be in there for a few minutes. No one will mind."

"I'll mind," said Maya firmly.

"Me, too," said Zhi. "Although, you could use Maya's mechanical carrier pigeons as a distraction for the clockwork surveillance ravens. We have four of the pigeons on board, and the fifth should be returning from your Godmother's home any day now."

Welli snorted. "Probably with more bile about King Louis being banished to his Prussian cousin's third finest castle. It's probably a good thing that she's decided to pack up the contents of her French château and head back to Yorkshire. It will take her mind off the genteel revolution, as the papers are now calling it."

Zhi nodded absently at Welli. "And of course, Lord Pendelroy's retired officer status and his silver tongue may allow him to talk his way into the Beefeaters' on-site tavern, the Yeoman Warders Club. The club has the weakest security in the Tower of London fortress, because who in their right mind would do anything nefarious within sight and sound of off-duty Beefeaters? They're notoriously tough and dedicated to their roles. If His Lordship could find a hiding place in the club, perhaps in the kitchen's vast pantry, he could sneak out after hours and plant harmless devices designed to distract the troops. Smoke bombs, glitter bombs, stench bombs, that sort of thing. The guards would be driven to distraction if they all went off in a timed sequence spread across, say, twenty minutes."

Welli folded his arms and scoffed. "That is absolutely not happening. None of it. Glitter bombs, I ask you. Not now, not ever."

Zhi jumped to his feet, his round face alight with joy at solving a seemingly impossible puzzle. "Please, your lordship, hear me out." He pushed his spectacles up on his nose and grinned manically. "What if we used one of our exo-suits to cause an almighty distraction? What a commotion it would cause amongst the Beefeaters and any nearby redcoat troops if they observed an exo-suit attempting to storm the fortress, say, through the ancient Traitor's Gate."

"The what now?" asked Hearn.

"The gate is comprised of giant oak doors that let out directly onto the River Thames. Ships used to enter the fortress this way, often carrying traitors to the crown. It's one of the fort's few weak points." He held up a hand to stop Maya interrupting him. "I know, my dear, weak is a relative term. But consider this—we could rig an exo-suit up with a short-term air supply, and someone—for instance, Mr. Trusdale—could walk it along the bottom of the river right up to the Gate. The royal submersible squid, *HMS Sir Inks-a-Lot,* is currently moored in a water-filled inlet on the inside of the Gate. Mr. Trusdale could bang the exo-suits' giant fists upon the ancient oak doors of the Gate. Or, perhaps more spectacularly, he could wield a blowtorch in each of the suit's hands and attempt to burn through the oak planks. Beneath the exo-suit's armor plating, he'd be safe from the guard's gunfire and the docked submersible's missiles that would no doubt be fired toward him. Unless you stole them in advance, of course."

Trusdale sat up, his almost-handsome face pale beneath his tan. "Oh no. I am not going to single-handedly attack the Tower of London in an exo-suit. No way, no how."

Zhi snapped his fingers. "Aha. I've figured out the next step. With all this mayhem going on under the cover of night, Mrs. Singh could fly the disguised *Lady Penelope* over the tower of the Jewel House. We can transform the airship to its air-pirate alter ego, the *Bad Penny*. With its black camouflage cloths and black armor plating, the ship should be difficult to spot against the night sky. As the airship drifts over the Jewel House on silent running, Mr. Singh could lower Miss Constance, Hearn, and Cawley down to the tower's flat roof. Hearn should easily be able to knock out the redcoat sniper who usually guards the roof."

Cawley and Hearn shook their heads vigorously. "We're not doing that," said Cawley. "Jumping off an airship on top of a redcoat? That's not in my job description."

Hearn sniffed. "I'm sorry to say that it *is* actually written into my job description, under 'taking out undesirables as needed from a moving vehicle.' Still, I don't want to do it from an airship in flight, if you don't mind, your ladyship."

Constance blinked at him, then turned her attention back to Zhi.

Zhi rubbed his chin, deep in thought, as Maya gaped at her paramour's newfound criminal creativity. He said,

"Once Constance, Cawley, and Hearn have secured the tower roof, they can pass down through the roof's trapdoor into the spiral stairwell. You could run down the stairs, bypassing the high security prison cells and any remaining warders, straight down to the ground floor jewel chamber. It's locked and barred from outside at night, with a dozen or so redcoat troops stationed outside. Assuming that the troops have been pulled away from the scene by Lord Pendelroy's explosions, and Mr. Trusdale's exo-suit attack—"

"Nope," said Trusdale. "Again, not happening. Absolutely not."

"—and also assuming that you, Constance, have secured the Enigma Key on your journey, you could let yourself out of the Jewel House and sprint for the walls of the fortress. You'd then take the nearest stairs leading up to the ramparts. If you can leap off the top of the walls, perhaps into something soft, or failing that, the Thames inlet that flows through the Traitor's Gate . . . well, there's a slim chance you'll make it out alive."

Constance applauded him with gusto. "I like it! Well done, Dr. Huang." The doctor bowed his head modestly. "That's a wonderful Plan with a capital 'P.' A few small tweaks, such as the fact that I can't possibly launch myself off the fortress's walls into the Thames, because I can't swim, you see, but other than that—"

She clapped her hands over her ears as every conscious being on board, except Zhi, started shouting at her at once. "All right, we'll work on the details. I can't think of a better plan, so if anyone has any better ideas, now's the time to share."

Cawley stood tall, swaying, with his shirt uncharacteristically untucked. "I'm sorry your ladyship, but you know very well that your father said you were never to go to London. Not under any circumstances. He forbade it, in fact."

He might as well have punched her in the stomach. The familiar emotional cocktail of fury, frustration, and a longing for approval drenched her as surely as the River Thames.

A memory of Papa, red-faced and furious at catching her reading Dickens again, telling her that she was forbidden to even read about London, never mind visit it, surfaced.

Her mother had stood by his side, dressed in her sky-blue silk travel gown, ready to go with him down to their London townhouse. A night at the opera was on the cards, with no place for a young Constance by their side.

Even today, the sweet sound of an opera aria made her heart break into a thousand pieces.

She tilted up her chin. "As Papa decided to gambol off to another dimension to spend his life with an alternate version of my late mother, I don't think that his opinion on this matter counts one jot, do you?"

She fixed Cawley with a steely eye.

The wrinkled retainer licked his lips, but his gaze was steady. "I've looked after you since you were a day old, miss. You're as close to family as I'd ever want to be around. But we promised the master—"

"We?" She glowered at Hearn, who buried his nose in a wine goblet.

"We," continued Cawley, "promised the Baron that we wouldn't let you go to London no matter how much you kicked and screamed about it. Whether you were seven, seventeen, or thirty-seven, that's what he said, and that's what we'll stand by." He lifted his own chin in defiance.

The crew gasped, glancing back and forth between the estranged mistress and servant as if they were at a tennis match. Hearn sank deeper into his wine goblet.

"And you, Hearn, are you going to *let me* go to London?" Her tone was ice cracking over a deep, dark lake.

The coachman gulped. "Well, miss, a promise is a promise. And then he made us promise not to tell you about the promise. Which I think we've just managed to break." He glared at Cawley. "But after that, he also made us promise not to tell you about the other thing either. The reason why you must never go to London. The darkest secret of the Haltwhistle dynasty—"

"Shut up, you idiot," snapped Cawley. "Ignore him, miss. Anyway, if the Baron said you're not to go, then I'll have to put my foot down with a firm hand. And nobody wants to see that."

Goosebumps rose along her arms, and she shivered. "So, my ever-loyal servants are still more beholden to my father than me? Did he . . ." her voice cracked. "Tell me the truth, right now. Was I an unwitting tool he used in his experiments to unlock the secrets of the Enigma Keys?"

Her eyes met Trusdale's. There, now the truth would be in the open. He would hear firsthand that in no way had her father ever . . ."

"Oh aye, m'lady," said Hearn. "Of course you were. Right from day one. You were even conceived atop the Keys. They were kept for the longest time under your father's marital bed—"

"Shut up, you idiot," hissed Cawley. "She doesn't need to hear that."

It was a gut punch straight to the corset. "You mean it's true? He knowingly subjected me to alien energy, knowing it was harmful? To what purpose?"

"To make you stronger, m'lady," said Hearn. "You father always wanted you to be the strongest, most powerful Constance out there. It was for your own good, he'd always tell us. But then, you didn't develop the way he wanted you to, so—"

She gasped. "Wait, are you telling I'm not only a lab rat, but I'm also a failed experiment? Is that why he left me?"

Hearn glanced between his mistress and Cawley, whose face was almost purple with rage. "I, well, I don't know why his lordship stopped coming home. Our job was to just to keep you safe, and away from London at all costs."

Her mind raced. "If my being a failed experiment isn't the deep dark secret, what is?"

"Oh well," said Hearn. "That would be about your great-great-great-great-grandmother."

Cawley groaned and flopped back onto his armchair. "Now you've done it, you cretin. Why don't you just tell her the whole damned story? What's a twenty-odd-year-old blood oath when stacked up against a barrel of absinthe punch?"

"My great-great . . . Who would that be? I can't remember the name—?"

"She's not on the family tree. Too secret for that. There's a false name in her place. No one knew about the wedding to Dudley, you see. By the time your ancestor was born, they'd fallen out, because she wouldn't let him tell the world about their marital state. In short, she divorced him as fast as she'd married him, and he plotted against her from that day on. She hid her pregnancy beneath her gowns, and she had her ladies-in-waiting sworn to secrecy. When her baby girl was born, she had her ferried away by Lady Haltwhistle, who claimed the child was her own. Her mother didn't want her to live the life she led, surrounded by men she couldn't trust. She wanted a better life for her only child. A noble sacrifice on her part, and a secret which has been carried down through the centuries until right here, right now. Your father said we could tell you when you either turned thirty, or got married. But the way things are going, I have my doubts you'll be doing either, m'lady, no disrespect intended."

Trusdale held up his hand. "Forgive me, but the American here needs a little help. Are you talking about—?"

"Her Royal Majesty, Elizabeth the First. As her only legitimate descendant, Constance Haltwhistle is the last Tudor."

The collective gasp that went up from the crew must have lifted the airship's balloon by at least three feet.

"I'm . . . the last Tudor? But . . . what does that have to do with me not going to London?"

"Queen Victoria knows of your heritage. By royal covenant, her line doesn't interfere with your line. She's descended from the Stuarts, and as far as the British public know, the Tudors died with Elizabeth. But Victoria isn't as popular these days as she once was. Storming parliament was a bold move, and although no one has dared to stand against her, if there was another claimant to the throne—"

"She might be threatened," said Cawley. "She might bump you off, especially with you looking so much like your royal forebear."

Maya clasped her hands to her face. "No wonder you looked so at home in your Elizabethan gown. Now I look at you, the resemblance is striking."

Everyone stared at her. Constance felt rage rising in her stomach. She kept her voice calm as she addressed the crew. "Well, this has all been most educational. If I ever manage to reconnect with my father through the aether mirror, I shall have some choice words to share with him." She swayed, aware that every eye on the ship was comparing her, favorably or otherwise, against her famous forebear. "I trust that you will all take this secret to your graves."

The crew nodded and mumbled acquiescence, too shocked to offer her any words of comfort. But what could they have said to make this situation any better?

Her father and servants had betrayed her.

Trust no one. No wonder Papa had raised her to be paranoid. She'd had an invisible target on her back since the day she was born. "My friends and family, I shall ask this of you only once. Will you come with me to the Jewel Tower? If so, please raise your hand."

Everyone raised their hands, even the two traitors. "My eternal gratitude to you all. However"—she fixed her gaze upon her servants—"Cawley, Hearn, you have done me a great disservice. One that I cannot forgive. I counted you as my closest allies, but you were never truly on my side. My father is lucky to have such loyal retainers. Sadly, I can no longer employ you in my service."

Hearn frowned. "Are you sayin'—?"

"We're fired," said Cawley. He gazed at his former mistress, tears in his eyes. "The minute we dock in London, we'll go. But know this, m'lady, whatever it looks like, we always loved you."

"That's the truth," said Hearn, his voice wavering. "And if I could turn back time and do things differently, I would. But I can't, and I'm sorry for the hurt we've caused."

She straightened her posture. "Perhaps in another dimension, I forgive you. But not this one. Not now, at least."

She waited for them to fight to win back her good opinion with genuine remorse and promises of better future behavior. Instead, the two men hung their heads, avoiding her gaze. Was this shame on their part, or had they secretly wished to leave her employ since the day she took charge of Haltwhistle Hall? Had she never been anything more than a burden thrust upon them by her father?

She bit her bottom lip to stop it from trembling. Had they never truly cared about her for her own sake? Was she that unlovable?

Tears stung her eyes, but she refused to allow them to fall. If she was to be a kingdom of one, then she would rule with an iron heart that no servant could ever break.

She said with all the hauteur she could muster, "Then I wish you well, Mr. Hearn and Mr. Cawley. This is the last time that you shall have to suffer my presence, or I yours." She glanced around the open-mouthed crew. "Now, I have pressing matters to attend to in my cabin. I do not wish to be disturbed until such time as I am required to participate in our mission. Is that understood?"

She did not wait to see them nod acquiescence as she swept as regally as she could toward the steps that led below deck. She passed by her former servants without so much as a glance.

It wasn't until she reached her cabin that she allowed the tears to fall.

And fall.

And fall some more.

Chapter 24:
A Tale of Two Constances

Constance raised her teacup to her alternate self, a warrior in plate armor with a jagged scar across her left cheek. The scar was a souvenir from a battle in which she claimed she'd struck down a cruel king.

She toasted, "To a better future for both of us."

Other Constance grinned, showing the gap where her front two teeth had been lost on yet another battlefield. "I'll drink to that." She raised her tankard of mead and drank heavily.

"So, your armies march ever north, and you're the new Queen of Prussia? I've recently found out that I have royal blood in my own veins."

"Then be careful it stays there. There's always some-one ready to stab you in the back when you're a queen. Trust—"

"No one? That seems to be a familiar refrain in our family across all of space and time. But I'm lucky to know at least one man I can trust."

"The last man I trusted gave me this," said other Con-stance, lifting up her neck to show a thin scar. "Knife blade as I slept. Idiot. He won't have the opportunity to do that again."

Constance decided not to ask for what she could only imagine were gory details. She glanced toward the near-est porthole, lit bright by the morning sun. "It's about ten o'clock now. We docked in London an hour ago. I heard a lot of banging and scraping from the furnace room, and then, silence. Mr. Singh brought me my morning tea and toast, so I'm assuming that Cawley and Hearn have left the ship. I know I should go out there, but . . . I'm scared."

"Of what?"

"That maybe they've all left me when I needed them most. I can't possibly storm the Tower of London by my-self."

"You'd need an army."

"Exactly. If I only had yours. They sound simply mar-velous."

Other Constance shrugged. "They're not bad gals. We've taken half of Europe, and their blood's still afire for more conquest. What more can you ask for?"

"Well, quite."

"If your army has left you, maybe you could round up some feisty locals with a nice big battering ram? You could bash your way in through the walls."

Constance tugged on her left earlobe. "Good idea, but I believe the walls are too thick. Fifteen feet thick at the base, and eleven at the top, from what I recall from my history lessons. Or was that just the walls of the White Tower? I'm not sure. Even my disintegrating ray gun can't get through that much stone."

The mirror shimmered. Constance made her apologies to the warrior as her fierce image disappeared to be replaced by an incoming communication. A brunette version of Constance in a delightful lemon lace gown appeared. She grinned. "Oh good, I've caught you. I did a little research as you asked, and no, there are no tunnels into the tower, at least none that have been documented. So, hopefully, your crew will be true to their pledge that they'll carry out Dr. Huang's plan. Have you gone up to see if they're still there?"

She shook her head. "Not yet. I'm terrified every one of them has gone, and I'm the sole resident on a ghost ship."

"Ugh, ever the drama. Pull yourself together and go and have a look." A male voice, high-pitched and nasal, called from outside the cabin. Other Constance bellowed, "In a minute. Lord help me, Pinkie—"

"Pinkie?"

"My husband. We're on our second honeymoon, but naturally I insisted on separate cabinets. He does so snore."

"Oh no. I . . . you . . . surely you didn't marry Lord Pinkington-Smyth? The man has no chin."

"It wasn't his chin I was interested in."

Heat flamed across Constance's cheeks. She lifted her teacup to hide her shock.

"No, not that. Where is your mind? It was his estate I was after. His older brother died in a hunting accident, and Pinkie inherited the lot. Title, land, houses. It was such a fortuitous death for me, I think."

Constance placed her cup and saucer down onto the iron bistro table she'd dragged in front of the mirror. She sat back and frowned at her other self.

"I can't believe you married Pinkie. I mean, he was nice enough, but . . ." She recalled the pallid, skinny youth her godmother had once introduced her to. He'd had a penchant for paisley vests and bowties, and an insignificant mustache that glistened with an overabundance of wax.

"Well, who else? Pinkie and I are as happy as any two people who enter into an arranged marriage with absolutely nothing in common. Four children so far, but sadly, the boys all have their father's looks."

"Four boys?" said Constance faintly.

"Yes. We're on our way back from our second honeymoon, actually, trying for a fifth son. Auntie Madge was kind enough to give us her estate in the south of France for a wedding present. That's where I found this old mirror frame packaged up in a closet. I had no idea I . . . that is, you . . . would talk to me through it. How utterly entertaining. I get so bored of Pinkie and the children. Perhaps we can make this a regular event?"

Constance nodded. "Absolutely. I should tell you a couple of things in case you choose to talk to other Constances. One, I'm clearly the nicest of all of us."

Married Constance laughed. "And two?"

"I've encountered some worlds where the alternate version of us has met an untimely death. Hunting accidents, assassins, being shot by the servants, it's just one thing after another. It's strange to think of all these dimensions with a Constance-sized hole in them."

The other Constance placed her teacup onto her marble-topped bistro table. "That is most chilling. Perhaps I won't try to communicate with anyone other than you, assuming you survive your trip to the tower, of course."

She nodded. "I suppose the mission does involve an inordinate amount of danger. I wonder how long it would take for the people in my world to forget me?"

Other Constance said gently, "Well, I won't forget you, if that's any consolation."

Oddly, it was. She grinned at her other self. "Thank you."

"You're most welcome. May I ask, have you tried to speak to your own papa? My father died from falling out of a homemade hot air balloon, but yours is still alive, albeit in the wrong dimension. I believe he owes you an apology for abandoning you to the care of his servants."

She shook her head. "He was happy enough to leave me here alone. I think it's time I moved beyond his shadow." She glanced over at the framed oil painting of Mama hanging over the fireplace. "And it hurts too much to see other versions of Mama. I've talked to one or two, but they're not *her*, you know."

"What about the torn-page letters you received? Maybe your true mother really *did* write them. Don't you owe it to yourself to go and find out?"

She shrugged. "I don't know. Maybe. If I survive the Tower of London mission, I'll consider looking into the situation."

"That sounds like an excellent idea. Now, to happier matters." Other Constance pushed away her own teacup and saucer. "If not Pinkie, who did you end up marrying?"

"Oh, well, no one yet."

Her alternate self's eyebrows raised. "Good heavens. But . . . surely you're the same age as me? Twenty-one? How can you possibly not be married? Are you planning to become an old maid?"

"Well, no. I just haven't met the . . . that is, I haven't met a suitable . . ."

Married Constance's jaw dropped. "But what about the family line? It's your duty to keep the bloodline going. Particularly now you know about our great-great- what is she again? I'll just say Elizabeth the First, for short."

"Marriages aren't that easy for me to come by. That said, it's not like I didn't have offers. I was engaged, actually, for a few hours. My fiancé was Queen Victoria's favorite grandson, Prince Lucien. But things didn't work out. Mostly because he kept trying to kill me."

It was somewhat gratifying to see a wave of envy sweep over the other Constance's face.

"A prince? Gosh. Is there any chance that you could win back his favor?"

"Well, no. He did plot to kill his grandmother and take her throne. The Queen frowns upon attempted regicide, even from her own grandson."

Other Constance gazed at her. "'Her Royal Highness, Princess Constance.' It certainly has a ring to it. To think, you were that close to becoming royalty. I mean you *are* royalty, I suppose, because of being the last Tudor. But what's the point of having royal blood if no one knows about it? Now, tell me, what did this Prince Lucien look like? If he *had* become king, would he have made a fine profile on the realm's coins and postage stamps?"

Constance considered the matter. "I believe so, yes. He was impossibly handsome, built like a roguish duke in a romance novel. Slate-gray eyes, angular cheekbones, and an aquiline nose that presided over an impeccably curled handlebar mustache. His wardrobe was to die for. But then again, everything about him was to die for, given his penchant for murder."

"Still, never say never," smiled the other Constance. "Even an evil prince is still a prince. Is there no one else who might save you from spinsterhood?"

Constance averted her eyes from her other self.

Married Constance leaned forward on her chair. "Oooh, there is, isn't there? Come on, spill the tea. Who is he?"

Constance rubbed her forehead, hoping a genie might appear to whisk her away from this part of the conversation. "No one, really. I mean . . . there's a tall American cowboy on board who, in certain lights, isn't entirely unattractive. He's brave, and funny, and I'd trust him with my life. But I'm not clear on what his intentions are toward me. And frankly, I'm not brave enough to ask him straight out."

"Oh, you poor dear, a cowboy. I suppose he shoots six-guns and lassoes things all day?" Married Constance picked up an ivory fan from her bistro table, flicked it open, and wafted herself vigorously at the very thought.

"He doesn't seem to be a fan of guns. Quite ironic really, given my own predilection for firearms."

"I loathe the things. Of course, that's how the Hall ended up going into receivership. I refused to take over the family business."

"On moral grounds?"

"No, I just didn't care for the paperwork. So many telegrams. Well, I wish you the very best of luck with your possible suicide mission. The sun climbs ever higher, and I must attend to Pinkie and the boys. They've probably worn out both the nanny and the cook with their breakfast antics. If you will excuse me?"

"Oh yes. Absolutely. If I survive the tower escapade, I'll look for you."

"Splendid," smiled Married Constance. She strolled out of the cabin to spend time with her family.

With a sigh, Constance walked out of her cabin to see whether the ship was deserted.

To her delight, Trusdale was waiting for her on the deck. "Finally. I was about to come and get you. Thought you might need a lie in after last night's drama. Are you okay? You look ill."

She could have hugged him. "You're still here. I was concerned I might be marching into the Jewel House alone."

"Well, you will be doing that. We've made a few tweaks to Dr. Huang's plan, but rest assured, we'll all play our parts in distracting the guards while you get dropped onto the tower roof by Mr. and Mrs. Singh."

The elegantly turbaned valet waved down at her from the upper deck. "My dear wife wouldn't hear of us not taking an opportunity to irritate the British crown. She has requested that any spare tiaras you might loot in the Jewel House be added to her wardrobe."

Constance nodded. "I'll see what I can carry out."

Trusdale grimaced. "Once again for the record, Mr. Singh, I'm not a fan of your, admittedly intimidating, wife, turning this escapade into a jewel heist. Maybe no one will notice a one-inch triangle of metal disappearing, but a tiara?"

Mr. Singh shrugged. "It's merely a request. From the woman who navigates our airship. I will leave it to Lady Haltwhistle to decide whether you wish to keep our getaway pilot happy."

"Ugh. So, I get it, your wife gets a new shiny hat or else. Like we don't have enough problems," grumbled Trusdale. "I guess this is the price we pay for getting everyone on board with this absurd plan." He gazed at her, his blue eyes as inviting as any ocean she'd ever seen. "It appears RATT won't stop hounding us until they either get their treasure back from Haltwhistle Hall, or they make themselves a brand-new mummy exhibit, courtesy of our corpses. It's do or die time, and we've chosen to do. We're all with you, your ladyship."

She gazed up at him with eyes blurred by tears. "You were right about my father. I was nothing but a laboratory rat to him. And the one thing that made me special, my royal blood, why, he even chose to keep that a secret from me."

Trusdale reached out and brushed a stray strand of hair away from her face. "That's never what made you special, Constance. The boldness in your step, even when you don't know what's around the next corner, and the way your smile lights up as bright as a sun when you're talking about your favorite novels. These are just two of the hundreds of things that make you special, and not one of them has to do with your ancestry. You're unique, Constance, one of a kind."

But she knew firsthand, she was only one of a crowd.

It was Trusdale who was one of a kind.

Chapter 25:
The Jewel House

Constance leaned over the prow of the *Lady Penelope* with brass binoculars pressed against her eyes. The moon was hidden by a thick blanket of clouds supplemented by the smoke that belched from London's industrial forest of chimneys. Even though they were less than a mile from the Tower of London, she could not yet spy the gas lamps flickering along the newly built Tower Bridge. The bridge's twin towers had quickly become an important landmark for the thousands of airship pilots that traversed the capital city's skies.

Even now, at midnight, cargo ships sailed across the darkness lit with battery-operated lights now required upon hydrogen-ballooned commercial dirigibles. Airship freight cranes bristled like weeds across the vast acres of slate-tiled rooftops. Landing platforms for both cargo and passengers topped every flat roof solid enough to bear the immense strain of a tethered ship. The Steamwerks' patented dirigible hook-and-anchor system had changed the landscape of British rooftops since its introduction two decades earlier. Now, thousands of airships bobbed like balloons against their chain or cable tethers, each secured by a three-foot-by-three-foot hook that locked into its rooftop anchor base.

Every hotel, train station, and even some wealthier homes now boasted one or more tethering anchors. Instead of traveling to crowded airfields, passengers could conveniently embark or disembark from a tethered dirigible at the rooftop of their choosing. A tall set of movable stairs was usually maneuvered alongside the airship on its port side. The number of deaths caused from leaping between airship decks and landing stairs had dropped dramatically with the advent of large trampolines being placed around the stairs. Many an heir's neck had been saved by a bout of bouncing. For some, a previously fatal fall had turned into an enjoyable bounce at the end of a dull flight.

No such niceties would await Constance when she jumped from the dangling hook of a moving airship onto the round roof of the brand-new Jewel House. Queen Victoria's custom-built treasure house and VIP prison was eighty feet tall but only twenty feet wide. Mr. Singh was tasked with lowering the dirigible's hook and chain to a discreet height, one that would carry Constance over the fortress's outer walls without drawing the guards' attention. He then had to avoid smashing her against the Jewel Tower's stone walls as he swung her hook over its roof. With the airship's engines cut to allow for silent running, his precision plus his wife's expertise in handling the gliding dirigible would mean the difference between life and death for Constance.

She lowered her binoculars and took in a deep breath of London's soot-saturated air. Her mouth instantly filled with the taste of ash. She coughed and wiped her suddenly tear-filled eyes. It was surely the smoke that caused them to water so. But she did feel so very alone. Only she and the Singhs remained on the airship as they flew toward the distant Tower of London. Trusdale had tried to fill her in on the tweaks of the plan, but her head ached so violently, she could barely focus on his words. Images of other Constances, other Papas, other Mamas, from other worlds, danced through her head, making her stomach churn like a cosmic whirlpool. Presumably, the crew was following Zhi's strategy of using harmless explosions, mechanical pigeons, and the exo-suit assault to give her time to exit the Jewel House with the Key in hand. That was all she needed to know.

"It's time," called out Rani Singh from the helm. Mr. Singh pulled up a hinged floorboard that blended perfectly with the other floorboards near the helm and reached down into a secret compartment to pull the hidden lever within.

With that single motion, the aristocratic pink-and-gold galleon of the *Lady Penelope* transformed into her pirate airship alter ego, the notorious *Bad Penny*. The pink side panels of the ship flipped to reveal black armor plating. Other panels slid back to reveal the black snouts of eight concealed cannons. It was a matter of pride for Welli that they had never been fired in battle. The sudden appearance of a pirate airship in place of a gaudy galleon had always elicited a quick surrender from nervous cargo captains.

It was a well-guarded secret that Welli occasionally allowed Mrs. Singh to fly his airship up to Scotland for a spot of light piracy, which Welli used to supplement his income with a sixty-forty split of any purloined goods.

Constance gazed up as the pink camouflage cloths that draped over the airship's balloon were drawn back to reveal the ship's true colors. The main balloon was as black as the sky around her, emblazoned with a skull and crossbones. As the final element of the airship's transformation, Welli's peacock-emblazoned standard was replaced by a skull and crossbones. No one could mistake the *Bad Penny*'s purpose. She was out to make a ruckus.

As was Constance.

A breeze picked up as the *Bad Penny* swung into its approach run toward the Tower of London. It gusted through the whisper-thin black silk gown Constance wore for modesty's sake over her battle attire. The skirt was daringly split up both sides to allow her to kick as freely as might be required. Beneath the gown, black moleskin trousers hugged her legs down into her knee-high laced boots. She'd sewn a pair of Welli's last-season pants to fit her own curvy, shorter frame with some success. They were a shocking addition to a lady's ensemble, and even slipping them on had thrilled her beyond measure. Pants gave one a sense of power that explained much of the overconfidence she encountered from the men in her life. She could only hope that, one day, all ladies would have the option to wear such potent symbols of equality and personal freedom.

A black leather battle corset, modeled after a diamond-studded version worn by Queen Victoria, was her choice for torso protection over her usual chainmail. The leather was lighter in weight, and frankly, if anyone got close enough to shoot her, her hope was for a quick death. She'd rather die instantly from a single shot than be captured alive by the Tower of London's Beefeater guards. Protestants, Catholics, rebels, saints, and more than one monarch had all met an untimely death within the tower's ancient walls. It had been a center for royal murders, torture, and executions for centuries, and she didn't want to add her own name to its long list of prisoners.

The *Bad Penny* finished her turn. Constance raised the brass binoculars and twiddled the focus dial. The yellow gas lamps of Tower Bridge were now pinpricks on the horizon. The Tower of London lay behind and to the right of the bridge, nestled beside the gleaming water of the River Thames.

She didn't have time to wonder about Trusdale, encased in the exo-suit, trudging his way along the river's muddy bottom. How she would have hated to have his job, surrounded on all sides by a watery grave waiting for its next body. Perhaps she should have listened to Cawley, all those years ago, when the old man tried to talk her into learning to swim.

She shook her head. No, she didn't have time to think about Cawley either. Or Hearn. Or Welli, setting his distraction bombs. Or the scientists, sending up their mechanical carrier pigeons to draw away the tower's clockwork surveillance ravens.

She set aside her binoculars and turned her attention to a black leather rifle case by her feet, kneeling down and clicking open its ornate silver lock.

This was her answer to the loss of Hearn and Cawley's roles in Zhi's plan. On a bed of purple velvet rested sections of the most beautiful firearm the Brass Queen had ever crafted. When assembled, the starlight sniper rifle was long and elegant with a flare reminiscent of a daffodil's trumpet at the end of its polished brass barrel. The marquetry design that traced along the rifle's slender ebony stock celebrated spring flowers and songbirds. A golden crown inside a cogwheel, the maker's mark that identified the gun as a Brass Queen creation, was set beside the trigger. The rifle was one of a trio she had crafted: one for Welli, one for her Irish pen pal Morrigan, and her own very special edition.

She expertly assembled the rifle's sections. As she clipped the silver starlight scope into place, she whispered in an archaic tongue, *"Deamhna Aerig."* The trigger words temporarily ignited a purple beam of light within the scope. According to her research with Daphnia, even though the Ma had been destroyed by the Enigma Keys' sabotage of their invasion of Earth, remnant globs of the shape-shifting species had been blasted across the world. Unable to bond with other elements of their form to take on their natural shape, most of the individual globs had withered into nothingness. But a few had landed on the Celtic isles and found a soft home within the peat bogs.

Rescued by the ancient Celts, the alien blobs had proven to be no more intelligent than a severed human foot. Oddly, they did twinkle in response to certain Gaelic words. Perhaps the lilting vibrations stimulated them like an electrical current?

Thanks to her discussions of the alien remnants with Daphnia, Constance now had a semi-scientific understanding of the starlight gel. Morrigan's gift of the three seemingly magical blobs had always stirred her curiosity. Morrigan herself remained a deeper mystery. But Constance wasn't the type of weaponsmith to look a gift scope in the mouth. With the rifle assembled, she inserted her magazine of nonlethal multistage projectiles.

Welli was the best shot she knew, but, armed with her starlight rifle, Constance could hit the eye of an oil-painted portrait of an ancestor at a half mile. As the *Bad Penny* moved ever closer to the tower, she pulled up her bistro chair and rested her elbows on the wide, teak handrail that ran around the prow of the ship. She cradled the butt of the rifle's stock into the pocket of her shoulder, just above her armpit. The glassy smoothness of the wood stock against her cheek chilled her as surely as if it had been carved from stone. She squinted down the sight, following the starlight scope's purple pinprick of light as it danced over the distant tower walls.

Constance raised the purple pinprick up the white stone walls of the fortress. There were twenty-two towers within the fort, but only six were designated as watchtowers. A single redcoat sniper, armed with binoculars, a polished brass pith helmet, and night vision goggles would be gazing at the London skyline from the top of each one. All she had to do was to quickly and quietly knock them unconscious with the tranquilizer darts embedded into the tip of her projectiles. Once fired through her ultralong silencer, the projectiles would spin toward their target, breaking apart at the last moment to allow only a harmless dart to penetrate the target's skin.

Even with technology on her side, making the shots wouldn't be easy.

She relaxed into her firing stance, breathing gently as the scope light danced to its first target. A sallow-faced youth gazed out over the river, no doubt dreaming of a night where something, anything, interesting might happen on his watch. This was his lucky night. Constance exhaled and gently tightened her finger on the trigger. The *pop* of her shot was softer than the sound of a cork popping from a champagne bottle. The youth slumped as her dart found its mark in his neck.

One down, five to go.

She moved rhythmically from one tower to the next, popping and swinging the long rifle barrel as smoothly as she'd once swung it from the battlements of Haltwhistle Hall down onto overripe apples in her orchard. The action was familiar and easy, even given the speed at which the airship was approaching the fortress.

Mr. Singh joined her, silently cheering her on as she lined up her final shot. As the redcoat fell to the pop of her rifle, the turbaned valet took three steps over to the chain winch at the ship's prow, which raised and lowered the steel anchor hook. "Sixty seconds, miss," he murmured.

Now for the hard part. Constance laid her rifle upon the deck, for once not taking the time to pack away the precious parts into their velvet-lined case. She walked to Mr. Singh's side and peered over the edge of the ship. Ten feet below, the landing hook was neatly clamped against the ship's hull. Designed to connect with anchor locks on rooftops, the hook was not an ideal mode of transportation.

But transport her into the fortress it must. As Mr. Singh released the hook from its clamp, she drew her black kidskin gloves out of her silk gown's ample pockets and put them on. They gave her some grip as she shimmied her way from the deck rail out onto the hook's chain. She cautiously climbed down the steel chain, scrabbling with her toes to find the landing hook at the end, trying not to think of what would happen if she didn't.

Knowing very well that she shouldn't look down, she did exactly that. Her stomach heaved at the hundred-foot drop below her.

Good. That's that out of the way.

"Thirty seconds, miss," called Mr. Singh. "Initiating silent running."

The airship's engines shut down, and the dirigible drifted on, powered only by its prior velocity and a helpful tailwind. The air whistled by her ears as the fortress's white walls loomed through the darkness. The stronghold was more imposing the closer she approached. It had certainly looked much smaller in her history books. Doubt gurgled in her stomach, but she ignored it as if it was the burbling one might expect from eating a past-its-prime pork pie. She'd knocked out the watchmen and the snipers, but scores of Beefeaters and redcoat troops regularly patrolled the castle's grounds. To approach safely, she needed a distraction.

She needed the rest of her crew.

"Ten seconds, miss." Mr. Singh set the winch in motion, and she dropped twenty feet in a heartbeat. The chain yanked to a halt, and she almost wobbled off the hook to her doom. She wrapped one leg around the chain and hung on for dear life with her gloved hands. With good luck and great helmsmanship, she would fly over the castle's outer walls and head straight for the solitary-standing Jewel House. That, or she would be flattened against the fortress's stone walls like an errant fly upon a carriage window. The crenellations that crested the Tower of London's outer walls raced toward her.

Was she too low?

She gulped.

She was. She was too low.

Three seconds.

Two.

One.

She closed her eyes as the outer walls filled her vision.

Bang! Crash! Boom!

Multiple explosions shattered the air as the airship soared up into the night sky. She opened her eyes to see the fortress's eleven-foot-thick external walls race below her boots. The airship continued its sweep upward toward the Jewel House, slowing its velocity as gravity tried to claim it as a prize.

Colorful flashes broke the cover of night across the fortress. Gas lamps that lit the main thoroughfares flickered into darkness. Presumably, her crew had added sabotage of the main gas line to the Plan with a capital "P," a brilliant touch on their part.

The quilted pattern of dark and light patches across the fort was carefully orchestrated to draw eyes away from the *Bad Penny*'s flight path.

Glitter flittered through the air, blown sky-high by Welli's well-placed devices. Maya's stench bombs wafted pungent farmyard fumes across the tower, making Constance gag. Years of raising pedigree pigs had not prepared her for the rotten perfume conjured by the Steamwerks' greatest scientist.

Maya's crowning achievement, a bulbous bronze-and-brass armored exo-suit, half emerged from the Thames to rage its solitary war at the Traitor's Gate. Constance prayed to any god who would listen for Trusdale's safety.

Water covered most of the suit's rounded glass cockpit, obscuring her vision of its pilot as the suit ignited a blowtorch in each massive hand. It set to work burning through the medieval timber of the Traitor's Gate. Nearby redcoat troops began to fire their rifles toward the semi-submerged exo-suit.

If only I'd had time to tell him . . .

It was too late. Her heart lurched at the thought of Trusdale encased in the velvet cockpit, staring out through the glass at the waves of troops determined to kill him.

And he was doing it to save her.

She lifted her head. No, he was doing it so that she could save them all. Her crew had completed their part of the mission. Now, it was her turn.

The roof of the Jewel House approached.

As the crenellated wall that ringed its roof swept beneath her boots, she jumped, tucking and rolling as best she could in a long silk gown. Fortunately, the comatose body of the redcoat sniper she'd knocked out cushioned her fall. The poor man would no doubt wonder in the morning what had happened that could have left him with bruises on his buttocks.

Hopefully, she wouldn't be present to explain his black-and-blue behind in person.

Winded, she rolled onto her knees and watched the *Bad Penny* labor toward the far side of the fortress. She wasn't supposed to wait to hear its engines roar into life, but as the shadowy ship swept over the outer walls of the fortress, she grinned as the familiar boom of ignition reached her.

Confident that the ship had a good chance of reaching the rendezvous point with the rest of the crew, she pushed herself to a stand and hurried to the tower's spiral staircase.

She kept her right hand running along the stonework as she rushed down the stairs, left hand holding up her gown. Fortunately, no one was around to see her outrageous flash of ankle. The stairs led into a storage room packed almost to the roof with crates branded with Queen Victoria's Royal Cipher, a calligraphy representation of her initials, VR. Some of the crates had been opened. Judging from the jewels and coins spilling upon the oak floor, these were the riches deemed not spectacular enough to make it into the Queen's Jewel Chamber at the bottom of the tower.

But that didn't mean the Enigma Key wasn't here. Constance wrote upon her mental blackboard, trying to connect with the new Key. She could only hope that this particular one was like Daphnia—loquacious, sophisticated, and willing to move to a new home.

Contact! The new Key drew a wavy representation of a human eye upon the blackboard.

Ugh. Creepy. Is it saying that it's watching me or that it's being watched?

She attempted to ascertain the Key's location in the tower.

Please be right here in this room. Please be . . .

She groaned as a shaky drawing of the state crown of Victoria appeared on the blackboard. So, the Key was most likely looking at the crown in the main Jewel Chamber. That had been her worst-case scenario.

Bother.

She ran down the next flight of stairs, attempting to illustrate her Plan with a "P" by drawing stick figures onto her mental blackboard . . .

A thick arm clad in a scarlet uniform walloped her across the neck, knocking her straight back off her feet and slamming her spine onto the hard edges of the stone steps. She clutched at her throat, choking, as pain flared through her back and she slid inexorably toward a large pair of black, polished boots attached to a stout, white-bearded Yeoman Warder. As she hacked and coughed, tears streaming down her cheeks, the Beefeater's meaty hands grabbed her and dragged her across the oak floorboards toward an iron-barred cell. She flailed her arms ineffectively, sobbing and trying to explain that this was all a ghastly mistake, officer, as the Beefeater opened the cell door. Close enough to smell the corned beef and ale that had served as the burly man's dinner, she hit the floor of the cell. She lay there, gasping, as keys jangled in a lock behind her. She peered back at the glowering warder.

He snarled, "In the name of our great Queen, you're under arrest, for whatever it is you were doing up there. If I find anything gone from them storage crates . . ." He thumped his right fist into his left palm. "Even so much as a single coin, I'll add theft to your charge of trespassing."

She croaked, "This is all a big misunderstanding. I lost my tour guide, and somehow . . ."

But the yeoman was already stomping his way up the stone stairs to check for signs of theft. If he extended his search up to the roof . . .

I'm done for.

With a whimper, she rolled onto her knees and blinked at a pair of burgundy-and-gold tasseled carpet slippers. The slippers were keeping the toes of a man in gold silk pajamas embroidered with a silver duke's coronet warm. Built like a wayward duke in a risqué romance novel, his slate-gray eyes, angular cheekbones, and aquiline nose presided over an impeccably curled handlebar mustache.

She gulped. Prince Lucien Albert Dunstan, third Duke of Hallamshire, thirteenth in line to the British throne and once Queen Victoria's favorite grandson, stared down at his former fiancée with shock written across his impossibly handsome face.

Chapter 26:
The Prisoner

Prince Lucien gaped down at the kneeling redhead. *Ugh. Is there anything worse than running into an ex-fiancée when you're not dressed to impress?* He brushed stray cookie crumbs left from his midnight snack off his silk pajamas and said, "My dear, darling girl. How lovely of you to pop by."

"Your Royal Highness," squeaked Constance. "You're looking . . . well." Her eyes were still as green as his favorite billiard table, now seized by the crown along with his thirty-thousand-acre estate, Wedgeworth Warbling. He stood before Constance as poor as a church mouse who'd once owned a cathedral.

The feeling was . . .

Humbling? Yes, there was the usual outrage and re-sentment, but beyond that . . .

Damn it all. Except for my title, I'm no better off than this wench.

His downfall had been caused primarily by this girl's interference. His wrath should be mighty as a dragon's, full of fire and fury. And yet . . .

He held out his hand to the downed debutante. She gaped at it as if he were offering her live haddock. He bestowed a thin-lipped smile and said, "I knew you'd come to your senses. No sane woman would break off an engagement with a prince of the realm and not regret her decision."

She opened her mouth, no doubt to apologize for her transgressions. He shook his head. "Let's not waste our short time together with regrets. I doubt the guards will allow a commoner to stay here in the VIP confinement area. They'll move you to some dismal dungeon. But over the last month, I've had time to consider what I would say to you if we ever met again. I've been informed that it was *you* who revealed my plot to assassinate the crown heads of Europe to my dear granny. Had you stumbled in here during my first week of incarceration, I would have strangled you on the spot."

She blinked and scanned the cell, perhaps for a weapon? How delightfully overconfident she was in her abilities.

She would find nothing here to help her. A barber was allowed into his cell once a day to keep his looks prince-perfect, and a royal chef brought him the finest in gourmet meals three times a day.

But other than his clothes, a few books, a gold chamber pot, and an oak four-poster bed draped with medieval hunting tapestries, the cell was bare.

He continued, "Betraying me was a clever piece of social climbing, especially if it leads to a title on your part. I'm . . . impressed at your self-serving determination to make the most of the little you've been given in life." He gestured at her black silk gown, voluminous and shapeless over what appeared to be a black leather battle corset. "You would have made me a fascinating wife. I regret our falling out."

Constance allowed him to pull her to a stand. A waft of her rose and orange-blossom perfume tingled his nostrils. She snapped, "Falling out? You tried to kill me, you brute!"

"Every couple has their little misunderstandings." He smiled, crinkling his eyes in the way that made even the primmest maid go wild.

She ran her gloved hand through her wind-blown bouffant hair. She pulled out two hairpins, and tendrils of flaming red locks tumbled about her shoulders.

Desire stirred deep within Lucien's belly. "Most charming, my dear, but I doubt we have the time—"

"I'll be quick," she said, scooting over to the door and falling to her knees with her back to him.

Constance was showing a whole new side to herself, and he liked it.

He rubbed his teeth with his index finger and smacked his lips. Now he could finally enjoy a taste of the honeymoon he'd never got to take with the unusual redhead. *Most excellent.*

He approached her, then halted. She had two hairpins stuck inside the door lock and was rotating them in a most curious fashion.

He smacked his forehead. "Ugh. I'm such a fool. Of course. You're here to break me out of prison, as penance for your betrayal. How utterly wonderful. Do you know, not one other person even came to visit me? Never mind breaking in here to help me escape. Not even Gunter Erhard, the yellow-livered toad. It was the least he could have done after all those years I tolerated his foreign presence in my court."

Constance stopped her lock-picking and glanced back over her shoulder. "Your man, Erhard, and his ax-wielding thugs have attempted to kidnap me twice this week. I assume you're behind his skullduggery?"

"Good lord, no. Murder, yes, but kidnapping? The only time I kidnapped anyone was those blasted Steamwerks scientists you insisted on rescuing. And I only agreed to that because King Oscar promised me an army in return for both them and that Enigma Key he's obsessed with."

Constance furrowed her brow. "So, Erhard might be working for Oscar now? Or, has he always worked for Oscar, and you were a means to an end?"

He considered the matter. "I always thought he worked for me and liaised with Oscar, but now that you mention it . . . good lord, has my good nature been taken advantage of? I'll cut them both into ribbons and feed them to my hounds." He rubbed his forehead. "That is, I would if I still *owned* any hounds. Granny has taken my entire estate as punishment for our little family squabble."

"You *were* plotting to kill her, her immediate family, and half the crown heads of Europe with a barrage of fire from an imperial dreadnought overrun with invisible abominations."

He shrugged. "All families bicker. Royal families just do so on a grander scale."

She blew out her cheeks and turned back to her work. "This lock is certainly grander than I'm used to. The Queen must have had Steamwerks engineers develop this contraption. They've put fourteen separate mechanisms in here. Talk about overkill."

He nodded absently, mulling over Erhard's possible treachery. It pained his heart to think that anyone would betray him before he betrayed them. A prime example of the falling standards in henchmen and retainers since his granny had entered her frail dotage. Once the old warhorse had reached her seventies, she'd positively mellowed, to the detriment of the entire commonwealth. It had been at least a decade since she'd burned down a major capital. Where was the bloody self-righteousness upon which she'd built her global empire? If only he'd managed to take her crown as planned . . .

Constance continued to click her hairpins in the lock as she mused, "But why would Oscar want to kidnap me now? The death threats I understood. We had a business arrangement that went south, and monarchs are notoriously revenge driven. But to switch from murder to kidnapping seems like a de-escalation on Oscar's part. It makes no sense."

Lucien snorted. "Oscar's obsessed with kidnapping. He even commissioned a special airship for it, some sort of stealthy dirigible with a soundproof cell. That's the Swedes for you." He raised his chin. "We Brits have the backbone to take our enemies out the old-fashioned way—with sword, gun, or bomb. Now that's civilization. Incidentally, I was woken from my slumber by a cacophony of explosions throughout the tower. I assumed anarchists were creating a ruckus, but was it you?"

She glanced back at him and grinned impishly.

He laughed. "Heavens, you're a spirited filly, Miss Haltwhistle. I certainly underestimated you. And I have to say, you're looking more like wife material by the minute."

Constance rolled her emerald eyes. "Keep looking, Your Highness. It's the single life for me. For now, at least. And it's Baroness Haltwhistle now, if you don't mind." She turned her attention back to the lock. "I'm on the last mechanism. If I can just turn it . . . Noooooooo!" The snap of a hairpin breaking unleashed a torrent of swearing from the girl that would have made a Beefeater captain blush.

"Now, steady on, my tart-tongued troublemaker. Perhaps I can help?"

She squinted into the lock. "It's jammed in there. I can't—"

She leaped back from the cell door and stood by his side as footsteps echoed from the spiral staircase that led down from the roof.

The Beefeater warder's cheeks were as scarlet as his overembellished Tudor uniform. He growled at Constance, "No theft, but you rendered a redcoat sniper unconscious." He wagged a meaty finger at the miscreant. "Oh, it's the gallows for you, missy." Through the Tower's thick walls, the muffled sound of gunfire peppered with explosions was joined by a tolling bell. "Ask not for whom that bell tolls. It's you. And probably His Highness there, once the Queen knows he plotted an escape."

Lucien held his hands open, pleading innocence. "I had nothing to do with this."

"That's true, he didn't," said Constance.

Lucien blinked at her in surprise. First, she came to rescue him, and now she was defending him? Her love for him must surely be boundless. The warder snorted and disappeared down the spiral stairs, presumably to tell his fellow guards of the foiled prison break.

Constance let out a string of truly exotic curse words, some of which he'd never heard before. She placed her fingers on her temples and closed her eyes. Her pink tongue poked indecorously from the side of her full lips as she seemed to be attempting to commune with spirits.

Lucien frowned. "If it's the dead you're trying to speak to, I'm sure you'll be able to do so in person soon enough. My dear granny is most efficient in these matters, unless she opts for torture. I must warn you, the food is adequate, but they only serve a third-class claret. And I've had not a single splash of good port since I got here."

"Is that the only torture you've suffered in this place?"

He stared at her. "Isn't that enough?"

She pursed her lips. "We're down to the wire. I've only got limited energy on this thing, so we're going to have to make it count. Hop onto the bed."

He gazed between her and the four-poster. "I must say, you modern women really take the biscuit."

"Get on the bed," she ordered. "We have to reach the ground floor before the warder, and we're not going to do that by chasing him down the stairs. Move!"

He'd never taken an order from a woman before. Somehow, he liked it.

He slid onto the bed and lounged, awaiting her attentions. "I'm ready if you are."

She pressed her fingers to her temples as she walked toward him. She murmured, "The Key now stares at two eyes."

"What is that, a riddle? The key stares at two eyes . . . oh, I get it. It's a lock. Very good. Now, come on up here." He patted the bed beside him.

She jumped feetfirst up onto the bed, standing over him, one hand rummaging in the pocket of her side-slitted gown.

He smirked. "I'm not sure where you're going with this, my dear, but I'm game."

Constance drew a tiny ray gun out of her pocket. "Don't move."

He sat bolt upright. "What do you mean—Waaaaah!" He screamed as the gun fired a flash of lurid green light that disintegrated half the bed and the floor below. Down fell the remains of the bed, his former fiancée, and himself in a stomach-turning tumble of blankets and pillows.

Down one floor, crashing through an empty cell.

Down another, smashing through splintered wood and stone.

Down into the Jewel Chamber, shattering the golden enclosure that arched over the crown jewels and blasting crowns, scepters, orbs, tiaras, loose jewels, and gold dinnerware across the chamber like priceless matchwood.

The air slammed out of his lungs, and he gazed, dazed, at the Yeoman Warder from his cell, caught mid-conversation with a slack-jawed scarlet-clad subordinate.

Constance howled like a banshee at the two of them, hurling her curvaceous form off the remains of the bed and toward the two men.

Lucien looked for a weapon to hand. He picked up the state crown—its jewel-encrusted frame was set off perfectly by its purple velvet cap trimmed with ermine—and flung it at the Yeoman Warder as Constance launched herself at the subordinate with a golden scepter raised like a club in her hand. She bashed the unfortunate man on the head as the Yeoman Warder sprang to catch the flying state crown. He fell onto his side, the crown cradled to his chest, as Constance slapped something drawn from her pocket into the neck of the cringing subordinate. He slumped to the ground, unconscious, as

Constance threw herself on top of the Yeoman Warder. He curled his body protectively around the crown as if it were as delicate as a newborn monarch.

The warder, too, slumped before Constance's onslaught. She turned to Lucien, her eyes bright and her grin captivating in the amber light cast by the chamber's gas lamp sconces. "Tranquilizer darts," she explained, pushing back wanton tendrils of red hair from her flushed face. She'd never looked more lovely—or more dangerous. Her flimsy gown was rent asunder, displaying her black leather battle corset, knee-high boots, and black pants.

Underneath it all, she's a cross-dressing Amazon. Who knew?

She jerked her thumb at the oak door. "You'd best get out of here, if you're going."

He stood unsteadily as jewels pilfered from a dozen nations slid from beneath his feet. He studied the pile of riches and sank to his knees, filling the breast pocket on his silk pajamas with loose diamonds and rubies. "What about you?"

She grinned at the golden scepter in her hand. A purple glow emanated from a triangular trinket set into the staff's bejeweled, crown-shaped head. "I've found my prize. All I need is a tiara to compensate my airship pilot, and I'm out of here."

He studied the pile of loot beneath his feet. He picked up a ruby tiara and what appeared to be Queen Victoria's famous miniature imperial crown. He chuckled and walked toward his ex-fiancée with his mementos in hand. "Here you are, my dear. You've earned these trinkets. One day, when I am King of England, I may crown you something even better." He reached her and gently placed Victoria's miniature diamond crown upon her head. "Seeing you wear this would kill the old battle-ax. Alas, only we shall ever know this happened."

She blinked up at him, her emerald eyes sharper than any jewel in the chamber. "It seems you've changed," she murmured.

"Prison does that to a man." He handed her the ruby tiara and knelt to pluck the large state crown from the Warder's slumbering grip. He placed the crown firmly upon his head and exhaled. "This crown is all I've ever wanted. Well, except for power, wealth, and an empire. You know, the usual."

"The usual." She smiled. And his heart lightened from a solid jet-black to a murky gray. His breath caught in his throat as he gazed at her. "A crown suits you, Baroness Haltwhistle."

"I rather thought it might." She grinned, and his heart uncharacteristically fluttered in response. She reached up to her bird's nest of a hairstyle, drew out two hidden hairpins, and secured her teeny diamond hat upon her head. "Come on. I have an escape route planned. As long as the distraction explosions continue outside, we . . ." She placed one ear against the studded oak door. "Oh, no."

The last bang of an explosion died away. Now, only the clang of alarm bells and gunfire pierced the shroud of night.

She slid back the door's iron bolt. "We're going to have to be quick. My crew should have left a large airship landing trampoline outside the wall near the Traitor's Gate. A ring of hay bales should disguise the trampoline from casual observers as they cruise by on the river. From there, we rendezvous with my airship. We're only a hop, skip, and a bounce from freedom."

Constance pushed the Jewel House's massive oak door ajar and peered out into the courtyard. She ducked her head back inside as a troop of redcoats, bayonets affixed to their long rifles, sprinted by. "Those troops should be heading for the main gate," she whispered. "We've got less than a minute of distractions left."

She picked up her torn silk gown in her left hand and bolted across the courtyard toward the outer wall. Clouds parted overhead, and moonlight glinted off Constance's miniature crown. He followed her, keeping his eyes as fixed on her crown as a shipwrecked man stares at a lighthouse's lamp while flailing in a stormy sea. At this moment, he'd never loved anyone as much as he did Constance. Except himself, of course.

His own crown must be sparkling in the moonlight, too, potentially giving away their position. But he'd rather die than take it off now. Not after all that he'd been through to get it. He might not yet possess royal authority, but, by the heavens, the crown sat upon his head. And that was half the battle.

They scrambled up stone steps to the crenellated ramparts of the outer wall. With the River Thames shimmering on their left and the White Tower glowing in the moonlight to their right, they scurried along the flagstone path. Below them on the roads and courtyards that covered the fortress between buildings, frantic troops ran back and forth. They shouted reports at one another as they searched in vain for the enemies that must surely be everywhere given the number of explosions that had rocked the fortress. The stench of foul air and, inexplicably, clouds of glitter, wafted around him as Lucien ran. They added to the dreamlike experience of escaping from his cell.

Is this a dream? If so, it's one of my best. And I'm even clothed!

He sprinted on, following the shapely behind of his rescuer, Lady Constance Haltwhistle. *What a woman she turned out to be.*

Together, they approached the wood and iron-barred Traitor's Gate, where someone piloting a Steamwerks exo-suit had sliced through with blowtorches and was now advancing on Granny's one-person mechanical squid submersible, the HMS *Sir Inks-a-Lot*, moored just inside the gate. Other than traitors, only the Queen herself passed through this entrance. She believed it to be the most secure exit from the Tower of London. Her paranoia had kept her alive through dozens of assassination attempts, so perhaps the old battle-ax was onto something.

Redcoat troops lined the Victoria Quay, shooting waves of ammunition that bounced harmlessly off the armored exo-suit. Three Beefeaters were standing atop the submersible's ten-foot-long wedge-shaped body, attempting to load the mechanical squid's head-mounted missile launcher. The glass cockpit door behind the missile launcher stood open to the stars, and a redcoat soldier lay on his belly fiddling with the launcher's controls inside. The squid's eight long arms and two fueling tentacles waved lazily in the air on standby mode.

Had the exo-suit damaged the squid somehow? Or had its missile launcher been sabotaged? Certainly, the Beefeaters seemed to be having a devil of a time shoving an explosive missile into the launcher. One scarlet-uniformed officer took the bold approach and reached inside the missile launcher, drawing out a cannonball that had been purloined from the tower's gatehouse cannons.

Ahead of him, Constance slowed her pace, staring at the exo-suit as it inched ever closer toward the squid under the hail of redcoat fire.

He asked, "The trampoline, my dear?"

"We're almost there. It's on the other side of the fortress wall. But that exo-suit is supposed to have retreated by now, and those troops should all be gone. I don't understand what's gone wrong."

He gently shoved her in the small of the back. "Jump now, think later."

"But, don't you see? This isn't the plan. Trusdale is piloting the suit. He wasn't supposed to burn through the gate, just provide a distraction. He should have left already, and those guards should be investigating a distraction at the main entrance. Why did he burn through the gate? Why is he still advancing into enemy fire?"

She slowed almost to a standstill. Irritated by her mention of Trusdale, Lucien pushed her again. "Not our concern. Show me the trampoline."

She waved her hand distractedly. "It's just up here, over the battlements—oh my god!"

The Beefeaters leaped off the top of the squid and its missile ignited, shooting like a comet straight into the exo-suit and blowing it sky-high. Flaming fragments of burgundy velvet and bronze scrap metal rained down, littering the stone walkway.

"Noooooo!" screamed Constance. She dropped to her knees and the scepter fell from her hand to roll along the flagstones. Ahead, a tall Beefeater loped up the stairs beside the Traitor's Gate and barreled down the ramparts toward them.

Lucien dragged Constance to a stand. She sobbed hysterically, as limp as lettuce, every ounce of warrior spirit sapped from her body. As the Beefeater loomed, Lucien shoved the girl with all his might toward the guard. "She's the one you want," he yelled. Constance smashed into the guard's broad chest, sending them both tumbling to the flagstones. Lucien dashed for the outer wall and launched himself over it, feetfirst. Whether the trampoline was there or not, he wasn't going back to his cell.

He plummeted over the wall, hurtling to the ground . . .

Then bounced.

He flew up into the air, in line with the top of the wall. The tall Beefeater was helping Constance to her feet. Her pale face, lit by the moon, gazed up at the guard in apparent surrender.

Women. Just when you think you understand them . . .

He plunged back down to the trampoline, locking his knees to avoid a second bounce. He clambered off the contraption and over its surrounding circle of hay bales, his silk pajamas snagging on the coarse straw. Then he sprinted as best he could in his tasseled slippers for the dark waters of the Thames. With one hand holding on to the state crown, he leaped into the icy embrace of the river. It swallowed him whole, shocking his system with its chill. For what seemed to be an eternity, he blinked up at the moon as he kicked his way back to the surface.

His head broke the waves of the tidal waterway, still wearing his shiny, precious hat. Gulping for air, he shoved it firmly down onto his head and started swimming for the far side of the river, and freedom.

He'd lost the girl, but he'd won the crown.

What devilishly handsome prince could ask for more?

Chapter 27:
What Lies Beneath

Trusdale couldn't decide what was more shocking. The fact that Constance had dissolved into tears on his chest, burying her face into the scarlet wool of his stolen Beefeater's uniform.

Or that she was wearing Queen Victoria's famous miniature crown. Or that she'd apparently broken Prince Lucien out of his well-earned incarceration.

It's gotta be the tears.

He wrapped his arms around the diminutive debutante, a full foot shorter than he, as she sobbed into his chest, her breath coming in ragged gasps. She wailed, "I thought you were . . ."

She suddenly pulled away, wiped her tears, and thumped his chest hard with both fists. He winced. "Ow."

"Don't you 'ow' me. I just saw you die in a horrible exo-suit explosion."

He shook his stolen Beefeater's hat. The round-brimmed "Tudor bonnet" was no substitute for a Stetson. He sure hoped Welli was taking good care of his regular clothes, particularly his precious duster coat and hat. He'd hate to spend more time than he'd have to running around London wearing a scarlet tunic embroidered with the gold initials of the Queen, a stiff white Elizabethan ruff, red knee breeches, and matching socks. Due to not finding the right-sized boots when he pilfered his uniform from the tower's laundry room, he still wore his Western boots. They were a dead giveaway of his interloper status should anyone give him a second glance.

He grinned at Constance. "Don't you worry, now, Miss Adventure. I'm not dead yet. I believe you just saw the *Lady Penelope*'s furnace automaton getting blown up. Maya rigged it to run the exo-suit, but we didn't have time to figure out a way to get it to retreat. It was a glorious end for ole rusty drawers."

She gaped at him, the moon gifting her the beauty of Artemis and the fury of Hera. "You idiot. You almost gave me a heart attack." She knelt and picked up a golden scepter that had fallen by her boots. A crown on the end of the gold staff bore many jewels, but none so precious as the purple, glowing triangle in its center.

"You found the Key," he breathed.

"Was there any doubt?" Her laughter carried a slightly manic edge. An overemotional Constance? The sooner he got her out of here, the better.

Trusdale scanned the twenty-or-so troops and Beefeaters who had been defending the Victoria Quay. Several men were in the water, scooping up the charred remains of the exo-suit. One by one, the rest were starting to move away, searching for the miscreants who had started all of this chaos. Only he and Constance should be left in the fort now.

"Won't be long until those troops are up here on the ramparts breathin' down our necks. It's time for us to bounce. Are you ready for a leap onto the trampoline?"

"I—"

Whether she was or not, he'd never know. From the far side of the wall, next to the river, a volley of gunfire tore the night air asunder. Trusdale raced to the crenulated wall and peered over. Despite the hay bales, a troop of redcoats had discovered their escape route. A dozen soldiers fired their rifles at a glittering object that was bobbing its way across the Thames. "Damn it. Our trampoline is compromised. We're not getting out that way."

Constance checked her crown, still perfectly centered on her bouffant hair. It had to be said, the woman was a virtuoso with her hairpins. As far as he knew, she'd never once lost a hat in battle. She said, "Well, as you and the crew have apparently gone rogue with Zhi's plan, please tell me you came up with an alternate escape route."

"We did. But you're not gonna like it. Pretend like you're my prisoner, hands behind your back. Start marching toward the squid."

"I—Hey!" she exclaimed as he spun her to face the Traitor's Gate and clasped her wrists behind her back.

"Walk. Look upset."

"I *am* upset," she snapped.

"Great. No acting required, then." He frog-marched her along the wall, keeping one eye on the troops circling below like scarlet sharks. "We'll see how far we get. Right now, we've got a semi-open water inlet and a closed off main entrance. Redcoat reinforcements are no doubt on their way. And may I ask, why the hell are you wearing Queen Victoria's crown?"

"Because Lucien took the state crown, I suppose." She exhaled. "You have no idea what I've been through tonight. It's been positively beastly."

I'm not gonna say it. I'm not gonna . . .

But his mouth had a mind of its own.

"Looked like you two were getting pretty chummy, before he threw you to the wolves."

"I honestly thought for a moment that he'd mellowed, but I suppose a leopard doesn't change its spots so easily."

"Or at all," he grumbled.

"You sound positively jealous," she said, a smirk in her tone.

"I think you've pinned that crown on too tight. Watch out, incoming." He put on his best military stride and pushed her toward three redcoats who had made their way up the stairs beside the damaged Traitor's Gate.

"Whatcha got there then?" asked the first redcoat, peering at Constance.

She let out a heartrending wail.

He groaned internally. *All right, don't overdo it.*

In his best working-class London accent, he said, "This silly sausage is the Yeoman Warder's daughter. She tripped over some of the loot the villains dropped, and thought she'd try on the Queen's crown for a lark. I'm taking 'er down to see her father right now. I'm sure he'll have some choice words for 'er 'ighness 'ere. But it's them lads cleaning out the Jewel House that need catchin', not this sprite. You get over there sharpish, and you'll be the boys picking up the medals for banging their 'eads together."

The redcoat nodded. "Fair enough, come on, lads." They pushed past Constance, none too gently.

Trusdale squeezed her wrists as she drew breath to perhaps say something about their rudeness. Fortunately, the Baroness held her tongue.

"Quick march, missy," he whispered. They hustled along the top walls to the stairs. There were now only two Beefeaters left guarding the quay, watching the damaged Traitor's Gate for further attacks.

Only thirty percent of the gate that had stood strong through the reign of monarchs both fair and foul had survived Constance's mayhem. The high tide lapped at its twisted frame.

Hopefully, the gate would be the only casualty this night.

He murmured, "I'm sorry, but I can't let you walk down the steps like this. That warder's daughter story won't wash with actual Beefeaters."

"So how am I supposed to get down the stairs?"

"Remember when I said that you wouldn't like this plan?" He spun her around to face him. "It'll be best if you can pretend to be unconscious."

"What are you— No!" She tightly held on to her crown and scepter as he hauled her up onto his shoulder like a sack of grain.

He said, "Seriously, Your Majesty, stop wriggling like a catfish. It's gonna be hard enough to get down there without you—"

"If that hand of yours 'accidentally' finds its way onto my derriere again, you'll pay for it."

"It wasn't on purpose. I was only trying to—"

"Just get on with the rescue, will you? I don't have all night."

He rolled his eyes at the watching moon and strode down the stone steps with the upright confidence of a military man.

The two Beefeaters guards eyed his unconscious prisoner, but it seemed that such a sight was common enough in the fortress that they didn't challenge him.

He drew alongside the squid submersible, its arms still lazily flailing and its glass cockpit door open to the stars. It seemed his hiding of the squid's missiles earlier in the day had not been the raging success he'd hoped for. Where had the Beefeaters stashed that final missile? But at least he'd managed to find Constance in the confusion of the exploding distractions. He'd wanted to help her get out of the Jewel House, but finding his way through the unlit fort had proved more difficult than he'd ever admit. Sometimes, being seen as a hero meant only that no one knew the full story of how badly the glitter had hit the fan.

The only way to escape the tower was via the river inlet, now guarded on both sides of the wall by troops. And a certain red-haired debutante couldn't swim to save her life.

As he took a sharp left onto the gangplank that led to the top of Queen Victoria's submersible, one of the Beefeater guards shouted, "Oi, you, get off that squid. That's a crime scene, that is. Somebody's coming by to pick up them bits of debris."

Waiting for a bullet in his back, he knelt with the slumped Constance still over his shoulder and peered inside the one-person submersible.

Inside, a black leather pilot's chair embroidered with the Queen's cipher looked mighty plush. Victoria sure enjoyed a comfy seat when she sailed her submersible up and down the Thames between her palaces. She was known to occasionally blast a missile through any ship that dared to get in her way.

It was for this reason that the shadow of a giant squid in the water below sent a wave of terror through the hearts of many a mariner.

Gently, he slid the seemingly boneless body of Constance down into the pilot's seat. "Godspeed," he murmured to her. She blinked up at him, comprehending the fact that this was a one-man submersible, and he was not going to be that man.

The Beefeater shouted again. "Get off that squid right now, or I'll shoot!"

He gazed down into Constance's shocked eyes for the last time and grasped the handle of the glass door, preparing to slam it closed so that she could make her escape through the broken gate.

"Oh, hell no," she said, grabbing him by his white Elizabethan ruff. She yanked him down on top of her, squeezing to one side so that he crumpled face-first into the seat custom designed for Queen Victoria's backside. Thank goodness Victoria enjoyed her cakes; the pilot's chair was plenty wide. With the leather crushing his cheek, and his body crumpled by pain, he stared underneath his own elbow as Constance reached up to hit the door's auto-close button. The glass bubble door slammed closed against the heels of his Western boots, driving him further into the seat as if he were a nail thwacked by a giant hammer.

He gurgled into the leather seat cushion as pain roamed his contorted physique, undecided as to which body part should hurt most. He tried to right his topsy-turvy self as Constance, pressed against him in all the wrong ways, slid down the wall of the cockpit, reaching for the controls on the mahogany dashboard. Shells from the Beefeater warders outside bounced like rain off the squid's bulletproof suprabronze armor. Made from the same ultra-alloys that protected the Steamwerks' exo-suits, the squid was designed to keep the most important person in Queen Victoria's world, Victoria herself, safe from any harm. Short of a missile or a cannonball, they were temporarily safe within the cockpit from all but crushed limbs and embarrassing body noises.

Had Constance not put her natural talents toward being a weapon-smithing, livestock-breeding, cider-brewing debutante, she could have been a gymnast. Somehow, she slid her arm between his crunched-up legs and managed to grab the silver flight stick. She shoved it forward, and the squid lurched up into the air, high-stepping on its tentacle-like arms toward the remains of the Traitor's Gate.

Trusdale almost broke his neck squirming to see out of the glass cockpit. "You're too high. You'll hit the stone arch." He gasped as Constance's black silk gown wafted across his face. The scent of her rose and orange blossom perfume was caught somewhere between oppressive and sweet in the cramped cockpit. Much like its wearer.

"Can't you move over a bit?" barked Constance. "I can't reach the . . ."

The metal-and-glass top of the squid scraped along the rough-hewn stones of the gate's archway with an ear-splitting shriek of technological anguish. Both Constance and Trusdale cringed in place, trying to cover their ears as the screeching wail reverberated around the cockpit.

Freeing itself, the squid lumbered on its many arms out toward the inky shadow and silver-topped waves of the Thames. The redcoats stationed next to the trampoline leveled a volley of gunfire at the squid as it staggered by. A storm of bullets pinged and cracked off the submersible's armor as it sank into the river. As Constance squirmed against him like a fish trapped in a net, he managed to drag his Western boots down from the ceiling, around her, and onto the burgundy carpeted floor next to the fallen scepter. A few more wriggles, and he found himself sitting right side up on the pilot's seat with an irritated Constance on his lap. She paid no more attention to him than if he was an exceptionally lumpy seat cushion. Her gloved fingers danced across the gilded controls as she played the switches and toggles on the mahogany dashboard as deftly as if they were a pianoforte's keyboard.

The squid lurched into deeper water, heading west, and the river sought to make a grand entrance into the cockpit via tiny scrapes and holes in the ceiling. Squirts of water shot down upon them, dampening their clothes and rinsing their faces. Mercifully, the damaged roof held back the torrent of water that would have brought an immediate, sinking end to their journey.

Constance heaved a groan almost as loud as the submersible had made scraping along the archway. "Dash it all. I'll try and keep us at surface level to avoid a flood. But of course, that will make us a target for enemy gunships and cannons. I assume we're still meeting the *Bad Penny* at the dock outside the Mardy Mare Tavern?

"That's the plan. But if we're late—"

"They'll take off without us. Quite right, too. And to think how close we were to getting this penultimate Key safely to my cabin. It's heartbreaking."

He gazed down at the crown-wearing pilot, drenched and dejected on his lap. "Hey, we're not dead yet. A half-mile voyage in the good ship *Sir Inks-a-Lot* and we're outta this town for good. Maybe fate's on our side."

"Maybe," sighed Constance, her usual confidence sapped by the surrounding water.

Drowning is probably the death she fears the most. She can't control the waves. "If, wait, I mean, *when* we get outta this current desperate situation, maybe I could teach you to swim?"

A smile ghosted across her pale face. "I'd like that. Well, I'll probably hate it at the time. But I'll give it a go. As long as we start very small, in a paddling pool, perhaps?"

The squid swam on toward the gothic-style towers of London Bridge, illuminated as if for a party by the warm amber glow of gas lamps. The landmark bridge bobbed in and out of visibility above the water line that cut across the submersible's cockpit window. The squid's ebb and flow propulsion system relied upon its massive arms pulsing rhythmically. The engine hummed discreetly behind the pilot's seat next to a gently hissing oxygen tank. The Queen certainly knew how to travel in style.

Constance's tone was as subdued as he'd ever heard from her. "Just so you know, I've left two letters on board the *Lady Penelope* in case I didn't make it back safely. The first letter is addressed to the British Museum. In it, I plead for their RATT squad to spare the crew's lives in return for both the Enigma Keys we've collected. Perhaps one day, they can locate two additional Keys for themselves. Then all they need to do is figure out how to open interdimensional portals, and they can haul Haltwhistle Hall and their missing treasure back through the void."

"I'm sure that will satisfy the Museum." *Another lie, but why stop now?* "Who's the second letter for?"

She turned to him, her cheeks glistening with more than river water. "The second is my apology letter to the entire crew for getting everyone into this mess. I am so very, very sorry about . . . everything." She blinked up at him. "And I'm sorry most of all to you. I should never have tried to spy on alternate versions of you through the aether mirror. It was a gross infringement of your privacy. You were so close to me, a few rooms away on board the ship, yet I chose a coward's way to try and sneak a peek at what makes you tick. I want you to know that I'm sorry for even looking. Especially as you didn't want me to use the mirror unnecessarily." Her lip trembled.

"Hey, it's all right. Don't cry, I forgive you. It's a pretty big temptation to get a handle on everyone around you. I just didn't want you to get hurt, that's all. This is nothin' but water under the bridge, literally." He pointed up as the dark shadow of Tower Bridge sailed over them. "I wouldn't have missed this escapade for the world. Meeting you has been a breath of fresh air—admittedly, occasionally deranged, always eccentric fresh air. It's been a hell of a ride, Lady Haltwhistle."

She grinned. "That it has, Mr. Trusdale. Or should I say, Liberty?"

"Why not? And dare I finally call you Connie?"

"We're not dead yet," she chuckled. "Let's see how close we get to the docks before we drop all sense of decorum."

He was trying not to notice the gentle curve of her neck, mere inches from his lips. "And here you are, stuck in here with me, and not a chaperone in sight. What would *Babett's Modern Manners* say?"

"I would imagine sitting on a cowboy's lap inside a leaking squid warrants its own chapter. Or at least, an addendum."

Distant cannons fired, and the squid lurched alarmingly as cannonballs plunged into the river around them.

They watched the sinking balls fall like comets, a silver trail of moonlit bubbles following their course down into the depths of the river.

"Isn't that romantic?" asked Constance wryly. "I assume we're under fire from the Tower Bridge heavy artillery emplacement. We'll no doubt be assaulted by cannonballs from every guard station between here and the rendezvous point. What a bother."

And there's that classic British understatement I've grown to love. Along with . . .

Do I dare say it? Those three little words that change everything. The three you can never take back. Lady Constance Haltwhistle, I love . . .

She gazed up at him. "So, now that you're a captive audience, I'm curious. Why did you stay with the crew when we first landed in Paris? You could have gone off to be a tourist again, but you stayed and never left. What's the . . . attraction . . . of being part of my crew?"

Technically Welli's crew, but that's neither here nor there.

Surrounded by water, his mouth was suddenly parched. *Should I tell her about God and Général Malaise? About them blackmailing me to get the Brass Queen to bring down Versailles? If that's not a mood killer, I don't know what is.*

The latest note God had mysteriously moved into his pocket in Rome had burned a hole in his heart. It contained a new mission, far from Constance. A mission he planned never to take. In response, he'd sent yet another resignation letter by carrier pigeon but had received the same reply as always.

Request denied.

Did God want to keep him on the agency payroll because she hated him, or because she needed him? Was he, in fact, her favorite son? Should he submit to God's design, or did he dare to fall from grace? Paradise beckoned in the arms of Constance.

Was he man enough to risk his body and soul for love?

He drew in as deep a breath as he could muster and spoke directly from his heart. "I guess the truth is that there's not an hour that goes by when I don't think of you. Even when you irritate the hell outta me. Perhaps then, most of all. You're like a storm on the horizon. I know destruction's coming, but I can't tear my eyes away from the power and beauty of an incredible force of nature. I might not survive meeting you, but I hope I'll always be brave enough to stand beside you, drinking in your smile, and watching your back."

She blinked up at him, her eminently kissable lips slightly parted. "Oh . . . I . . . gosh. I had no idea you could be so poetic."

"Me neither." *And that's the truth.* Perspiration was making its presence known beneath the scarlet wool of his uniform. His Elizabethan ruff itched, and his boots weirdly felt three sizes too small. But Constance gazing up at him in the soft glow of the lights from the dashboard made every ounce of discomfort worthwhile.

Dying with her was better than living with anyone else.

"I have something to tell you, too." She blinked up at him.

He held his breath. "Yes?"

"Even though I looked, I couldn't find another version of you in any other dimension. Not a single one. Now, there are a plethora of interdimensional variables that I can't compensate for, but from a scientific perspective, it appears that you and I are not fated to meet anywhere but here. Destiny appears to have given us only one chance to be together. It's logically improbable that this is the case, and yet, here we are."

He blinked at her. "What?"

"I'm saying that *you're* the unique one, Mr. Trusdale, one of a kind. And as such, it would be foolish of me not to treasure you and hold you dear."

"I'm not sure I'm getting . . ."

She stretched up toward him. He closed his eyes as she kissed him on the lips with the gentleness of a butterfly landing on dewdrop. He responded with a kiss of his own, a little firmer, but filled with tenderness. A volley of cannonballs rocked the waters around them as they melted into their embrace. A second volley thundered down upon the submersible roof, smashing its armor and springing a thousand leaks.

They gazed into one another's eyes as the water rained down.

Neither of them moved a muscle.

"You'll have to swim for it," murmured Constance.

"I'm not leaving you. Not now, not ever," he said softly.

She straightened up and fixed him with a glare as the water flooded around their knees. "That's an order. Abandon squid, Mr. Trusdale. I insist."

"Oh, now we're getting formal again? I'm not leaving you here to die alone. So, forget it. I'm stayin'."

She scowled and contorted her body downward, reaching into the freezing water around his knees and pulling up her glowing scepter. "I'm going to be the distraction. This submersible appears to have an ejector button for this chair. I'll fly up into the air, grabbing every rifleman's attention, while you quietly swim for the shore with the scepter in hand. There's no point in us both dying horribly."

She pushed the scepter at him as the water reached their waists. "Go on, release the door and swim out. I'll give you as much time as I can to get away. Once the water reaches my neck, I'll push this button—"

"Which button?"

"This one here, the one marked ejector— Oh no you don't! Don't you dare!"

He dared. She slapped frantically at his hands as he slammed his palm onto the button. The overhead glass door's percussive bolts exploded, shooting the door out into the night. Icy water flooded into the cockpit, and the submersible sank beneath them.

With water lapping at her throat, Constance shrieked, "That's not the Plan with a capital . . . Wheeeeeeeeeeee-eeeeeeeee!"

The pilot's seat shot up through the empty hole in the ceiling, soaring for the stars.

They held on to each other for dear life as the force of the ejector system blew them and the chair as high as the tower tops of London Bridge. At the apex of their flight, there was a brief moment of stillness as the twinkling lights of London spread around them like a celestial eiderdown. It was stunningly romantic. He listened with a smile as Constance cursed him to the ends of the universe and back again.

What a woman.

He pulled her even closer as they plummeted toward the river. A loud bang heralded the inflation of a golden airbag beneath the pilot seat. They crashed down onto the water with bone-jarring force, but thanks to the inflatable cushion, no permanent injury was sustained.

They bobbed almost regally on Queen Victoria's watery throne. Perfectly upright, and somehow, very British.

Imperial gunships were incoming. Redcoat troops sprinted along the embankment, shouting, pointing, and occasionally firing their rifles toward them. "Well, this is a fine how-do-you-do." Constance pouted at him with those luscious lips. "You should have swum for it. You at least had a chance of getting away. Now every eye is upon us."

"Let 'em look," he said, leaning in for one last kiss.

"You're incorrigible," she smiled and raised her lips to his.

"Get your filthy mouth off my cousin," screamed Welli through what sounded like a megaphone.

They froze, searching the river for an irate Lord Pendelroy. Constance pointed up at the sky behind them. A looming black shadow was fast approaching, blocking out the stars. It was the *Bad Penny* on silent running. Welli leaned over the prow of the ship, and a large deep-sea fishing net swung from its landing hook.

"Oh no," said Constance. "Surely he's not going to . . ."

But he was. The fishing net scooped up the floating throne and trawled them up toward the moon's splendor. The *Bad Penny*'s engines roared into life, and the airship soared over the top of London Bridge with its fishing net swinging like a hammock.

The catch of the day, Lady Constance Haltwhistle, thrust her hands up to the heavens and cheered. "Hooray! Destiny blows us one more kiss. Thank you, great goddess!"

But the only goddess Trusdale cared about was sitting on his lap, wearing her stolen crown with a panache Queen Victoria could only dream of.

Chapter 28:
The Traitor

Constance wriggled her way out of the fishing net and collapsed, laughing, into Welli's waiting arms. The deck of the *Bad Penny* seemed to spin around her as if she'd drunk too much of Haltwhistle Hall's infamously strong hard cider. Effervescent bubbles of joy fizzed through every atom of her being. Joy at being alive, joy at being rescued, joy at securing another Enigma Key.

But most of all, joy that Liberty Trusdale had returned her kiss.

She couldn't believe she'd been so bold. The squid's missile had shattered the protective ice around her heart as surely as it had exploded the exo-suit. A world without Liberty Trusdale was not one she'd want to live in. He was the sun to her moon; he opposed her, complemented her. Together, they would be an unstoppable force of nature.

She hugged Welli, burying her face into his ruffled pink shirt, breathing in the warmth and comfort of family. Tears of delight blurred her vision as she blinked up at him. "Well met, cousin. Thank you from the bottom of my heart for swooping in with my ship—"

"My ship," he corrected absently, staring over her shoulder.

She howled with laughter, almost louder than the *Bad Penny*'s engines, which were straining to lift them far above cannonballs and sniper fire. "You're such a card. Honestly, I've never been so happy to see you."

He frowned down at her. "Have you been drinking?"

"Only the sweet liquor of life. It's been a wild night. I honestly thought I'd never see you again, any of you." She beamed around the deck, but apart from Rani Singh at the helm, pushing the airship to greater speeds and height, only Mr. Singh was there to greet her. The moonlight frosted his uncut beard and lit his white shirt to silver. He was as elegant as ever in a green turban and gray pants. But the curved dagger that was usually tucked into his sash belt was shining from his left hand. In his right, the ambidextrous Sikh warrior held his wife's second-favorite cutlass. A gold and silver masterpiece purloined from a maharajah's flagship. Its curved blade glittered as if stardust had kissed it.

No doubt, he was prepared to fight off the Queen's troops should they be boarded. Cawley and Hearn were . . .

Oh, that's right, they've abandoned me.

Yes, she'd ordered them to leave the airship, but still. Their betrayal stung as sharply as if Mr. Singh had plunged his dagger straight into her heart.

"Where are Maya and Zhi?" she asked.

"They're manning the ship's engines. They've rigged up a replacement automaton for shoveling coal, but given our need for speed, they're helping it out by tossing nuggets of supracoal into the furnace. It burns hotter and brighter, but give it too much—"

"And we explode. I'll have to wait until later to thank Zhi for his brilliant plan. Your additions were a bit of a shock. But sacrificing the old automation and sending Trusdale in undercover helped me to secure the scepter that contains our second-to-last Enigma Key. I couldn't have escaped without his help."

She gestured back at the tall cowboy, who was still extricating himself from the fishing net wrapped around Victoria's aquatic throne. At his feet, the scepter glowed faintly purple, casting an eerie alien glow onto his Western boots.

She grinned. "And you'll be delighted to hear, dear cousin, that I know where we can find the final Key in our quest to bring back Haltwhistle Hall. And none too soon, as five o'clock this afternoon is our deadline to return the British Museum's missing treasure."

She stepped back from Welli and turned to face the struggling Trusdale. She called out, "You should hear this too, Liberty. Do you recall the flashing red dot we spotted on the aether mirror map? That anomalous dot seemed to be trailing us, which explains why you always felt we were being followed."

"Uh-huh," said Trusdale, glancing up from his bondage. It seemed he'd got his boot entangled in the netting and was trying to remove it. He suddenly froze, staring at Mr. Singh's drawn cutlass. Worry lines marked his brow beneath the brim of his Tudor bonnet.

Constance continued, "Well, before I single-handedly knocked out the snipers at the Tower of London"—she coughed modestly—"I took a last look at the aether map. The flashing red dot has become a steady purple dot. It must be a stray Enigma Key. But instead of following us, it's now moving away slowly, leading us toward the east coast. Given that Prince Lucien just told me that King Oscar has a stealth airship set up to transport his kidnap victims to Stockholm—"

"Wait, what? Prince Lucien? The Queen's favorite grandson?" said Welli.

"Not so favorite now, I believe. Anyway, we got chatting when I was in his cell—"

Welli ran his hand back through his forelock. "And why were you in his—?"

"May I *please* finish my story? Anyway, it appears that Oscar commissioned a stealth airship. So, given that he's been trying to kidnap me, and given that we know he's been searching the globe for Enigma Keys for years, unsuccessfully as far as I'm aware, it stands to reason that he's trying to lure me into a trap. Consider the letters from Stockholm, Welli, and the trajectory of the stealth ship. Everything is leading to Stockholm. But if we know that a trap's been set, we'll be able to avoid stepping into it. Isn't that wonderful?"

Welli frowned down at her. "Nothing you just said meets my criteria for being wonderful. And good lord, what are you wearing?" He gaped at her miniature diamond crown. "Please tell me that's a replica you picked up in a joke shop somewhere."

She huffed. "As if I'd wear costume jewelry."

He looked her up and down. "Well, you do seem to be dressed in a sky-pirate costume."

She reviewed her attire. The loose silk gown she'd worn for modesty's sake was torn asunder. She tut-tutted at it and ripped it apart, letting the gown fall to the deck. She stepped out of it, revealing the full glory of her black leather battle corset, moleskin pants, and knee-high laced boots.

Welli gawked at her shockingly visible legs. "Are those my trousers?"

At that precise moment, one of Maya's mechanical messenger pigeons fluttered over the deck, a message tube clutched in its silver claws. It circled once, twice, and then flew down to perch upon Constance's right shoulder. She grinned at the silver-plated pigeon. "Ahoy, matey. Who's better than a boring old pirate parrot any day, eh?"

The pigeon cooed, remarkably realistically, from its clockwork-driven voice box. It dropped the message tube into her outstretched palm. She peered at the dial that indicated the intended recipient.

Somewhat disappointed that that recipient wasn't her, she said, "Welli, it's for you."

He reached for the tube, unscrewed its cap, and let it dangle from its tiny chain as he drew out a rolled message. He unrolled the parchment and groaned. He turned the message to Constance so that she could see it. It read, *Then we'll see you in court.*

"That's from your bloody suffragette friends. I've been in constant communication with them, but they absolutely refuse to stop printing libelous articles about you. Apparently, they've been following us in a chartered airship, and another dirigible leased by three unidentified women is following them. What do you have to say about that?"

She shrugged. "It's good to be popular? Anyway, back to the stealth airship that is carrying our final Enigma Key. It's meandering its way along the Thames heading for the coast. Presumably, this ship is intended to draw us to Stockholm where Oscar will have an elaborate trap set up for me."

Welli groaned. "And what makes you think this trap will be elaborate?"

"When does a king *not* show off? It stands to reason that any trap would be completely over the top. Then again, I could be mistaken. He may intend to entice us to fly across the open waters of the North Sea. He could have warships out there waiting to shoot us down. But that wouldn't help him kidnap me, now would it?"

Trusdale cleared his throat. He had unraveled himself from the net and was standing with the glowing scepter in hand, his eyes fixed on Mr. Singh. He said, "If I might chime in on this absurd conversation, walking into a trap is always a horrible idea."

She laughed. "In this case, it's a superb idea because they don't understand the brilliance of our ship and crew.

We have the *Bad Penny's* cannons, two ex-Steamwerks scientists, two working exo-suits, one ex-air-pirate queen." She glanced down at herself. "And I suppose, one air-pirate queen in training—me." She gestured at Welli and Mr. Singh. "Plus two ex-redcoat soldiers. And last but not least, an ex-US cavalry officer, one Liberty Trusdale. Throw in a few mechanical pigeons and whatever automaton Maya and Zhi have bolted together in the furnace room, and we have a veritable army of heroes. Oscar will never know what hit him."

She waited for applause that didn't happen. *What is wrong with everyone? Why has their desire for adventure fizzled like a damp firework? Have I missed something?*

She studied Trusdale and Mr. Singh with a furrowed brow. The two men were eyeing each other like gunfighters at high noon, except that it was the middle of the night and neither possessed a gun. "Are you two even listening to me? So, to continue, we spring Oscar's trap with our combined fabulousness, grab the final Enigma Key, and then, bing, bang, boom! I open an interdimensional portal and we snatch Haltwhistle Hall back from the void. Cheers ring to the rafters! Champagne all around! A grand party on the airship back home to Yorkshire! What could be finer than this last escapade on our glorious grand tour?"

Welli was watching Mr. Singh and Trusdale. "It sounds simply marvelous, old girl. But I think you'd best go and explain your new Plan with a capital 'P' to Maya and Zhi. Get their input. Let them explain the thousand and one ways it won't work. Off you go, now."

She gaped at him. "Are you shooing me away? I will not be dismissed off the deck of my own ship."

"My ship," said Welli, with an undercurrent of irritation she'd never heard from him before. His eyes were still focused on Liberty. "Mr. Singh, kindly give Mr. Trusdale his luggage."

Without taking his eyes off the cowboy, Mr. Singh sidestepped over to a shadowy mound of items on the deck. It appeared to be Trusdale's Stetson, shirt, and duster coat neatly folded atop the American's battered leather suitcase. Mr. Singh shoved the suitcase and its garnish of appalling clothing with his foot. It slid across the boards to Trusdale like a solitary soldier crossing no man's land. The cowboy stopped its progress with the heel of his Western boot.

The penny dropped for Constance. "Oh, for heaven's sake. Is this because you caught us . . . I mean, it was only a kiss."

Now Trusdale stared at her with hurt writ large across his face.

"I mean it wasn't *only* a kiss . . ." Welli glared at her. She licked her lips. "That is, we thought we were about to die horribly. You can't go all 'pistols at dawn' for my honor with Liberty just because of a kiss or two."

"Or two?" Welli's eyebrows disappeared into his forelock. "This has nothing to do with your improper conduct. Or even your questionable attire. That, we'll discuss later. This is about trust and betrayal. Nothing more, nothing less."

To her surprise, he snarled at Trusdale. "Remove that Beefeater's uniform. You're not fit to wear Her Majesty's cipher."

Trusdale dropped to one knee and laid the glowing scepter gently upon the deck. He stood tall, pulled off his Tudor bonnet, and tossed it down next to the scepter. Slowly, he unbuttoned his scarlet Beefeater tunic. "I didn't mean anyone any harm. Please allow me to explain—"

"I think not," said Welli. Trusdale's tunic fell to the ground to reveal his impressively muscular bare chest, a most magnificent sight above his stolen scarlet breeches. "You should know that Maya and Zhi are absolutely gutted by your duplicity."

"His what? What are you talking about?" asked Constance.

"Why don't you put on your duster coat, Mr. Trusdale?" Welli's tone was as sharp as Mr. Singh's dagger.

"It's astonishing how many secret pockets one garment can hold. And don't search for your miniature gun. It's stored safely in my cabin. The same cabin you had the audacity to share with me on this voyage of misadventure. A cabin I shared with you because I thought I could trust you."

Trusdale shrugged on his black duster, leaving a sliver of his bare chest illuminated by a silver moonbeam.

Constance's cheeks burned with embarrassment for his state of disarray. "Will someone please tell me what's going on?"

The deck boards beneath her boots trembled as Mrs. Singh engaged the autopilot machinery and the airship chugged to a dead stop. Rani walked to her side and handed her a manilla folder stamped with the Brass Queen's symbol: a crown set inside a cogwheel.

Constance stared down at the one-inch-thick folder. "This isn't mine."

Trusdale's voice held an edge of desperation. "You have to believe me; I had no choice. They would have sent someone else in my place if I didn't take the mission. Someone who didn't care about this crew. I was trying to protect you all."

She opened the folder. By the light of the moon, she scanned through names, dates, and places. The speculation that Dr. Maya Chauhan was secretly the high-end bespoke weapons designer, the Brass Queen. The plot to blackmail Maya to take down the Palace of Versailles. If she didn't, the lives of the *Lady Penelope*'s crew would be forfeit. And most damming of all, the speculation that she, Lady Constance Haltwhistle, was a gullible, naive girl who, due to her close relationship with Maya, could be used as a tool to manipulate Maya into compliance. All that was needed was a seasoned American spy, code name Captain Cowpoke, to turn Constance's head and heart to make her an unwitting accomplice in the mission.

Trusdale's voice cracked as he said, "I could have told them that Maya wasn't the Brass Queen. I could have sold out Constance. I could have walked away from the whole damned mess and tried to forget you all. But I didn't. I tried to help you as best I could without revealing—"

"The truth," said Constance numbly. It was as if her ribs had turned to solid ice, freezing her from the inside out. "You could have revealed the truth to us, to me. But you didn't."

"I thought it was safer if you didn't know."

"Safer for whom?" asked Welli.

Anguish contorted Trusdale's almost handsome face into a macabre moonlit mask. Cast half in light, half in shadow, he stuttered. "I-I tried to resign my commission numerous times. I swear I sent my cold-hearted handler letter after letter, begging to be released from my contract. But the only responses I ever received were a handful of typed notes that read, *Request denied.* You must have found them in my pockets."

Welli snorted. "You probably typed those notes yourself as an out in case you were discovered. How foolish do you think we are, Captain Cowpoke?" He held up his hand. "No, don't bother to answer that. You clearly played us all for the fool. Some of us more than others." He glanced meaningfully at Constance.

Trusdale shook his head. "No, you've got me all wrong. I truly love Con—"

"Don't you dare," she roared, a wounded lioness, as the shock that had frozen her in place melted before an inferno of rage. "None of it was real. You were using me, just like Papa. To think that I trusted you. And all the time you were laughing at me behind my back."

"That's not true," said Trusdale. "You have to believe me. I love—"

"Enough," interjected Welli. "Haven't you done enough damage, Cowpoke? Well, I'm sure your handler can find you a whole new group of people to betray. We're going to drop you off at the next port, and for your sake, I hope we never see you again."

"That's it?" said Constance, her heart pounding in her ears as her body trembled. "That's what he gets for breaking my heart? I don't think so."

"We've all been wronged here," said Welli. "But we're not—"

"You're not Haltwhistles. But I am. And I shall answer this betrayal with all the strength my ancestors bestowed upon me." She strode to face Mrs. Singh, eyeing the gold cutlass the pilot wore at her hip as an adornment to her gorgeous red-and-gold sari. "May I?" she asked.

Rani's dark eyes glittered with understanding. "Of course, your ladyship." She drew her cutlass and presented it to Constance handle first with the curved blade laid across her bent arm.

Constance grasped the leather-wrapped handle of the cutlass in her right hand and hefted its weight. She admired the gleam of moonlight along the blade's razor-sharp edge. Still holding the Brass Queen folder in her left hand, she tested the blade's sharpness with her left thumb. She winced as the cutlass bit into her flesh and wiped a thin line of blood across the folder.

She felt the power of her villainous ancestors burn through her. *Trust no one, Papa always said.*

Her father being proved right cut her far deeper than any blade ever could.

She nodded at Rani. "I assume you know what I'll need next."

Rani nodded grimly and headed for the port side of the ship. She pressed a hidden button underneath the

handrail on the ship's side and a panel slid back to reveal a control stick and several buttons. The ex-air-pirate
queen pressed a button and an engine beneath the deck
hummed into life. Rani leaned over the handrail and
peered down at one of Baron Haltwhistle's favorite additions to the *Bad Penny*'s box of tricks. The one Constance
had helped him to build almost a decade before.

Hell hath no fury like a Haltwhistle deceived.

Trusdale placed his Stetson onto his head. He picked
up his suitcase and cradled it to his chest. He gazed, ash-
en faced, at Constance's growing rage. "I know I've done
you wrong. I'll spend the rest of my life regretting—"

"Silence, traitor." Constance set her jaw and pointed her cutlass directly at Trusdale's heart. "Walk over to
Mrs. Singh, right now."

Trusdale's shoulders slumped. He shuffled like a con-
demned man to stand beside Mrs. Singh. She jerked her
thumb over the edge. "Hop on, traitor."

He leaned over the handrail and stared down. "What
is that?"

Constance, Welli, and Mrs. Singh joined him at the
side of the ship. Constance peered over too, knowing exactly what she would see.

And there it was. Papa's Precarious Plank of Plung-
ing. A ten-foot by two-foot length of teak with tiny rockets attached to its base.

Trusdale stared at Constance. "You're making me walk the plank? From an airship? I'll die."

She shrugged. "Probably not. In theory, the plank will levitate you down to water level. How slowly or quickly depends on Mrs. Singh's light touch on the controls. Over you go."

Trusdale's jaw dropped low enough to hit the river below them, plank or no plank. "Again, I can't say enough how very sorry I am—"

"You're right, you can't," said Welli. "And Constance has a point. Dropping you at the next port wasn't enough of a punishment for what you did, although perhaps never seeing her again would have added to your pain." He shrugged. "Or not. That's the point, isn't it? We'll never know what you truly felt for Constance, or for any of us, will we?"

He pleaded, "On all that is holy, I swear I never meant to hurt any of you. You're the closest thing I've found to family outside my own. I'll do anything—"

Constance pointed her cutlass at his throat and snarled. "Not one more word, you lying snake. Get off my ship."

Just this once, Welli didn't correct her.

Reluctantly, Trusdale clambered over the side and dropped onto the plank. He walked to the center and turned to gaze at her. It might have been the moonlight, but she could almost swear that tears glistened in his eyes. The tears of a serpent.

She nodded at Mrs. Singh. The pilot hit the release button. Before the plank could fall, the mini rockets on its underside roared to life with a wind so ferocious that Trusdale's Stetson blew clean off his head and back onto the deck. The hatless cowboy stood there on the levitating plank, holding his suitcase like a newborn. A hundred feet below, the dark water of the Thames shimmered in the moonlight. Mrs. Singh spun the mini rocket's control dial, and Trusdale's plank dropped like a stone.

Constance watched him all the way down until Mrs. Singh guided the plank into a hover a few feet above the river. The ex-pirate queen flipped the plank over, tipping the traitor into the drink with a splash. He treaded water, gazing up as the plank flew back to the waiting airship.

Constance knelt and picked up his Stetson, gently blowing dust from its wide brim. Then she leaned over the edge of the ship and screamed, "Don't forget your hat!"

She flung it with every ounce of strength she had after the cowboy who had shattered her heart.

Down it fell, down, and down.

But she turned away long before it hit the water.

Because it no longer mattered to her.

Not now.

Not ever again.

Chapter 29:
The Stone Gallery

With his Viking warriors marching by his side, and a wriggling Boo clamped tight to his chest, Erhard strode through the empty kitchen of the Royal Palace of Stockholm. Where once chefs, scullery maids, and gold-liveried servants bustled in their never-ending quest to feed the court of King Oscar II, only the echo of his men's boots stomping on the flagstones remained.

It was here in the kitchen that he'd hoped to glean gossip as to what had been going on at the palace in his absence. But it seemed his network of eyes and ears had disappeared as if someone had waved a magic wand.

Was this Lady Nay's doing? His throat tightened. They marched on, along corridor after corridor, through the deserted throne room, heading for the stone gallery. As their airship had landed, he'd observed that the gallery's French doors had been flung wide open to the palace's central courtyard. This was unusual given that the city was blanketed by angry clouds from which strange purple snow drifted down to smother all. The sun seemed to have long since abandoned Stockholm to suffer winter's gloom in early June.

Perhaps Nay was truly the sorceress he sometimes suspected her of being?

There was no sound as he and his men drew close to the gigantic oak doors that guarded the stone gallery. They halted as one unit, and Ludwig stepped forward to place his meaty hands upon the carved royal shields that adorned the door. With a grunt of exertion, he shoved the oak doors inward. They opened silently on well-oiled hinges.

Forty of Nay's ladies-in-waiting milled about the gallery, sweeping the chessboard pattern floor tiles clean with the long trains of their crinoline ball gowns. The aristocratic women seemed to glide as if over polished ice, with barely an ounce of effort on their parts. Was it his imagination, or did none of the court ladies seem to cast a breath into the chilly air? Perhaps they were too genteel to breath heavily.

Their faces were familiar, yet he couldn't recall seeing them at Oscar's court. There were oil paintings of great, not-so-great, and downright tawdry aristocrats hung throughout the vast palace. Nay's ladies resembled the women in those portraits. Their alabaster skin, pink lips, and hairstyles from across the centuries could have been brushed in oils by an old master that very morning.

As if by an invisible cue, every lady gliding through the stone gallery halted. They turned to stare at Erhard and his men. No one breathed a word in the silent chamber.

Boo stopped wriggling against his chest and whined plaintively.

Icy sweat trickled down Erhard's spine. He licked his lips beneath the scrutiny of Nay's ladies-in-waiting, but it was their mistress's emerald eyes that struck true fear into his heart. With her long, dark hair framing her porcelain-pale face, she stood in the center of the chamber in a scarlet ball gown that pooled like blood on the checkered marble floor. She far surpassed the cold beauty of the exquisite statues that lined the monochrome gallery. A work of art in its own right, the gallery's stately ionic columns supported the arched ceiling of the long chamber. The tall French doors down one side of the gallery were still cast open onto the palace's square central courtyard, large enough to allow a thousand guests to dance through the night at the summer balls of old.

There were no courtiers left now to dance in the deserted square. Flakes of purple snow drifted down from a vortex of unnatural clouds that crowned the palace skies. The snow—or could it be ash?—blanketed the square with tiny violet crystals. Amethyst drifts shone with a faint violet light that cast strange shadows across the marble gods and goddesses, frozen forever on their raised pedestals inside the gallery.

Not one of the ladies-in-waiting cast an eye toward Nay herself. Perhaps they didn't dare to? She stood beside three large iron cages, empty of prisoners, and a small golden cage with an open door. Beyond the cages, a brown canvas drop cloth covered what might be four or five large furniture pieces.

The only other furniture was the King's red-and-gold baroque throne. King Oscar was slumped upon the throne, almost invisible in his frailty. In days of old, he would have sat tall, a golden crown upon his head, surrounded by guards, servants, courtiers, and his adoring children and grandchildren.

Now, both his crown and zest for life had disappeared. The good man who had once saved Erhard from a life of despair was nowhere to be seen. The Vikings exchanged glances, their lips tight and unsmiling.

Boo uttered the tiniest of snarls as Lady Nay swept toward them with an icy smile. "Ah, gentlemen, well met. And is this creature Constance's puppy? How delightful."

She peered at the terrier, whose snarl grew into an angry bark.

Before Erhard could react, two ladies-in-waiting swooped in to wrest the dog from his arms. One glassy-eyed woman held the squirming puppy with its back against her chest, as the other rubbed a paint-stained handkerchief against Boo's flailing front paws. Nay herself stepped close and grabbed the puppy's left front paw, stamping its tiny paw print onto a printed page torn from a book. "There. Proof of life—or at least, proof that we have her hound." She handed the page to the handkerchief lady. "Send this with the other letter to Lady Haltwhistle's ship by carrier pigeon immediately."

The lady swept away, page in hand, as her companion carried Boo over to the small golden cage. She pushed the puppy inside none too gently, causing Lars and Johan's hands to reach for the handles of the axes stuffed inside their belts.

Erhard held out his hands toward the two men, silently commanding them to not do anything rash. He smiled warmly at Lady Nay, dropped into a courtly bow, and swept off his feathered hat with a flourish. "Your ladyship, well met indeed. We return ready to carry out our King's commands. What, pray tell, *are* those orders?"

He kept his eyes trained upon her, the smile stretching his lips tight against clamped teeth.

She narrowed her eyes at him. "You have no questions for me? That's so unlike you, Colonel."

He nodded. "I know which way the wind blows, my lady. We are here to sail with the tide, not to fight the inevitable."

A serpent's smile lit up her face. "Excellent. In these final hours, I will make use of your services. Know this, I'm sending the puppy's paw print to Constance so that she is aware that we hold her dog in captivity. This will unhinge her mind as completely as any other cruelty I could have administered. You have my thanks for snatching the beast." She half bowed her head, keeping her eyes fixed upon him.

"It was our pleasure." He placed his hat firmly back upon his skull.

She said airily, "Of course, I was planning on torturing her two former servants before her very eyes to bring her into a state of anguish, but fear for the puppy's safety might be easier to manipulate."

He put as much admiration as he could muster into his tone. "You captured Cawley and Hearn? We did wonder where they'd—"

"The two drunken fools sat in a pub, discussing ad infinitum how best they might once again put themselves into Constance's good graces. It was a *simple* matter to have my agents chloroform them and bring them here."

He didn't care for the implied criticism of his own team's failure to chloroform Constance. But the potential risk to his men, the King, and little Boo if he chose to defy Nay now was too great. Reluctantly, he let the insult slide.

Nay continued, "It's vital that the two servants do not set eyes upon me until I have Constance exactly where I want her—emotionally, that is. Physically, she shall be placed in that cage over there."

She pointed at the collection of cages. "When the servants are brought in in chains, I will appear to be a prisoner myself, trapped in the cage next to Constance." She held up her hand to stop him from interrupting. "Fear not, Colonel. There is no cage known to man that can hold me. I will be there merely to stoke the girl's emotional furor to such a height that I can trigger her powers. She doesn't know it yet, but young Lady Haltwhistle is the key to unlocking an interdimensional portal that will ensure King Oscar's dominion over this world." She waved a hand in Oscar's direction. The slumped king lifted his head slightly in response. Apparently, he was still alive, if not well.

Erhard straightened his shoulders. "Most excellent, my lady. But I do not understand—?"

"The more emotional turmoil we can stir in young Constance, whether good or bad, the better my chances of manipulating her to open doors to other worlds. In one of those worlds, my army stands ready to conquer the Earth. King Oscar shall rule over this world, I guarantee it. And you and your men, Erhard, will be given control of this never-ending army. You will become the four henchmen of the apocalypse, and none shall dare to stand against us."

Erhard wiped his brow and tried his best to look suitably delighted at the prospect of an interdimensional invasion. With effort, he could look almost as thrilled as he'd appeared while managing deranged invisible assassins for the vile Prince Lucien. Not for the first time in his life, he regretted his career choice of professional henchman. "And all this will come about because Constance Haltwhistle is concerned for her dog's safety?"

Lady Nay laughed. "Heavens, no. The paw print letter is merely a tool to encourage her to rashly attack the palace without thought or care. If there's one thing I've learned from watching a thousand different versions of this girl across as many realties, she is nothing if not a slave to her emotions."

"Which makes her vulnerable?" asked Erhard.

"Which makes her human," smirked Lady Nay. "And that will be her undoing."

Chapter 30:
The Lady in Red

Constance ducked as a cannonball whistled over her head and sailed across the deck of the *Bad Penny*. "Return fire!" she bellowed into the speaking tube set beside the brass telescopes on the ship's prow. Hopefully, her cannon crew could hear her belowdecks through their end of the tube. Their understanding of her order would be a miracle given the thunder of heavy artillery firing from the Palace of Stockholm's verdigris roof.

So far, it appeared that Oscar's cannoneers were remarkably bad shots. None had managed to make a mark upon her airship's black armor plating. It was almost as if they were firing to annoy rather than to harm. Half of the *Bad Penny*'s eight cannons roared their response,

their reduced shooting capacity a reflection of her severe-
ly reduced crew. With herself as lookout and Rani at the
helm, manning the cannons had been left to two retired
scientists, her cousin, and his valet. She'd never missed
Hearn and Cawley more. But she was determined not to
miss a certain treacherous cowboy, no matter how handy
he could be in a fight. This fight was for Haltwhistle loyalists only, not backstabbing servants and spies. Win or
lose, she only wanted people she could trust beside her.
Of that, she was certain.

The *Bad Penny*'s cannons roared again, shooting
their newly crafted ceramic cannonballs, each filled with
a knockout amount of chloroform gas. Constance had
no more desire to damage the red brick and sandstone
main palace, or its offshoot wings and gardens, than
she would Haltwhistle Hall. Built around a large square
center courtyard, the palace was renowned for its art
collections. According to her *Social Climber's Guide To
Winsome Courtly Wiles,* the statues and paintings of the
court rivaled even Versailles's magnificent artworks. Not
to mention, the Brass Queen only dealt with nonlethal
weaponry now, and standard cannonballs were notoriously bad for people's health.

She peered through her brass binoculars at several
women in pastel ball gowns abandoning their cannon
emplacements. As one elegant unit, the ladies swept into

a stairwell and disappeared inside the palace. Only four men now remained to guard the roofs.

Erhard and his Viking thugs. Ugh. Let's see how they like being chloroformed.

She shouted into the speaking tube, "Fire again, targeting the emplacements at each corner of the palace roof."

Boom, boom, boom, boom.

Her ears rang like church bells as the balls arced toward their targets, passing in midflight a single, red-glowing cannonball shot from the roof below.

She gaped at the unusual ball, and yelled, "Evasive maneuvers, Mrs. Singh."

The *Bad Penny* lurched portside, turning to avoid the cannonball while speeding inexorably toward the roof.

Constance blinked as the red glowing ball matched their flight change in both course and velocity. She yelled to Rani, "Could you be a bit more evasive, please?" The airship plunged down forty feet, sending her stomach into her knee-high laced boots. The red cannonball followed their dive and accelerated unnaturally, a blazing comet against the dark purple skies.

At least the strange snow had stopped falling.

Constance yelled, "It's following us. Go left . . . I mean port . . . that is . . . oops!"

The ball slammed into the hull of the *Bad Penny* with a force that slapped the airship into a vicious tailspin.

Constance crouched, hanging on to the teak handrail as the sky whirled around the ship like a vortex. A red glow shimmered across the ship as it fell toward the palace's center courtyard.

She'd almost forgotten she was walking into a trap. But seeing Boo's inky paw print on the torn page of a letter from her long-lost mama . . . she'd know that paw print anywhere. How many times had little Boo walked across her letters as she wrote, leaving her ink-stained prints on everything she touched. And maybe, just maybe . . . if Boo was here, perhaps her Mama was here too.

She had to seek the truth of whether Boo and Mama were truly being held as prisoners at the palace, as the last mysterious letter she'd received had claimed. Their lives might depend on her actions, and she certainly wasn't going to let them down.

The *Bad Penny* whirled like a sycamore seed on the breeze. The centrifugal force was powerful enough that the two empty bronze-and-brass exo-suits, kneeling upon the deck like supplicants, slid several feet. The four-hundred-pound behemoths scraped grooves into the teak that would surely never buff out.

Down the ship plummeted, to the point that she regretted her choice of a full English breakfast of delicious salty-smoked bacon, sage and onion sausage, fresh eggs, mushrooms, and a fried tomato. It was the perfect meal to enjoy before what could be one's final battle, assuming one didn't end up corkscrewing to the ground in an out-of-control airship.

She groaned and cradled her battle-corseted belly. She was still dressed as an air-pirate queen with her stolen imperial crown. After all, if today's enemies could potentially bring about one's demise, one might as well go out in style.

It was easy to be blasé about death when you barely cared whether you lived or died. That's what Trusdale's betrayal had done to her. She was as numb to the beat of her heart as if it had been removed and replaced by a block of ice. Except for protecting the lives of her diminished crew, nothing mattered to her anymore.

She closed her eyes and waited for the inevitable crash that would flip fortune's coin toward life or death. The ship spun wildly, tilted alarmingly to forty-five degrees, and then . . .

She flicked her eyes open just in time. A flash of red light froze her in place as surely as if she were a butterfly trapped in amber. She couldn't move, breathe, or even blink. Yet somehow, she was alive, conscious, and furious.

What genius is at work here? A freeze ray that can be compressed into a cosmic snowball and flung at passing airships? Why didn't I invent this?

The ship skewed heavily to the right as it neared the courtyard. If she hadn't been frozen in place, she would surely have fallen onto her side. But here she was, an oddly angled statue, crouched as if she were about to relieve herself on an unfortunate patch of grass.

It was an embarrassing position in which to meet death. If she did now encounter the grim reaper, she would have a few choice words for him, her, it, or them. She might not care whether she lived or died, but she certainly cared about how she looked while doing it. What kind of coffin would accommodate her body in its new contorted shape? Perhaps they would skip the coffin completely and roll her into a large sack?

Ugh. Auntie Madge will kill me for dying so inelegantly. I hope I'm the only one in this predicament.

She mentally placed her hands into a position of prayer.

Please God, or gods, or sprites, or pixies, or anyone out there who can hear me, please, let my friends and family be spared this dreadful frozen fate. I remain your faithful servant, et cetera et cetera, Lady Constance Haltwhistle.

Her letter to the heavens brought no discernable response. So perhaps she could speak to someone a little closer to home?

She drew on her mental blackboard a picture of her current position to Daphnia.

Daphnia responded with a red chalk scribble ball in the center of the blackboard that grew and grew until the entire chalkboard was nothing but red lines.

Perhaps Daphnia was telling her that her sight was blocked by the red light? Ah, that made sense, even if nothing else about this did.

A resounding crash that rattled her back teeth informed her that the hull of the listing airship had potentially smashed into the palace courtyard's flagstones.

Oh, I can still hear. Excellent.

A rustling noise that sounded as if a dozen silk ball gowns brushing across the hull seemed to be heading toward her. She strained with all her might against her invisible bonds, to no avail.

Irritated, she tried to glower menacingly as swathes of pastel silk entered her peripheral vision. Many hands set upon her body, and she was lifted, still frozen in her crouched position, onto her side. She was passed like a luggage trunk over the edge of the hull into the waiting hands of four weird women in fabulous ball gowns from a bygone age. At last, the final resting place of the *Bad Penny* was revealed. The airship had indeed landed somewhat heavily on the flagstones of the Palace of Stockholm's center courtyard.

Dozens of women in pastel crinoline gowns were gliding over the ship without using their arms. Their motion reminded Constance of octopuses gliding over rocks, if the octopuses wore crinoline gowns to hide their moving legs.

What has Oscar got himself into here?

She was carried without ceremony across the square toward a long row of open French doors. The women slid in through the doors, turning Constance right side up as they did so. Three large cages, one occupied by a slumped woman in a red dress facing away from her, dominated the sculpture gallery. A joyous yapping came from a tiny golden cage beyond her.

Boudicca. Mummy's coming, Boo. Stay strong, my brave little pup.

A brown drop cloth appeared to be covering furniture next to the empty cage toward which she was being propelled. King Oscar sat upon a golden throne, fast asleep, with his white beard unkempt and his withered hands crossed neatly in his lap. His frail form shocked her to the core. Where was the villainous monster she'd anticipated would be waiting for her in this room?

The women pushed her inside the center cage and locked the door. Without a single word spoken, they slid out of the statue chamber. As soon as the last lady exited the chamber, the red light that kept Constance's body frozen dissipated. She flopped against the metal bars of the cage, coughing, hacking, with tears streaming from her sandpaper dry eyes. Her heart was thudding in her ears more loudly than a drum. It was almost as bad as the hangover she'd suffered after drinking Welli's absinthe punch. She clutched at her aching ears and groaned as she rose unsteadily to her feet.

She scanned the gallery. She noted Boo's cage, the slumped woman in the cage to her left, an empty cage to her right, a superb collection of classical statuary, a sleeping king and . . . silence.

It was the silence that struck her as being particularly odd. All those court ladies in crinolines, and nobody was gossiping? That was beyond peculiar. The air should have been rife with scandal, sarcasm, and intrigue. More than their anachronistic gowns, hairstyles, and picture-perfect makeup, this was a dead giveaway that something bizarre was afoot.

But bizarre was her middle name. Or at least, it would have been if Mama hadn't put her foot down to Papa about it when she was a baby. It was one of her favorite stories about her parents' early days together. Back when Papa would listen to people other than himself.

Constance sighed and reached up for two more hairpins. Hopefully, this lock would be easier to pick than the one on Lucien's cell. She moved to inspect the device, her fingertips running over the icy cold metal. It was beyond cold in the gallery. Her breath was frosting the air, and purple snow had gusted in through the open doors to the courtyard. Even so, the lock's metal was exceptionally chill to the touch. It was as glass-like as the metal used for the Enigma Keys.

Interesting.

Still, if it was a lock, she could probably pick it, given enough hairpins and time.

A groan emanated from the caged slumped woman. Keeping her eyes on the lock, Constance called out, "Don't worry, madam. I'll help you out of there in a moment. I have an escape vehicle . . . sort of." She glanced into the courtyard at the stranded *Lady Penelope*, a sad shipwreck in a sea of drifting alien snow. No strange ladies appeared to be slithering upon the ship anymore, so that was a plus. "And I have a crew. Who may or may not be conscious at this point. Still, don't panic, because the cavalry is here."

A vision of Trusdale in his blue cavalry uniform, as painted alongside his family inside his silver fob watch, danced through her mind.

Focus, you fool.

She pouted at her own harshness to herself and slipped her hairpins inside the lock.

"Constance?" asked a woman's voice.

"Yes, I'll be with you in a moment, madam." She swore vividly at the uncooperative lock.

"Constance, language. *Babett's Modern Manners* states that a young lady never swears. Doubly so in the presence of royalty."

Constance groaned. "I almost had it open then. Will you please keep . . ." she glanced up at the dark-haired woman in her scarlet gown. Her words died on her tongue, and she swallowed hard. "Mama?"

The older Lady Haltwhistle clutched back a sob and slid down the bars of her cage, paler than a sheet of fine embossed stationery. "Oh, you can't truly be here, Constance. You're probably an illusion created by those . . . beautifully dressed creatures. I can't possibly have been returned to the side of my sweet little nutmeg."

The sword of memory plunged into Constance's guts and twisted its blade. *Nutmeg.*

Logic dictated that this was not her deceased mother. Perhaps she was a doppelgänger from another dimension?

She took a deep breath. "I'm not your Constance, Mama. It's difficult to explain, but there are many different versions of ourselves across the universe. I'm sure wherever you are from, there's a Papa, and a Constance, or maybe a Constantine—that's the male version of me, who honestly sounds like a total nightmare every time people speak of him. But I digress. You are currently located in dimension seventy-seven—"

"Seventy-seven-three-nine-b. My original dimension, my home. And I know my only daughter when I see her, Constance. How long has it been? Years, I know. But you still carry the same fire in your eye. I'd know you above any other version of you. I've traveled so far to find my way back to you. When your father decided to trade me in for that sweet, compliant version of me . . . and a male heir rather than you . . . oh, it broke my heart."

Constance gaped at her. "Papa wouldn't have done that, surely?" But the seeds of doubt were cast upon a well-plowed field of resentment. Hearn had admitted that Constance had been an experiment of Papa's from the start, hadn't he? Even Trusdale, betrayer that he himself was, had questioned Papa's care for her. As had Welli. It was an undeniable truth that Papa had left her alone time after time during her childhood. Wasn't it possible that he could have abandoned Mama too?

Mama sniffed and dabbed delicately at her eyes just the way that Constance remembered she did after a disagreement with Papa. Over her, usually. "Our travels took us far beyond this world. We used the Enigma Keys to explore every dimension we could find. But the more we traveled together, the further we drifted apart. We argued in a distant realm, and he left in a blaze of aether. I've been searching for Keys to help me to travel back here ever since."

"Did you manage to find any?"

Mama shook her head, her dark hair tumbling about her shoulders. "You know me. I've never been a scientist. That's your Papa's passion, not mine. The strange ladies here are working for King Oscar. They helped him to bring me here, back to my own dimension, so that you and I could set the universe back on its correct course. It seems that by opening all those portals, your Papa created multiple rips and tears in the fabric of time and space. Your father attempted to mend these tears as best he could. But Henry is not the cosmic seamstress he thinks he is, and his stitches are coming undone. Oscar believes that you and I can help persuade Henry to return here, thus closing the original anomaly. If we don't help, Oscar believes that our entire world will be destroyed by chaotic energy exploding from the void between dimensions."

The sleeping king let out a loud snore. Constance frowned at him. "The king who tried to kidnap me, the same man who put both you and me in cages, is the hero of this hour? It's hard to believe that he only wants to save the planet from destruction."

Mama nodded. "I know, but trust me. A king without a land to rule over is just a very lonely man with a shiny hat. He wants to save the world for his own selfish reasons, not altruism. But does that matter, as long as the world is spared destruction?"

"I suppose not."

"There you go then. But I must warn you, my sweet nutmeg, that the strange court ladies you see here are not human, no matter how closely they resemble our form."

Constance turned back to the lock. "I thought as much. I mean, the outsized trains on those dresses are clearly hiding something. Probably tails or claws or tentacles."

"Well, these creatures are themselves victims of your Papa's interdimensional shenanigans. Henry's damage to the void created a portal through which they were dragged all the way to Stockholm. As far as I can tell, they are not very communicative. They don't seem to know how to ask nicely for help getting back to their home. One might almost say that their manners are poor."

Always with the manners is Mama.

"All they want is for Henry, the man who abandoned us, to be brought back here to his original dimension, thus plugging the original tear in the void he unwittingly created with his travels. Oscar has said that if you cooperate with bringing your father back home, he will set us all free. And maybe we can try to become a family once more."

Constance rubbed her temples. "This is a fiendishly complicated development. I need time to think—"

The King jerked from his slumber and croaked, "Guards! Where are my . . ." His frail body shuddered as he was racked with a hacking cough. When he spoke again, his speech was that of a younger, stronger man. It was as if he were a ventriloquist's dummy. But Oscar sat in no one's lap that she could see.

His eyes wandered the room, settling upon the two caged women. "Ah, the Haltwhistles. Splendid. Then we can begin."

Scores of the weird silent women slid into the room from all directions.

For the first time in her life, Constance felt fear blast through her like lightning from a misfired battle mitten.

Chapter 31:
The War of the Worlds

King Oscar's alien court was truly a sight to behold. Almost two hundred weird ladies stood in neat rows, as if waiting for a play to begin at a theater. Their oddly painted eyes were fixed on the aged King. Constance had never attended a royal court event, but as far as she could tell from books, this was the usual routine. Courtiers watched the monarch, waiting for a chance to drop a word in the regent's ear for power, money, or favors. The difference here was that these courtiers were waiting for an interdimensional portal to be opened.

Does that make me the floor show?

Oscar clapped his hands. "Bring in the laboratory assistants."

Six ladies in pink crinolines slid in from the far end of the chamber. In the center of the group shuffled two male prisoners with their hands bound behind their backs. The first sported a bald head, a walrus mustache, and a red-and-white striped shirt stretched to bursting over his muscular frame above black woolen pants and hobnailed boots. The second stalked behind his burly compatriot with the air of an angry crane that has taken to wearing a tweed three-piece suit. Constance barely recognized them without their livery uniforms.

"Cawley, Hearn!" she shouted. Both men's eyebrows raised, but overall, they didn't seem too surprised to see her in a cage surrounded by ball gown-wearing alien beings. That's the kind of backbone that was developed by long-serving retainers at Haltwhistle Hall.

They did, however, gape at Mama as if they'd seen a ghost. Their troop escort halted beside the empty cage.

King Oscar waved his hand at Constance and said in his unnervingly young and vigorous voice, "Lady Haltwhistle, I have abducted your assistants in order to help you perform a simple task for me. I insist that you—"

"Open an interdimensional portal and bring my father here, so that your ladies can go back to their home, thus repairing the damage to the space-time continuum and making you the hero who saves the world from destruction in the void?"

The King's jaw dropped. "How did you know that?"

Constance shrugged. "Lucky guess. May I ask, why do you have an empty cage here?"

"It's to hold whichever assistant you do not need. You only require one to power your dimensional device, do you not?"

"Dimensional device? I don't have a—"

Two weird ladies approached the brown drop cloth draped over items in the center of the room. They drew the cloth back with a flourish to reveal a flat-bottomed trailer that may have once served as the bottom of a horse-drawn carriage.

Upon the trailer were a collection of state-of-the-art scientific contraptions that she recognized all too well. A four-foot-tall brass control console bristled with levers, switches, and dials. A penny-farthing bicycle on a wood-slat treadmill stood beside a copper bathtub. The tub held a trunk-size apparatus crafted from cogs, gears, and chain drives. The makeshift kinetic generator was hooked to the brass console via a black telegraph cable that snaked across the trailer's boards. From the back of the console, a blue wire ran across the trailer to a leather-topped writing desk. It wound its way up the leg of the desk and connected to a copper birdcage placed as the desk's centerpiece. The top of the birdcage had been opened on its hinge, as if to prepare for cleaning. A ring of five silver candlesticks surrounded the birdcage. From the tops of two candlesticks glowed the red light from two Enigma Keys that had been inserted where candles usually stood.

In totality, the items were a reasonable copy of the fractal generation laboratory that her father had built in the dungeon of Haltwhistle Hall. It required only three more Enigma Keys to complete the candlestick circle, thus endowing the objects with the potential to open a rift in the void.

From the palace courtyard, in blew a violet gust of snow carrying Gunter Erhard and his Viking cohorts. Constance scowled at the Austrian as he walked by her cage with the ostrich feather on his cocked general's hat bobbing triumphantly. He carried a scepter, a rosary, and a small triangular prison . . .

Daphnia! Constance drew a heart on her mental blackboard to the imprisoned alien. The giant water flea drew blobs of water across the board. Or were they teardrops? Was she sad?

Constance couldn't blame her. It had no doubt been a rough ride down in the airship for all on board. She blurted to Erhard, "My crew, are they . . .?"

She didn't dare finish the sentence. The Austrian leered at her, but his eyes didn't hold the same venom that she'd witnessed in their prior encounters. "They're alive, for now at least."

She exhaled, "Thank you."

"They're tied up, awaiting the King's pleasure. And they had a few choice words to send to you for leaving them there."

She huffed. "It wasn't as if I had any other option."

"Even if they tried to free themselves from their bonds," Erhard continued, "it would take them at least ten minutes—I mean, ten hours—to escape and remove the ship's anchor clamp. So, Connie, there's no hope of rescue for you. You're stuck here with us."

He laughed diabolically, joined in his mirth by the guffaws of his blond Vikings.

Connie? Only Welli calls me Connie. Was that a cryptic message from Welli that he'll be free in ten minutes, or is Erhard being his usual human equivalent of a migraine?

The Austrian henchman narrowed his eyes at her.

Migraine; definitely a migraine.

Erhard stepped onto the trailer via the mounting step leftover from its days as a carriage. He walked to the writing desk and placed Daphnia's prison into the top of one of the candlesticks, before tucking the Key that dangled from the Celestial Rosary into the top of another. He attempted to pull the final key out of the golden scepter without success. He asked her, "What will happen if I leave this Key in the scepter?"

"I suppose it will add a little glamour to the table."

He thudded the scepter down onto the table unnecessarily hard and went to stand behind the King's throne with his henchmen.

Constance reviewed the laboratory setup and said to Oscar, "I will need both of my laboratory assistants to manipulate this equipment, so please release them from their bonds. And we should conduct this experiment outside. If I make an error and accidentally release a rogue blast of aether energy, the entire roof here could collapse upon us. Will you allow us that precaution?"

The King waved his affirmation.

One of Hearn and Cawley's pink-gowned guards removed the men's handcuffs as the remaining ladies surrounded the trailer.

Good, now I'll see how physically strong these creatures are.

"Oi, hold up," called Hearn. "Allow me." He strode over to the trailer and shoved it hard toward the courtyard, sending it flying outside on its carriage wheels. "No point in you ladies getting your pretty dresses all dirty, is there?" he grinned at his jailers.

Ugh. It's like he's developed affection for them, even though they held him hostage. The sooner I get him out of Stockholm, the better.

She said, "And release my dog. She has no part in this." The King nodded. Boudicca was set free and came bounding toward Constance with her tail wagging. "No, Boo. Go and find Uncle Welli. Go on, get out of here."

The puppy whined pitifully.

"Be a good girl, go get him. Go find Welli."

As the disconsolate puppy trotted off toward the downed *Bad Penny* airship, Constance thought, *At least I've got one of us out of danger for now.* "And I'll need my Mama to help me press the buttons, so please release her too."

The King gazed at Mama and nodded.

The pink-clad jailer released both mother and daughter from their cages. Lady Haltwhistle walked toward Constance for the first time in a decade. She hadn't changed one iota. She was every bit as beautiful as the portrait in Constance's cabin, even down to the scarlet ball gown. Constance's heart beat a tattoo so loud that she was sure everyone in the gallery could hear it.

Every human and alien eye in the chamber was on her as she ran into her mother's open arms.

She buried her face in her mother's soft hair and breathed in the scent of roses.

Roses! Not paint, not . . .

"It's you. I thought you were a painted lady, but it's you!" she blurted. Tears welled as her mother's arms clasped her tightly against her warm bosom.

"Of course it's me, you silly sausage."

"I thought you were one of them . . . the odd ladies . . . I thought . . . oh, Mama!" Constance slumped against her mother and sobbed like a toddler who had rolled off a cushion. It was uncommonly decent of Oscar to allow a prisoner to wear their favorite perfume. Perhaps he really did want to save the world? After all, it wasn't as if she was a great judge of character.

Trusdale was proof of that.

She set her jaw. *Stop thinking about him, you fool.*

She could be so blunt with herself sometimes. If anyone else ever spoke to her as she talked to herself, she would slap them.

"So much has happened since you left." She sniffled. "I missed you every day. I kept the Hall farms running as best I could. I got engaged to a prince. Well, that didn't work out. But then I met a cowboy . . . actually, that didn't work out either. Oh Mama, nothing ever goes right for me. No matter how hard I try."

Mama stroked her hair and hummed a lullaby from long ago. "Hush, my dear. Everything is all right now. We have each other. Nothing will ever separate us again."

"About that . . . should our immediate problems be resolved, I should probably tell you about this RATT problem I have to deal with."

Mama sighed. "My poor baby. Everything has been so hard for you."

"I know, I could just scream half the time. But, stiff upper lip and all that. I wonder if it's possible to attempt to pull both Papa and the Hall back at the same time?"

Mama's brow wrinkled. "I don't know. Let's give it a whirl, shall we?"

Constance grinned and grasped her mother's hand. "Yes, Mama. Let's go and find Papa, to read him that riot act that's so long overdue." She felt giddy, furious, exhausted, and somehow, lighter than air. She had always believed that Papa was wrong to make his home in another reality. Clearly, it wasn't how things were meant to work. It was as if Mama was inside her head, holding her close, making her feel . . . loved. Truly loved, with an intensity she could almost taste.

Mama gave a wistful smile. "My only hope is that somewhere, deep down, he will be happy to see us again. We have so much healing to accomplish. The three of us. Together."

Together.

The word imprinted on her brain almost like when an Enigma Key communicated with her. But this felt different, like the words were being written in champagne bubbles directly onto her soul.

"I'm so angry at him. Did you know that I'm merely an experiment that's gone wrong? Or that I'm related to—"

"I know enough to understand, my dear. I've imagined your life unfolding in my dreams, every day since we've lost touch."

Her mother had never truly left her. She'd been there, just out of reach. And she loved her child like no one else could. Constance could feel it in her bones. Whatever Mama wanted, Mama should get. She released her mother's hands. "Let our grand experiment begin."

"There's my little scientist," Mama cooed.

Constance and Mama walked out into the courtyard, following Hearn, Cawley, and the trailer laboratory. The court ladies followed silently, gliding across the purple snow to stand in a four-alien-deep circle around the laboratory. Erhard and his henchmen helped the frail king to walk out into the courtyard. The old man gazed up at the purple skies as if he were seeing them for the first time.

Constance scanned the *Bad Penny* airship for signs of life. A large yellow anchor clamp held its docking hook firmly, but at least now the ship was fully aloft and bobbing on a two-foot length of chain above the flagstones. The crew was nowhere to be seen. But as a light breeze gusted through the courtyard, blowing purple crystals into sculptural drifts, she could have sworn she heard the bleats of Haltwhistle sheep from the airship's hold.

Constance stepped up onto the trailer. Her head was bursting with memories of Mama, her heart trembling between joy and fear. This was her chance to bring her parents back together. It was time to set her parent trap, and hope that her father would willingly step into it.

She flicked the switches on the brass console. "Mr. Hearn, would you be so kind as to mount the penny-farthing? Mr. Cawley, you may begin dusting the table."

The ex-servant pulled out a handkerchief from his pocket and moved toward the desk to commence the entirely unnecessary cleaning. This task was the only one she could think of to keep him from being locked in a cage. But as usual, it seemed he didn't appreciate her generosity.

Above the circle of candlesticks, the air shimmered. "This device essentially creates a virtual aether mirror. If you cast the viewing circle wide enough, you can view thousands of dimensions at a time. Millions, probably, if you expanded it wide enough. But the larger the circle, the more unstable the aether energy becomes. Please keep a light touch on the controls, Mama."

"Of course, dear."

"Good. Once we spot the correct dimension, I will create the smallest hole possible through which objects or people can fall. There's a certain amount of intuition and luck guiding which dimensions you encounter. The Enigma Keys are generating the energy, but they're guided by the emotion of the operator. The more emotionally connected you are to your outcome, the higher the probability that you will see the dimension you want to see."

Mama nodded. "And I want to see the correct dimension very badly indeed."

Constance grinned. "Then we should have no problems. Once we locate Haltwhistle Hall and Papa, I will cast open a doorway to their dimensions to try and physically draw them through. Hopefully, Papa won't fight me. But be warned, if I leave the doors open for too long, we risk the Enigma Keys breaking."

Mama's face hardened. "We wouldn't want that."

"Not to be bossy, but everyone needs to do exactly as I say in order to avert disaster, up to and including destroying the entire world. Mama, could you please turn that dial to seventy percent." Constance pointed at the console, and Mama complied. "Mr. Cawley, keep dusting. Mr. Hearn, keep pedaling. Mama and I will keep watch over the static as it expands above our heads. I warn you, once the static switches over to moving pictures, the images can be positively mesmerizing."

Mama's eyes were as large as cannonballs as she stared at the static sphere that crackled into life above the candlesticks. The sphere rose to hover twenty feet above the trailer.

The weird ladies surrounding them gasped in unison as Constance fiddled with her controls. "All right everyone, watch that space. We're looking for the Hall and my Papa."

The static sphere flickered into a hundred different moving images, each contained in its own hexagon, fitting together like a cosmic honeycomb. Constance scanned the images. A dozen alternate versions of herself drank tea and read novels. Several versions of Trusdale's engineer brother, J. F., worked alone in their laboratories. The notorious gunslinger, young Freedom Trusdale, shot his way in and out of trouble across the four different versions of the Wild West. A dimension entirely filled with floating chamber pots flashed before her eyes. Multiple Haltwhistle Halls flickered above her, but one in particular drew her attention. The rose gardens surrounding the Hall were badly in need of pruning. This was a Hall without a Constance, or even a gardener. This was the Hall she'd been forced to send spinning into the cosmos so that Prince Lucien's troops didn't burn it down, with her in it.

This was home.

She mentally tagged the image with a golden star and continued to search for Papa, reaching out with her feelings of anger and rage; his betrayal burning through her heart as surely as the energy from an Enigma Key.

From the corner of her eye, she saw him, ethereal behind a camouflage shield. Had he been hiding from her all this time? She roared in fury at the heavens, ripping asunder his cosmic veil, bringing him into the sharp focus he sought to avoid.

"Papa," she cried. "How could you leave me here? Was I never more to you than a lab rat? You knew the Enigma Keys' energy could be harmful, yet you exposed my mind and body to their effects for years. How dare you treat me this way?"

Papa's monocle dropped from his eye as his cheeks flushed as red as his beard. Henry the Eighth, reborn. She could see the family resemblance now in every line on the face she'd once loved but now despised. No wonder he treated the women in his life so badly. He was descended from a man who had murdered his wives when he tired of them. Really, why *wouldn't* he find a son to replace his mere daughter? The apple hadn't fallen far from their family tree. "I hate you," she screamed, as a newfound power coursed through her, darker than night and as bright as the stars, and she was in control.

"That's it, Constance, you're doing so well," cooed Mama. "Pull him back, and fix the tear in all our hearts."

"My dear girl," said Papa. "You look upset. I presume those idiot servants of mine have blabbed about my experiments on your poor mother's corpse? I tried to bring Annabella back from the dead, but failed horribly. That's why we buried a coffin full of rocks at her funeral. There was nothing left of her physical form. And then I tried to make you mentally strong by exposing you to alien energy via the Keys. In retrospect, perhaps this wasn't one of my better ideas."

"You . . . what? How could you . . . you're an absolute monster!"

Her father's eyes flicked to Mama beside her. "I'm the monster? That creature has been spying on us in every dimension. Surely you don't believe that's truly your mother? I've been hiding from it in the void, creating false images for its mirrors, leading it on a merry trail to try to keep you safe."

"Since when did you ever keep me safe?" she yelled.

He sighed. "Constance, I've made mistakes, with you most of all. But the second woman I've ever loved, the alternate version of your dear departed mother, has opened my eyes to how badly I've mistreated you. I'm sorry, dear girl. You deserved better. I thought my experiments were making you strong. Strong enough to break through all realities to help me find another Annabella to be my wife. In the end, I found her, but in the process, I caused you great harm. Please, if you can't forgive me, at least try to understand that I'm a changed man. And I'll always love you."

Trust no one, he'd always said.

"Make him prove his love of you in person," hissed Mama. "Bring him back. Shatter the cosmos if you must, but let your emotions run free."

What fine English lady would condone such a thing? Certainly not a woman who lived her life by the words of *Babett's Modern Manners*.

Memories flooded into her mind of Mama and Papa together. The Shetland pony on which the two of them had led her around the estate. The teddy bear tea parties they'd helped her to lay out. And then: Papa sobbing alone in his study every night. Papa spending weeks and months in his laboratory, seeking ways to reach other worlds. Papa, a broken man without his wife beside him.

If the woman beside her was truly his first love, then Papa would have torn apart the cosmos to be with her. But he wasn't here.

A strange peace descended over her. An acceptance of the inevitable truth that we all lose people we love. But our memories of those people help them live on forever in our hearts. She had to trust the most untrustworthy person she knew to tell her the truth.

Herself.

No matter how much it tore her apart.

Howling like the storm she felt inside, she pushed her energy against her father's image, pushing him off the cosmic chessboard that was developing in the skies. Not because she hated him, but because she loved him and wanted to protect him. And for the first time, she could sense that, in his own way, he loved her too.

Constance turned on the graceful doppelgänger who had dared to rip open an old wound. "You are not my mother," she said with the sort of exacting hauteur under duress that would have filled her true mother with pride—a lady shaped as much by *Babett's Modern Manners* as she herself had come to be.

The doppelgänger chuckled at her anguish. "Thank you for your power, my dear. It's a shame you never understood what you held inside you all along. You could have harnessed this energy, but instead you waste your focus looking outward, never inward. You're the worst of all the Constances I've encountered through my aether mirrors. I talk to them as Mama, and they tell me all their secrets. I know everything about you, girl, and now I shall harness your unique energy to rule this earth. I've already eaten of the power you used to reach your father to open a portal of my own. There they sit, your home and mine. But yours is dead and mine is full of life. Specifically, an army of creatures just like me, ready to move their gelatinous might into this world to take it for our own."

The two images grew larger in the sky, Haltwhistle Hall and an alien world, overpowering the other dimensions as aether energy surged into them and the Enigma

Keys ignited into full power. Purple and red lights converged upon the two images, until they hung over the watching court as large as omnibuses. The fractal generator hummed into top gear as Hearn pedaled and Cawley dusted like a madman.

Constance snarled at the creature, "Of all the filthy tricks, pretending to be my dead mother. That's beyond the pale, even for a giant alien jelly. I assume you're one of them—one of the Ma. But still—"

She stopped and gazed at the circle of weird ladies around her. "Your form isn't big enough to be a giant jelly. Those . . . things . . . are you, aren't they? They're blobs of you. Like a severed finger or toe. Yuck. And why did you give them such appalling ball gowns?"

"To cover their blobby shape, you cretin. Do you think it's easy to maintain that level of control? Do you have any idea how many townspeople I had to consume to create so many body parts? It's been positively exhausting. Once my family invades and destroys your species, I'm taking a very long vacation. Probably by the sea. I do so love the ocean. Don't you, daughter dear?" The Ma roared with cruel laughter as the images above rose and grew ever larger.

Cracks in reality flashed out like lightning from around each image as the portals began to open. Constance could do nothing to stop them now.

Damn and blast it. How could I have been so foolish as to allow my heart to rule my head?

Constance shouted, "Hearn, stop pedaling. Start thumping." The carriage driver sprang off his penny-farthing and advanced toward the Ma. The weird ladies swarmed toward him at astonishing speed, bouncing the big man between their jelly crinolines as he struggled to reach the Ma's leader.

"Should I stop dusting, miss?" asked Cawley.

"What? Yes, please do. Perhaps you should run for cover, Mr. Cawley. I fear things are about to get ugly."

"Very good, miss." The aged retainer stepped down from the trailer and halted as the weird ladies slid toward him *en masse*.

"Oh no, not on my watch," snapped Constance. She glared at the head Ma. "This is your one chance to retreat. Or I'm going to find myself a very large spoon and . . . well, I won't be held responsible for the outcome." Not exactly her most spine-chilling threat, but what else would a giant jelly fear?

The Ma chuckled. "Do you believe I should tremble before you? You're no goddess."

A gruff American voice shouted from the direction of the *Bad Penny*, "I'll have to disagree with you there, ma'am."

Constance spun on her heel. With the backdrop of the gently bobbing airship behind him, Trusdale walked toward her with his pistol in hand. And he was leading an army, of sorts.

Constance clutched at her chest as her heart fluttered with surprise, excitement, and more than a little joy. Trusdale's Brass Queen-armed militia consisted of two scientists, one cousin and his valet, one ex-pirate queen, and a yapping Yorkie puppy. But they were followed by well-armed reinforcements. Four twill-clad suffragettes swinging their truncheons, three well-dressed ladies in jewel-toned bustled gowns with double katana swords drawn, and twelve muscular men in tweed suits, all wearing tortoiseshell spectacles and carrying multishot Orphanator Mark VII blunderbusses.

RATT?

The incongruous cavalry had arrived. And not a moment too soon. Two hundred weird ladies swept toward the army in a wave of enraged jelly. Their weapons were their natural form as they sought to engulf and suffocate their prey. The blob courtiers around Hearn had almost enveloped the carriage driver's legs. When he punched at their viscous goo, it splattered over the entire trailer and Constance.

Yuck! Constance wiped the goo from her cheek and shook it off her hand onto the trailer. That should have been enough to end the threat, but to Constance's extreme annoyance, it crawled toward the Ma instead. Her fake mother absorbed the slime and grew just a little larger. Throughout, her hands remained on the brass console's instruments as she appeared to ignore the battle raging around her. Her eyes, remained fixed on the two growing portals overhead.

Constance held up her right arm, extended toward the creature. "It may interest you to know that I've been conducting experiments involving electricity. A certain gadget I own had a tendency to misfire, but I realize now that its chaotic nature was linked to my own internal turmoil. My energy, my power, were not focused enough to allow the device to operate as it should. In essence, I got in my own way every time I used it. I'd like to thank you for your assistance in helping me to resolve this situation."

The Ma turned her head. "What are you babbling on about?"

"May I demonstrate the Kinetic Storm Battle Mitten #004?" Constance clenched her fist and focused her mind. She opened her fingers, and a net of pure white electricity flew from her fingertips over the Ma.

Mama exploded in a wave of sizzling slop that covered Constance from head to toe.

Yet her body parts fought on, unaffected by their leader's possible demise.

Constance grimaced, wiping off the alien remains and scanning the crowd. To her surprise, Erhard and his Viking horde had joined the fray, but on Trusdale's side. Even the doddering king had risen to his feet and was swinging wild punches at the jellies, his strength clearly returning as theirs diminished. *Most splendid!*

Turning away her attention from the raging battle, Constance reached out mentally to Daphnia and drew her an image of her most audacious Plan with a capital "P" yet. As Daphnia communicated with the nearby Keys, Constance gazed at the open portals above. Both had now reached a critical size, huge and ominous in the darkened sky.

"Now!" shouted Constance at the Keys. Purple lightning crackled between the artifacts on the writing desk, and Haltwhistle Hall burst through its portal out into this world, full-sized and fabulous. Soil dropped down from the plateau upon which it sat. It was Yorkshire dirt, the finest of all the earths on Earth. "Go get 'em," screamed Constance up at the Hall, willing the aether energy still vibrating through its atoms to guide its path. The stately home rotated once, then flew into the jelly's portal, bouncing to squash the jelly army flat. The crenellated mansion levitated above the gigantic pool of multicolored goo in triumph. The jellies molten mass slid into a full retreat toward the inner reaches of their alien world, like a sea of slime drawn away by a tidal low.

Haltwhistle Hall burst back through the portal, hovered overhead for an uncomfortable moment, then shot up into the stratosphere and headed for Sheffield.

Her home was heading home. Hopefully. If not, well, maybe it would land by a nice beach somewhere?

Her crew and assorted helpers were still battling an ever-decreasing number of weird ladies. Several of the downed blobs were slithering back toward Mama's wide puddle of goo, which quivered as they approached. Perhaps they could rejoin and revitalize her, making the Ma effectively immortal.

That was all she needed. An eternal enemy from another world with a grudge against her family.

There was only one thing for it. Constance drew for one last time on her mental blackboard to Daphnia. *It's been my honor, oh great giant water flea.*

Daphnia drew a pair of lips. A final kiss between friends. Purple and red energy crackled across the writing desk between the Keys. As one entity, they tore themselves free from their candlesticks and scepter and rose toward the still-open portals above. Their energy circle spun faster and faster, creating a vortex whirlwind of cosmic energy that tunneled down to the courtyard. Every weird lady, every scrap of Ma, was sucked up into the base of the whirlwind. The Keys whipped the purple vortex over to the open portal that led to the jellies' world. A gigantic boom rang across the sky, and they shot the slime back to its home world.

As the goo stream ran dry, the Keys flew into a tight ball to perform their own jail break. Combined and united, their raw power surged, and a massive cosmic explosion flashed through the air with an electronic bass note that rang Constance's ears. The boom left a high-pitched whine that would surely last for quite a while. Leaving the buildings and people below intact, three giant semitransparent water fleas and two kraken drifted away into the newly clear sky.

Constance rubbed her ears and turned to inspect her troops. The crew of the *Bad Penny* were laughing and clapping each other on the back. To her surprise, one of the backs being clapped belonged to Trusdale. *So, it only took him bringing an army to a battle for them to forgive him?* She was made of sterner stuff.

She stepped down from the trailer and addressed Hearn and Cawley. "Well, well, well. Taking our own grand tour of Europe, are we?"

Hearn sniffed. "We got grabbed in London by that jelly's handmaidens. Right embarrassing it was. We thought we were goners."

"And the worst part is, we were going to die with you being angry at us," said Cawley.

She quirked an eyebrow. "*That* was going to be the worst part of dying?"

"Apart from the actual death bit," said Hearn. "Anyway, we talked about it in our cell, and agreed if we did happen to survive, we'd tell you face-to-face that we're sorry we deceived you all those years. Yes, we owed allegiance to your father, but as you so rightly pointed out, we owed you loyalty too."

"Aye, we're sorry, truly," interrupted Cawley. "And should you ever be looking to hire—"

"I *am* looking, and you *are* hired." She smiled, her spirits lifting to the heavens above. "Welcome back to the crew."

Cawley groaned. "The crew? You mean we're staying on that bloody airship? When I saw the Hall flying about up there—"

"The *Lady Penelope*'s next mission will be to go and find out where Haltwhistle Hall has landed. We're going home, gentlemen, once we've established exactly where home is."

The retainers beamed. "Oh, that's smashing, miss," said Hearn.

Boo bounded over, barking with joy. Constance picked up the puppy and smothered her with kisses as she wriggled, trying to lick her mistresses' face. She snorted. "My heavens, someone needs a bubble bath. Did someone bite a few nasty jelly ladies in the bustle? Yes, I thought so. Cawley?"

The elderly retainer groaned and took the Yorkie from her hands. She crooned and tickled the dog under her chin. "I promise I'll come and play with you later, my tiny terrier. You've been braver than the greatest Great Dane, and I'm proud of you."

The puppy yapped her delight.

Constance chuckled and continued her path toward her crew. Welli and a certain cowboy-spy were shaking hands. It appeared that Trusdale was once again wearing his Stetson.

I should have thrown it in the furnace when I had the chance.

The twill-clad suffragettes swarmed around her, stopping her in her tracks. As the sturdy Anne clapped Constance on the back far too vigorously, Emmi gushed, "Oh, Miss Constance, you were magnificent."

"So were you. How on earth did you ladies end up in Stockholm?"

Emmi grinned. "Well, as Mr. Trusdale told us when we fished him out of the Thames—"

Constance blinked. "That was terribly nice of you."

"Gosh, what lady doesn't want to fish a handsome cowboy out of a river?"

Constance sniffed. "I've always considered him to be *almost* handsome."

The ladies disagreed. Emmi simpered, "Those sky-blue eyes."

"And them brawny biceps. Phwaargh!" added Anne, making a very unladylike motion with her hips.

Constance's brow quirked as Emmi continued, "Mr. Trusdale informed us that you had requested assistance from the Sheffield Sisterhood of Suffragettes. Naturally, we raced after your airship as quickly as the *Shoulder of Mutton* allowed. We were more than happy to allow Mr. Trusdale to use our carrier pigeons to contact the British Museum regarding the treasure you were locating for them."

Ah, so that explained why a posse of RATT agents was heading her way.

Constance nibbled her lip. "And what else did Mr. Trusdale share with you?"

"Only that you were in dire danger, as usual, and that he'd do anything to help you. It was terribly sweet."

The ladies nodded their straw boaters in assent.

"Sweetness isn't everything," grumbled Constance.

In her broad Yorkshire accent, Anne said, "And might I add, you've inspired us beyond measure with your victory over those weird blobby things. Do you have any advice we can share with the readers of the Sheffield Suffrage Gazette?"

Constance tugged at her earlobe. "Trust your instincts in all things and carry a concealed weapon. Preferably a Kinetic Storm Battle Mitten #005, a new, slimline gauntlet that I'm thinking of developing that may specifically be of help to you ladies as you fight the good fight to win the vote."

The ladies *oohed* and *aahed*.

All four drew black notebooks with attached pens out of their highly sensible skirt pockets and started scribbling.

"Until we meet again, ladies. Thank you again for your assistance." Constance curtsied politely and strode once more toward her crew. Maya was giving Trusdale a hug, while Zhi nodded and grinned.

Everyone's so forgiving of his transgressions. Does one raised army cancel out a spy mission? I think not.

A dozen muscular men in tweed suits and tortoiseshell spectacles were the next to block her way.

Constance blew out her cheeks. "Look, I'm doing my best to meet your wretched deadline. I almost had your missing treasure in hand, but it sailed off toward England in Haltwhistle Hall's cellar. At least give me twenty-four hours to go and find it for you."

The RATT agent in charge, burdened in life by an excessively bushy ginger mustache, bowed his head. "Lady Haltwhistle, in light of your involvement with what appears to have been some sort of invasion of Earth by creatures unknown—"

Constance exhaled. "They're called the Ma. Nasty, shape-shifting bunch. I'm sure they'll try again. Their sort always does."

The scholar-thugs exchanged glances.

Mr. Mustache said, "And that device you were using to open the portal? May we add it to our collection of oddities?"

"I suppose you won't let me say no."

The men conferred. Mr. Mustache said, "You are correct. We're taking your laboratory."

I'll say this for the British Museum. Their collection policy remains consistent.

He gazed up into the sky. "And those triangles that appeared to turn into monstrous airborne creatures—?"

"Oh, they're harmless enough. They like to live far above our atmosphere. They're probably on the moon, if you want to go looking for them." She smirked, knowing full well that space travel in search of cosmically exotic artifacts was high on the Museum's to do list, with little hope of ever getting it done.

"That's a pity, your ladyship. Do let us know when we may stop by your abode to retrieve our treasure."

"That's it? No, 'you've missed the deadline by five minutes so now we're going to remove a body part' kind of thing?"

His ginger eyebrows raised. "We're not unreasonable. You could have always asked for an extension. Good day, miss."

"But, but . . ." Constance spluttered after them as they turned and marched away across the square toward the statue gallery. *Why didn't I think of requesting an extension? What a twit I am.* No doubt King Oscar would wake to find that his most prized works of art had mysteriously disappeared overnight. And the British Museum never left IOUs for the items that mysteriously fell into their hands. *Poor Oscar. I hope he has everything insured.*

The King was talking to Erhard and his blond associates. The once haggard monarch had seemingly de-aged by several decades. His cheeks were flushed, his eyes were bright, and he was shaking the Vikings' hands most vigorously. *Is there any chance that he's dropped his vendetta against me?*

She caught Erhard's eye. The Austrian took off his cocked hat and swept into a low court bow toward her. He stood and smiled in a way that wasn't entirely filled with malice.

Still, she had no desire to make his acquaintance on a deeper level. Once almost chloroformed, twice shy. She nodded her head in acknowledgment of the bow.

His grin widened.

Well, that's enough cavorting with evil for one day, I believe.

Her crew was drifting toward the *Bad Penny*, rounding up stray farm animals that had escaped from the hold as they went. Mr. Singh was helping Hearn to free the airship from its yellow anchor clamp. Cawley and Boo had already disappeared inside. The Singhs waved at her, the scientists cheered her on, and Welli applauded her as she approached. Only one man now stood between her and her crew.

A man in a black leather duster coat and a Stetson.

A man with his back to her.

She blew out her cheeks and walked toward him.

Trusdale turned, his ridiculously blue eyes clouded with pain and regret.

"Constance, I'm so very, very sorr—"

"You found your hat, then."

He blinked and reached up to touch its wide brim. "Well, yes."

"I still believe you should widen your repertoire of *chapeaux*. Deerstalkers are very popular this year. You could blend in with a wider crowd. No doubt that would be useful, given your career as a spy—"

"Not anymore." He held up a piece of paper, neatly typed with two words. *Request approved.* "My handler has set me free. Heaven only knows how this note found its way into my pocket on an airship full of suffragettes. God sure works in mysterious ways. But the point is, I'm my own man once more. I joined the agency to escape the pain of losing my men on the battlefield. But I didn't know what pain was until my work caused me to lose you too. All I want is the opportunity to earn your trust once more."

She nodded. "I see."

Trusdale glanced over her shoulder. "While you think on that, I should give you a heads up that there's some finely dressed ladies heading this way at a fair clip."

"I've already given the suffragettes a printable quote. Surely that's more than enough." She turned to see three feather-hatted fashionistas in jewel-toned gowns approaching. Double katanas were strapped to their backs, their hilts poking up like angels' wings. "Are these women more combatants in your rag-tag army that I should thank for their service?"

Trusdale stepped up alongside her. "They ain't nothin' to do with me. Watch your step here. They look like they mean business."

"I can take care of myself, thank you very much."

He gazed down at her. "I know. But katanas can put a quick end to even the bravest warrior queen."

"Queen?" She reached up and ran her fingertips over Queen Victoria's diamond crown. "Good lord, I'd forgotten I was wearing this."

"It still suits you," he grinned.

A smile she wasn't sure she should share tugged at her lips.

The elegant ladies drew close and stopped. "Baroness Constance Aethelflaed Zenobia Haltwhistle?" asked a tall brunette in a ruby-colored gown of impeccable taste.

"Who's asking?" she replied, eyeing the woman's dress appreciatively.

"Her imperial majesty, Queen Victoria, requests that you and your entire crew attend her upcoming jubilee ball. She wishes to discuss your ancestry, your continental adventures, your ability to pay for the reconstruction of her submersible squid, and most importantly, the whereabouts of her favorite grandson."

Constance's head spun. "Prince Lucien? I don't know where he is. The last I saw of him, he was swimming across the Thames being shot at by Beefeaters."

"And yet somehow, he miraculously escaped, and was last seen boarding a steamship bound for America." The brunette scowled at Trusdale.

He said, "Oh no, that has nothin' to do with me. I'd have sooner you shot the blighter."

The women's eyebrows rose in unison.

Constance laid a hand upon Trusdale's arm. "What my security consultant here means is that, of course, we mean no harm to a member of the British Royal Family. No matter how disgraced they are, or how far they have fallen in our great Queen's esteem. Naturally, we would be delighted to attend the jubilee ball."

"We would?" said Trusdale.

The brunette fashionista said, "The invitation is for the entire crew of the *Lady Penelope*. You are crew, aren't you?"

"Am I?" he asked Constance, his eyes wide and wondering.

She gazed into his ridiculously blue eyes. "I don't see why not. Only a crew member would raise an army that helped to save all our skins. Such loyalty should be rewarded."

"I should add," said the brunette, "that not accepting Her Majesty's invitation will lead to a summary execution." She smiled sweetly and reached up toward her back.

Constance and Trusdale inhaled and moved closer together, each ready to defend the other if required.

But the lady did not draw her katana. Instead, she miraculously produced a gilt-edged, embossed, letterpressed party invitation so grand it put King Louis XVIII's party invitation to shame.

Constance gingerly took the card from her. "Nonesuch Palace? I've never heard of it."

"Attire is formal," said the brunette, looking up and down at Trusdale's cowboy ensemble with disdain. "And speaking of formal attire," she held out her hand to Constance expectantly.

Constance heaved a sigh and reached up to loosen her remaining hairpins.

Her auburn hair tumbled about her shoulders as she removed the diamond crown. "I was keeping it safe for the Queen. There's an awful lot of villains about these days. May I inquire as to your name, Lady . . .?"

"You may not. Good day, Lady Haltwhistle. We'll see you at court." The ladies turned and walked away, their katanas and bustles a fashion inspiration she would love to imitate.

Trusdale blinked down at her. "You really want me back on the crew?"

"I need a security consultant, and you appear to be the best man for the job. For some reason, the universe keeps sending villains after me, and I need someone to watch my back. Plus, I have a wonderful design in mind for the Kinetic Storm Battle Mitten #005. And I need my partner's input to make sure the device is safe for both wearer and target. I certainly never meant to hurt anyone." She gazed up at him.

"Me neither. And I'll spend the rest of my life making sure you're safe, if that's what you want from me."

She winked mischievously. "Well, that will do for a start."

He chuckled. "I never know what's coming next with you, Constance. Does this mean we're . . ." His eyes settled on her lips. "Is there any chance we might one day . . . be more than fellow crew members?"

"Honestly? Time will tell. But for now . . ." She stood on her tippy-toes and kissed him gently on the cheek. "Thank you for not giving up on me."

He grinned. "I swear I never will, Lady Haltwhistle. You have my word."

"And you have my trust, Mr. Trusdale," she smiled.

They linked arms and strolled to board their pirate airship with their heads close and their hearts even closer.

And everything was right in the world.

·⁓ THE END ⁓·

About the Author

British native Elizabeth Chatsworth lives with her husband and rambunctious Yorkshire Terrier, Boo, in the picturesque town of Tamworth in New Hampshire, USA. Elizabeth enjoys steampunk cosplay, gardening, cooking, and playing video games until the wee hours of the morning. She loves to write science fiction and fantasy stories that celebrate rogues, rebels, and renegades across time and space. From Victorian sensibilities to interstellar travel, she aims to send you on a cosmic adventure filled with quirky characters and a touch of humor! Find out more at her website:

www.elizabethchatsworth.com

Acknowledgments

My heartfelt thanks go to my wonderful editors, Cassandra Farrin and Helga Schier. Thank you to my creative writing coach, Rhonda Douglas, for her inspirational insights. Many thanks to James A. Owen for his fabulous illustrations for the entire Brass Queen series. I'm eternally grateful to the entire CamCat Publishing team who worked so hard to bring this book to you today. Special thanks to my friend, Gabi Coatsworth, for her support throughout the years. And finally, thank you to my husband and family for helping me to see the magic in every dawn.

If you liked
Elizabeth Chatsworth's
The Brass Queen—Grand Tour,
consider leaving us a review to help our authors.

And check out
The Shabti by Megaera C. Lorenz.

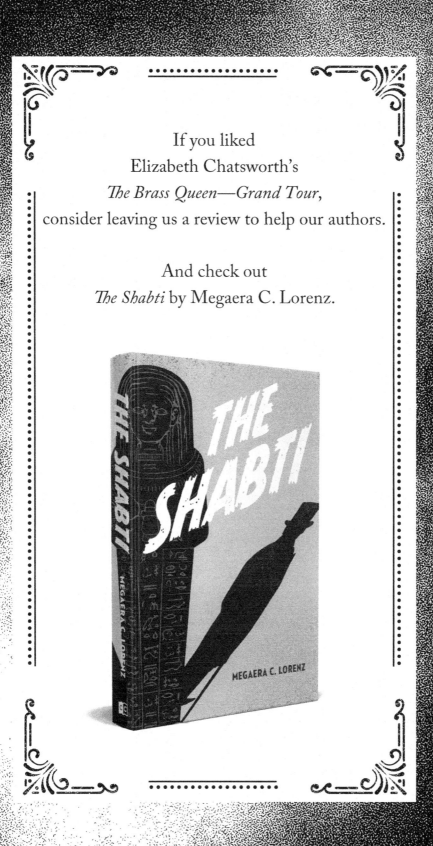

CHAPTER
1

Dashiel Quicke sat at the center of the stage, his head bowed, a shimmering stream of ectoplasm flowing from his open mouth. As the ethereal discharge cascaded over his lap, it seemed to borrow its own luminescence from the white-hot arc lamps that blazed overhead. Perspiration prickled his scalp and soaked his shirt collar, but he welcomed the punishing heat of the lights. He'd spent enough time working under the cover of darkness. He was a man with precious little left to hide.

The watchful eyes of his audience bore into him. The atmosphere was thick with their morbid curiosity. Even at a demonstration like this one, Dashiel didn't shy away from theatrics. If tonight's crowd of gawkers took nothing else from the experience, they would at least leave entertained. His shoulders heaved and he swayed in his seat as the ectoplasm continued to unfurl, pooling on the floor at his feet in a filmy heap. His hands, resting on his knees with the palms facing up, twitched spasmodically.

Someone in the audience let out a low whistle. Another onlooker, seated closer to the stage, groaned in disgust.

"Holy cats, mister," said a voice from somewhere in the middle seats. "How much of that stuff you got in there?" A handful of the speaker's neighbors broke out in raucous laughter.

Dashiel pulled the tail end of the ectoplasm out of his mouth, then rose to his feet and moved to the edge of the stage. He held it aloft in front of him, spreading it out wide between his hands. The ends trailed down on either side of him, sweeping up dust and grime from the battered floorboards as he walked.

"I hope you're all duly impressed by what you've seen here tonight, ladies and gentlemen," he said. "Your average Spiritualist would tell you that it's impossible to produce ectoplasm under these conditions. It's sensitive stuff. Disintegrates under full light, you see. The theory has it that light disrupts the ectenic force that the spirits use to manifest it out of the medium's body."

He paused, waiting for the crowd to settle. There was a smattering of whispers and laughter from the gaggle of hooligans in the middle seats. A young woman in the second row snapped her gum with a sharp crack.

Her neighbor swatted her arm and giggled.

"What they won't tell you," Dashiel went on, "is that it's made of common cheesecloth. Or muslin, if you're the type of medium who likes to live large and spring for the good stuff. It doesn't really matter which one you use, though. Either one looks mighty impressive if you've got a dark séance room and a strong will to believe. They're both just about infinitely compressible—perfect for hiding in tight spaces, away from the prying eyes and hands of doubters and debunkers. And to answer your question, young man," he added, smiling in the direction of his heckler, "unless the fellow at the general store shorted me, it's exactly three yards."

Satisfied that everyone had gotten a good look at the ectoplasm, Dashiel walked back to the center of the stage. Paint splatters, scuffs, and the faded remnants of spike marks from past theatrical productions marred the dark floorboards, which creaked beneath his feet with every step.

Like most campus theaters where he had performed, this one was a humble affair. It held enough seats for about two hundred spectators. Only a battered chalkboard sign outside the front entrance served to announce Dashiel's performance that evening. *Tonight Only*, it proclaimed, *Acclaimed Ex-Spirit Medium Dashiel Quicke Unveils the Dark Secrets of the Psychic Flimflam Racket!*

"My spiritual instrument is speaking to me again," Dashiel said. With nimble fingers, he wound up the trailing ribbon of muslin ectoplasm as he spoke. The length of cloth vanished within seconds into a bundle small enough to fit between his cheek and his gums. "I'm receiving a very strong impression. The spirits have a gift for someone who is here in the theater tonight."

Someone in the audience snickered. Dashiel blithely ignored them. He tossed the roll of muslin onto the rickety table that stood at the center of the stage, where it joined several other tools of his trade—a dented tin trumpet decorated with bands of phosphorescent paint, a stack of cards inscribed with forged spirit messages, and a fluffy drift of white chiffon veils. He turned his attention to the audience, squinting at them past the glare of the footlights and the bluish fog of cigarette smoke that hung low and heavy in the air beyond the stage.

The spring of 1934 was proving to be a cold and dreary one, and that always meant good business. The house wasn't packed, but there was a decent crowd. Except for a lone middle-aged gentleman in brown tweeds seated in the front row, the audience was overwhelmingly youthful. Bored college boys and girls filled most of the seats, their dreams of necking with their sweethearts under the mellow April moon dashed by the chilly weather. So far, they had reacted to his routine with rowdy enthusiasm.

To these people, Dashiel was an amusing curiosity, a rainy-day diversion that they'd likely soon forget. He could only hope that he'd serve as an edifying cautionary tale for some of them as well.

A few short years ago, he'd drawn a different sort of crowd indeed. Throngs of affluent true believers once sat through his demonstrations in the chapel at Camp Walburton with breath bated, eyes shining with devotion, entranced by his every word and gesture. When he closed his eyes, he could see himself there again, dressed in a pristine white suit and wreathed in the scents of fresh-cut chancel flowers and sandalwood instead of sawdust, cigarettes, and half-dried paint. No point in dwelling. This was the path he'd chosen for himself.

"Is there," he asked, pressing his fingers to his temples, "a Professor Hermann Goschalk among us?"

It came as no surprise to Dashiel when the man in the tweed suit rose to his feet. He clutched his hat to his chest and cleared his throat, glancing around as if he expected some other fellow to step up at any second and identify himself as the person in question.

"Um, I beg your pardon," he said at last. "That's my name. Do you mean . . . me?"

Dashiel smiled. "Unless there is more than one Hermann Goschalk in the audience, then I think I must. Join me on stage, if you please, sir."

Professor Goschalk made his way to the stage, accompanied by scattered applause, whoops, and whistles.

In Dashiel's experience, there were few things that a collegiate audience liked better than the prospect of a faculty member making a spectacle of himself on stage, and this crowd proved to be no exception. The professor didn't seem to mind. He trotted up the steps and stood smiling shyly at Dashiel like a starstruck kid meeting a matinee idol.

"Hello!" he said.

"Good evening, Professor," said Dashiel, with a brief bow. "Please, be seated." The professor nodded, blinking owlishly under the blazing lights, and took a seat in one of the two folding chairs that stood in the middle of the stage beside the table.

Hermann Goschalk was a little gray mouse of a man, about fifty years old. Dashiel guessed that his well-worn suit was at least half as old as its wearer. His rumpled brown hair was generously streaked with silver, and he had large, uncommonly expressive hazel eyes—an excellent asset in a sitter. The more demonstrative the face, the greater the sympathetic response that the unwitting shill would arouse in the audience.

"Thank you," said Dashiel. He sat down in the other chair and fixed the professor with a penetrating gaze. "Before we proceed, I hope you don't mind if I ask you a few questions, just to get my bearings. I want to be absolutely sure I do have the right Hermann Goschalk, after all."

"Of course!"

"Wonderful. Now, stop me if I'm mistaken in any detail. You are a member of the faculty here at Dupris University, a professor of Ancient Studies, specializing in the language and civilization of the ancient Egyptians. Is that right?"

"Yes, that's absolutely correct," said Goschalk, with an enthusiastic nod.

"Very good." Dashiel inclined his head and squeezed his eyes shut for a moment, as if trying to draw his next morsel of information from some deep and inscrutable well of hidden knowledge. "Is it true that you used to keep a black cat in your younger days, back when you worked as an assistant druggist at that pharmacy in—"

"Milwaukee, yes!" Professor Goschalk's astonished expression couldn't have been more perfect if he'd rehearsed it. "Good heavens, you even know about old Tybalt?"

"I do," said Dashiel, with a solemn nod. "He must have been quite the beloved companion."

The professor chuckled. "Oh, he was a terrible little yungatsh! He'd lie there in the windowsill soaking up the sun and hissing at anybody who dared to get too close. Did a fine job keeping the store free of mice, though." He smiled fondly. "Papa always said a pharmacy without a cat was a pharmacy without a soul."

"Ah yes, that's right. He was the drugstore cat. Your father owned the pharmacy, and he was hoping you'd carry on the family business. But you longed for greater things. You decided to pursue a degree in Egyptology. Once you completed your studies, you came to work here . . . about fifteen years ago."

"Gracious, yes! But how on Earth did you know all these things?"

"Before a second ago, I knew hardly any of it," said Dashiel. "All I knew was that you once worked in a pharmacy and had a black cat. Just enough detail to impress you—and get you talking. It wasn't too hard to put the rest together from there." He winked and patted the professor on the shoulder. "I daresay you'd be a plum customer in the séance room, Professor Goschalk."

Goschalk gaped at him. "Well, I'll be a son of a gun!" he said. A ripple of laughter erupted from the audience.

"Thank you, Professor, you've been very obliging," Dashiel went on. "But if you don't mind me taking just a little more of your time, there's one more thing I'd like to ask you before I let you go. At this moment, the spirits are telling me that you recently lost something of great sentimental value. Is that true?"

The professor nodded. "As a matter of fact, I have. Gosh, how uncanny! It was a cabinet card of my mother. I've kept it on my office desk for years, but I noticed it was gone not two weeks ago. I can't imagine what could have happened to it."

"That is too bad. But perhaps we can help you find it again." Dashiel rose and moved to stand behind Professor Goschalk, resting his hands lightly on the man's shoulders. He gazed out at the audience and spoke in a booming, authoritative tone. "Ladies and gentlemen, you are about to witness one of the most powerful forms of mediumistic manifestation. But I must ask for your help in amplifying the potency of our connection to the spirit realm. Please, raise your voices in a hymn of praise."

He nodded to the elderly organ player stationed at stage right. She curtly returned his nod, then began to grind out a shaky but serviceable rendition of "From the Other Shore." Three or four voices in the audience piped up with gusto, while a handful of others mumbled along uncertainly.

It was hardly the sort of performance he would have gotten from his regular Sunday evening congregation back at the camp, but it would have to do. Dashiel let his eyes flutter closed and allowed his head to loll back as if he were falling into a trance.

"Dear ones who have passed beyond the veil," he intoned above the drone of the organ, "we beseech thee to reunite this gentleman with his lost portrait of his beloved mother. Keep singing, ladies and gentlemen! I am sensing a vibration from the other side. The spirits are with us!" He raised his arms in a dramatic, sweeping gesture, and as he did so, an object tumbled into Professor Goschalk's lap.

"Oh!" said the professor.

"Oooh!" echoed the audience.

Dashiel lowered his arms, letting his hands come to rest on the back of Goschalk's chair. He nodded again to the organist, who stopped playing. "Thank you, Mrs. Englebert. Please, Professor Goschalk," he said, "tell us what you have just received."

Goschalk pulled a pair of wire-rimmed glasses from the inner pocket of his jacket and slipped them on. Slowly, he picked up the item in his lap and squinted at it. He turned in his seat and blinked up at Dashiel in amazement. "Why . . . it's my photograph!"

"The same cabinet card of your mother that used to sit on your desk?"

"The very same, down to the faded spot in the corner. Oh, that is magnificent. Absolutely phenomenal!"

Dashiel bowed and smiled graciously as the audience burst into whistles and hearty applause.

"Thank you, Professor. Ladies and gentlemen, what you have just seen is known in the spook business as an *apport*. Impressive, yes? But of course, like everything else I have demonstrated this evening, a complete hoax. I hope you'll forgive me, Professor, when I explain that this photograph was stolen from your desk, in broad daylight, by one of my own personal agents—someone who is, what's more, entirely corporeal and very much alive."

"I'll be damned!" said Goschalk, his eyes more saucer-like than ever.

"It was a simple matter for me to obtain a list of the names of people who bought advance tickets for tonight's demonstration. Having selected your name from the list, I sent my young assistant to gather some basic intelligence. Your students and colleagues were happy to share a few choice tidbits of information with someone who, they assumed, was a prospective pupil in the Ancient Studies program."

There were some crows and hoots of amusement from the middle-seat gang. "Oooh, Professor," one of them called out, "he got you good!"

Dashiel raised his voice, speaking over the brief uproar of merriment that followed. "That, Professor Goschalk, is how I learned of your position in the department, your time as an assistant druggist, and yes— even old Tybalt. As for your photograph, all that my accomplice had to do was to pay a brief visit to your office, posing as a student with a rather vexing academic question. When you got up to consult one of your books, he quietly purloined the cabinet card from your desk. Thank you. You may return to your seat."

Professor Goschalk rose, clutching hat and photograph, and toddled off the stage, still looking delightfully befuddled. Dashiel was conscious of a pang of wistfulness. Had he still been in the business of fleecing the rich and bereaved, this was exactly the sap he would have wanted front and center at every service.

A stinging wind had picked up by the time Dashiel wrapped up his act and wandered out of the theater. He turned up his collar and huddled against the wall by the side entrance, debating whether to hail a cab or brave the walk back to the modest room he had rented a few blocks away. Absently, he drew one of the last two cigarettes from the crumpled packet in his coat pocket and placed it between his lips.

"Those things are terrible for you, you know," said a soft, pleasant voice from the shadows.

Dashiel turned, slowly and deliberately, doing his best not to look alarmed. He'd managed to make himself a number of enemies over the past few years, what with one thing and another, and he didn't relish being crept up on in dark alleys. When he saw that it was the little professor from his demonstration, his shoulders slumped with relief.

"So my doctor tells me," he answered with a wry smile. "But you can only ask a man to give up so many vices at once." He slipped the unlit cigarette back into the package and put it away.

Professor Goschalk chuckled. "I suppose that's true," he said, looking like a man who had little experience with vices, much less giving them up. "That was all very impressive, by the way, Mr. Quicke. *Very* impressive. If you hadn't explained how it was done, you might have made a believer out of me."

"Well, if I had, you would've been in good company, Professor," Dashiel assured him. "I've hoodwinked everyone from medical doctors to bishops."

"Please, call me Hermann." He extended a hand, and Dashiel gave it a firm shake.

"Dashiel. It's a pleasure."

Hermann's fingertips lingered on Dashiel's for a moment as the handshake ended, and his brow furrowed with sympathy. "Oh, gosh, your hands are like ice! It is awfully cold, isn't it? Well, this is what passes for spring here in Illinois, I'm afraid. Do you have far to go? I can give you a lift."

"That's very kind of you. I'm just over on Fifty-eighth and Crestview."

Hermann beamed, and Dashiel realized that he was handsome, in his understated way. He wasn't sure how it had escaped his notice before.

"Perfect!" Hermann said. "There's a nice little diner on Crestview. Please, let me treat you to dinner. Unless you have other plans, of course."

"No plans," Dashiel admitted with a hint of wariness. In his experience, this sort of amiable generosity tended to come with strings attached. However, the ex-medium business wasn't a lucrative one, and he was in no position to balk at the offer of a free meal. Besides, it had been a while since he'd dined with anyone socially, and the notion appealed to him. "Dinner sounds swell."

They were hailed with a chorus of friendly greetings the moment they stepped into the Nite Owl Diner, one of those sleek little modern establishments that looked like a converted railcar. They sat across from each other in a cozy booth, lit by the yellowish glow of an incandescent bulb hanging overhead.

With Hermann's hearty encouragement, Dashiel ordered a dinner of roast lamb, buttered corn, and whipped potatoes that seemed extravagant by his recent standard of living. Coils of fragrant, shimmering steam wafted invitingly from the plate.

He willed himself to take small bites, resisting the urge to scarf it all down.

"You must be quite the regular here," he said.

Hermann looked a little sheepish. "I suppose I do come here a lot. But their tongue sandwiches are truly the gnat's whiskers, especially after a late evening marking papers."

"This lamb goes down easy, too. Much obliged, by the way."

"Not at all!"

Dashiel took a sip of coffee before going on, in a casual tone, "So, the missus doesn't mind all those late evenings at the office, eh?" He was still casing the man, like one of his marks. In the old days, he would have gone home and written up a nice little file after a social tête-à-tête like this. Personal information, no matter how trivial, was a medium's true stock-in-trade, and old habits die hard.

"Oh, there's no missus," said Hermann, his cheeks pinkening. "I suppose I'm what you'd call a confirmed bachelor. No, it's just me and Horatio."

Dashiel raised his eyebrows questioningly. "Horatio?"

"My cat."

"Ah."

"Didn't the spirits tell you all this?" Hermann asked, blinking innocently. "Oh, don't mind me, I'm just making fun. What about you? Do you have any family?"

"Just my sister, back in Tampa. But I haven't heard from her in some time."

"Ah," said Hermann. "A Florida man."

"That I am. Born and raised in Tarpon Springs. My work took me all over, though. Before I left the business, I spent several years at one of the big Spiritualist camps in Indiana. But you heard about that at my demonstration."

Hermann nodded. He paused, as if weighing his words. Dashiel fancied that the flush in his cheeks grew a little deeper. "You mentioned an accomplice before. The person who purloined my photograph. Do you always work with a partner?"

"Oh, no. That was just a kid I hired for a couple of bucks to do the job for me before the act. These days, I'm on my own." He hoped this answer would be enough to satisfy Hermann's curiosity. The evening had been pleasant so far, and he had no desire to sour the mood by discussing the details of his former working arrangements. That way lay a morass of painful memories he'd rather not retread.

Hermann scraped some horseradish sauce over a slice of bread, lost in thought. When he spoke again, Dashiel was relieved that he had moved on to a different subject. "What I can't understand," he said, "is why you decided to give it all up. As good as you are, you must have made a mint!"

"And how," Dashiel agreed, a little wistfully. "But I suppose even the most vestigial conscience starts to get a bit inflamed when you're bilking little old ladies out of their inheritance day in and day out. I just plain got sick of it."

"Hmm. And now you've made it your life's mission to expose all that fraud and humbuggery to the world. It's kind of poetical, don't you think?" Hermann leaned forward, his big hazel eyes shining with enthusiasm.

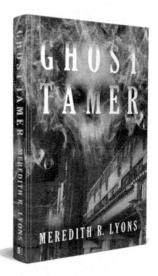
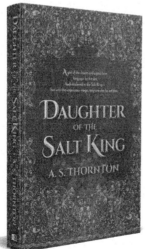
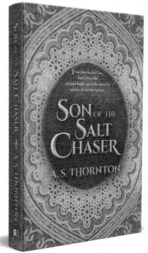

CamCat Books

VISIT US ONLINE FOR MORE BOOKS TO LIVE IN:
CAMCATBOOKS.COM

SIGN UP FOR CAMCAT'S FICTION NEWSLETTER FOR
COVER REVEALS, EBOOK DEALS, AND MORE EXCLUSIVE CONTENT.

CamCatBooks   @CamCatBooks   @CamCat_Books   @CamCatBooks